Praise for Kristyn

Half of What

"Detox from the holidays with Kristy
and well-to-do Virginia town, its meddlesome residents,
cades of secrets within its walls." —*InStyle*

"The fast pace and intriguing mystery make this one perfect for fans of *Big Little Lies.* A compelling look at the power of small-town gossip." —*Kirkus Reviews*

"Fans of Emily Giffin and Sally Hepworth will appreciate this enjoyable family drama." —*Booklist*

"A character-driven, dishy, gossipy, fun read. . . . A fine story that will move readers to look for other books by this talented author."
—*New York Journal of Books*

"An astute, exquisite account of a gossipy small town. . . . Mesmerizing and entertaining." —*Washington BookReview*

"Exciting and addicting. . . . You'll have a hard time putting it down this holiday season." —Women.com

"The story won't end where you expect it to, and its strong women's-relationships theme underscores many truths." —NJ.com

"This engrossing novel has everything: a web of secrets, gossip, and lies, and a heroine you'll be cheering for. . . . Delightful."
—Jennifer Close, author of *Girls in White Dresses*

"A delicious, insightful page-turner set in a genteel Virginia town where everyone knows your secrets."
—Kristin Harmel, international bestselling author of *The Room on Rue Amélie* and *The Sweetness of Forgetting*

"Imagine a Liane Moriarty novel served with a tall glass of sweet tea and you'll have *Half of What You Hear*. . . . Utterly captivating."
—Camille Pagán, bestselling author of *Woman Last Seen in Her Thirties*

"Incredibly intriguing, *Half of What You Hear* is a must-read that artfully delves its way through the layers of gossip, secrets, and lies of the small and seemingly charming town of Greyhill."

—Liz Fenton and Lisa Steinke, bestselling authors of *Girls' Night Out*

Praise for *Save Me*

"Lewis gets it just right in her examination of how tiny cracks can shatter in a marriage that gets 'cemented in the fable' of what being together is supposed to be." —*Publishers Weekly*

"An emotional roller-coaster of a read. . . . It's a testament to Lewis's great writing and is an absolutely fantastic read."

—*RT Book Reviews*

"As thought-provoking as it is thoughtful. . . . Absorbing, compelling, and a pleasure to read, this book is a page-turner."

—Taylor Jenkins Reid, author of *Daisy Jones & The Six* and *The Seven Husbands of Evelyn Hugo*

"Kristyn Kusek Lewis defines heartbreak with deep understanding and compassion in *Save Me*. . . . Lewis portrays neither angels nor demons, but the aching reality that marriage can become, along with the possibility of grace that love offers."

—Randy Susan Meyers, author of *Accidents of Marriage*

How Lucky You Are

"Fans of women's fiction about enduring female friendships will relate to debut author Lewis's vivid and genuinely written protagonists. A good choice for readers who enjoy the novels of Kristin Hannah."

—*Library Journal*

"Charming and achingly real. . . . I'm certain it will become a book club favorite."

—Sarah Jio, *New York Times* bestselling author of *The Violets of March* and *The Bungalow*

Perfect Happiness

ALSO BY KRISTYN KUSEK LEWIS

Half of What You Hear

Save Me

How Lucky You Are

Perfect Happiness

A NOVEL

KRISTYN KUSEK LEWIS

HARPER

NEW YORK • LONDON • TORONTO • SYDNEY

HARPER

This is a work of fiction. Names, characters, places, and incidents are products of the author's imagination or are used fictitiously and are not to be construed as real. Any resemblance to actual events, locales, organizations, or persons, living or dead, is entirely coincidental.

HarperCollins books may be purchased for educational, business, or sales promotional use. For information, please email the Special Markets Department at SPsales@harpercollins.com.

FIRST EDITION

Designed by Jamie Lynn Kerner

Library of Congress Cataloging-in-Publication Data has been applied for.

ISBN 978-0-06-296663-6 (pbk.)
ISBN 978-0-06-300846-5 (library edition)

20 21 22 23 24 LSC 10 9 8 7 6 5 4 3 2 1

For Ginger and Cate

ONE

It is just past eight o'clock on Saturday morning when Charlotte McGanley hears a strange rustling and looks up from her coffee cup. She is sitting outside on her back porch, at the weathered, wooden IKEA picnic table that she and Jason bought fifteen years ago, just after they married. Her journal is in front of her. She's trying to indulge in what has always been one of her favorite rituals of the season: a few moments alone outside with her coffee, in the finally warm sunshine of early spring, the house to her back still quiet.

When her daughter was younger, this was a time Charlotte cherished. Jason would keep Birdie inside, occupied with *Sesame Street* or cinnamon toast or Chutes and Ladders, and Charlotte would scribble away, her thoughts pouring out of her so easily that by the time she came back inside, she felt cleansed. Light and serene, like she'd just emerged from under the hands of a very good masseuse. But lately, even though she has plenty on her mind, the words won't come.

She sighs, her pen hovering over the page. Her intentions are good. Writing in a journal, or *journaling*, as they say, which makes it sound more physical (but also a little pathetic, she's always secretly thought), is one of the core habits that she prescribes to her students and readers. Not only has she personally found that it works (back when she and Jason tried to have a second child and ultimately failed, it was actually one of the things that got her through) but the research clearly supports it. People who journal are happier. More resilient. More grateful. Just last week, she told her undergraduate students that keeping a journal is the psychological equivalent of taking your vitamins.

And yet . . . The only thing she's managed this morning is a doodle of a trailing flower vine along the upper right-hand corner of a blank page. *What's that phrase*, she thinks. *Squeezing water from a stone?* That's what she feels like lately: the stone. Quick, like a lightning flash, her mind flickers on Jason, how the night before, he'd called her "cold." An awful thing for a man to call his wife. Too close a side step to "frigid."

She hears the sound again and looks up. What *is* it? And then it stops.

She flips back to the last time she wrote and, noting the date on the entry, feels a sense of defeat. It was nine days ago, and even then, it was a half-baked gratitude list, consisting of three unimaginative items, bullet-pointed with little ballpoint-pen stars:

- Coffee
- Slept through the night
- No rain today

The rest was a scribbled smattering of reminders in the margin of the page: *Call orthodontist—Birdie checkup reskedge, window washers?, Amazon: laundry detergent.*

Did I remember to put the new checkup appointment in my calendar? she thinks. And then she hears the noise again—louder this time—and jumps, a little yelp escaping from her mouth.

Jesus, settle down, she scolds herself, running her hands over her face. Maybe she's off because of the extra glass of wine last night, she thinks, feeling a twinge of shame for having drunk it only because it was Friday and she was bored sitting on her end of the couch, scrolling through Instagram while Jason watched the hockey playoffs. (*Was* this why they both worked so hard all week? she'd thought. For this?) She feels a sinking darkness, like she's slipping underwater, remembering their bickering before bed, how she'd caught a glimpse of Jason rolling his eyes at her just before she turned out the light.

Hearing the rustling again, she takes a last gulp of lukewarm coffee (from a mug with "Do more of what makes you happy" printed on its side), and stands, determined to find the cause. When she steps off the porch, the wet grass tickles her feet, dampening her slippers, and she reconsiders for a moment, glancing toward Mr. Marchetto's house, where she can see her neighbor in his open window preparing breakfast. *But that sound . . .*

It's almost like cellophane crinkling, but there's a chirpy squeaking, too. Maybe chipmunks? She's used to spotting all sorts of animals in her yard. People back home in Georgia can't believe her when she tells them, but even though she's barely five miles from the DC line, she frequently sees deer, raccoons, and families of foxes frolicking in the grass. Mr. Marchetto even saw a coyote in their driveway once. The wildlife tortures Sylvie, their elderly golden retriever, and Charlotte's relieved that the dog is still inside, having taken over her spot in the bed the minute Charlotte got up.

Once upon a time, they wouldn't have let Sylvie on the bed, and for a while, she was banned from the room, due to her tendency to sit right beside the bed while they were having sex, watching them so intently that it was like she was a judge on one of those TV dance competitions. But now, it seems like a moot point. The last time they had sex was seven months ago, and even then, it felt more like an obligation because it was Jason's birthday. *Over seven months*, Jason had said last night, when she pushed his hand off her hip. *I'm too tired*, she said. *I had too much wine.* She turned off the lights and they turned their backs to each other, and in the tense awful dark, she reached out for him, feeling guilty. She's told him that it bothers her, too, how they never even try anymore, but that's a bit of a lie, because while she misses the closeness they once shared, and the intimacy that was more than just physical, not having sex actually feels like a tremendous relief, one less thing on her to-do list. He didn't respond to her hand on his shoulder blade last night, her half-attempt at an apology. She turned back over. She went to sleep.

The sound, Charlotte realizes as she makes her way through the damp yard, is coming from the other side of the deck. She crouches, taking tentative steps, remembering the time years ago when they were having dinner on the porch and watched a fox snag a squirrel right off the trunk of one of the oak trees. Or the time when Jason, digging ivy out of the flower beds, discovered a copperhead coiled just feet from where Birdie had been jumping rope less than an hour before. Charlotte begged him to call animal control, but he refused, instead insisting that the best thing was to just leave it be and let it go on its way. "I'm a keeper at the National Zoo," he'd said, laughing as he followed her into the house. "You really think I'm going to call the morons at animal control?"

She takes one final step around the deck and then she sees it.

"Oh!" she gasps. There is not just one animal beside the deck but . . . she counts . . . *one, two . . . Four bunnies! A perfect little bunny family!* They're huddled together, three big ones and a baby, and they are feasting on the leaves of her rhododendron. Instantly, her hand goes for her phone in the pocket of her robe.

She stretches her arms out to take the photo—it's a flawless shot with the pink petals in the background, like something you might see on a wall calendar in a pediatrician's office. When the clicking camera sound punctures the air, the bunnies freeze, their paws poised perfectly in front of their little chests, their big gumdrop eyes trained on her, the middle one—the smallest one—with a triangle of green leaf poking out from its mouth.

Yes! It's perfect. The bunnies scurry off, and she walks back to the porch, a wave of satisfaction settling over her for the first time today. She opens Instagram, composing a caption in her head. Birds chirping, sun shining, and these little guys making my backyard feel like something out of a Disney movie today, she types. Happy morning, friends! She hits share and then immediately begins swiping down; one time, and then another, and then another. Within seconds, there are 153 likes. Her 93,000 followers love these sorts of posts. Simple. Wholesome. *Happy*.

She sits, picking up her pen and opening the journal again. It's pale green. She bought it at an airport newsstand during a layover on her way back from giving a talk at a women's luncheon in Dallas last month. The trip had been a hit. They all were lately, which she attributed to how she had tailored the boilerplate talk she'd been giving since her book, *Perfect Happiness*, came out two years ago. She'd learned that it was important to play to your audience, that they warmed to you more quickly if they could relate to you. So when she went to Dallas, she hit Drybar first and had her white-blond bob blown out, and wore a hot pink dress she'd bought in Savannah, something she'd never wear to speak to a crowd in Chicago or the Northeast, where she wore charcoal and navy, and kept her hair simple and her nails neutral.

In Dallas, her nails matched her dress. During her talk, she'd improvised with some extra bullet points about the importance of self-care, and scanning the tables of well-preserved women, she made a quip about day spas: "I don't know about y'all," she said, her voice taking on the accent she'd almost completely shed since leaving the South nearly twenty years ago. "But the aesthetician I see does as much for my well-being as any antidepressant could." She also squeezed in just the tiniest mention of her Baptist upbringing, although she hadn't been a regular churchgoer in decades. Some people might think she was pandering, but to Charlotte, none of it was insincere. She just felt that it was far easier for people to digest her message if they were comfortable with her. And she meant every word she said.

She puts her pen down on the still-blank page and picks up her phone again. 3,452 likes.

She's been studying positive psychology—the science of happiness—since she was an undergrad psych student at Emory, where she stayed for a PhD. After graduation, she moved to Washington to teach at Georgetown, a move made much easier by her then-fiancé's decision to sleep with somebody else. She got a little studio just off campus, and when she got homesick, her sweet brother, Aaron, shipped her Tupperware containers of boiled peanuts and pimento cheese via Next Day Air. One afternoon, just months into her new life, she got trapped in a thunderstorm while out for a run on the National Mall. She sprinted up the steps of the Lincoln Memorial, waiting out the rain under Abe's solemn gaze, and then, while reading the words of the Gettysburg Address inscribed on the wall, she took a step back and bumped right into another runner who was doing the same thing. Two years later, she married him. Birdie, conceived on their honeymoon in Costa Rica, came just after her thirtieth birthday.

Home, at that early time in their family's life, was everything she'd wanted it to be, almost too good to be true. At work, she hustled. She stood barely five feet tall, hardly a demanding presence, and when she first arrived at Georgetown, fellow faculty members often mistook her for a student. This only fueled her desire to outwork and outpublish them, which she did, building up a following of dedicated students who lapped up her theories about happiness and what she called "living a contented life." She churned out research papers, publishing on her main area of focus: the idea that people can manifest positive emotions through deliberate action instead of letting their feelings be their guide. On the weekends, she and Jason drank beers on the back porch with their neighbors, the baby monitor on the table beside the chips and guacamole. They went for family bike rides, strapping Birdie into a little plastic seat on the back of Jason's bike. Their little girl suddenly turned three, and then four, and then went off to kindergarten, her giant backpack dwarfing her as she climbed the steps onto the school bus. Jason told funny stories over dinner about the orangutans he cared for at the zoo. Charlotte was awarded tenure. Her mother continued to call and ask when she was coming home.

She sailed along for a while, doing her thing, juggling work and marriage and motherhood. She actually felt like she'd become the epitome of Susie Sunshine, which her father used to call her sometimes, because she really was the picture of happiness, always with a smile on her face, always doing her best to make the people around her feel good. People sometimes asked her, "Are you *ever* in a bad mood?" and she responded honestly—of course she got down sometimes. But from the time she was young, when her mother's mercurial moods could change the tone of the house in an instant, her fake-it-till-you-make-it strategy had worked. Smile through the tears. Keep your focus forward.

And she had been tested. First, with her father's death when she was in college. Then with Reese, her childhood sweetheart and fiancé, who'd been carrying on an entire relationship with another woman as he and Charlotte were brainstorming wedding venues and honeymoon destinations. And then, just when she'd built such a nice family, career, and life for herself in DC, she and Jason found they couldn't conceive again. They tried and tried, racking up credit card debt on treatments, injecting Charlotte with an endless number of syringes. It was the hardest time in her life. She smiled at herself in the mirror and told herself it would be okay. To cope, she poured herself into work, and the outcome—her salvation, really—was the Intro to Happiness class she dreamt up during that time. It became a different sort of baby.

It is the most popular course in the university's history. The *Washington Post* even ran a feature about it in the Sunday paper, with quotes from her students evangelizing about how much better they felt since taking the class, now that they'd learned strategies like unplugging for an hour every day, or getting more sleep, or spending face-to-face time with friends instead of just texting. And then, barely four years ago, she got the email that would change everything. It was from one of the organizers of the TEDxMidAtlantic conference, asking her if she'd like to speak.

At Georgetown, Charlotte had given a dizzying number of lectures over the years, but for some serendipitous reason, that TED talk sparked something. She started it the same way she started the Intro to Happiness class each semester, when she looked out at her lecture hall full of students—in hoodies, bedheads, and vegan leather sneakers—and said, "Rule Number One: If you want to be happier, you have to stop thinking so much.

"Stop wondering whether this is the life you should be living.

"Stop second-guessing your choices.

"Stop worrying about where you are or what you're doing relative to those around you.

"Stop thinking so much about yourself.

"Stop thinking, period.

"Facts before feelings," she said during the talk, which had just over four million views on YouTube the last time she checked. "You can soul-search, go deep with your vulnerability, spend your summer vacation at an ashram seeking out your higher calling, and sure, that stuff might work." In the video, she pauses here, and flashes a conspiratorial smile. "Oprah and Gwyneth and Deepak will tell you that it works." Chuckles erupt throughout the audience. "But that's not for me.

"*No, no*," she says. "I might *look* like Susie Sunshine," she jokes, smiling a wide smile and tucking a lock of her hair behind her ear, and the crowd laughs because she really does, like a "human Tinker Bell," her brother used to say, resting an elbow on the top of her head. "But I need hard facts. I need research. I don't need more thinking and feeling. I don't *have time* for more thinking and feeling." More laughter. She waits for the crowd to quiet. "Listen, I'm not just being cheeky here," she says, speaking slowly, thoughtfully. "Science is very clear about what makes people happy: time in nature, a daily gratitude practice, regular contact with close friends, exercise, more sleep. Et cetera . . . et cetera. We've all heard these things a million times. But do you do them?" She pauses. "Do you *do* them? Or do you sit around wondering why you *feel how you feel*?" She holds her hands out to her sides, the tips of her fingers pressed to her thumbs like those of a yogini, and closes her eyes for a moment in faux introspection. "Honestly, the why-you-feel-the-way-you-do is a waste of time. It doesn't matter so much. What matters is that you *do* something. Action first, feelings later. Fake it till you make it. Follow the facts."

It wasn't three weeks before an email popped up in her inbox from Wendy Harmon, a literary agent at one of the top agencies in New York, who said her mother had forwarded her the now-viral video. She wanted to know if Charlotte had ever considered writing a book, which of course she had. There isn't a college professor on Earth who hasn't.

What Charlotte never banked on was becoming a guru. The book (or, *The Book*, as she'd come to think of it) chronicled her attempt, according to the jacket copy, as a "frazzled wife and mother, to apply cutting-edge 'positive psychology' research to better her own life." Not that she really felt that she *needed* to better her own life at the time, but Wendy and the editors at the publishing house who bought her manuscript thought that the secret sauce for the book's success would be a personal approach. So she rewrote the draft she had initially submitted—essentially a regurgitation of the class she taught—with more anecdotes from her own life. This was much harder than she anticipated, the irony of course being, as she said to Jason, that writing a book about her personal quest for more happiness was actually making her a little bit miserable. (Also, she hated that the book cover called her "frazzled," which made her feel like Cathy from the comics. Had any of her male colleagues ever been described as "frazzled"?)

Whatever, she told herself. She chose (naturally) to focus on the positive. It was an instant hit. She sold a zillion books, and the royalties were enough to knock out the IVF debt and finally complete the kitchen renovation they'd spent years saving for. And what was inside the book *was* mostly true. She wrote that she wasn't depressed, and there wasn't anything exactly wrong, but she wanted, as she stated in the introduction, "a deeper sense of satisfaction that she was living life to the fullest." She promised her readers less stress, less fretting, that they wouldn't end each day feeling they were crawling across a finish line. *Life is more than a series of chores and tasks to be completed*, she wrote. *And while it's totally unrealistic to expect to roll through each day in a state of bliss, aren't we at least entitled to rest our heads on our pillows most nights feeling solidly content?*

Sometimes, late at night, she thinks back on that final sentence from the introduction, the words returning to her like angry pinpricks, and she wonders what her life would be like had she never written them. Because the truth is, most nights now, when she pulls her covers up to her chin and turns off her light, she doesn't feel as happy as she ought to be. Or as she once was, before all of this madness with the book began. If she's downright honest about it, becoming a happiness guru has made her as unhappy as she's ever been.

She picks up her phone and types a hashtag into the search field, one that she coined just after the book came out: *#happyhighfive*, the practice of identifying five things that you're grateful for each day. She scrolls through the entries. @Betsy423 has posted a photo of her green smoothie. @CaliJenna is grateful for last night's Pacific Coast sunset (and rightfully so, Charlotte thinks, examining the postcard-perfect view of the ocean beyond the woman's infinity pool). She looks down again at her journal and sighs, then she turns her attention back to her phone, tapping the icon on its screen that will take her back to her profile. Her picture of the bunny family has now racked up 8,482 likes.

Just over an hour later, she and Jason are eating breakfast at the kitchen counter, shuffling sections of the newspaper back and forth, when she takes a bite of her avocado toast, picks up the Saturday real estate insert, and notices the date on the top of the page.

"It's April Fools' Day," she says, shifting on the stool.

Deeply involved in the opinion page, he doesn't answer. He runs a hand over his head, scratches the back of his neck. He buzzed his hair short last year, when his bald spot became too noticeable to ignore any longer.

"Hey," she says, waving a hand in front of his face.

"What?" He looks weary, his mouth turned down at the corners.

"It's April Fools' Day," she says again, more pointedly this time. *Nine hours of sleep and he's still tired?*

"Oh," he says, barely glancing up.

"That's it?"

He shrugs and wiggles the side of his fork into his fried egg. "It's not like it's Christmas."

"No." She sighs. "It's not."

"What?" He looks up at her, defensive.

"Nothing. I just wish we'd remembered to pull a prank on Birdie. But it's no big deal."

"Huh?"

"A prank. Remember? Like we usually do? Was it last year that we froze her bowl of cereal the night before, with the spoon inside?"

He cracks a smile. "A classic. I can't believe she fell for it again."

"We could still do something." She turns and looks at the clock on the microwave. "She'll be home from Hannah's soon, but we have enough time."

He nods his chin toward the sink. "We could tape down the handle of the sink sprayer thing."

"She knows that one." He goes back to reading. "We should have done something," she mutters to herself, looking around the room. *Food coloring,* she thinks, opening a cabinet. *What could I do with food coloring?*

Out of the corner of her eye, she sees Jason shake his head, furrowing his eyebrows as he lifts the newspaper and flips the page, snapping it into the air to straighten it. She once found the habit endearing; it reminded her of her dad, whom Jason had never met. Now the snapping drives her crazy, along with the loud way that he chews, the way he can't eat an egg without dousing it in sriracha and getting half of it on his freckled face, and the fact that he hangs on to pit-stained ratty T-shirts that are older than their marriage. She glances at the one he's wearing today, from the Cherry Blossom 10K in *1998*.

She picks up her phone and sees that her friend Stephanie has texted, saying she'll drop off Birdie on the way to her daughter Hannah's soccer game. They'd met back when the girls were infants and in the same playgroup, and fortunately for the adults, who'd become fast friends, the girls had remained inseparable long past the point of the two women forcing them together with side-by-side dates in their jogging strollers, group Kindermusik classes, and joint memberships in the same Girl Scout troop. Now, they're nearly through their freshman year of high school, and despite Birdie having her first boyfriend—a fact that Charlotte, in particular, isn't thrilled about (wasn't it too soon?)—the girls still seem to be as close as ever.

She starts to go to her Pinterest app to look for an April Fools' idea but opens Instagram instead. Birdie isn't allowed to use social media yet, though according to her, she is the "last living person in Arlington" without it. (Actually, just last week, she told Charlotte that not letting her get on Snapchat is as old-fashioned as if she made her wear "those pads with belts from the 1950s.") Charlotte gets it. A lot of Birdie's friends have had Instagram accounts since fourth or fifth grade, and over the years, Birdie's tried every argument under the sun: Hannah's mom lets her have an account ("Every family makes their own decisions," Charlotte tells her), Charlotte has an account ("Only because I need it for work," she says), following her cousins' and aunt's and uncles' accounts would help them stay in better touch ("You're welcome to call them anytime," she says). The conversations always end the same way: Charlotte starting in with "The research shows—" and Birdie interrupting her, lamenting, "I know, I know! Why do I have to be a psychology professor's kid?" Charlotte knows that her standing firm makes Birdie a Luddite among her friends, but she doesn't care. The research *does* show, and Charlotte's read enough about teenage girls and social media to stand firm. The skyrocketing anxiety, depression, and suicide rates are more than enough evidence for her. On several occasions, Stephanie has justified Hannah's Instagram and Snapchat and TikTok accounts by saying that her daughter's posts provide a window into her life unlike anything their own parents had when they were growing up, and while Charlotte isn't convinced, she has no problem using Birdie's friends' accounts, most of which are public, for her own intel. She makes a point not to actually like or comment on anything they post; that would be over the top, like one of those parents from her own childhood who tried too hard to befriend the kids, singing along to Guns N' Roses in the car and offering to buy them wine coolers, and because none of Birdie's friends have ever mentioned the fact that she follows them, it feels anonymous somehow even if it's not.

Still, she worried she was crossing a line when she found Birdie's new boyfriend's account, @tucklaxlife05, a few months ago. As her students trickled in for her eleven o'clock lecture, she stopped one of her favorites, a redhead from Indiana who wore knee-high striped Pippi Longstocking socks, and asked her if it would be weird for her to follow her daughter's fifteen-year-old boyfriend on Instagram. Becca gave her the best answer she could have, saying that most kids are more concerned with the number of followers they have than who they actually are, and that he honestly might not even notice, or care. It *had* surprised Charlotte how many followers Birdie's friends all had, with numbers in the thousands. She checked Tucker's account—the kid had fourteen hundred followers—so she went ahead and hit the follow button, never mentioning it to Birdie.

Today, she types Tucker's username into the search field, and sees that he hasn't posted anything in three days, not since the photo of him and his lacrosse teammates standing sweaty at the edge of the field after their win over W&L. But when she taps on his profile picture (a fuzzy pic of his hands gripping a lacrosse stick) to see if he's posted any stories, a choppy video pops up onto her screen. At first she can't tell what it is, the video is too dark, and it looks like he was running with his phone in his hand when he took it, but she realizes it's just wet grass. Then it jerks to several silhouetted figures in the distance. All teenagers, clearly, but they're so far away and the picture is so dark that it's impossible to make them out. She looks at the time stamp on the video and sees that it was taken eight hours ago. *After midnight*, she calculates, trepidation sinking in. *How am I supposed to feel about my daughter dating a fifteen-year-old boy who is out somewhere that late?* She glances at Jason, to confirm his eyes are still on the paper, and clicks to move the story to the next frame, and her breath catches in her throat. It's a foot, a boy's sneakered foot—dirty slip-on checkered Vans like her brother wore in the late eighties—kicking a beer can. *Fuck.* And then in the next shot, a boy she doesn't recognize is shown in shadow, the glowing tip of something in his hand. An e-cigarette, she realizes, and a split second later, she remembers something else her student Becca told her, how most kids have "private" stories, too, that only close friends can see. If this is what Tucker is posting in public, then what is he posting privately?

She clicks to Hannah's account. Nothing new since her last post, from around 8:30 last night, when she posted a photo of herself with Birdie and two other friends, the four of them standing outside of La Moo, a local ice cream shop, arms wrapped around each other's waists, all four of them in oversize T-shirts and those high-waisted mom-jean cutoffs that Charlotte thinks are horribly unflattering even on beautiful teenage girls. *See*, she thinks, an angry pulse beating behind her ears, *Birdie should be dating a boy who posts pictures of ice cream, not—*

"Stop spying on her," Jason suddenly says. When she looks up, his eyes are still on the newspaper.

She taps quickly back to Tucker's video and holds her phone out to him.

"What?" he says, throwing his hands up like she's showing him something she just found on the floor.

"Look." She nudges the phone toward him. "Look at what Tucker posted last night."

He takes the phone and shakes his head, confused. "What are you—"

"Here." She takes the phone back and taps the screen to replay it, pointing at the evidence. "Do you see that?"

"Are you sure that's Tucker?" he says, squinting at the screen.

"It's his account," she says. "I don't know if it's his foot kicking the can but he posted it."

"Yeah, but . . . show it to me again," he says, and she studies his face as he watches it a second time. "For all we know, it's not their can. It could be something they found on the ground."

"Jason, come on. Look," she says, tapping to get to the kid with the Juul or whatever the stupid thing is. "It's an e-cigarette, Jason. Do you know what those do to kids? To their lungs? Kids end up with irreversible damage. They end up in the ICU. They did a whole thing about it on the *Today* show when I was there last week. I was in the greenroom with the doctor."

He shrugs. "I don't know. They're fifteen."

"Jason."

"It's not good. I'm not saying I like it, but at least the kid holding the vape pen isn't Tucker."

"But what about the beer can?"

"I don't know." He rubs his hand over his mouth. "I don't know what to tell you."

"He's dating your daughter," she says, and when he doesn't react, she repeats herself. "He's *dating your daughter*."

"I'm not saying I like it, Charlotte, but this . . ." He sighs. She can tell he's more rattled than he wants to let on. "This is our reality now. Teenagers do stupid shit. We have to accept that fact a little bit, right? Not every kid she dates is going to be an Eagle Scout."

"Why is your first instinct to protect him?"

"Why is your first instinct to think the worst of him?" He picks up the newspaper.

"Forgive me for parenting," she says under her breath.

"What?" He drops the paper.

"Never mind." She walks to the sink to rinse her coffee cup. She does not have the desire or energy to fight with him today.

"It would be awesome if we could make it to lunch without you telling me something I'm doing wrong," he says.

"Jason, please." She turns off the water. "You started this."

"Just give her some space, Charlotte," he says. "Or spend some *actual* time with her, instead of spying on her through your phone."

She freezes. "*What* did you just say?"

He stands, his eyes boring into her for just a moment before he looks away and walks with his dirty plate in his hand to the sink, where he lets it clatter into the basin.

"Are you *actually* accusing me of not spending enough time with Birdie?" she says to his back. He's standing in front of the refrigerator, filling his glass from the water spigot on the door. "Because I'm pretty sure that I'm the one who picked her up from practice twice this week, once on a day when I had to leave a department meeting early to do so, not to mention all of the lunches I packed, the dinners I made, and the clean laundry folded in the basket in the hall upstairs—"

He holds a hand out, stopping her. "I'm so sorry, Charlotte," he says. "How could I accuse you of anything? Not when you were actually here last week."

She clenches her teeth, feeling a familiar anger build inside her. "I do not neglect Birdie," she says evenly. "You know that. My entire life is this family."

He turns to her, making a face like what she's just said is incredibly amusing, and her stomach goes hollow. They both know that her schedule would suggest otherwise. Since the book came out, she's been on the road constantly, slotting speaking engagements into the open spaces outside of her teaching schedule. The university has been happy to accommodate this. Actually, they sort of insist on it, realizing the opportunity that her newfound popularity presents: The more attention she gets, both in the classroom and on the road, the more they can use her as a selling point to get wealthy alumni to donate money to the school.

Nobody, least of all Charlotte, expected the momentum to be so strong two years later. Her department head now clearly resents her absence, which isn't surprising since she's never exactly been Charlotte's biggest fan. What's been harder is the change in Jason's attitude. He seems to hate how much she's gone, but he won't come right out and ask her to stop taking these gigs, Charlotte suspects, because of the money they bring in. For an hour onstage, she can now earn five figures. It feels almost illegal, a stupid amount of money for something so small. The first time it happened (Google offering her eighteen thousand dollars for a breakfast seminar), they celebrated with champagne. Now Jason barely acknowledges her when she rolls her suitcase out to the car.

"If anything, I beg Birdie to spend more time with me!" she says. "And you're talking out of both sides of your mouth! Two minutes ago, you told me to give her some space. Now, you're saying to spend more time with her. Which is it, Jason?"

He turns. "You're right, you're right. You spend plenty of time with her," he says, in a condescending tone she hates. Like he's talking to a fool. "But if you're so worried about what she's up to, you could ask her instead of checking Instagram or Snapchat or whatever."

"Got it," she says. "Because teenagers are so forthcoming with their parents about what they're actually doing and feeling and thinking. Especially when they have their first boyfriends." She pauses. "Boyfriends who are a year older."

"Oh, come on!" He groans. "It's not like he's twenty-five and sneaking her into bars. He's fifteen."

"It makes a difference. And his fam—"

"There's nothing wrong with his family," he says. "I've known Finch since high school."

"Going to the same parties with Tucker's dad twenty-five years ago doesn't mean you *know* them. I've seen the mom around, Jason. They're not our kind of people." Charlotte bites her tongue, thinking about the rumor that Stephanie told her about Dayna, Tucker's mom, that she goes around town bragging about all her conquests on Capitol Hill when she first moved to DC after college, as if sleeping with a congressman from Florida is on par with bedding George Clooney.

"Then why the hell are we having dinner at their house tonight?" He starts down the hall and Charlotte follows, watching as he turns for the stairs.

"Because they invited us!" She groans, her frustration taking over. "Because our daughter is dating their son!"

He turns, his hand on the banister, his face scrunched up like he's in a commercial for migraine medication. "Why are you yelling? What are we even fighting about? Tell me, Charlotte! You're the expert!"

She wipes her hands over her face. He's been throwing this *expert* word at her lately, knowing how much she hates it. "Stop it, Jason," she says, closing her eyes for a moment and taking a deep breath. Outside, she hears the sound of a car door slamming. *Birdie.* "Why do we fight over every goddamn thing?" she whispers, saying it as much to herself as to him. "Why do we even bother?"

He shakes his head. "I don't—"

The door opens.

"You're still in your pajamas!" Charlotte says, compensating for the tense atmosphere with too much enthusiasm.

"Hey, Mom!" Birdie says, smiling and sleepy in a Yorktown tennis T-shirt and flannel pajama pants, closing the door behind her. Her backpack slides off her shoulder and onto the floor behind her. "Hey, Dad!"

"How was it?" Jason says. "Did you girls have fun?"

Charlotte goes to her, wrapping her arms around Birdie's blanket of long, unbrushed hair. Sometime last year, Birdie passed her in height. Charlotte inhales her daughter's familiar scent; residual hair product, fruity bubble gum. And, this morning, the faint scent of maple syrup. Steph must have made pancakes.

"Yeah, we had a good time," Birdie says. "We went to La Moo and then watched a movie. An old one. Hannah's mom said you'd know it. *Ferris Bueller*?"

"Danke Schoen!" Charlotte hears Jason sing behind her, imitating Matthew Broderick. *"Darlin', danke schoen!"*

"Oh, God, Dad!" Birdie laughs, shaking her head.

"What?" He feigns innocence, smiling at her in a way he hasn't smiled at Charlotte in months. *Can he just turn it on and off that easily?* she asks herself, knowing that it's a stupid question, because if there's anything she's an expert at, it's faking a good mood.

"Please, Dad, just get all of your embarrassing behavior out of your system before tonight," Birdie says, letting go of Charlotte and starting down the hall toward the kitchen. Charlotte watches her, thinking of Tucker's Instagram. *Has she tasted beer before?* she wonders. She had, by the time she was Birdie's age, but that was a different time and place.

"Tonight?" Jason jokes. "What's tonight?" He glances at Charlotte and his expression straightens.

"Dad!" Birdie yelps. "Stop!" She laughs again.

"I'm gonna go change and mow the yard," he says, starting up the stairs.

Feeling calmer, Charlotte follows Birdie into the kitchen, and clears her throat. "Are you hungry?" she asks her daughter, who's disappeared into the pantry. "I can make you something." She reaches for her phone on the counter, taps a familiar dance with her fingertips across the screen. Her bunny picture has 31,437 likes.

TWO

The North Arlington section of the city, where Jason and Charlotte have lived since their wedding day, is full of ramblers, the mid-Atlantic term for what Charlotte always knew as ranch houses, as well as bungalows and the ubiquitous Broyhill Colonials that were marketed to families after World War II. For decades, the landscape stayed basically the same, minus the occasional 1960s split-level or orangey-brick 1980s Neo-Colonial. But now, in North Arlington on any given day, and on any given street, there is the inevitable sound of a bulldozer gnashing its way through an old house's foundation, or the clink of hammers nailing together an addition. The colonials, like Jason and Charlotte's, grow appendages; two stories out the back and the sides, more space to accommodate the needs (and desires) of modern young families who have been steadily swarming into these hills for the past twenty years, lured by the excellent public schools and proximity to DC. The ramblers get replaced with six-thousand-square-foot behemoths built out right to the edge of the property line (no need for a backyard, of course, when the kids are too busy at practice and/or padding their college résumés). Space is precious and real estate is competitive and expensive. The conversations at PTA meetings, on the soccer sidelines, next to the potluck table at neighborhood block parties: *Are you digging out the back? Total reno? How many times were you outbid before you got your place?* Homes go under contract, inspections waived, before they hit the market. The real estate agents all drive luxury cars. The builders make a killing.

Finch Cunningham took over his father's construction business right after he graduated from Hopkins, and pulling into the circular drive in front of the Cunninghams' home, Charlotte recalls the stories she'd heard when they built the house a few years ago. Unable to find a piece of land large enough to accommodate their wishes, they talked the elderly residents of three adjacent lots into selling, the rumor being that they gave the families a million each *in cash*. An airy stucco mansion, the Spanish Colonial style a nod to Dayna's upbringing in Montecito, California, went up on two of the lots. A turfed, regulation-size sports field for Tucker was built on the third.

Waiting for the Cunninghams to open the door, Charlotte notes the large potted lemon tree on the front terrace, pointing out the tiny green fruit to Birdie, and then glances beyond the house to the left, where a row of tall Leyland cypress trees outlines the field. The house is barely two miles from their own, and though she's passed it many times while out walking the dog, she's never been on the property. Through a separation in the trees, she can just barely make out markings on the grass.

"Are those Tucker's initials?" Jason says, taking the words

out of Charlotte's mouth. She can't help but laugh at the ostentatiousness of it—the kid's monogram on his field—and when her eyes meet her husband's, she feels a glimpse of their old connection, the first she's felt in days.

"Oh my God, you guys!" Birdie whines. "*Please* don't be weird!" Charlotte can tell she's nervous. She's been snippy all afternoon and changed four times, once because Charlotte told her she could not wear ripped jeans to dinner (she realized, as the words were coming out of her mouth, how much she sounded like her mother).

"Best behavior," Charlotte promises, reaching and pinching for a stray hair that's caught in Birdie's lip gloss, and then, hearing the faint tap of approaching footsteps, she glances back at the field, remembering Tucker's Instagram story. *Maybe Jason's right*, she thinks, eyeing the manicured green. *Maybe just a bunch of boys hanging out, being silly. Maybe it was nothing. Harmless*, she tells herself. *Nothing more than that.*

Up close, Dayna looks like the kind of woman who knows every corner of every luxury department store in the DC metropolitan area. *She* is wearing ripped jeans, though quite clearly not homemade like Birdie's, and a white tank top that shows off her commitment to Orangetheory or CorePower or whatever it is that keeps her lithe and lean. When she hugs Charlotte, air-kissing the space just beyond her ear, Charlotte notices that she smells cosmetic, like a combination of heavy floral perfume, powder, and body cream.

"Come in, come in!" Dayna says, hurrying them inside. "I can't get these . . ." She turns back toward the long corridor behind her, the marble floor gleaming beneath her leather wedges. "Boys! They're here!" She turns back to them and rolls her eyes, and then seeing Birdie, she freezes, her ample lips forming a surprised O like she's just discovered something precious and pleasing, a cupcake on a paper doily, a kitten with a satin bow around its neck.

"You are just . . ." she starts, shaking her head, her eyes passing over Birdie from head to toe and back up again. With Charlotte's prodding, Birdie had finally settled on a blue gingham top from J.Crew and white jeans, though she's pushed the top's elasticized sleeves off her shoulders a little farther than Charlotte would prefer. "I mean, I know we've met at school, Birdie, but look at you! You are *adorable*!" She shakes her head. "I am *so* not surprised that my son fell for you!"

Birdie dips her head down, her cheeks turning a deep red, and Charlotte winces inside. Her daughter is rarely self-conscious or timid. This is new, and Charlotte doesn't like it. She looks down the hall, wondering where Tucker is, thinking to herself that if he were her kid, she would have made him come to the door to greet them, too.

Finch suddenly emerges from beneath one of the archways, wiping his hands on a striped dish towel. "Hey, hey!" he yells, his voice bellowing. "My apologies, I was just getting the grill going!" He does a little jog toward them, then claps Jason on the back. "Nice to see you, buddy!" When he shakes Charlotte's hand, stuffing the dish towel under his other arm before he does it so that he can grasp her hand with both of his, she thinks to herself that he's huskier looking than in the head shot she'd seen on his company website. Shorter, too. *Above all, Finch Cunningham believes in the power of home*, the copy next to his bio said, a statement so trite and cheesy it felt immediately untrustworthy, like the opening lines in a political ad. He's sweating along his hairline, and his ruddy complexion matches the orangey red hue of his polo shirt.

Suddenly, Tucker slides into the hallway in his athletic socks, dressed in khaki shorts and an untucked oxford shirt. His dark hair is wet, the comb marks running distinctly through it. "Sorry! Sorry!" he says, a wide smile materializing on a face that resembles his mother's. His eyes pass over all of them as he approaches but he goes to Jason first, shaking his hand, looking him in the eye. *Good move*, Charlotte thinks, and then: *Too smooth?*

"Nice to see you again," he says, giving Charlotte a faint hug that matches the one that he then gives to Birdie, who giggles a little, and Charlotte wonders how they greet each other at school, that it's likely kissing but *what* kind exactly? And how much?

Birdie and Tucker became official after Valentine's Day, when she came home with an armful of red carnations that he'd sent to her through one of those school fund-raisers, with different colors symbolizing the gift's significance: yellow for friendship, red for love. Charlotte's only met Tucker in person twice since then: once, when she picked up Birdie after a basketball game at school this winter, and the second time, just a few weeks ago, when she dropped off Birdie and Hannah to meet Tucker and a group of friends in Westover for pizza and ice cream. Jason had asked why there hadn't been any official dates yet, why she and her friends only seemed to travel in packs, and

Birdie had looked at him like he'd asked whether Tucker was going to give her his letterman's jacket.

They all move into the kitchen and Charlotte tries not to gawk. She's been in plenty of nice homes before; at trustees' dinners for the university, for instance, and her own brother's house back in Savannah is so gorgeous that *Southern Living* featured it a couple of years ago. But this is something else, if only in the sense that it seems like the Cunninghams want their home to scream, *We have lots and lots and lots of money!* She notices the glass-front refrigerator and twelve-burner stove and starts to ask Dayna whether she cooks but her hostess is already speaking.

"So this is a really good Pinot Gris," she's saying, lifting the nearly empty crystal glass that Charlotte had noticed the moment they'd walked in the room. "We went to Sonoma over Columbus Day weekend. A miracle we could go anywhere at all, given Tucker's lacrosse obligations." She rolls her eyes up to the ceiling like this is a tremendous inconvenience, but Charlotte knows that this is meant to impress her. Parents around Arlington use their kids' athletic achievements as social currency starting as early as kindergarten, and as much as she'd like to believe otherwise, Charlotte knows she's done it, too, with Birdie and tennis. "Would you like a glass?"

"Charlotte never met a glass of wine she didn't like," Jason pipes in. All of the adults laugh—Tucker and Birdie have already escaped to the periphery of the room, where they're looking out the French doors toward the pool—and Charlotte manages to smile and make a jokey grimace at her husband's remark, but the comment annoys her.

"Well, that makes you my kind of girl!" Dayna giggles, handing her a glass.

"That's for sure!" Finch quips. "Dayna has a tank top that she wears to SoulCycle—What does it say, honey?"

"Coffee till cocktails!" She laughs.

Charlotte throws her a polite smile and takes a sip. The wine is in fact delicious, much better than the glass of grocery store chardonnay she poured for herself while she was getting ready.

"It's great," she says, aware of Dayna's eyes on her as she lowers the glass.

"Yes," Dayna says. "It is. Too bad for Finch that I like it so much. We have to have it shipped by the case from California."

Finch raises his eyebrows in an amused way and holds up a hand, rubbing his thumb and fingers together. "Every goddamn thing she likes is expensive!" He goes to his wife and wraps his arms around her shoulders, craning his neck to kiss her cheek. "She's worth it, though!" Charlotte sneaks a look at Jason, sure he finds this whole display as over the top as she does, but his eyes are locked on Tucker across the room, his expression stony. When he finally turns back to them, their eyes meet, and she can see it all over his face. For all of his pronouncements this morning about her overreacting about Tucker's Instagram, he doesn't like the kid either.

Finch releases his wife, pats the side of her hip, and she giggles. "Come on," he says to Jason, waving him toward the doors that lead out onto the patio. "Let me show you my new toy!"

As the doors close behind them, Dayna makes an exasperated face. "We have a pizza oven out there, a smoker, two grills, a rotisserie, but he's never gotten as excited about anything as that damn Kegerator!"

"A *Kegerator*?" Charlotte says. She hasn't heard of anyone having one since she was in grad school and the Georgia Tech students who lived across the street installed one in their kitchen. She remembers the sour smell of it when she stopped in on their parties, the sticky feel of the linoleum floor under the soles of her shoes.

"Yes," Dayna says, leaning against the edge of the kitchen island and plucking a slice of cucumber from the overflowing tray of crudités in the center. "I finally relented and got it for him for his birthday last month. Not that a forty-eight-year-old man needs a Kegerator, but guys are impossible to shop for, aren't they?"

"Sure." Charlotte nods, thinking to herself that she and Jason gave up on birthday and anniversary presents years ago, instead putting the funds toward household things like landscaping, a new HVAC system. At first this felt like responsible adulting, but now it kind of feels like one more aspect of their relationship that they maybe shouldn't have let go of so easily, like date nights, or kissing each other hello and goodbye at the beginning and end of the day.

"I mean, he'd prefer a new Tesla," Dayna says. "But . . ." She flits her hand to her side. "Tucker, come here!" she says, calling to where he and Birdie are talking low beside the windows. "You two come eat some of this, chat with your mothers." She smiles at Charlotte.

Tucker pulls out a stool from under the counter for Birdie and then sits beside her. He digs his hand into a pile of cubed cheese and deposits the cheese on a cocktail napkin printed with tiny navy crabs, the greedy gesture reminding Charlotte of her three nephews. Birdie takes a water cracker and nibbles on the edge.

Charlotte watches Tucker, noticing the smattering of freckles across his nose and cheeks, seeing the adorable little boy he must have been not so long ago. When she first met him at school, picking up Birdie after that basketball game, he'd leaned in the passenger-side window and introduced himself to her just after closing the door for Birdie. Charlotte had watched him for a moment after he walked away, noting that though he was shorter than the others in the group of friends he was with, she could tell from the way he carried himself that he was the alpha. She could always pinpoint this with her students; it was in the way that they talked (excessively loud, to be sure everyone heard them) and the casual, assured gait.

"So how is your weekend? How is tennis going, Birdie?" Dayna says.

"Great!" Birdie nods politely, her hands clasped tightly in her lap. "Our coach is super nice."

"You're the only freshman on the varsity team, I hear?" Dayna says.

"Not only that, but she started practicing with them when she was still in middle school," Tucker says, looking slyly sideways at Birdie and nudging her in the waist. "She's their best player."

Birdie smiles. "Tucker . . ."

Charlotte purses her lips. She never sees Birdie like this, so demure, so modest, and she understands that her daughter is nervous—this is a first for all of them—but she still doesn't like how Birdie seems to be making herself small.

"Birdie picked up a tennis racket for the first time when she was three, when we were at Jason's parents' place in the Outer Banks," she says.

"Oh, they have a house there?" Dayna asks.

"Just a little condo," Charlotte says. "In one of those little golf communities."

"We have a house in Duck." Dayna laughs. "Right on the water. I told Finchy that was a huge mistake, what with the hurricanes, but—" She crosses her fingers. "We've been lucky so far. Honestly, it wouldn't really matter. We *never* get there. We prefer to spend the summer out west, at our place in Jackson Hole. Then, of course, last summer we were in the Seychelles. And before that, it was Tulum." She rolls her eyes.

The insanity of it all, Charlotte thinks, grinning at her host. *Poor thing.* "Anyhow," she says, clearing her throat. "We were in North Carolina and we'd brought Birdie to the court with a tote bag full of toys to keep her occupied while Jason and I played—nothing serious, just messing around—but tennis was all she wanted. We spent the rest of the vacation on the courts. She didn't want ice cream, mini golf, anything. Just tennis. And it's pretty much been like that ever since." She reaches out to smooth the back of Birdie's hair but when she does it, her daughter dips her head out of the way.

"Fabulous!" Dayna says, draining her wineglass. She walks to where the bottle is chilling in an ice bucket across the room. "You want more?" she says.

Charlotte eyes her glass and is surprised to see it's nearly empty. She didn't realize how fast she'd been drinking. "Sure," she says. "Why not?"

"Well, tennis is a sport you can play forever," Dayna says. "And the outfits are so cute!" She looks Birdie over and then turns to Charlotte. "Where did she play before high school? Are you guys at Washington Golf?" she says, referencing the country club up the road.

"No."

"Congressional?" She tilts her head, her brow furrowed in confusion. "Army Navy?"

"We just go to Overlee," Charlotte says, referencing the pool club that Jason's family has belonged to since he was a kid.

"Oh." Dayna frowns.

"I just always played through the county," Birdie pipes up, her eyes meeting Charlotte's. "At Tuckahoe Park or the courts at Yorktown or wherever."

"Well, if you're good, you're good," Dayna says with a shrug. "I mean, just look at Serena Williams and her sister and where they came from." She makes a face like she's just smelled something awful. "I'm from California, and *trust me* . . ."

"Serena's my favorite player," Birdie says, gently kicking Charlotte under the table. Charlotte reaches down and squeezes her daughter's leg. Inside, she's beaming. *We're still on the same team.*

"Birdie's had a poster of Serena on her bedroom wall since she was in third or fourth grade," Charlotte says. "She actually has a similar style, that's what her coaches always say. *Powerful.*"

"How fast did you say your serve was the other day?" Tucker says.

Birdie grins, seeming more like herself now, and reaches for a slice of Brie. "Ninety-two."

"Ninety-two miles per hour!" Dayna exclaims, shaking her head. "Wow." She looks at Charlotte. "I mean, *wow*! I don't even know if my Lexus goes that fast!"

Birdie kicks Charlotte again under the table. "Trust me," Charlotte says. "She doesn't get it from me."

Tucker stands. "We're gonna go outside, okay?"

"Had enough of us, lovebirds?" Dayna says.

"*Mo-om*," he singsongs, and they split for the backyard, practically sprinting.

"Gosh, she's adorable!" Dayna says, watching them as they go. "She gets those highlights from you? Or do you take her somewhere?"

"What?" Charlotte says, her eyes still on the kids. Their heads are dipped together like they're in on a secret, and she feels a nervous flutter, trying to imagine what it might be. "Oh," she says. "No, that's natural."

"Well, to the happy couple." Dayna raises her glass and then Charlotte does the same, taking a big swig, pushing the wine past the lump in her throat. *Happy couple.* This isn't an engagement party, for God's sake. She's *fourteen*.

"I've never seen Tucker like this with a girl before," Dayna says, reaching toward the overflowing veggie tray and picking up a tiny perfect carrot stick, the green fronds still attached like something out of Beatrix Potter. "He is head over heels! Normally, he doesn't say a thing about the girls at school, but ever since school started last fall, it's been Birdie-this and Birdie-that."

Normally? Charlotte thinks, plastering a big smile on her face. "Has Tucker had a girlfriend before, or . . . ?"

"Oh, well . . ." Dayna shrugs. "Nothing serious. Last year, he took a girl to the homecoming dance, and then I took them to the movies a couple of times after that before it fizzled out. That alone surprised me. You know kids these days, it seems like they're far more interested in just hanging out in one big group."

"Exactly," Charlotte says. "Jason and I talk about that all the time."

"But then I found out a little bit more about the girl, and I started to understand why Tuck wanted to be alone with her in a dark movie theater."

Charlotte feels her breath catch in her throat. "I'm sorry?" she says, fighting to keep the cheer in her voice.

Dayna gives her a conspiratorial look. "*Elizabeth Stephenson*," she whispers, as if there's anyone else in the room.

"I don't—" Charlotte shakes her head, her mind still stuck on the dark movie theater.

"Oh, you know the Stephensons. You *must*!"

"I don't."

"Really? Eric and Susie?" she says, in a way that feels so juvenile and judgmental that Charlotte's reminded of something Stephanie says, about how living in North Arlington can sometimes feel like being back in high school, where every parent is a former class president or prom king or star athlete, and intends for their children to be the same.

"Anyway, the Stephensons, they're a big Washington Golf family." Dayna takes a step toward Charlotte, looking back over her shoulder at the kids outside as she does. "And I know for a fact that Elizabeth's mom has enjoyed a few extracurriculars besides tennis and golf in the ladies' lounge . . ." She pauses, eyes widening. "You know there's a group of parents who do coke in the bathrooms there."

"Oh, I never believed that old rumor," Charlotte says, enjoying it when Dayna's expression predictably crumples. She surely expected Charlotte to be wowed by this bit of blue-chip gossip.

"Anyway," Dayna says. "I was happy when that little relationship ended. When I used to pick them up from the movies, both kids' faces looked like they'd been rubbed raw. As if I couldn't tell what they'd been up to." She laughs but immediately stops when she sees the way Charlotte's flushing despite her best efforts. "I'm sorry!" she says, reaching out to grasp Charlotte's arm. "I didn't mean to . . . I'm sure it's so different, having a girl."

"Well, it is," Charlotte says breezily, trying to play it off. "It seems like just yesterday that Birdie was playing Legos and poring through the American Girl catalog. This boyfriend stuff is all a little new for us."

"Well, not to worry. Tucker is a *total* gentleman. A really, really great kid." Dayna smiles then, her tongue visible between her teeth, and Charlotte can't deny it, something about the pointedness in her voice feels aggressive, like she's challenging her to think otherwise. "You have nothing to worry about, Charlotte," she says. "Honestly . . ." She puts her hand to her chest in faux modesty. "Forgive me for saying it but you kind of hit the jackpot."

Charlotte finishes her last sip of wine. She knows that the condescension in Dayna's remark isn't a mistake. This is an offensive move; she's establishing a pecking order, just like Jason's animals at the zoo. "The feeling's mutual," she says, putting down her glass. "Anyway, they're so young . . . I'm just happy they're having fun."

"And so great about them both being only children, right?" Dayna says. "I bet that's part of their connection. Were you like me? One kid's enough? Or was it not by choice that you had just one?"

Charlotte's so stunned by Dayna's gall that it takes a few beats to find her words. "Um," she says. "No, it wasn't *by choice*, I guess, but we're more than grateful for Bird—"

Dayna cuts her off. "I'd say we're better off, don't you think? Did you do fertility treatments? I didn't even bother. The number it can do on your body!"

Heat prickles behind Charlotte's ears. *Who talks like this to someone they barely know?* "Dayna, I don't—"

"Never mind," she says, lifting her glass. "None of my business. Though I will say, I think it's better for the kids, not having to share us, you know? And it's probably good for our marriages, too. Finch already says I devote too much time to Tuck. You want a tour of the house?"

"Sure," Charlotte says, dizzied by the exchange. "Sure."

Dayna leads her around for the next fifteen minutes, past paintings of Tucker she's commissioned, through the his and hers offices crammed with leather-bound books that have probably never been cracked open, and Charlotte thinks to herself that she hopes Birdie will just get this first relationship out of her system. She wants her to keep her options open, to put boys last on her list of interests, not to get too attached.

Maybe she's focused on Birdie keeping independent because she herself didn't. It was different, of course, but ever since Birdie first mentioned Tucker, she keeps thinking of Reese, the one and only boyfriend she had before Jason, and the person who haunts nearly all of her memories of her pre-DC life. She and Reese met in preschool, dated all through high school and college and most of graduate school, the two of them choosing to stay at Emory, where they'd both gone to undergrad, so that they could be together. He proposed just weeks before she defended her dissertation, on the dock behind her childhood home. Even though it feels like an entire lifetime since their relationship ended, like she's an entirely different person than the one she would have been had she stayed in Georgia, she still feels a little burn deep down in her chest when she thinks of Reese, remembering how he'd ruined everything they'd planned, how they'd been engaged barely a month when she found out he'd been cheating. And not just cheating but brazenly dating another woman for almost a year before he proposed, living an entirely different existence apart from hers, with dinner dates when she thought he was studying for the boards and romantic weekends away when he said he was roadtripping with buddies to football games. She had just come home from a run when the woman—a fellow medical student studying pediatrics named Tricia—knocked on the door of her apartment and tearfully confessed their relationship, the morose disappointment all over her face as she took in the ring on Charlotte's finger. She told Charlotte that they'd had a fight, and Reese had finally come clean about everything, confessing that Charlotte wasn't, in fact, an old flame who couldn't get over him and still called him sometimes. She also told Charlotte that Reese would never think she'd have it in her to come tell Charlotte about the two of them, and sure enough, that evening, when Reese came over expecting takeout and a movie, he actually tried to deny it at first.

For the longest time after she left him, the thing that bothered Charlotte the most was not that she'd been duped but that the person who'd done it had been someone she thought she knew so completely. She realized that it didn't actually matter how long you knew someone. People change. Sometimes not for the better.

"Where does Birdie's name come from anyway?" Dayna says as they return to the kitchen and she pulls another bottle from the wine fridge under the counter.

"It's a nickname. Her full name is Beatrice, after my grandmother."

"Oh." Dayna nods, a vacant expression on her face like she hasn't heard the answer or doesn't really care. "Cute. Well, let's go outside," she says. "See what kind of trouble the boys have gotten themselves into."

Dinner is served at a round wooden table under a trellis on the Cunninghams' patio. Birdie sits across from Charlotte between her father and Tucker, and Charlotte takes the lucky middle seat between Dayna and Finch, who wipes his glistening forehead with the inside of his wrist just after he rests a massive porcelain tray heaped with burgers, grilled chicken, and hot dogs in the middle of the table.

"So!" Dayna says, placing a napkin on her lap. "I've bought your book, Charlotte, but I confess, I haven't gotten to it yet. I *love* to read but there's just never any time!" She looks around the table, her eyes wide like she's searching for confirmation. Birdie nods politely at her. "Anyway, it's on my nightstand! I can't *wait* to dive in."

"So are you just happy all the time?" Finch says, clamping a hand on Charlotte's shoulder. "I'm sorry, do people constantly ask you that?" he says, leaning in so close that Charlotte can see a speck of pepper between his teeth.

"They do," Birdie says, taking a bite of her burger.

Charlotte winks at her, happy that her daughter finally seems relaxed. "It's true," she says, gearing up to give her usual explanation.

"So you just, what, never have a bad day?" Dayna says, her palms to the sky. "I mean, it seems that way!"

"Seriously!" Finch says, gesturing toward Charlotte. "You just *look* like a happy person!"

"So cute!" Dayna says. "Like a sweet little doll!"

Jason laughs. "Looks can be deceiving!" he jokes, the tone in his voice so lighthearted that the bite behind it doesn't register to anyone but his wife, who narrows her eyes at him ever so slightly to communicate her displeasure. "Trust me, she's not happy all the time!"

"Oh, well, that's a relief!" Finch laughs, clapping his hands together. "So you *are* normal!"

Charlotte clears her throat, giving Jason a pointed look, and delivers the answer she must give at least twice a week. "Of course I'm not happy all the time. Nobody is. But what we know from the research is that while everyone has a very clear . . . the psychology community calls it a 'happiness set point' . . . there are a lot of simple things we can do in our daily lives to bump up our overall satisfaction. That's what I'm focused on—the concrete, easy, achievable strategies that fit into our lives."

"Does drinking wine count for one of those strategies?" Dayna laughs, raising her glass.

"Absolutely!" Charlotte says, raising her own.

"But you must have a high set point!" Finch says, pinching her arm.

Charlotte shifts in her seat. She wonders if Finch is a little drunk or if he's just like this all the time.

"Wait! I want the husband's perspective," Finch says, pointing his fork at Jason. "What's she really like at home? Does the mask come off?"

"Happy wife, happy life!" Dayna says, to everyone and no one.

Charlotte's chest tightens, but she pushes past it, hoping that the actual tension between her and Jason isn't obvious to the others—most of all, to Birdie. "*Nobody* should be happy all the time," she says. "That's not the goal. The goal is feeling like you're ultimately headed in the right direction." She looks at Jason, realizing, as the words are coming out of her mouth, that that's exactly the problem. *She's not sure she feels like they're headed in the same direction anymore* . . . Their eyes linger on each other, and she knows he's heard her the same way, as clearly as if she'd just come out and said it.

He sits up in his seat, breaking the spell. "Charlotte's actually spent her entire career studying this stuff," Jason says, giving her a weak smile. She can't remember the last time he said something nice about her job, and she feels a warmth flood over her.

"I thought it would be more fun to study happiness than the alternative," Charlotte says, using another one of her frequent lines.

"Well, from what I've seen, it certainly seems to have paid off!" Finch says. "I see your book *everywhere*."

"Oh my God!" Dayna suddenly exclaims, clapping excitedly, like the cheerleader she must have been. "I just remembered something! I saw you on the *Today* show once! Last year, I think? I remember talking about it with some moms later. You're, like, famous!"

"No, I'm—" Charlotte starts.

"She was on the *Today* show again last week," Birdie interrupts, and looks at Charlotte and smiles.

"No way!" Dayna says, her eyes wide. "No way! With who? Savannah? Hoda?"

"It was the third hour," Charlotte says, downplaying it. "With Craig Melvin."

"Oh, him!" Dayna says. "Oh my God, he's so hot!"

Charlotte laughs and looks again at Birdie, smiling softly at her.

"That's incredible!" Dayna says. "Just incredible!"

"And she's speaking at Grey Browning's annual summit this month," Jason adds.

"You're kidding," Finch says. "At his ranch in Montana? That's amazing."

Charlotte glances at Jason. "Thanks," she says. "I'm actually pretty nervous—"

Finch interrupts her. "Have you read your mom's book?" he says, pointing his fork at Birdie.

"Yeah," she says, wiping her mouth with a corner of her napkin. "I have. It's really cool."

"Has some of her advice rubbed off on you?" Dayna presses. She's still studying Charlotte—the *Today* show appearance apparently impressed her—and it pleases Charlotte, she has to admit, that this status-obsessed nitwit seems a little bit awed by her.

"Oh," she says. "Sure." Charlotte watches her daughter tuck a lock of hair behind her ear and remembers how Birdie kept a gratitude journal for a while after the book came out. She was in seventh grade then, and Charlotte used to sneak peeks at what she had written in the little rainbow-patterned notebook she kept in her nightstand: *Dad bought me a pack of Sour Patch Kids at CVS*, an entry would say. *Hannah liked the picture I drew for her birthday.* Back then, all three of them made a concerted effort to go on walks together after dinner ("Exercise! Time in nature! Quality time!" Charlotte would extol, joking around, as they set off down the trail near their house), but the habit had somehow fallen off. Probably because they got too busy.

"I guess now," Dayna says to Birdie, looking back and forth between her and Tucker, "you have something new to make you happy!"

"Mom, God!" he says, squirming in his seat, and Charlotte

studies him again, looking for signs of trouble. She looks over at Jason, who raises his eyebrow ever so slightly, and she wonders if he's doing the same.

As dinner winds down, the kids flee, walking down to the pool holding brownies from the tray that Dayna brought out with a lame joke as she set it down about how she worked *so hard* to buy them. The conversation circles back, once again, to lacrosse. It's become clear, given how much they've already talked about it tonight, that the sport is the gear that drives their family.

"With all of the money we've spent on this fucking sport," Dayna says, a slight slur in her voice. Charlotte eyes her own glass, which Dayna and Finch have taken turns refilling all evening. Somehow, she still feels mostly sober, though she knows she must be pretty buzzed. "I'll go ballistic if he doesn't have a scholarship secured by this summer."

"When did he start playing again?" Jason asks.

He was four, Charlotte thinks, annoyed that he's encouraging them. *We covered this earlier.* She's tired and ready to go home.

"You know, the Cunninghams are lacrosse legends around here," Jason says to Charlotte. "All four of the brothers!" He turns to Finch. "Your brother, man! No offense—you were awesome, too—but Thomas . . ." He shakes his head in disbelief, as if seeing Finch's brother play would be like seeing the moon landing.

Suck-up, Charlotte thinks, smiling as she lifts her glass. The wine is warm now. Too acidic on the back of her throat. She eyes Jason's beer, still nearly full. *He'll drive home,* she thinks, remembering that he said as much on the drive over as she reaches for the bottle chilling in the middle of the table and pours a little in her glass. *Just a splash*, she thinks, *to get through this*.

"Speaking of brothers," Finch says. "How's yours?"

"Oh, Tate," Jason says. "He's doing really well. Lives out in Portland."

"Seems like the right place for him," Finch says, laughing. Charlotte's eyes fly to Jason, wondering if he'll call Finch out on this, which is so blatantly mean-spirited. It wouldn't take a rocket scientist to discern that Jason's gay brother and Finch Cunningham might not have been best buds in high school.

"He's really happy," Jason says. "He and his partner—"

"Like business or . . ." Finch says.

"Both actually," Jason says. "They run an architecture firm and they just got married a couple years ago."

"Sounds cozy." Finch laughs again and knocks Charlotte's arm with his hand.

"Right," Charlotte says flatly, scooting away from him in her chair.

"So, as you can see, it's not like any child of ours wasn't going to play lacrosse," Dayna says, steering the conversation back to her family, which is apparently far more interesting. "I remember when we had our first ultrasound . . ." Dayna starts giggling. "Remember, Finchy, how you joked that you saw a little lacrosse stick on the monitor!"

Jason starts laughing along, as if this is the funniest thing he's ever heard. Charlotte steals a peek at her watch. She looks down the lawn to where Tucker and Birdie are sitting with their feet in the pool and wonders what they're talking about.

"Just to be sure," Finch says, reaching across the table for Birdie's plate and clawing his fingers around her leftover hunk of burger. Charlotte watches, struggling to keep her expression neutral as he drags it through the puddle of ketchup on the plate and pops it into his mouth, the piece protruding out the side of his cheek as he talks. "When Tuck was in preschool we had his body type analyzed to see which sport he'd be most likely to excel at."

"Wait, *what*?" Charlotte says.

Dayna cocks her head at her like she's concerned. "You haven't . . . ? There's this state-of-the-art facility up in Gaithersburg. Lots of Tucker's teammates did it. My girlfriend back home, she had all three of her girls tested. And, wow, has it paid off."

"Her daughter's going to the Olympic swim trials next month," Finch adds. "Butterfly. Though . . ." He dips his chin and lowers his voice. "The poor girl, you should see the size of her back . . ."

"*Not cute*," Dayna says.

"I mean, why not set your kids up for success, right?" Finch says. "Birdie gonna play tennis in college? What are the best schools? Who has the best team? What's your plan?"

Jason sits up in his chair. "Yeah, yeah," he starts. "Fortunately, like with lax, some of the best schools for tennis are great schools regardless. We're talking Vanderbilt, Chapel Hill . . ."

"Scouts started looking at her?" Finch asks.

"Oh, scouts, well . . ." Jason's saying. "Not yet, but we feel pretty confident—"

"It's her freshman year," Charlotte interjects, annoyed by how they're trying to outdo each other. "We just want her to have a good adjustment to high school, first and foremost. If that includes playing on the tennis team, great. If not, great." She shrugs.

"Yeah, but . . ." Jason clears his throat. "*Of course* she's going to play! We wouldn't let her not play."

"It's not really a case of letting her or not," Charlotte says, adding a grin for good measure.

"You know what I mean," Jason says, an edge in his voice. "We wouldn't want her to lose an opportunity."

"Of course," Charlotte says. "But if she changes her mind down the road . . ."

"She's a good student, isn't she?" Dayna says, and for once, Charlotte is happy to hear her interjecting. "Tucker told me she's super smart!"

"Yeah," Jason says. "She's always liked school."

"Tucker, too, but honestly, who gives a shit?" Finch laughs. "You should see the way the kid handles a ball down the field."

"Ultimately, we just want our kids to be happy, though, right?" Charlotte says, unable to take any more. "I see how stressed out my Georgetown students are, and they're all high-performing kids. There's such immense pressure to perform," she says, noticing the slight grimace on Jason's face as she repeats herself slightly. "I just want Birdie to feel satisfied with her choices. Whether it's tennis or academics, or—"

"Oh, come on!" Finch groans. "I'm so tired of hearing about kids these days feeling under pressure. I mean, my dad was shipped off to Vietnam when he was eighteen. That's pressure! What do these kids worry about? How many likes they get on Instagram?"

"Is Tucker on Instagram?" Charlotte asks, glancing at Jason. As expected, he doesn't look pleased by her question.

"Well, they all are, aren't they?" Dayna says.

"Not Birdie," Charlotte says. "We're just not comfortable with it, given all of the research about social media and self-esteem, especially with girls."

"Well," Finch says, reaching over to grab her arm for the millionth time tonight. "You would know what's best, Dr. Happiness, wouldn't you?"

Charlotte doesn't love his tone, but she musters a smile. "At the end of the day, we're all just trying to do the best we can, right?"

"Jason, you work at the zoo?" Dayna says, changing the subject. "Tell me about that!"

As he fills her in, Charlotte begins to tune out, not because she's not interested but because she's heard these stories a thousand times, about how Jason was obsessed with the National Zoo as a kid and always knew he wanted to work there. She looks out at Birdie and Tucker again.

Finch knocks her arm with his knuckles. "Hey, I'm sorry," he says, under his breath. "I didn't mean to offend you just there." He leans in, his face close to hers.

"Oh, it's fine," she says. "I'm used to—"

"*Really,*" he says, and she notices the glassiness in his eyes. "I'm sorry if I . . ." His hand is still on her forearm, and suddenly he takes his finger, tracing a line up her arm, before dropping a hand to her thigh.

"What are you doing?" she yelps, leaping up from the table.

"What?" he says, swaying a little in his seat. "I didn't . . ." He puts his palms up and laughs. "Totally forgot where I was for a minute, man." He pushes his glass away. "Too much bourbon, I think." He laughs. "I was thinking you were Dayna. I'm so sorry!"

Charlotte's eyes meet Jason's. She taps her finger against her wrist. "Let's go."

"What happened?" Dayna says. "Did somebody spill—"

"Your husband, um—" Charlotte begins. "He was . . . I don't know what he was . . ."

Dayna starts to giggle. Charlotte's mouth falls open. She looks at Jason, who is standing now, clearly uncomfortable and not sure what to do.

"Oh, Finch," Dayna says, putting an arm around him. "I'm so sorry, you guys. My husband gets a little handsy when he drinks . . ."

"I really didn't mean anything," he says, wincing animatedly, like a clown. "I'm sorry."

"Trust me, he didn't mean anything," Dayna says, rolling her eyes. "This . . . happens."

"Okay, so . . . why don't we go?" Charlotte says, stepping away from the table. "It's getting late."

"I'm really sorry, man," Finch says to Jason.

"It's fine," Jason says, forcing a smile. "Really, totally . . ." He slices his hands through the air, crossing them in front of his body. "No worries. But I think we'll head out."

Dayna laughs and pats Charlotte's shoulder. "Please don't be offended."

"Oh, I'm not," Charlotte says, laughing it off, quickening her pace. *If we could just get out of here.*

"Geez, Finch, I hope they're not worried that Tuck takes after you!" Dayna says after they've rounded up the kids and are heading for the door.

"What?" Tucker says, turning.

"Nothing, honey." Dayna winks at Charlotte.

"Great to have you," Finch says, then has the gall to lean in for a hug, but Charlotte turns for the door, her hand on Birdie's back as they head out.

When they reach the car, she waits for Birdie to slip inside. "That was awful!" she whispers to Jason.

"It wasn't that bad!" he mouths, reaching for his door handle.

She glares at him. "Are you kidding me?"

"Just . . ." He presses his lips together like he doesn't know what to say. "I don't know, Char. Just let it go."

THREE

“What on earth are you doing?”

Jason looks up from his spot on the conference room floor, where he is working on a new project for one of his animals. He has pushed a table from the center of the room against a wall and is struggling to uncoil a bundle of fire hose that is approximately the size of a small dinghy.

“Oh, hey,” he says, breathless from his effort. His coworker Jamie is standing in the doorway, wearing a pair of gray cargo pants and the polo shirt with the zoo’s insignia that all of the keepers wear. She absentmindedly knocks her ever-present giant plastic Nalgene of water against the wall. “I got in really early so I thought I’d get to work on this while it’s still quiet.” He stops and rubs his forearm across his forehead. He’s sweating like crazy. “Now I understand why firefighters are so buff. This is so much heavier than it looks.”

“I think you’re man enough to handle it,” she says with a smirk, stepping into the room.

"Very funny," he says. "Thanks for the ego boost."

"Is this for the hammock?" She kneels beside him and touches the rope, and he catches a whiff of her coconut shampoo. It's a smell he's accustomed to, since she showers in the office locker room each morning after she bikes into work from Bethesda, and her brown curly ponytail is usually wet until lunchtime.

"Yeah," he says, rocking back on his heels. "For Niko, the new sloth bear." When he speaks to groups at the zoo—field trips or camps or the occasional corporate event—they're always surprised to learn that a big part of a keeper's job is to find creative ways to keep the animals entertained, mentally stimulated, and able to exercise their natural instincts while under human care. "It's not like I can go into the giant panda section of Petco," he usually jokes, a line that always gets a laugh.

"Oh, he'll love it!" she says. "So, what, you're going to weave it together?"

"Uh-huh. Hopefully. Remember the video I showed you of the one they did out in San Diego?" he says. "I talked to the keeper there a few days ago. Seems pretty simple once you get started. You want to help?"

She looks at her Ironman watch. "Sure, I can for a few minutes. I need to go check on Lucy before long."

"Great," he says, handing her the printout of the PDF the San Diego keeper had emailed him. "Here's the general idea."

She scrutinizes the instructions as Jason starts cutting the hose with the carpet knife that was recommended, and they fall into the kind of easy silence that comes with working side by side for almost twenty years. They were hired as keepers just six months apart—Jamie was first, she likes to point out—and for years, they were both in the Great Ape House. A few months ago, though, the longtime keeper of the Asia Trail exhibit finally retired and Jason was given the spot on the glowing recommendation of his predecessor.

He was a shoo-in for the job, which he had openly coveted since the summer he was eleven and saw the giant pandas for the first time at his day camp at the National Zoo. In addition to the pandas, he cares for sloth bears, red pandas, clouded leopards, small-clawed otters, and fishing cats.

"I can't believe how well Lucy's doing," he says. Lucy is Jamie's orangutan, who gave birth just last week. All of the orangutans are strong-willed, but Lucy is especially independent, and nobody was sure how she'd take to becoming a mother. Jamie and Jason had worked with her for over a year before they even considered trying for a pregnancy, just to see if she was up to the task.

"She's doing beautifully," she says. "Still no signs of rejection whatsoever."

"I'll swing by later and see her," he says, the word *rejection* ringing in his ears. He thinks of Charlotte the other night, how she pushed his hand off her hip.

"Try to come by three or so, if you can," Jamie says. "I'm leaving early today for a doctor's appointment. Lucy will be so excited to see you."

"Well, she always preferred me over you."

"Yeah, okay, whatever," she says, then pauses before adding, "Can you finally admit that Bobo did his job?"

Jason forces a smile. He'd been teasing Jamie throughout Lucy's pregnancy about Bobo, the stuffed animal orangutan that she'd procured from the zoo's gift shop to help get Lucy accustomed to caring for an infant and the fact that she would have to give her newborn baby to her handlers on a very frequent basis for checkups and the like, especially right after the birth. Jamie and Jason had spent countless hours teaching Lucy to place Bobo in an open-topped metal box that they had built into one of the Plexiglas walls of her pen so that the zoo's veterinary staff could access the baby for its assessments.

"Speaking of Bobo," he says. "Does the actual baby have a name yet?"

"Not yet." She rolls her eyes. Linda, their boss, is notorious for trying to make every event a publicity opportunity and has decided to hold an online vote to name Lucy's offspring. "Too bad he isn't a girl. We could have just named her Linda."

"That would be an insult."

"To the baby."

"Exactly." He laughs. "Though, I don't know, I think I'd love to have one of the animals named after me."

"Hmm, I can see it. Perhaps one of the sloths?"

"You're so funny today," he jokes, starting to weave together pieces of the hose. "All right, so I think if we just take turns passing this back and forth . . ."

"So you said you came in early?" Jamie says, picking up the PDF again.

"Just past seven."

"Eek, why?" she says.

He shrugs and turns away from her. "Couldn't sleep last night. Figured I might as well just get the day started." The truth is, he'd barely slept since Saturday night, after he and Charlotte got into a huge fight when they got home from the Cunninghams'. She was pissed that he wasn't more bothered by Finch's transgression and wanted to know why he didn't "stand up for her." But what could he have done? Of course it bothered him. Finch is clearly not the best guy, Jason's known that forever, but he isn't dangerous and he had apologized, and given that he was drunk and his wife was right there, Jason really didn't think he meant anything by it. Charlotte had every right to be angry but she herself was a little drunk and, as usual, she was overreacting.

"Everything okay?" Jamie says.

"Yeah, of course," he says. "Why?"

"I don't know," she says. "You look a little . . ."

"I'm fine," he says, pushing his thoughts away. "Really."

Even though Charlotte herself openly calls Jamie his work wife—they've worked together longer than he's been married—he and Jamie don't really confide in each other in any serious way. There was a time, absolutely, especially in the early years of their marriages, when they would gripe to each other about their spouses, though nothing major. Then, last year, Jamie's husband, Warren, died. He'd had a heart attack on the GW Parkway, right there in the car, with Jamie in the passenger seat and their twin eleven-year-olds in the back. They were on their way home from seeing *Hamilton* at the Kennedy Center, a show she'd been so excited to see that months earlier, she'd taken the day off to stand in line for tickets. She hasn't told Jason about the accident, but he knows that she was able to at least take over the wheel and get them safely to the side of the road. Still, Warren died before the ambulance arrived. It was one of those terrible, senseless things. He was barely forty-five, with a great family, great career, and he was one of those ascetic, ultramarathon-running health nuts who should ostensibly live forever.

Jason sneaks a glance at Jamie, knowing he could never tell her that the real reason why he arrived at work so early is that he was desperate to get out of the house. He knows she would give anything to have Warren home, no matter that he sometimes forgot to flush the toilet and treated the inside of his car like a dumpster. Jason feels a wave of guilt settle over him. In the moment, his fights with Charlotte feel so urgent and all-encompassing, but afterward, the general malaise of their marriage feels stupid, like a waste of what they could actually have if they could just figure it out. If something happened to her—say, if her plane went down during one of her business trips, or a shooter burst into her classroom, both things he sometimes has flashes of worry about—he would tear himself apart with regret for not cherishing every moment they'd had together.

He looks at Jamie, biting her thumbnail while she reads over the instructions for the hammock, and thinks back to Warren's funeral, which was held at a little church by the water in his and Jamie's hometown on the Eastern Shore. After the service, he and Charlotte stopped at a little roadside place for a late seafood basket-and-beer lunch, and talked about the things you talk about after such a tragic thing happens—how fleeting life is, how important it is to appreciate what you have while you have it—but the next morning, it was business as usual, the two of them alternately bickering or avoiding each other completely.

After their fight on Saturday night, they'd managed to do the latter all day Sunday, and he'd hoped that everything would just blow over. Charlotte took Birdie to the mall for some new clothes for spring, and he'd gone for a run, and then to his parents' place to mow their yard and water the plants, since they weren't due back from the Outer Banks for another month or so. In the evening, Charlotte pulled a lasagna from the freezer, and they'd all had a pretty nice dinner, talking about Birdie's big match coming up against Marshall, the top-ranked team in the state, and the big conference that Charlotte is speaking at in a couple of weeks at a gajillionaire tech CEO's ranch in Montana, which he can tell she's nervous about from the way her face pinches whenever the subject comes up. He told them about the hammock for Niko, and Birdie, who rarely shows as much interest in his job as she did when she was younger (he was unquestionably the star at every career day while she was in elementary school, which had always felt like redemption for the sliver of a paycheck he got compared to the defense contractor dads and corporate attorney moms), actually seemed really into it, and even asked to see the plans that his zookeeper friend had sent over.

But then, later, while he was doing the dishes, and Birdie was splayed out on the couch in the living room reading *The Canterbury Tales* for school, he heard the distinct sound of Charlotte lifting the wine bottle out of its slot in the refrigerator door. She'd already had a glass at dinner (maybe two?), and while he didn't want to be monitoring her (it's not like she's been pouring vodka into her morning coffee), it did seem like she was drinking more than ever lately, and he had started to notice a correlation: The more she drank, the more they fought.

Sure enough, after Birdie went to bed and Charlotte took over her spot on the couch, he was watching the Caps game in the chair across from her when she looked up at him, her laptop balanced on her legs, and laid into him *again* about how he had kissed Finch's ass all night Saturday night. He told her—*again*—that he was just trying to be a good guest. Of course he knew that Finch Cunningham was a blowhard and a prick (how many times had they been over this?), and he also told her, for possibly the millionth time, that he didn't love the idea of Birdie dating Tucker either, but that the worst thing they can do is try to pull Birdie away from him, because then she'd only want to be with him more. And it got worse from there.

It was infuriating, how the fights just came out of nowhere, as intense and sudden as summer thunderstorms. There'd been a time when they knew better, when they would rationally talk things out, using the techniques that Charlotte had learned in her psych classes as an undergrad—no blaming, no finger-pointing—but now it almost seemed like they were too far gone for that. Worse, it felt like they both knew as much, that it was the unspoken thing between them, and what did it say that neither of them was trying to do anything about it?

"This is a nightmare," Jamie says, trying to keep the hose in place as Jason pushes the pieces together to close the gaps. The weaving reminds him of those pot holder craft kits that Birdie used to get for birthday gifts when she was younger.

"Hold on a sec." Jamie lets go and takes a big swig from her Nalgene, and when she lifts the edge of her shirt to wipe her lips, Jason unwittingly catches a glimpse of the slice of skin above her waist. He feels an involuntary little surge and looks away.

Jamie's attractive, outdoorsy and muscular, like the rock-climbing women in the Patagonia catalogs that come in the mail. He'd be lying if he said he hadn't had the occasional lazy fantasy about her. It's only natural given all of the time they spend together, and Charlotte is so constantly and increasingly irritated by him that Jamie is, in some ways, a sort of escape valve, but he'd always felt intensely guilty when he'd thought of her privately, in the ways he knew he shouldn't, so he tried to just not let his mind go there.

"So did you do anything special this weekend?" she asks, sitting cross-legged next to the hammock.

"Not really," he says, reaching for the PDF to study it once more. He glances up at her and she's looking at him oddly. Suspiciously. "What?"

"You seem weird," she says.

"Weird how?" he says, leaning back and wiping his palms on the front of his pants.

"You seem edgy," she says. "Stressed."

"Compared to you, everyone seems edgy and stressed." More than once, Jason has teased that she's in the wrong part of the country—she belongs out in Boulder or Southern California, among laid-back people like herself—but Jamie has always said that being the most easygoing person in DC would probably make her the most uptight person in one of those places, and she's probably right. How would Charlotte handle it, he wonders, if an ape came at her full speed, throwing its own shit right at her? Would she turn and laugh, like Jamie had a few weeks ago? Unlikely.

"I told you, I just didn't sleep well. And this thing . . ." He gestures toward the hose.

She tilts her head to the side, squinting at him. "Jason, c'mon," she says, reaching over and giving his arm a quick squeeze. He notices the little silver ring she wears on her middle finger, a simple knot with a turquoise stone in the middle. She told him once that Warren gave it to her when they were teenagers. "Seriously, what's wrong?" She sits back on her heels, biting her lip like she's thinking something through. "If I can be honest . . . ?"

"What?" he says, feeling a squeeze in his stomach. They never talk like this.

"I can tell that something's up. You haven't seemed like yourself for a while now."

A heavy silence falls over the room. He doesn't know what to say.

"Listen, it's none of my business," she says. "But I've spent a lot of time in therapy this year so I feel like I'm developing kind of a sixth sense. You just seem . . . sad." She pauses, then chuckles. "Dude, I'm the one who lost my husband. If either one of us gets to mope around and be miserable . . ."

Jason looks away, feeling himself flush. *This is exactly . . . Oh, fuck it.* He takes a deep breath. "Charlotte and I aren't really getting along that well lately."

"What?" she says, her tone kind. "I never would have known."

"I know," he says, then shrugs. "Actually, I don't know . . . I don't . . . It's stupid."

"What do you mean?" she says. "What happened?"

He shakes his head, wishing he had a good answer. "Things just haven't been ideal between us for a long time."

"I'm so sorry," she says.

"It's fine," he says, not letting his eyes meet hers. "It'll work out." He can feel her watching him, studying him. When he looks up, she is still watching him, like she's waiting for him to say more.

"You know, you can always talk to me about stuff," she says, smiling.

He nods. "I keep thinking it will pass. That it's just a rough patch."

"Right," Jamie says.

He runs his hand along the hose. "Charlotte's just been so . . ." *Stop talking, Jason*, he tells himself, but it's like there's this tiny part of him that suddenly wants to get this out. "She used to be this . . . fun person . . . but everything with her job is so crazy now. I thought the intensity would die down a little but it hasn't, and I'm worried about the toll it's taking on her, and on us. You can't imagine how much it's changed her."

"Charlotte?" Jamie says. "The happiness expert?"

Jason rolls his eyes. "Yup, that's Charlotte, all right; Little Miss Sunshine, met with thundering applause wherever she goes. She jets all over the country, signing her books, staying at five-star hotels. She goes on national television, gets interviewed in newspapers all over the world." It's like a dam has broken, he can't stop now that he's started . . . "And I don't think she enjoys one iota of it. All she fucking does is complain."

Jamie narrows her eyes at him.

"What?"

"Well . . ." she says.

"What? Tell me."

"Honestly, you sound a little jealous, Jason."

"I'm not jealous!" he barks, a little too insistently.

"Don't get—" She lifts a palm. "Don't get mad, but is it possible you resent her success just a little?"

His ears burn. "How could I be resentful? Her success is our success, right? She does well, we all do well."

"You sure?"

He shrugs.

"Maybe she feels under pressure, now that she has this image to uphold? Or maybe working so much has made everything harder for her."

He thinks about the way Charlotte constantly talks about how tired she is, how every "how are you?" he tries is met with something like "exhausted" or "stressed." And then there's the drinking, the constant replenishing of the wine supply. "I know." He nods. "Trust me, that's crossed my mind. And it's not like we haven't talked about it . . . or . . . I've thought about it. She gets so defensive . . ."

"It's been a big year for you guys, with Birdie starting high school, and you starting Asia Trail."

"Yeah," he says. *Not that Charlotte ever asks about my job,* he thinks. "You're right, I'm sure it's all related. I just don't understand why she's decided to make me the . . ." He pauses, running his tongue along the inside of his bottom lip. "She just seems like she hates me. Honestly, Jamie, we can barely be in the same room." He looks up at her for just a moment before he looks away. There's a part of him that's horrified that he's revealing all of this; he doesn't talk like this with anyone; the only person he's ever really confided in is Charlotte, and on very rare occasions, his brother. But it also feels good, finally getting it all out. "It's really bad."

"Are you thinking . . . I mean, when you say 'really bad,' how serious is this? Are we talking, like . . . separation?" she asks.

"I don't . . . No," he says. "Definitely not." He's thought about it, fleetingly, what it might look like if things were to get to that point: a sad single-dad apartment in one of the generic high-rises in Ballston. Nights alone, the creepy old guy at a bar, surrounded by twenty-somethings. "No, that's not what I want."

"What about counseling?" she says. "Honestly, I don't think the boys and I would be able to get out of bed without it."

He sighs. "No." The truth is that he'd asked Charlotte once a few months ago if she would go to a marriage counselor and she refused. "How would that look?" she'd said. "For me, given my so-called expertise, to be in counseling?" He could tell, once the words were out of her mouth, that she was embarrassed to have said it, to have thought that her sort of fame was the kind that would make her so instantly recognizable.

"Wait," Jamie says, lowering her chin. "Is there someone else?" she whispers.

"What? No!" he says. "No, of course not." He shakes his head. "I would never, and Charlotte is married to her job. That's the other thing she said about counseling: When would she find the time?"

Jamie scrunches her lips to the side, thinking this over.

He puts his hands out. "Don't get me wrong, it's not that I'm not excited for her, or proud of her success, it's just . . . it's hard to explain. I don't mean to put it all on Charlotte," he adds. "It's me, too. I just need a break. I think we both need a break. I'm sorry, I shouldn't be . . . This feels stupid, talking to you like this."

"No, no, please," she says. "Don't ever say that. I know how hard marriage is. What happened to me didn't erase that. I remember feeling the way you do. I used to fantasize about getting my own secret apartment, or a little houseboat somewhere, a place to go where nobody could find me."

"Really?" He laughs.

"Oh, yeah," she says. "All the time. I had the whole place decorated in my head. And I had a *Vespa*."

"You're kidding?"

"I'm not." She laughs. "You should get your buddies together. Go on a golf trip or something. Go down to your parents' place at the beach, I don't know . . . what do a bunch of forty-something dads do when they need to blow off steam? Actually, don't answer that. I don't think I want to know."

Suddenly, his phone vibrates in his pocket. He pulls it out and looks at the screen. "Speak of the devil," he says, holding it up to Jamie.

"Be nice," she says.

He puts his hand to his mouth. "I really didn't mean it that way," he says, standing and walking out of the room as he answers.

"Jason, *fuck*!" Charlotte screams into the phone. "You won't believe this." He can tell from the whooshing hollow background noise that she's in the car.

"Is everything okay?"

"Yeah, yeah, I mean, it's not okay, but there's no emergency. I was just on my way in and Stephanie called. You won't believe this!"

"What?" he says. "What is it?"

"The other night. Friday? When Birdie slept over with Hannah?"

"Yeah?"

"They snuck out of the house!"

"Snuck out of the . . ." The images flicker before Jason's eyes: Birdie, walking along a dark street, or in a random Uber headed into DC. *Oh, God.* He'd done plenty of stupid things as a teenager: climbed the fence at the pool to swim in the middle of the night, egged a few houses with his friends, used a fake ID to get into Mr. Henry's, a bar on Capitol Hill where everyone was underage. But *Birdie*? "How did Stephanie find out?"

"Another mom told her at her exercise class early this morning. That kid Morgan Duncan, who used to be in Birdie's Girl Scout troop? She felt guilty and confessed to her mom. Our daughter, on the other hand, did not."

"Where did they go?"

"According to Hannah, there was a group of five of them—the other girls were all sleeping over at another kid's house—and they went to the playground by the Knights of Columbus pool to meet up with some boys."

"What boys?"

"Who do you think, Jason?" she shouts. "Tucker and his friends, of course! His Instagram account, remember? You'd told me to stop spying, but I knew in my gut something was off, Jason! I knew it!"

He closes his eyes and rubs the bridge of his nose with his thumb and forefinger. "Okay," he says. "So this obviously isn't good, but at least they didn't get into any trouble. At least they weren't, you know, out in DC or something, or didn't encounter anyone who could've . . ." His voice trails off as he remembers the stories that sometimes show up in the daily local news email he subscribes to, about some drunken guy exposing himself or groping a young woman as she walks home from one of the bars in Clarendon. To think that Birdie . . .

"Jason, she's never openly lied to us like this before!" Charlotte wails. "She's never done anything like this before! She waltzed into the house on Saturday morning and said they went out for ice cream and watched *Ferris Bueller* and went to sleep! And then she and Tucker sat right through that dinner on Saturday, the two of them! After they'd been doing God knows what on that playground the night before!"

"I know, I know . . ." he says, his mouth going dry. "It's not good."

"*Not good?* That's an understatement! We have to ground her, Jason. She can't think for one second that this is remotely okay."

"I'm with you," he says, pacing back and forth in the narrow hallway. "One hundred percent."

"Okay," she says, some of the force leaving her voice with a sigh. "Okay. So will you promise you'll help me with this tonight? You won't back down with her?"

"What?" he says, incredulous. "I do realize that the parenting of our child is half my job. Of course I'm going to handle this with you! And of course I'm not going to 'back down.' What makes you . . ." He sees someone down the hall—Alan, opening the door to his office, a thermos of coffee in his hand—and he realizes that he can't get into this now. Not here. "Never mind."

"Okay," she says, her voice clipped. "Well. I guess I'll see you at home then."

"See you then," he says.

He shoves the phone into his pocket and turns the corner back into the conference room.

"Well, you won't believe this," he says to Jamie, who miraculously, in the short time he's been on the phone, has almost half the hammock woven. He relays the details of Charlotte's call, and when he's done, nervously tapping his fingers against his side, still thinking of Birdie in the dark with that damn kid, Jamie bursts out laughing.

"This is funny?" he says, a contagious smile materializing on his face despite what he's just learned.

"Of course it is!" she says. "Don't you remember being a teenager? Your first love? I mean, obviously you need to ground the poor kid, but Jason, come on . . . We all did stuff like that!"

"You did?"

She nods. "You bet your ass I did! Warren and I snuck out and met up so many times in high school. Those are some of my best memories!"

"I guess you're right," he says. "But were you *fourteen*?"

"More or less." She shrugs. "Give or take."

He nods. "I know you're right, but try telling that to Charlotte."

"She's pissed?"

"Out of her mind."

Jamie sticks out her bottom lip, a sympathetic pout. "I'm sorry," she says. "You guys are just . . . You and Charlotte will work this out, I know you will."

"I hope so," he says.

"Just be . . ." She pauses. "Not to be all . . ." She tilts her head toward the ceiling, like she's weighing whether to say more. "Life's too short, Jason. You never know what's around the corner."

"I know," he says, feeling guilty. "I'm sorry for—"

"Please!" She stands and grasps his arm again, but this time she leaves her hand there. "What are friends for?" And then, for only the second time in their two decades of working together, the first time being the day she came back to work after burying her husband, she leans into him and hugs him. Hard. *Too hard?* Jason freezes. This isn't a platonic side hug like you'd give a co-worker. He can feel her chest against his, her torso against the bump of his belt buckle. He feels a prickling chill run over him. It is weird and a comfort, all at once. "I'm here for you," she says as he starts to pull away, her voice a little too soft in his ear.

FOUR

"Dammit!" Charlotte screams, banging the heel of her hand against the steering wheel after she hangs up with Jason.

She moans into the hollow cocoon of her Volvo SUV, bumping the back of her head against the headrest. This is the first nice new car she's ever owned, a present to herself on her birthday last year when Loretta, the sputtering Subaru Outback that she bought during grad school, finally died. Unlike so many of the people she knows in Arlington where even the high school parking lot, packed with hand-me-down Audis and BMWs, looks like a luxury car dealership, she and Jason had never really been car people. But now that they had the money for it, she'd decided that her daily battle with DC traffic was enough reason to go for something nice. Plus, she reasoned, aside from her office in White-Gravenor Hall, her car (which Birdie nicknamed "Serena," no surprise) was the only space that was truly her own. She could zone out, tune out, and often, when she arrived somewhere, pulling into the parking garage at work or the driveway at home or the grocery store parking lot, she'd realize she'd been riding along in hermetic silence.

She is sitting in bumper-to-bumper traffic on the Key Bridge over the Potomac River, the spires of Georgetown's stone buildings on the bluff just ahead of her. She adjusts the vents on the dashboard, punching up the AC to full blast, letting the clean cool air blow right into her face, settling her. It's not like there's something she wishes Jason had done when she reported Birdie's transgression to him, but the problem, like so many things in their home life these days, is a task she'd like to be able to just delegate to him, the way he handles cleaning the gutters and mowing the yard. Sometimes she just feels so fucking alone when it comes to all the things she's juggling, and when something unexpected comes along, it feels like a fireball hurtling toward her.

Charlotte edges her car forward, trying to encourage the Camry in front of her to *move* already. She can see the driver's head tilted down, probably scrolling through the latest inane top ten list on Facebook or something, and she tightens her grip on the steering wheel, visualizing herself just *ramming* into the bumper. *What's that TV show about women who lose it?* Breaking Point? Snapped? One rainy Saturday morning last year, she was speaking at a wellness conference in Connecticut, and the time management expert onstage before her asked the audience to make a list of all of the responsibilities, big and small, that they dealt with regularly: shuttling kids to their various activities, running meetings and writing reports, buying toilet paper, paying bills, doing the laundry. Backstage in her metal folding chair, she played along, jotting her list in the margins of the speech she was holding in her lap. When she finally finished, looking down at the ballpoint scrawls, she didn't feel relieved or justified or proud. She felt an immense heaviness, one that made her want to burst into tears and crawl into bed, have somebody give her a spoonful of something and run a palm across her forehead. Jason didn't seem to get that. She'd tried to explain it to him months ago, how it felt embarrassing to admit it, but she yearned for someone to take care of her, for a change.

She thinks of the day ahead, the weight of its responsibilities settling on her chest: the class she'll teach, the doctoral student she'll counsel, the emails and voicemails and emails and voicemails, the notes she'll work on for the big talk out in Montana, the preparations for the trip she's taking tomorrow to Savannah, et cetera, et cetera, et cetera. And then, when she finally returns home, rumpled and tired, her feet aching and sweaty in the flats she wears to work, the biggest mountain of all: how to address the issue with Birdie.

Her eyes flick to the clock on her dashboard, knowing her mother's probably wondering why she hasn't called her yet for their standing morning chat. Charlotte can picture her now, sitting in the brick courtyard behind her home on Wright Square in one of her loud silk caftans, her breakfast (a porcelain teacup of Maxwell House, two Splendas, no cream) beside her, picking the crinkled dried petals from her gardenias while she bitches about how the gardener isn't watering them enough. Her mother's not the person to go to if she's craving nurturing or encouragement. Her mother has the maternal instincts of Cruella De Vil. She considers dialing Stephanie instead to powwow on punishments for the girls.

On her right, a few kayakers are setting out on the Potomac, and a rowing team, maybe from one of the high schools, is gliding back toward the boathouse just on the other side of the bridge. Beyond, the Kennedy Center gleams in the yellow morning light, the Washington Monument in the haze just behind it. Back when she and Jason were first dating, she made this trip constantly, back and forth from her place on O Street to his apartment in Arlington, and this very view made her feel such a sense of peace about her decision to leave Georgia. Her heart was full, every facet of her life a piece of evidence leading to the conclusion that she had made the right choices and had an incredible future ahead of her. She was so happy back then. *Happy, happy, happy.* She hates how that word has become so loaded for her now.

The Camry starts moving, then stops short again. "Fuck!" Charlotte screams, piercing the quiet. She lays on her horn, then glances out her rearview and guns the gas, weaving around the guy, who's now flipping her off. "Asshole!" she screams, flying through the light at the end of the bridge just as it's turning red, barely making it, and then her phone buzzes through her speakers. Fancy Nancy, the caller ID on the dashboard says.

She takes a deep breath, taps the green answer icon. "Hello, Mother," she says over the speakerphone.

"I've been waiting for your call."

"I'm sorry, we got a little bit sidetracked this morning." In the background she hears yipping; Paisley, her mother's Havanese, ten pounds of hell on earth, and known, on more than one occasion, to drag the bodies of the stray cats that roam downtown Savannah onto her mother's cobblestoned patio. Charlotte hates the dog, but then again, she hates lots of the things that her mother loves.

"Oh?" her mother says. "What's happening now?"

Charlotte clenches her jaw. Her mother always acts like Charlotte's life is a circus designed to amuse her, like she's lying on a chaise, getting fanned by someone holding a massive peacock feather, while a tiny Charlotte sprints in a hamster wheel on a table beside her. "It's Birdie, Momma," she says, knowing this admission might be a mistake. "She snuck out on Friday night when she was sleeping over at Hannah's house."

"Oh, Charlotte!" Her mother's cackle fills the car.

"What's so funny?"

"How worked up you are! How—Oh, Charlotte!"

"Are you kidding me?" Charlotte says. "I distinctly remember your demeanor during my and Aaron's teenage years and it wasn't particularly calm."

"Oh, I remember!" her mother says. "I remember all right! And it sure wasn't fun, having you run all over the city of Savannah and every barrier island and Lord knows where else with Reese Tierney!"

"That was different," Charlotte says. "It was a simpler time. And Savannah isn't a big city like DC. There were only so many ways I could get into trouble, and given that everybody knew everybody, I didn't even try."

"My ass, you didn't," her mother says, laughing. "I have a long memory, don't forget."

"Oh, I haven't," she says. *If anyone can hold a grudge . . .*

"Birdie will be fine," her mother says.

"I know, I know," she says, pulling onto campus, the dappled sun through the trees making her squint.

"This is what being a teenager is all about."

"Uh-huh," she says. "I know."

"And she's falling in love!" her mother says. "You can't deny her that experience, Charlotte, or the fact that she's growing up. She deserves those memories. Everyone does."

"When did you become so rational?" Charlotte says, scowling. "You sound like the wise old matron in a Lifetime movie."

"Oh, well, thank you, Charlotte," her mother says. "There's nothing I enjoy more than being called old and matronly all at once."

"You're welcome," Charlotte says, pulling into her usual parking spot. She starts gathering the pile of notebooks and papers from her passenger seat and shoving them into her bag.

"Speaking of young love, I was at a luncheon yesterday and heard that Reese's divorce is final."

Charlotte stops what she's doing and sits back in her seat. "Oh?" she says. "Well . . . good for him."

"Mm-hmm," her mother says.

Charlotte waits a beat or two for her to elaborate, but of course she doesn't, because this is the kind of conversation her mother relishes. Rather than just come out and give her all the details, she'd rather have Charlotte ask for them.

Charlotte closes her eyes. "Who told you?" she finally asks.

Her mother laughs, just faintly enough. "Bryn Howard, that woman who has the little gallery on Abercorn. She said he's keeping his place out on Wilmington Island but I'm sure that girl took him for all he was worth."

"Well, that's hardly surprising. Wasn't that more or less her intention since the day she met him?" Charlotte says, remembering the wedding announcement from the *Atlanta Journal-Constitution* that her mother had clipped and sent in the mail a few years ago. Over the past twenty years, Reese had become a sought-after plastic surgeon in the Southeast. The bride had been his patient, a former University of Georgia gymnast who'd done a few rounds on the pageant circuit before homing in on him.

"That's awful, Charlotte," her mother says, though she'd probably said the same thing herself.

"Momma, why else would a girl her age—what is she, twenty-six? Twenty-seven?—marry a man in his mid-forties?"

"Maybe they fell in love."

"Oh, come on."

"I just hope he's not too heartbroken," her mother says, and Charlotte feels her ears start to burn. Her mother's never come right out and said that she thought that Charlotte made a mistake by not taking Reese back, but she's made her opinion crystal clear.

"Well, why don't you bring him a goddamn casserole?" she says, yanking her bag onto her shoulder and stepping into the parking lot, slamming her car door closed with her foot.

"Charlotte! Language!"

"He's not that great, you know," she says. "Don't forget what he did to me."

"Well . . ." her mother says, leaving it at that, the silence enough to communicate everything she wants to say.

Ten minutes later, Charlotte strides down the dim hallway in the psychology department, still smarting from the phone call, when her coworker Liza comes out of her office with an overstuffed messenger bag slung across her middle.

"Heading to the lab?" Charlotte says, pushing her mother's voice out of her mind.

"Yup," Liza says, her shoulders slumping like she's a balloon being deflated. Liza is actually a lovely person, one of only a few colleagues that Charlotte would call a real friend, but she's also whiny, which is funny given that she spends a lot of her time with little kids, studying their response to media, mainly cartoons, and how it affects the way they learn. "Hey, I saw your *Today* show clip!" she says, straightening the strap on her bag. "It was in that weekly PR email. Great job!"

"Oh, it was?" Charlotte frowns, thinking of the email that's blasted to the school's employees, students, and alumni. "I mean, thank you . . ." Unlike some of her colleagues—academics are a snippy sort, no matter how you cut it—Liza has never seemed anything but genuinely happy for Charlotte's success, or even mostly indifferent to it, which is a huge relief.

Before they can say goodbye, Tabatha, their department chair, comes out of her office, narrowing her eyes at Charlotte. "No TV crews today?" she says, arching an eyebrow. "We don't need to reserve the conference room for hair and makeup?"

Charlotte purses her lips, digging her fingernails into her closed fist at her side. "No," she says, exchanging a quick glance with Liza, who waves quickly and steps away, muttering that she's late.

"It's amazing you get any work done, with all of your media commitments," Tabatha says, and crosses her arms. She has been the chair of the psychology department at Georgetown for a little over a decade now, and she's never liked Charlotte. Her specialty is the mechanics of memory, and she's a sturdy woman, tall and almost rectangular, with salt-and-pepper hair that is always pulled back in the same kind of velvet headband that Hillary Clinton used to wear. She is serious, which is normal for a university faculty member, but her crime is that she's humorless. When Charlotte first started working with her, she yearned to be able to ask her father how to handle her, because after a lifetime with her mother, he knew better than anyone how to mess with someone who couldn't take a joke.

Instead, when Tabatha passes over her at department meetings, or looks at her the way she's doing now, like Charlotte's presence is as vaguely amusing as that of a mediocre street performer, Charlotte finds herself taking up the slack, ingratiating herself in a way that makes her feel like a poodle in a carnival, balancing on a ball on its hind legs with its tongue hanging out. *Like me! Like me!* Why she bothers seeking out this woman's approval is beyond her, but it pisses her off, how Tabatha behaves toward her, because there is no basis for it. If anything, she should be grateful to Charlotte for the attention—and funding—she's brought to the department.

"Just headed to my office," Charlotte says, smiling up at her boss. "Need to run through some emails before class."

"You have that big talk in Montana coming up?"

"Yes," Charlotte says, her nerves flaring at the mention of it. This talk—at the ranch of a Silicon Valley bigwig during his annual "thought summit"—has her on edge, not only because of the intimidating invite-only audience but because of the heavy media coverage it gets. Charlotte has pored over articles about it, in the *Atlantic*, the *New York Times*, *Vanity Fair*, and it still baffles her a little bit that they want her there at all—last year's speakers included a Nobel Prize–winning chemist and a former secretary of state—but according to her agent, the organizer is a fan who's kept a stack of her books in his office to give to guests since it first came out.

"And you'll be out later this week, yes?" Tabatha says.

Charlotte knows she's doing this just to toy with her but it isn't any less irritating. "Yes," she says, sighing. "Tomorrow and the next day. But I'm leaving *after* my class. I won't miss anything."

"Of course you won't," Tabatha says, turning back to her office. "Have a nice day."

Charlotte's little office at the end of the hallway smells dusty and stale, and looks predictably industrial, but she's done her best over the years to make it more welcoming, both for herself and for the students who come to her with questions, or debates, or tears, depending on the day. There is a busy rug, in blues and greens that remind her of the shoreline of her childhood, on the floor that hides the ugly tan carpet beneath, and the books in the shelves that line one wall are arranged by color—red, orange, yellow, and so on—a project that she and Birdie took on two summers ago after they saw a picture in a magazine.

She hangs her bag on the yellow hook she fastened to the wall just inside her door and walks to her computer, her mind drifting again to Birdie, and how she'd brought up Charlotte's latest *Today* show segment the other night at the Cunninghams'. She feels duped now, jilted. Was Birdie just buttering her up? Throwing a little extra honey her way in case she was found out?

She distracts herself for the next thirty minutes, flying

through her emails, then stops, taking her hand off the mouse, when she lands on the message that Wendy, her literary agent, had sent last week, just four minutes after she'd gone off air, on the ball as always. PHENOMENAL. BLEW ME AWAY. YOU'RE A NATURAL. She'd read the message when it first came in, of course, but now she reads it again, her eyes scanning the words over and over, like her fingertips over a string of prayer beads, wanting the easy praise to make her feel better, but it doesn't. She'd sent back a quick reply last week (Thanks! Glad you liked it!) conveniently ignoring the sentence at the end of Wendy's message saying that they really need to talk. Charlotte's agent has been on her case for weeks now; emailing, calling. "The publisher isn't going to wait around forever for your next book," the last voicemail said.

She scrolls through her unread messages and finds the email from the university's public relations department, where a still from her appearance is featured just below the introduction. She'd chosen a peacock blue blouse, a shade that the personal shopper she'd enlisted at Saks a year ago had accurately told her was her best color, and right before air, she'd wiped off half of the bright pink lipstick that the heavy-handed makeup person at the studio insisted would look great on camera. The segment was part of a weeklong series about mental health, and it was her first on the morning show where she was the sole expert, a promotion from past appearances when she'd shared the couch with everyone from a goofy dating expert who seemed barely old enough to drive a car to a trio of sweet centenarians who'd shared their secrets to a long life.

She clicks on the video, remembering, as Craig Melvin introduces her, that she'd wondered, despite the smile in his eyes, if he was just going through the motions, counting the minutes until he could get back to "real" reporting instead of running through her tips for creating a daily happiness "routine," an idea from the producer who'd called her the week before to book it. When she starts speaking in the video, her voice explodes into the room, and she ticks the volume down on her keyboard, her cheeks warming, embarrassed at her on-camera enthusiasm. She hardly ever watches these things. She can't stand the sight of her amped-up self, the way she overdoes it, the pitch in her voice rising higher, her hands windmilling in front of her as she speaks, the eager way she sits so close to the edge of her seat that it almost seems as if she might launch herself into the host's lap at any moment.

This isn't the image she wants for herself. *Susie Sunshine.* It's not who she pictures when she thinks of who she really is, deep down. And yet, minutes after she went off-air, while she collected her things in the greenroom off set, she watched as her number of Instagram followers ticked up and up and up, from just under 90K to almost 93K, and felt weirdly redeemed. And then later, riding home on Amtrak, the messages from her reliable superfans: You were fantastic today, Char, they said, like they were old friends. The blue looked great on you! I've already started implementing that tip about a midday break—I actually left the office at lunch for the first time in ages and browsed a bookstore—just for me! It made her feel a little bit nauseous, but of course, also validated. The praise made it easier, and there were worse things than peddling her kind of medicine. Why not just keep going, her own feelings be damned.

She closes the link to the *Today* show website and checks

the time, then stands and smooths her skirt, pretending not to notice the thoughts that keep circling in her head about how many faculty members might have found the PR email in their inboxes and, seeing her name, thought, *Oh, God, her again.* How many of them think of her the way Tabatha does? How many can see right through her? She picks up her phone off her desk and, leaving the office, closing the door behind her, she swipes at the screen as she begins to walk, looking for an email to answer, a post to like, something—anything—to distract her.

Her class becomes the day's bright spot. Though they are hurtling toward the end of the semester and the students are typically restless, ready to head into summer, today was different. They spent the ninety minutes sharing the results of one of her recent assignments, where she'd had her students write letters of gratitude to people who'd made an impact on their lives: coaches, parents, grandparents. At one point, Josiah, a prep school kid hailing from the Upper East Side of Manhattan (whom Charlotte had, until today, always thought was a bit of an asshole) silenced the room with his story of the oncologist who'd helped him beat his childhood leukemia. It was one of those special, unexpected moments in the classroom that reminded Charlotte why she loved teaching. Not speaking, not writing. *Teaching.*

She walks back to her office, checking her phone to see whether any of the eighty students whom she's just left have tweeted anything interesting during class. The university generally doesn't allow students to use their phones in the classroom, but because her course has become such a press win for the school (with a photo of her lecturing, arms raised enthusiastically, on the cover of this year's alumni-giving mass mailing to prove it), her students are allowed to comment on her lessons online, often even live-tweeting statements as they come out of her mouth.

At first, when the class was taking off in popularity, this was great. It was instant validation and feedback when a student tweeted out a point she'd made in class, especially on days when it didn't seem the kids were engaged and she'd leave the room feeling frustrated, like she'd just spent an entire lecture throwing pebbles into a dark canyon, wondering whether anything she'd said resonated. Now, it sometimes feels a little too public, especially since she knows that a lot of her students' parents are monitoring her every move.

There are just a couple of tweets today: a Bart Simpson GIF from Marcus Gromley, a Hurricane Katrina survivor who is one of her best students, showing the cartoon character cartwheeling with a caption about the surprising benefits of generosity, and a tweet from Susan Thompkins, a mild-mannered premed student whose parents are a nightmare, with a link to a study Charlotte had referenced about the correlation between doing good deeds and overall life satisfaction. Back when she started teaching, she might get one or two overinvolved parents each year. "Helicopter parents," they called them then. Now, the term is *snowplow parents.* She gets emails from them every single week, wanting her input on how their kids are doing in class, complaining about something she's taught them ("How is meditation going to get my kid into law school?"), asking her for deadline extensions on their children's behalf. It amazes her that these adults—often high-achieving ones with busy schedules; diplomats and doctors, bankers and attorneys—find the time to email their kids' college professors, but they do. *And Jason has the gall to tell me* I'm *overinvolved*, she thinks to herself, sitting down at her desk. She feels a chill run through her, thinking again of Birdie sneaking out, what she could have been doing, and how deceiving them so blatantly didn't seem to faze her at all. She keeps getting images of her worst possible fears. Birdie in some dark corner, on a squeaky metal swing, Tucker pressing himself against her, pressuring her, whispering insistently in her ear. She also knows she's *catastrophizing*—the very thing she tells her anxious grad students not to do when they tremble in the chair facing her desk, certain they're going to fuck up and flub their dissertations—but she just can't help it. How can any mother?

Birdie's probably just finishing lunch. Charlotte feels the urge to drive back to Arlington and pull her daughter out of school and talk to her now, filled with something she's never really felt before as a parent, a weird mix of anger over the way Birdie flat-out lied to them and an underlying yearning to hold her close, to protect her from the things that might have transpired on the playground the other night. Tons of families they knew, including Stephanie's, were members at that pool, and they had spent a lot of time there as a family when Birdie was younger, often for Friday night cookouts on the lawn that separated the pool from the playground, the kids climbing all over the swings and the monkey bars, their hands sticky and their faces Popsicle-stained. She picks up her phone and shoots Stephanie a text: Did you decide on a punishment for Hannah yet? We should probably conference on this.

Immediately, a message comes back: Probably should, she says. What do you think? Draw and quarter them? Public stoning at

Starbucks in front of all their friends? Charlotte laughs. Seriously, though, Stephanie texts again. I feel terrible that it was my house they snuck out of.

Stop, Charlotte types. She pictures Stephanie, who's retired from the Army but works part-time doing marketing for a veterans' charity, sitting at her kitchen table in comfy clothes. Next time, though, it's totally fine with me if you feel the need to punish them with whatever hell you went through during Basic Training, she types.

Got it, Stephanie replies. But hopefully, there's no next time. Gotta go. Conference call.

Charlotte puts down her phone and digs a granola bar out of her desk drawer, then looks up at her computer monitor. There are forty new messages since she left for class less than two hours ago, including one from the university PR office, telling her that the reporter from *U.S. News & World Report* who was going to sit in on her class next week has to cancel, but that another one, this one from *Good Day L.A.*, would like to do a segment with her at the end of the month. Again, like the tweets, it's the kind of thing that would have thrilled her a few years ago, but now it's just one more item on a long list of things to handle. She thinks of Tabatha, ribbing her this morning for her media attention, and closes out the program and grabs her phone instead.

She hasn't Instagrammed anything since the bunnies on Saturday, and she tries to post something at least every couple of days. *Maybe a quote*, she thinks, scrolling through the cache she keeps bookmarked. She finds one from *To Kill a Mockingbird*: "People generally see what they look for and hear what they listen for." She types out a caption that she knows is too cheesy—So focus on the good!—and tags it #MondayMotivation.

She's about to close out the program when she notices a little red icon at the top of the screen, indicating that she has a new direct message. She gets several a day, most from readers simply thanking her for the book that are easy enough to answer with a quick "Thanks!" and a smiley face emoji. This one is from somebody named @KGpartyof5. She squints at the little photo on the woman's account, trying to see if she's one of the people who regularly message her, but this woman—big glasses, a denim shirt, living in Muncie, Indiana—has never contacted her before. And that's a good thing, she realizes, her pulse rising as she reads the message, which is essentially a long catalog of insults.

Who the fuck do you think you are, it reads. I am raising four kids on minimum wage, one of them with severe special needs that our public school doesn't have the capacity to deal with. My husband runs his father's dry-cleaning business but every day it's like we might have to close up shop because with so many people out of work around here, nobody needs their work clothes cleaned anymore. My main babysitter, my sister-in-law, has a severe opioid addiction after getting prescribed painkillers for knee surgery a couple of years ago, so she can't help anymore. And you want me to sit down every day and write about what I'm grateful for? You want me to go breathe in fresh air when I don't have an extra minute in my day? You want me to "consider generosity"—Charlotte smarts, remembering the drawing of two hands clasped together that she'd posted last week—when every fucking thing I do all day long is for somebody else? I watched your TED talk after one of the waitresses I work with sent it to me and I thought it was bullshit. I wasn't impressed. "Action first, feelings later"? Try that when you meet with your kid's teacher and find out there isn't any funding for the special ed services you're supposed to be entitled to by law. ANYWAY. Just thought you should know that I see you and you're completely out of touch. Have a nice day!

Charlotte drops the phone. It's hardly the first negative message she's ever received, but this one's a little harsher than usual, or maybe it burns because of where her head is today. She turns in her chair and looks out the window, feeling tempted to write back, though she knows better, when she hears her phone start buzzing behind her.

She picks it up and, seeing the caller ID, puts it back down on her desk. It's Wendy, her agent. *Fuck*, she thinks. *Fuck, fuck, fuck, fuck, fuck. When the hell am I supposed to find the time to write a follow-up?* she wants to scream. *And about what?* Her mind zips back to @KGpartyof5. *I see you*, her message said. She swallows, a lump forming in her throat, and hears a ding signaling that Wendy's left a voicemail.

Reluctantly, she picks up the phone to check the message.

"Jesus, you're hard to pin down these days!" Wendy says. "Listen, I know it's the end of the semester, but we really need to talk strategy for the second book, okay? I'm coming down to DC for lunch. Next week. Wednesday? Call me back or at least shoot me a message to confirm. Thanks, love."

Charlotte swipes back to Instagram, where there are forty-six comments on her post. Heart emojis, heart-eye emojis, rainbows, and smiley faces. Thanks! they say. Just what I needed! OMG, exactly! Somehow, it doesn't make her feel any better.

FIVE

Jason is lifting a paper take-out container from a plastic bag on the kitchen counter when he hears the garage door opening.

"Thanks for getting that," Charlotte says, turning in to the kitchen, and he feels his shoulders drop. She sounds like she's in a pleasant enough mood, or at least a better one than this morning.

"Sure," he says, opening one of the containers. She throws her bag down and reaches across the counter for one of the yucca fries he picked up along with Peruvian chicken and salad and plantains. "Crisp & Juicy?" she says, referencing the place around the corner. There are dozens of Peruvian chicken places all over the DC area but this is their favorite, in rotation since Birdie was still in diapers.

"What else? How was your day?" he asks.

"Long," she says, walking to the refrigerator. "I need a glass of wine."

"Actually, grab me one," he says.

"Really?"

"Why not?" he says, shrugging, trying to keep the mood light.

"You almost never drink with me anymore."

He purses his lips, telling himself it's not a dig. *Don't react*, he thinks to himself, though what he wants to say is that she just drinks all the time now, with or without him.

She places the glass of white wine next to him. "How was your day?"

"Fine," he says. "Good, actually. We put the hammock we built in the sloth bears' enclosure and they really seemed to take to it. Niko even ate his meal in it."

"Niko?" She squints, trying to place the name.

"The sloth bear," he says, certain he told her about him.

She shrugs. *Of course she doesn't remember*, he thinks. *Her job stuff crowds everything else out*. "So where is she?" she says.

He nudges his chin toward the ceiling. "In her room."

She sits at the counter, watching as he pulls plates from the cabinet. "How'd she seem?"

"Normal as always," he says. "She was walking up to the house from practice just as I was getting home. Had her head in her phone, as usual."

"Texting Tucker?"

"Yup," he says.

"So what did you say to her?"

He looks at her, blank-faced. "Say to her? I didn't say anything yet. I wanted to wait until you got home."

Her eyes widen, and any optimism he had about the evening fades. Just when he thought they might be able to do this without arguing . . . "So, what?" she says. "You just pretended like everything was normal?"

He grabs three forks from the drawer, telling himself not to react. "No, Charlotte," he says. "Like we talked about this morning, I thought we were doing this together. I thought we'd wait until you got home." *And you would have totally lost your mind if I did this without you*, he thinks.

She sighs and takes another drink, her face settling into its familiar scowl.

"What?" he says.

"Just don't make me be the bad guy," she says. "I don't want you to just sit off to the side like you usually do, letting me do the dirty work."

"Seriously?" he says. "That's what you think I do?"

She rubs an invisible little circle into the space between her eyes with her fingers, and for a moment, he's reminded that there was a time when this was his signal. She'd be worn out from a long week or an argument with her department head, or despondent after taking another pregnancy test, and he would see her do this and walk up behind her, pull her hair off her neck, and rub her shoulders. He wonders if she remembers this now and if she misses it. *Unlikely*, he thinks.

They sit there in silence, the tension building. He can hear the faintest thrum of Birdie's music on her iPad upstairs. "Why don't I go get her?" Charlotte finally says, lifting herself from the kitchen stool, like it's a herculean effort.

"Shouldn't we talk about this first?" he says. "Decide on a punishment?"

"Well, she's grounded," she says.

"But what are the specifics?" he asks, thinking back to this afternoon at work. He'd gone over to the ape house to see the baby orangutan, and he and Jamie and Ian, one of their other coworkers, got talking about Birdie, which led to a funny conversation about the various punishments they received as kids. Ian had literally had to stand in a corner with his nose touching the wall. Jamie's dad made her take an actual bite out of a bar of Irish Spring when he overheard her call her brother an asshole. Jason hadn't had much to add to the conversation. His parents were so mild-mannered, and his older brother, Tate, was really the one who had been the troublemaker, getting caught with a bag of weed under his mattress, skipping class constantly. Jason was in his sophomore year of high school when Tate finally came out to them, and his parents, both lifelong Catholics, were so caught up in getting used to the idea that Jason had managed to stay under the radar and out of the way.

"We could take her phone," Charlotte says.

"But she needs it in the afternoons," he says, thinking through the logistics. "If she needs to reach us after school, or if a practice runs long or is canceled."

"Right," she says. "Well, it needs to be harsh. We need to scare her straight so that this is a onetime offense. If she ever does anything like this again, she's toast."

A slight smile appears on Jason's lips. He can't help it. There was something about the conversation at work today that made him feel like this isn't such a big deal. Charlotte's intensity, in comparison, is kind of funny.

"What, Jason?" she says.

"More than likely, she's going to do stuff like this again, Charlotte. Maybe she won't sneak out, but maybe she will."

"So, what?" she snips. "We just let it go?" She shakes her head, looking at him like he's a moron.

"Of course not!" he says. "Listen, I'm as pissed as you are." He thinks of Tucker, the little prick, and heat rises up the back of his neck. "But we both know that if we really lay down the law, she might not hear that we also don't want her doing this stuff because it's not safe. I don't want her to think we're just punishing her for the sake of it, you know?"

She nods and he finds himself doing the same. *Okay*, he thinks. *Getting somewhere.*

"Maybe we shouldn't let her see Tucker anymore," she says.

"Charlotte, you know what that will do."

"I'm just saying," she says. "If we really want her to learn her lesson." She gets up to pour herself more wine. "You want?" she starts, nudging the bottle toward his glass on the counter before she realizes he's barely drank any. "Never mind." She leans against the refrigerator after she's closed it, her arms crossed over her chest. "Well," she says. "You don't seem to like any of my ideas, so *you* come up with something. I'll follow your lead."

"Fine," he says, saying it not so much because it's what he wants but because he just doesn't want to deal with *this* conversation anymore. Honestly, a part of him feels like dealing with Birdie will be easier.

"So you said *nothing* to her?" she repeats again. "She has no idea what's—"

"Charlotte," he says, his annoyance finally building to the

point where he can no longer hide it. "I saw her for like thirty seconds before she ran upstairs to shower and start her homework."

"Okay, okay," she says, raising her palm to him as she leaves the room. "Got it."

When Birdie walks in for dinner, she's wearing last year's Christmas pajamas, which Jason's mother had left on their front stoop on the morning of the twenty-fourth in a handmade drawstring bag, a felt Santa sewn onto the front. After two boys, she's always gone a little overboard with the girlie stuff for Birdie, and the gifts in general, but Jason never minded it. Nancy, his mother-in-law, has been such a lackluster grandparent, visiting them only once in the past several years (and complaining the whole time about the weather, the traffic, the people), that he was happy to have his mother take up the slack. The pajamas are hot pink flannel with a Frosty the Snowman print, the pants too short now, exposing Birdie's ankles. She's fresh from her postpractice shower, running a brush through her long hair.

"You should have seen my serve today, Dad," she says, reaching for a plate. He takes a step back, watching her fill it, her head bobbing to some song she's singing in her head, and that's what does it. He was disappointed before, but now, seeing the overt duplicity, the fact that she doesn't seem to care at all that she totally lied to him and Charlotte . . .

"What?" she says, turning and smiling at Jason. "What is it, Dad?"

He looks at Charlotte for just a moment, coming around to her point of view more with every second that passes. "Nothing," he says, pretending to be casual, trying out a strategy that's just occurred to him.

Charlotte lifts an eyebrow. He watches as she uses a pair of tongs to grab a chicken breast out of the container, placing it on the plate in Birdie's hands. She looks at Jason, then back at their daughter. "How's Tucker?" she says, not a hint of anything sour in her voice.

"He's fine," Birdie says, flopping down in her usual seat at the kitchen table, straightening one of the straw place mats that Charlotte puts on the table in the spring. "All lacrosse, all the time right now."

Jason's eyes meet Charlotte's again. He remembers something he once heard, on a stand-up special on Netflix or something, about the difference between men and women when it comes to aggression: With men, it's all physical; you see a guy try to pull one over on you, you want to punch him in the face. But with women, it's worse: one hundred percent psychological warfare.

"Is that so?" Charlotte says.

"Yeah. But, you know, it's totally fine and everything. I get it," Birdie says, waving her fork around as she talks. "With me and tennis . . ."

"Uh-huh," Jason says. He sits and wipes his palms along his lap.

"But actually . . ." Birdie raises a finger, pausing to finish a bite of chicken. "I need to ask you guys something."

Jason's eyes meet Charlotte's across the table.

"What is it?" he manages, unfolding his napkin on his lap.

"Tucker's best friend, Colin, is turning sixteen in a few weeks and Tucker is going to have a pool party for him," she says, her forehead wrinkling above raised eyebrows, eyes wide in nervous anticipation. "Would it be okay if I go? His parents will be there and everything."

Charlotte sits up straight in her chair, resting her elbows on the table, crossing her hands at her chin. She narrows her eyes at Birdie. "Well, I'm pleased that you asked," she says.

Jason lowers the drumstick he was about to bite into. "Birdie, we need to talk to you about something," he says. Her eyes flicker for a split second. Part of him wants to see how long she's willing to go before she confesses. Whether she'd fess up if they didn't say anything. Birdie lifts her fork and then puts it back down, then reaches for one of the little plastic containers of mayonnaisey sauce that came with the meal and starts turning it in her hands.

"What is it?" she says, her eyes darting back and forth between her parents.

Charlotte reaches for her wineglass.

Jason clears his throat. "Birdie, we found out something a little troubling today," he begins, but as Charlotte lowers her glass, it clatters against her plate.

"Birdie, what on earth were you thinking?" she suddenly says, cutting him off.

"Wha—" Birdie stumbles, her eyes widening, her cheeks reddening.

"You and Hannah? Sneaking out of her house? Do you have any idea what could have happened to you? Did you really think we wouldn't find out?"

Birdie squeezes her eyes closed, a look on her face like her stomach is cramping, and Jason feels a sudden unexpected pang of sympathy for her. She's never lied to them, not in any serious way, at least not that he knows of. When he looks over at Charlotte, she's staring at him, an annoyed, expectant look on her face.

He clears his throat. *So now she wants me to jump in.* "We're really disappointed, Bird," he tells her. "And your mom's right, something terrible could have happened."

Her hands fly to her face and he can see that they're shaking. She starts to cry. "We didn't even do anything!" she suddenly wails.

"Well, that inspires the question, doesn't it?" Charlotte begins. "What *did* you do?"

"We heard you went to—" Jason starts, but Charlotte puts her hand out.

"Let *her* tell us," she says, crossing her arms over her chest.

Birdie's face is deep red now, her eyes filling with tears. "We didn't do anything, really! Just walked around! Me and Hannah and then some girls who were sleeping over at that other girl Izzy's house. It was stupid."

"Just walked around?" Charlotte says. "Are you sure?"

Birdie nods. "Yeah, Mom. I'm sure. We just . . ." She pauses, sighs. "We went to the Knights of Columbus playground." She shrugs. "I don't know why. It was dumb. I'm so sorry, you guys! I'm so, *so* sorry!"

"And that's it?" Jason says. "Absolutely nothing else you need to say?"

Birdie's knitting her fingers together in her lap. She swallows. "Some boys met us. Tucker and some of his friends. I . . ." Tears start rolling down her cheeks. "I'm sorry!" Her face crumples. “I don’t know why we did it. They texted us and we just . . . I’m sorry!”

Her eyes meet Jason’s, searching, for just a second, to see if she’s been absolved, it seems.

“You are so incredibly lucky that nothing happened to you,” he says. “That’s the first thing. And neither of us are thrilled about you openly defying Hannah’s mom by sneaking out of her house. But what really bothers me . . .” He looks at Charlotte. “And your mom . . . is that you lied to us, Birdie. You did something you knew you shouldn’t, and then you kept it from us.”

“Do you know what it was like to learn that from another parent?” Charlotte says.

“Mom, I—”

“Was there drinking?” Charlotte asks.

Birdie’s eyes widen, genuinely stunned. “*Drinking?* No! Why would—”

“Birdie, listen,” Jason says. Charlotte seems amped up now and he doesn’t want this to get worse than it needs to. “We know you’re going to test things. We know that being a teenager means that you’re probably going to want to push your limits, and you’re probably going to mess up. But you absolutely cannot lie to us. Under any circumstances.”

She nods.

“Your dad’s right,” Charlotte says, looking at him. “We were both teenagers once, believe it or not, and we messed up, too, but that doesn’t mean you’re not going to get punished for this. So, no, you absolutely cannot go to the party. That’s the minimum.”

Birdie starts to cry harder. She wipes her nose with the back of her hand.

"In fact, you're grounded," Charlotte continues. "For the next few weeks, you will do nothing besides school and tennis. No social plans. No seeing Tucker."

"But, Mom!" Birdie suddenly wails. "What am I . . ." She looks back and forth between them. "How long?" she asks, panic in her voice. "If I can't see him—"

"What?" Charlotte says. "If you can't see him what?"

"Never mind!" she screams, jumping up from her seat. "You guys just—"

Jason's heartbeat quickens, little tap-tap-taps. This isn't his daughter. She is *such* a good kid. People used to make jokes when she was little. "Watch out when she becomes a teenager," they'd say. It always pissed him off. Charlotte, too ("What? Little girls aren't allowed to get angry or act out?" she'd say. "Is that the problem?"). But now . . .

"Your mom and I will talk about exactly what this grounding is going to look like," Jason says.

"I want you to really think about whether Tucker Cunningham is the right boy for you," Charlotte says, her voice ratcheting up in volume, her priority clearly elsewhere. "If this is the kind of thing he's encouraging you to do—"

"Mom!" Birdie says. "He's not doing anything! This is not his fault! Don't blame him!" She flies from her chair and races out of the room. A moment later, her bedroom door slams.

They sit there, silently for a minute, neither of them saying a word.

"Well, that went well," Charlotte finally says. She lifts her fork and then puts it down again. She finishes the last bit of wine in her glass.

"Yeah" he says, exhaling. He didn't realize he'd been holding his breath.

"Yeah, what?" she says.

"I guess we'll just see how it goes?"

"Jason, I don't want her anywhere near that boy."

"So you've mentioned," he says.

"I can't believe you don't agree with me."

"I agree with you!" he says. "But—" He closes his eyes for a moment, collecting himself. "Listen, I get where you're coming from," he whispers. "But we can't forbid her from seeing someone. This isn't Romeo and Juliet."

"Oh, please." She stands and goes to the refrigerator. "It's called *parenting*, Jason." He watches as she serves herself another glass of wine.

He's not sure why he says it but he does: "Healthy pour."

"What?" she says, whipping around.

"You really need to drink that?" he says.

"You're kidding, right?"

He shrugs and pushes his plate away. "It's Monday night," he says.

"Exactly," she says. "And it's been one hell of a Monday. I think I deserve a little wine."

"That's your third glass," he says.

"You're tracking how much I drink now?" she says.

"Maybe somebody ought to be," he mutters. He doesn't want to hurt her, he really doesn't, but he's so tired of this. He's so sick of her getting home and sinking into a bottle, how she lashes out at him after she's had a couple of glasses. *If she could just—*

"I can't believe you're actually going to get on me about the amount of wine I'm drinking right now," she says. "After I, as usual, did all of the heavy lifting when it came to that conversation with her."

"Please, Charlotte," he says. "Maybe you could try letting me get a word in."

She shakes her head. "I can't deal with you tonight," she says, walking out of the room with her glass.

"The feeling is mutual," he says, knowing how stupid it sounds, how immature, how impotent. He listens for Birdie upstairs, hoping she hasn't heard them.

The only other time that Charlotte can remember Birdie overtly lying was four years ago, when she was ten. She'd begged them for a pair of Converse high-tops, and they'd seen an opportunity to teach her a lesson about earning money. One of the things she and Jason talked about often back then, when their financial situation was different—and they actually talked—was how they didn't want their daughter's view of the world to be skewed by the overt wealth that she was growing up around. Birdie had plenty—Jason's and Charlotte's jobs were good ones—but lots of the kids that Birdie went to school with had their own en suite bathrooms and movie theaters at home. They had second (and sometimes third) homes, passports full of stamps.

To earn the sneakers, Birdie did chores around the house: feeding the dog, keeping her room tidy, folding clothes with Charlotte and Jason in the family room while they watched *America's Funniest Home Videos*. And then after about a month, they all made a special trip to the mall together to get the shoes. She'd chosen a bright turquoise pair, and she was so excited about them that they had the salesperson cut the tags off so that she could wear them out of the store. For the next several weeks, the only places she didn't wear them were bed, the bath, and her tennis lessons (and that had been a bit of a battle, requiring her coach explaining to her why they weren't appropriate for the courts).

And then all of a sudden, she stopped. Charlotte asked her why she wasn't wearing the shoes and Birdie gave all sorts of excuses: She wasn't in the mood to wear them, they made her feet hurt, she wanted to wear something other than sneakers on the days she didn't need to wear them for PE. Charlotte worried that a kid at school had made fun of them, but when she asked, Birdie insisted that wasn't it.

One afternoon, she finally, tearfully, came to Charlotte with the shoes behind her back. She confessed that a few weeks earlier, she was messing around and tied the laces of the shoes together while they were on her feet. She tied not just one knot, but a bunch of them, and ended up tying them so tightly that she couldn't get them undone. She didn't know why she did it, she just did, and she'd finally had to cut the laces with scissors to get her feet out. When she told Charlotte this, she wouldn't look her in the eye. She cried, her shoulders shaking, and confessed with a solemnity that would make you think she had done something truly despicable—cheated at school or been cruel to a friend. Charlotte had to fight to keep a straight face and hide her smile as she pulled Birdie in for a hug and assured her it was okay.

How did they get from there to here, she wonders now, sitting at her desk in the little living room they'd converted into a home office, looking out the window at the dark street. Birdie's upstairs doing homework, Jason's upstairs avoiding her. She is attempting to work on her notes for the Montana talk—her usual speech doesn't feel like enough for this crowd—but all she can think about is her daughter.

Birdie refused to talk to her after dinner. Charlotte had tried, speaking in a soft voice on the other side of her bedroom door, but Birdie said she wanted to be left alone. She knew it was unrealistic to expect that they'd get through all eighteen years of Birdie's childhood without a snag, but this was not what she wanted for them. She wasn't one of those lenient mothers who wanted to be her kid's best friend—that didn't seem to benefit anyone—but she'd never wanted to replicate how her own mother had straitjacketed her with antiquated rules about the way girls were supposed to behave. There had been white-gloved cotillion classes, teaching her how to waltz and identify a salad fork. There were strong admonitions about what she was to wear and how she was to speak. And then there were the weigh-ins: From the time Charlotte was ten until she finally started refusing around age sixteen, her mother had made her stand on a scale each morning, then wrapped her shoulders tightly with an Ace bandage before she put on her Savannah Country Day School uniform so that she would learn good posture. Jason had thought she was lying the first time she told him about this little routine. He was sure it was something she had seen in a movie, not her actual life.

Charlotte didn't want to be that kind of mother. If anything, she wanted to parent the way her father did. Her sweet daddy had been her mother's foil: gentle, quick with a joke, a sparkle in his eye. For her and her brother, he had been the benevolent undersecretary who balanced their mother's dictatorial reign—or, at least, that's how Charlotte likes to remember him, his flaws buffed out of her memory. She chooses to focus on the good things: how he was in the stands at every single one of her softball games. How he taught her to catch and gut a fish, and how to keep proper score of a baseball game. He'd died her senior year at Emory, from a melanoma tumor on the back of his neck that spread before they could catch it, which was not a surprise at all given how many years he'd spent on his boat in the high Georgia heat without a speck of sunscreen.

Birdie, she thinks, sipping from her glass. *Fuck Jason. Fuck him and his judgment.* Who did he think he was? She almost wants to have another glass just to spite him, but that would mean opening another bottle, and there's a deep down part of her that knows that if he sees an empty bottle in the recycling bin the next morning, and another bottle open in the fridge, it will confirm . . . She twirls the stem of her glass between her fingers. She doesn't need it anyway. Not with the flight tomorrow, work . . . She feels a sinking sense of dread, her stomach clenching when she thinks of how upside-down it is to be getting on a plane in the morning to speak to a bunch of strangers about happiness when her own daughter is miserable. *You're out of touch*, that message said today. *I see you.*

Her eyes well up with tears. She leans down to pet Sylvie, who's lying on the floor beside her, and the dog starts to stir, yelping in her sleep, dreaming. Charlotte looks at the time on her monitor. It's nearly 11:30. She scans her professional Facebook page, which she never really wanted to have to manage but which her publisher insisted she use as a "tool to connect with readers." Earlier in the day, before leaving the office, she had posted a question, a low-effort perennial that her followers loved nevertheless: *What do you do to make your Mondays brighter, better, happier?*

She scrolls through the comments—eighty-seven of them, about going to movies, taking bubble baths, going out to dinner, going for a run—and tries to will something witty to type in return, but she just can't do it. She scrolls through her news feed, looking at the posts—senior prom pictures, requests for donations, sweaty finish line photos, vacation pics—and before she can think it through, she enters Dayna's name into the search field. In the photo on her profile page, Dayna's standing between Finch and Tucker on a boat. The photo is old—Tucker barely clears her shoulder—but Dayna looks much the same, though the large sunglasses she's wearing obscure much of what Charlotte can see. Tucker looks different—a little goofy, neck too long, teeth crooked—the way boys do as they're heading into puberty. Finch and Dayna are not exactly smiling, instead conveying self-satisfied smugness.

Before she closes the browser, Charlotte types in another name: Dr. Reese Tierney. She and Amanda, her lifelong best friend and now sister-in-law, had made a joke of it when they learned that Reese was opening his own practice. They wondered whether he would become one of those doctors on the billboards lining the highway that snaked into Savannah, his likeness in scrubs looming next to before and after photos of a woman's saddlebags. It was an easy thing to latch onto, to make Charlotte feel better about the fact that he had hurt her, even though she knew deep down, from the conversations she'd had with Reese so many years earlier, late at night, that one of the reasons he chose the dermatology specialty he did before he went into plastic surgery was her father's illness. Reese had been close to him, too, the three of them fishing together, going out on the boat, shooting the breeze in the backyard for hours on end. Reese was the one who comforted her when they learned how extensively her father's skin cancer had spread. Reese had been the one who cried along with her, his hand linked tightly in hers as her father's coffin was lowered into the ground.

He doesn't have a personal Facebook page, just a business one that links to his office website, which she clicks through to. She hasn't looked at this in a while, though she has called it up before. She studies the photo of him next to his bio, remembering what Amanda said the first time they saw it because it is so true. He looks like a soap opera doctor. *Dr. McCheaty*, they'd called him.

He'd sent her pleading emails after she moved to DC, begging her to reconsider. She'd kept them for a while, in an email folder marked "Personal" that she finally deleted one day when she was pregnant with Birdie. There would have been all kinds of problems had she gone back to him. They might live next door to Aaron and Amanda, raising their kids alongside each other like they'd always said they would, but she would always worry about him and whether he'd be capable of deceiving her again. God, he'd hurt her.

On the other hand, it would be an easy life. A simple life. She wouldn't have the career she has now, that's for sure, though given what it's been like lately, that almost sounds like a relief. She and Amanda would go for long walks in the mornings, they'd meet for lunch and mani-pedis and prowl the stores on Broughton Street.

I should stop, she thinks, staring at his photo. *I should go to bed.* She knows better than to let her mind wander back to a place that can look idyllic in retrospect, a phantom life that wasn't meant to be. She doesn't think so, at least.

Her daughter is upstairs sleeping. Her husband is upstairs, too. She looks at Reese and she remembers the two of them, moonlight shining, their bare feet side by side on the dock, all of the promises he made to her, all of the ways he said he'd make her happy. She closes the browser and grabs her glass, putting it to her mouth, practically sucking out the last sip, knowing, of course, that it's empty.

Upstairs, in the dark bedroom, Jason can't sleep. He scrolls through links to articles he's already read: the latest about more wildfires in California, a gruesome news story about more violence in Venezuela. He swipes over to Charlotte's Instagram account. He doesn't post any photos himself, but he'd signed up when her book came out, to watch the wave of excitement as it unfolded, to cheer her on from the sidelines, and to follow the zoo's account, of course.

At first, it seemed like something she had to do. She had to present a more polished version of herself. Wittier. More together. But now, it pisses him off, because the distance between who she is and who she claims to be has grown. He looks at the time stamp on the photo and sees that she posted it three hours ago, around the time she was done slamming the dishes into the dishwasher, clanking around the first floor angrily, furious at him once again. The photo is of the pile of stuff that Birdie left on the mudroom floor when she came home from school: her tennis racket and duffel bag, a backpack, the purple hoodie she's been wearing instead of a coat. Life with teenagers, the caption says. I could tell her to pick up her things—what I usually do—or I could remind myself, just this once, that the day will come when the house is too quiet and I will miss this.

He knows it's different now, more voyeuristic and duplicitous, checking in to see what his wife is putting up, in this alternate online life that she leads, separate from him and their family. The thing is, it almost always confirms for him what he's already thinking in his ugliest moments. She is faking it.

He puts his phone down on his chest, the blue light glowing in the dark, and stares up at the ceiling.

And then he starts to cry.

It comes out of nowhere, surprising him like a hiccup, but when it starts, it doesn't stop. He can't remember the last time he did this, but it comes like a flood, loose and out of control, all of the frustration and tension that's been building up, everything not like it should be, the way it is supposed to be, the way he thought it would be.

He hears Charlotte's footsteps on the stairs and wipes his face, hurrying to collect himself, his breath shuddering as he turns away from the door, putting his phone facedown on the nightstand. He yanks the comforter up to his chin. He closes his eyes as if he is asleep.

Charlotte tiptoes past the bed and closes the bathroom door quietly, then flips on the light. While she's brushing her teeth, she grabs her phone and scrolls through Instagram, not even really thinking about the fact that she's doing it. She spits into the sink and looks back at her direct messages, the one from @KGpartyof5 looming at her like it's outlined in neon.

She taps on it. *I'm the kind of person who writes back,* she tells herself, *even when the feedback is critical.* She stumbles a little and leans against the sink. I'm sorry that you feel the way you do about my work, she types. I can assure you that science supports my theories about "acting first, feeling later" but I also totally get your frustration. Yes, compared to bigger challenges like the ones you mention, some of the things I post can seem trivial, but I really only mean to be a help. Trust me, I get it when you say I seem out of touch. I really do. I have my own problems. I doubt myself all the time. I don't have everything figured out. She pauses, questioning whether she ought to delete this, but then continues on anyway. I apologize if I gave you the impression that I have all the answers, because believe me I don't. I'm just trying to help. Thanks.

SIX

The minute Charlotte steps out of her Uber and onto the circular driveway in front of her brother's house, she can hear her nephew John Martin's new drum set, which Amanda had warned her about.

"I cannot tell you how happy I am to see your face!" Amanda wails from the doorway. She is dressed in her usual head-to-toe athleisure—a tight-fitting tank top and a pair of plum-colored leggings with mesh cutouts that crisscross over her thighs. "Please, for the love of all things good and holy, could you bring some estrogen into this place?"

Charlotte hoists her roller suitcase up the stairs and when she gets to the top, Amanda embraces her tightly. "Your hair's cute," Amanda says, tugging at the ends. "Shorter?"

"Yeah," Charlotte says.

"I wish I could do chin length," Amanda says, wrapping a long ringlet around her finger. "But I don't have your cheekbones."

"Well, I'd rather have your ass," Charlotte says, slapping her sister-in-law kiddingly as they go inside. "So the music lessons are paying off then?" she jokes, noticing the vanilla Glade plug-ins scent that Amanda has never been able to give up no matter how many times she says it's probably slowly killing them all.

"Sixty-dollars an hour and this is what we get," Amanda says, pointing toward the ceiling. "It's all your brother's doing, by the way. Drums! For a boy with a hyperactivity diagnosis!"

"Actually, now that you say it, maybe it *is* good for him," Charlotte says, though the banging is so loud that she can feel it in the soles of her shoes.

"You sound just like Aaron. We did always say that he wanted one of the boys to be musical. I guess I just hoped for a pianist. A chill acoustic guitar player at the least."

"Where are the other two?" Charlotte puts her purse down on the upholstered bench just inside the entryway, trying to remember if it was here when she last visited or if it's one of her sister-in-law's latest purchases.

"Oh, who knows!" Amanda rolls her eyes. "One's probably sledgehammering the walls while the other stuffs the toilet with his clean laundry. Come on, let's get you something cold to drink."

"The house looks good," Charlotte says, following behind, reaching out and touching the leaves of an orchid on the round pedestal table in the middle of the bright foyer, where a huge staircase curves around one side of the room to the second floor. "I don't know how you keep these floors so clean with three boys and two dogs," she says, noticing the gleaming hardwoods as they walk down the hall to the back of the house.

"It's called a housekeeper," Amanda says. "And also, while

you're out making the world a better place, I'm starring in my own private Swiffer commercial."

"Right," Charlotte mutters, Amanda's words stinging despite her good intentions. "That's exactly what I'm doing." Birdie barely managed a goodbye before she raced out of the house for school, never once making eye contact, and Charlotte was barely able to brush a kiss across her daughter's cheek before she was gone. Jason, once again, left early for work, taking off without a goodbye while she was in the shower. She follows Amanda into the kitchen, and through the glass wall at the back of the room she notices a stripe of gray storm clouds lining the sky. "It looks like I got here just in time," she says, looking out on the wide swath of green grass that leads to the Intracoastal Waterway, Aaron's boat bobbing in the slip next to their dock. She pauses, gazing out at the yard, the tableau of grass and sea and marsh in the distance as much a part of her as her own fingerprints.

"So what's happening with you?" Amanda asks. "How's Jason? Birdie? The boyfriend?"

Charlotte wrinkles her nose.

"That good?" Amanda says.

"I'm just not sure Birdie's ready for all of this."

"Oh, come on," Amanda says. "She's in high school now. Get over yourself."

Charlotte shrugs. "Everyone seems to be telling me that, but walk a mile in my shoes and then tell me what you think. Is John Martin showing any interest in anyone yet?"

Amanda bursts out laughing. "Please," she says. "He's even more awkward than Aaron was at that age. He's dating those drums. And his video game console."

"Well, just you wait," Charlotte says, spinning around toward the kitchen. "Honestly, though, let's change the subject. I could use a break from reality."

"Done," Amanda says. "I'm so glad you got this talk booked down here. Anything to force you back home for a few days."

Charlotte raises an eyebrow. "You sound like my mother."

Amanda laughs. "True. But I'd still take your crazy one over the one I've got."

Charlotte reaches across the counter and squeezes Amanda's arm. "Haven't heard from her, I assume?"

Amanda shakes her head. Charlotte and Amanda were born two months apart and spent nearly every moment of their childhood together, even after their mothers fell out when they were just starting elementary school. Amanda's mother was an alcoholic, though they didn't have the word for it when they were kids. All they knew was that she often slept past lunchtime and then, when she was awake, they got one of two people: Either she was ranting and raving, her unpredictable anger crackling over some nonsensical thing. Or she was the life of the party, dancing, laughing, yelling at them to turn the stereo louder, no matter that it might be four o'clock on a Tuesday afternoon and she was the only one up for a good time. Either way, dinner was never made, the mail went unopened, the laundry piled up on the bedroom floors, weeds took over the patchy yard. Her father got fed up and moved out, then moved back in, then moved out; establishing a pattern that would last for the entirety of Amanda's childhood. Neither of her parents seemed to care what this was doing to their daughter, and she more or less moved in with Charlotte's family, sleeping over several nights a week, and even spending holidays with them most years. Amanda's mother never got sober, and is living, last they heard, somewhere in Texas. She's refused every bit of help that Amanda and her father have tried to offer her, the occasional birthday card that shows up every few years the only acknowledgment that she cares for Amanda at all.

The life she has now, Charlotte has thought, is Amanda's direct attempt to right the way her childhood went off course. When they were growing up, Amanda had never so much as breathed in the direction of Charlotte's brother, Aaron. But then, in their mid-twenties, while Aaron was working on his PhD at Georgia Tech, she started hanging around at his apartment. They were all in Atlanta then—Charlotte and Reese and Aaron all working on graduate degrees, and Amanda floating around, working a so-so marketing job, trying to figure out what to do next. Her mother was at her worst then, and she started spending a lot of time with Aaron, cooking meals for him when he stayed up all night working on his dissertation, doing his laundry. Really, it was her calling; she'd always been a nurturer, and as she and Aaron began to fall in love, she'd say to Charlotte: *Do you think it's awful, if the only thing I really want to do with my life is marry your brother and have some babies?* Charlotte thought it actually made perfect sense. Amanda had devoted herself to creating the family home she'd always deserved, and she was really, really good at it.

Everyone had always assumed that he would end up a professor somewhere, living in some little bungalow, but Aaron had become obsessed with an idea he had for a new kind of dispenser that pharmaceutical companies could use when bottling their medications at the factory stage. Everyone tuned out when he talked about it at Christmas dinner and Easter brunch, nodding absentmindedly while he rattled on about dosages and whatever else, but then he got a patent and started an LLC. It wasn't long before the big pharma companies came calling, and Aaron's little invention made him a fortune.

"Where's the talk again?" Amanda asks, sitting across the counter from her.

"Tomorrow morning, downtown at the convention center. *The Southern Women's Show*. I have no idea what to expect but hopefully the crowd will be friendly. My guess is that it will be heavy with the over-fifty set."

Amanda gives her a deadpan look. "Friendly to you? Don't be humble. They'll eat you up."

Charlotte reaches for a cracker and drags it through the little bowl of spicy pimento cheese that Amanda always makes for her, knowing it's her favorite. "This is delicious, as always," she says, reaching for a second cracker as soon as the first is in her mouth. When she looks up, Amanda is staring at her.

"What?" she says, wiping cracker crumbs from her bottom lip.

"You have a funny expression on your face. Everything okay?"

"Yeah, yeah," she says. "You know . . . just tired from traveling, the end of the school year . . ."

"Charlotte, come on," Amanda says, tilting her head. "I can tell when something's up."

She sighs and raps her knuckles on the counter. "Things have just been a little rocky at home. Nothing serious. Nothing . . ." She shakes her head. "It's nothing. Really."

"You sure?"

"Yeah, yeah, it's fine. Jason and I just seem to be operating on different planes these days. We'll figure it out."

Amanda gives her a concerned look. "Okay," she says. "But if you need to—"

"I'm fine, Amanda. Really."

"All right."

"Just don't say anything, okay? To Aaron? I know you would never but sometimes he slips to my mother. And you know how Nancy gets."

"Oh, I know," Amanda says, raising an eyebrow.

"I need to steel myself. I haven't seen her since Christmas."

Amanda laughs. "She says as much every time I see her."

Charlotte sucks in her breath. "Does my brother realize how lucky he is, having you to put up with her?"

Her sister-in-law shrugs. "I know how to deal with her. Don't forget, she practically raised me."

"Didn't we raise ourselves?"

"I don't know what's worse," Amanda says. She puts her palms up, lifting them up and down like she's weighing two options. "Raging alcoholic, raging narcissist . . ."

Charlotte laughs but that word—*alcoholic*—makes her think of Jason and his silly accusation the night before. She'd been thinking about it: His own parents were virtual teetotalers, *maybe* treating themselves to a thimble-size glass of wine at a party or on an anniversary. In contrast, her own father had a cold beer on his boat most Saturday mornings. Charlotte and Jason, she decided, just had different perspectives. He'd never seen a *real* alcoholic like Amanda's mother, who was literally falling-down drunk most of her waking hours. He didn't know what he was talking about.

Amanda turns to look at the clock on the far wall. "Speaking of your mother, we're expected there around six-thirty."

"Well, shit, that's just forty-five minutes," Charlotte says.

"Don't worry," Amanda says, turning for the refrigerator. "I got your wine open for you already." She twists the cork off a bottle of sauvignon blanc and pours them each a glass. "If you drink fast enough, you can have two before we go."

Charlotte takes the glass and sighs, thinking to herself how nice it is to be there, with somebody who truly understands her. "It's good to be home," she says, raising her glass.

SEVEN

Charlotte never in a million years would have thought that her mother would give up the home she was raised in, a grand Low Country–style place on the water that had been in her family for generations, but when she got engaged to Emmett, she did just that, moving into his row house downtown. Charlotte looks up at the chandelier looming over their heads, tiers and tiers of dangling crystals and gold curlicues. *Trumpesque*, she thinks, a notion that leads her to glance at Emmett, her mother's husband, who still proudly sports a Lock Her Up bumper sticker on his F-150.

He catches her looking at him. "So how much do they pay you to give these speeches?" he asks, taking a final forkful of chess pie and washing it down with his bourbon.

Charlotte turns to look down the table at her mother, waiting for her to admonish Emmett for asking a question so *gauche*, a word that might be the crowning jewel of Nancy Dalton's predictable vocabulary. Unlike her husband, she fancies herself the picture of propriety, a beacon of traditional good taste in a coarse, crass world. "Miss Manners," Jason called her. Behind her back, of course, because he didn't mean it as a compliment.

Nancy, who has dressed herself in a coral raw silk sheath dress with lipstick to match, smiles at Charlotte, waiting for her to say something. The narrow slice of pie in front of her (served on her spring china, ringed with little blue and yellow flowers, and only in service, as she would say, from Easter through Labor Day) sits untouched, save for the single indentation she has made at the tip of the slice with the tines of her fork. This is as close as she will come to indulging.

"It's enough to make it worth the trip," Charlotte says, reaching for the wine bottle in the center of the table.

"Aw, come on, you can tell me. We're family!" Emmett says, licking his full lips. Charlotte peers at him—the gin blossom nose, the beady alligator eyes, and wonders for the millionth time why her mother has anything to do with this man.

She knows her brother, sitting across from her, is thinking the same thing. Her mother started dating Emmett barely a year after they'd sprinkled her father's ashes on the Wilmington River. She is a product of the time and place in which she'd been raised, and still believes, Charlotte is certain, that marriage is what makes a woman. She's also sure that Nancy chose Emmett Dalton not because she fell in love with him, but because he was the only eligible bachelor in her social circle. Nancy and Emmett, like everyone else in Savannah, had known each other forever, and Emmett's wife, who was on the flower committee at First Baptist with Nancy, had succumbed to a lung cancer diagnosis the year before they got together. Emmett's line of work only sweetened the deal. The Dalton Jewelry chain has been a local fixture for generations, with a big, three-story shop that takes up a city block on Broughton Street, and Charlotte's mother, now perpetually draped in diamonds, is a walking advertisement for the business. Aaron jokes that she ought to have armed guards with her whenever she leaves the house.

"It's a shame, given that they fly you down here and all, that Jason can't join you," Emmett says, his eyebrows creeping up into his forehead as he looks at her over the top of his glass.

Charlotte feels a sudden rage, a fluttering in her chest that he has the unique ability to conjure. *He just can't help himself*, she thinks, knowing that he only brought it up to be hostile. This is precisely why she would never mention that life is anything less than perfect at home. Nancy and Emmett are vultures, especially on the topic of her husband, and it would be like handing them a side of raw meat.

For many, many years, Jason had ingratiated himself to her mother. He brought her gifts—boxes of chocolate, a patterned scarf that Charlotte helped him pick out, hand-painted note cards—like he was making an offering to the Gods, and still, she froze him out. She should have been pleased that Charlotte had a doting husband (doting at the time, at least), but Jason wasn't good enough for her. He wasn't, as she finally put it, during one of the many arguments leading up to Charlotte and Jason's wedding, *the proper match*. Charlotte knew what she meant without her having to say anything, because she had alluded to the specifics dozens of times. Jason wasn't southern. His career didn't have the kind of earning potential that Nancy would prefer. And on and on. In short, he wasn't Reese Tierney.

"Jason can't travel with me because he can't take the time off work," Charlotte says, steeling herself for the inevitable comeback.

"Oh, of course," her mother says, a thin smile spreading across her face. "Of course he has to work."

"Does he come home smelling of the animals?" Emmett says, glancing at Nancy before his eyes find Charlotte's, his gaze like a housefly landing on her skin. This isn't the first time he's asked this question.

"Of course not," she says.

"And how are his pandas?" her mother says, smirking at Emmett.

"Fine," Charlotte says, taking another gulp of her wine.

"Oh, well, good," her mother says. "How delightful."

Charlotte squeezes the linen napkin in her lap, which has been starched so severely that it feels like construction paper in her hands, and tells herself that at least Jason isn't here to witness this. It used to bother her at first, how he complained about coming down here, how even though she understood, how even though he tried, for years, to let her mother's commentary roll off his back (Nancy must have asked him ten times in their first year together why he couldn't have at least considered veterinary school), he still let it get the best of him. No matter how many times she told him she was on his side—she'd been raised by the woman, after all—he still made Charlotte feel like it was her fault. Like there was something she could do to stop it. But of course her mother is unstoppable. Charlotte's told him all of the horrible stories from her childhood. He knew that the reason her handwriting was so perfect was because her mother made her practice traditional cursive until her fingers ached from the effort. He knew why her posture was flawless. He knew why she never let her smile fade in social situations, always striving to make other people comfortable. He knew.

"Well," her mother says, lifting her chin, gazing around the table. "Hopefully Jason will be able to make it down at the end of the month. Do you think he can get the time off?"

"The end of the month?" Charlotte asks. *Is there something the end of the month?* Amanda kicks her under the table, and when Charlotte looks at her, she sees the expression on her face, the wide-eyed *I'm sorry I forgot to mention this.*

"Emmett and I are throwing a party. I wanted to tell you in person."

"A party?" Charlotte asks.

"To celebrate the best ten years of my life," Emmett says, tipping his glass toward Nancy.

Charlotte's heart sinks.

"We've decided to have an anniversary party!" her mother says, her eyes sparkling in the candlelight. "A ten-year-anniversary gala!"

Charlotte feels like she might be sick. An anniversary party. For her mother and Emmett. A familiar sensation falls over her, the one she feels so often lately, like an invisible weight is being plunked on her back. With everything she has going on right now, this is the last thing she needs.

"Isn't it wonderful?" Nancy says.

"Momma, did you say a gala?" Aaron coughs out, and with good reason. Whatever Emmett doesn't agree to cost-wise, she'll just guilt Aaron into covering, the same way she did with the Jaguar convertible in the alleyway behind the row house.

"Well, you know, just a big party," their mother says, sliding the yellow diamond pendant back and forth along one of the chains draping her neck. "We've already booked the club."

Emmett snaps his fingers. "Nance, I just had the best idea! How about a vow renewal, too?"

Oh, Jesus, Charlotte thinks. She looks at Amanda across the table. Simultaneously, they raise their glasses, both to drink and to hide their expressions of horror, but Nancy misreads it.

"Oh, yes!" she says, putting her hand to her chest. "Let's have a toast, everyone!"

Emmett stands slowly, holding on to the edge of the table as he raises himself up. "To my bride!" he says.

"Oh, Emmett! How romantic!" Nancy says.

Charlotte drains her glass. Out of the corner of her eye, she sees her brother squirm in his seat.

"Charlotte!" Nancy says.

Her head snaps toward her mother. "Yes?"

"I know! You can help me write my vows. That is . . ." She pauses for emphasis. "Assuming you can make it."

"Of course, Momma," she says, kicking Amanda this time, the way she has so many times over the years. "Of course, we'll be there."

Later, in the cocoon of Aaron and Amanda's guest suite, Charlotte climbs up onto the four-poster bed, remembering how Amanda commissioned it from a craftsman in Asheville after falling in love with a similar one on their honeymoon in Indonesia. It occurs to her that if almost anyone else—say, Dayna Cunningham, the most obvious example—told her about doing such a thing, it would make her want to throw up, but Amanda's extravagances never bother her. Perhaps because she knows how much Amanda deserves and appreciates the nice life she has now.

She pushes her laptop aside for a moment, not quite ready to go over her notes for tomorrow's talk, and lies back on the pillows, grateful for the four-hundred-count Egyptian cotton sheets, the locally made Lake pajamas that Amanda had waiting for her on the settee, and the soundproofing that her brother put in around the guest room. After they got home from dinner, she'd spent an hour catching up with her nephews, meaning that she sat beside them while they played Fortnite, and the electronic beeps and dings are still pinging in her head.

As usual after an evening with her mother, she's exhausted. On the drive home, while they rehashed the dinner and their mother's insufferability and Emmett's overall horridness (he was exactly the kind of guy who'd get caught in a prostitution ring, Amanda joked), she came precariously close to telling them more about Jason and how this rut between them felt different, like something they might possibly not make their way out of. There was a part of her that wanted to unload everything—about Jason, about Birdie, about her own constant exhaustion and stress, how some days the simplest chores—putting dishes in the sink, making a phone call—felt insurmountable. But then she heard the familiar refrain in her head, her own voice sounding so much like her mother's: *What do you have to complain about? Fake it till you make it. Action first. Smile your way through it.* She flicked away a tear in the dark backseat.

They came to a stoplight and she noticed how pretty the Spanish moss hanging from an old oak in someone's front yard looked, a silhouette against the navy sky, and she gave in to the distraction. She snapped a quick picture while Aaron prattled on about Emmett's shortcomings (his pinkie ring, his bourbon breath) and uploaded it to her Instagram. Spanish moss, still taking my breath away forty-four years later, she typed. Love being back in my hometown. #savannah #georgia #georgiaonmymind #family #nofilter.

She reaches for her phone on the nightstand and notices that there's a missed call from Jason, who must have tried her while she was in the bathroom getting ready for bed. She looks at the time—nearly midnight—and dials him back.

"Hey." He answers immediately.

"Is everything okay?" she says.

"Uh," he says. "I don't know. I think so."

"What?" Her stomach drops. "Jason, what's going on?"

"I just got a weird email about an hour ago. From Birdie's coach. Did you see it?"

"Birdie's coach?" she says, feeling a tingling in her fingers. "What did it say?" She lunges across the bed for her laptop, cradling her phone between her chin and her shoulder while she hurries to log in to her email account.

"It said she missed practice. Did she have something going on that I forgot about?"

"No!" Charlotte says, the tingling moving up her arms, down her spine. "No! She didn't have anything." She punches the power button on the laptop. "I'm waiting for my computer to come on. Do you have it right there? Read it word for word."

"Yeah, it's right here," he says, a biting urgency in his voice that she can't place. *Is he irritated with me*, she thinks, *or the situation?* "Okay. Here—" She hears rustling, then his voice on speakerphone. "It says, 'I'm writing to check on Birdie. She wasn't at practice today and I want to make sure everything is okay. As you know, we have a big match later this week. If she's sick and/or unable to play, I'll need to readjust the roster. Please let me know at your earliest convenience.'"

Charlotte pictures the coach, an affable guy in his mid-twenties, originally from New Zealand, whose curly hair that poofs out behind the Adidas baseball cap he always wears makes him look like a young Pete Sampras. In her effort to be unlike the overbearing parents she deals with at Georgetown, she has spoken to him only casually, once or twice at the start of the season. Birdie adores him, more than most of the coaches she's had over the years. But even with the ones she didn't particularly like, she loved the sport too much, and was too responsible and conscientious a kid, to just up and skip practice. This is about as unlike her as could be.

"I don't understand, Jason," she says, her eyes scanning the email now that it's in front of her. "What did she say? Where would she have gone?" she asks, images of Birdie and Tucker lurking in the shadows of her brain. "What did she say?"

"She didn't say anything because I didn't ask her," he says. "She was already asleep when I got the email. But, Char, when

I got home from work, she was freshly showered, just like she'd been to tennis. And when I asked her about practice, she said it was fine."

"*Shit*," Charlotte says. "Shit!"

"I know."

"You know who she must have been—"

"I know," he says. "I know, Charlotte."

"Dammit!" she says. "I'm tempted to have you wake her up."

"I'm not waking her—"

"I'm not asking you to. But I'm tempted," she says. "To show her how serious this is."

"Yeah," he says. "I know. Do you think there's any other possibility? Tucker would have had lacrosse practice, so . . ."

"He must have skipped, too. Or, I don't know . . . What did you tell the coach?"

"Nothing yet. I wanted to talk to her first. Maybe there's a possibility she had to stay after at school for something. Maybe there was a test or a . . ." His voice trails off.

"No," she says.

"I know."

"All right, well," Charlotte says, sighing deeply. "We need to get back to him soon."

"I'm aware," he says. "I can write him back right now. Or call first thing in the morning. I know you're busy."

"Jason, I wasn't—"

"I can handle it, Charlotte."

"Okay," she says, not wanting to bicker. "My talk's at eleven tomorrow. Update me as soon as you can."

"Yup."

As soon as they say good night and hang up, she finds her way to Instagram to check Tucker's account. No new post, but when she clicks on his story, there's a video of him hopscotching to the lacrosse goal in his yard, making a shot, and then doing a blooper-reel-like roll across the grass. Somebody else is taking the video, and in the last few seconds of it, she hears an unmistakable blip of a sound: Birdie's laugh. She watches it again, then again, then again.

She reaches for her phone. "Jason," she says, as soon as he answers. "I just watched his Instagram story. She was at his house. I could hear her laughing."

"Okay," he says, his disappointment evident in his voice. "All right, I'll call you first thing, right after I talk to her."

"Should we get in touch with the Cunninghams?" she says. "Should I message Dayna?"

"Charlotte, I . . . What is that going to—?"

"Never mind," she says.

After they hang up, she watches the video over and over, racking her brain for an explanation or excuse, but of course there isn't one. At least not anything other than the fact that her daughter is fourteen, and this is what teenagers do. *Other teenagers*, she thinks, a sickening anger creeping over her as she considers that what she saw is only fifteen seconds of the afternoon that Tucker and Birdie spent together. She's tempted to send him a direct message through the app but talks herself out of it. The repercussions are too great. And then she has another thought: If he actually pays attention to who watches his stories—with over fourteen hundred followers, she's really not sure—he must know that she's watching, and that's even worse, because it means he doesn't care.

She sits there in the silent bedroom, trying to figure out what to do, then stands, nervous energy pulsing through her veins. She knows she shouldn't, but . . . *What's the big deal?* she asks herself. *I need to sleep. It will help.*

The kitchen is dark. She tiptoes through, thankful for the soft slippers Amanda keeps in the guest room for her, and finds the bottle of sauvignon blanc from earlier this evening. She pours a bit into her water glass (*why dirty another glass?*), and then, judging the amount, pours a little more. She takes a deep drink, the crisp tang tasting of relief, and slips back upstairs. She already feels better.

Her photo of the Spanish moss has nearly four thousand likes, she sees, closing the bedroom door.

Gorgeous!

Stunning!

Wow, so jealous!

She climbs on top of the bed, scrolling through the comments, trying to ward off her craving to watch Tucker's video two, four, ten more times. A few of the commenters mention that they'll be at the talk tomorrow, and she tells herself she ought to go to sleep. She has to speak to two thousand people about her tenets for a happy life, rattling off her canned advice about action over feelings. A year ago, this would have spurred her to overprepare, read through her notes again and again while she paced the bedroom, waking up extra-early to make sure she was ready. Now she just can't wait to have it over with. She takes another sip from her glass and notices a little red icon appear on the top corner of her screen, indicating that she has a new message.

@KGpartyof5

Fuck, she thinks. *Just what I need.*

So I got off my shift at the restaurant where I work just in time to get home and have my oldest kid tell me that she wants to kill herself, the message begins. She's fifteen, and she told me she's been looking up ways to do it on the internet. Want to tell me how to act my way out of that one?

She puts her hand to her mouth, and before she can think not to, she responds: No, I don't. I'm sorry. I can't imagine how you must feel.

The response comes back almost instantly: Of course you can't. You don't know problems like mine.

Charlotte knows she shouldn't engage—the woman is obviously taking her frustration out on her, using her as a punching bag for problems that may or may not actually exist—but something in her wants to set this straight: I have plenty of problems, I've never claimed otherwise, she writes. That's part of my whole deal, to plow through them, to do the right things in spite of what's holding you back. She hits the little paper airplane send icon, feeling a rush of satisfaction, and then she types some more: Also, I have a teenager, too. I know it's not easy.

Oh yeah? Congrats, the message comes back. Let me guess: Honor roll student, star athlete, never misses curfew?

Heat rises up Charlotte's neck. The woman isn't far off the

mark, it's true, but Birdie— Her problems are nothing like what this person's dealing with, assuming she's being truthful.

Hardly, she writes back. So what did you say to her?

I didn't know what to say, the response says, when it comes a few seconds later. I was terrified. All I could think of was to hug her. I didn't say it, but I would have stayed like that forever, all through the night and into next week, if it would make her feel better.

I know, Charlotte types back, tears springing to her eyes. I know just what you mean.

Do you, though? the woman types.

Charlotte's tempted to give her proof. To tell her about what her life actually looks like inside the walls of her house. She thinks of Jason and Birdie and takes another sip of wine. Just trust me, she types.

She waits for a response to come but nothing shows up. Eventually, she scoots herself under the covers and turns out the light, checking her phone one more time in the dark. One last time, and then another, replaying Birdie's laugh, over and over again.

Nearly twelve hours later, Charlotte puts down her laser pointer, applause erupting around her as the lights go up in the auditorium. Attempting to be discreet, she glances down at the phone resting on the podium next to her notes. Nothing from Jason or Birdie regarding her missed practice. How could he not have called her by now or at least answered one of the zillion texts she'd sent first thing this morning? She'd called and texted Birdie, too, and also received no response. She smooths her hands against her yellow dress and sweeps her eyes across the room, surveying the mostly female crowd. They look pleased, like always.

"I'd love to take any questions you may have," she says, her voice as bright as she can get it.

They ask different versions of the same question: *Is Charlotte happy all the time?* (*No,* she answers, giving them the same answer she gave Finch last weekend at dinner.) *What does she do to be happy?* (*Spend time with friends and family,* she chokes out. *Make sure I get time to myself each night, to have a glass of wine and relax*, she says, relieved when several women laugh and nod.) Charlotte smiles her way through it, trying to sound enthusiastic, but the truth is that she's said these things so many times, it feels robotic and meaningless, like the words coming out of her mouth are just sounds. She's wondered if this is what it must feel like to be a singer having to belt out the same hit over and over and over again, relentlessly, for years—Dolly Parton and "Nine to Five," Billy Joel and "Piano Man."

After the Q & A wraps up, a slope-shouldered volunteer in a pale green linen jacket escorts her to a banquet table just off-stage.

"A wonderful talk!" the woman says. She seems to be in her sixties, and Charlotte can tell she's nervous. Not about her, exactly, but, it seems, about doing her job correctly. Her hands shake as she pushes a bottle of water across the table, and she keeps eyeing the crowd lining up just beyond the X that somebody's placed on the floor with duct tape.

"Thank you," Charlotte says.

"I really liked what you said about the definition of a happy life," the woman says, her eyes scanning the space around them, nervously checking the details like a party host just before the first guest arrives. She straightens the row of Sharpies on the table and puts her arm out, inviting Charlotte to sit. "About how finding your happiness doesn't have to be this big philosophical question . . . that it can be just . . . a series of happy moments. That it's the little things you do, every day, that add up." The woman leans in and whispers. "I lost my husband six months ago. Before that, he lived ten years with dementia."

"I'm so sorry!" Charlotte says, leaping up to give the woman a hug.

"No, no." She pats Charlotte's arm. "It's okay. He's in a better place now. We both are. I have you, in part, to thank for that."

"Me?" Charlotte says, putting a hand to her chest. "No!" It isn't the first time somebody's told her that her book got them through the death of a loved one, not by a long shot, but it's always tricky to figure out how to respond.

"My neighbor gave me your book just after Hank died. It really helped me, just going through the motions, doing those little things you talk about. I'd go to a water aerobics class in the morning and the exercise and the sense of community really helped. I'd talk to my daughter every afternoon. She lives in Seattle."

"Ah," Charlotte says, thinking to herself that it's been weeks since she's gone for a run, and that she wishes she could make a joke with the woman about how those mother-daughter chats aren't always everything they're cracked up to be. "Well, I'm so glad it helped."

The volunteer nods. “Do you have children?”

“A daughter.”

The woman puts her hand to her chest. “We’re lucky, aren’t we? My daughter is my best friend! What I’d give to have her here locally with me.”

“That sounds familiar,” Charlotte says, thinking of her mother the night before, holding court at the dinner table. “My mother says the same thing.”

“How old is your girl?”

“Fourteen.”

The woman clasps her hands together. “Wonderful!” she says. “So exciting. Well, I know I don’t have to tell you this, but treasure every moment with her. She’ll be out of the house in a blink, and then it will just be you and your husband. That’s fun, too, of course. Just different.”

“Just different,” Charlotte repeats. “Right.”

“Anyway,” the woman says, pointing a finger toward the line, which is now twenty or thirty people deep. “I didn’t mean to take up your time. Your family must be so proud of you! It must feel so good, spreading the message you do!”

Charlotte lunges for the water bottle across the table. “I’m sorry,” she says, taking a deep gulp. “My throat is dry from all that talking!”

“Well,” the woman says, her smile pleasant. “Your fans await!”

“Yes,” Charlotte says, downing one last gulp. “Okay.” She stretches her arms out, grinning, then raises her voice to the crowd. “Well, hello! Let’s do this!”

The first woman in line clutches the book in two hands, the

pages decorated with a fan of Post-it notes. Readers often reference the book when they meet her, even open the cover and finger through it to show her the passages that helped them the most. It should be gratifying, but the truth is that it feels awful, hearing their incredibly sad stories. The best friend who died in a freak accident. The house fire that destroyed everything. It's easy for Charlotte to accept the validity of her work with her students—that job is to spell out the research, to tell them in very clear terms what science says about emotion. But to meet these real people out in the world, with their jowly chins, their burnished gold wedding bands, their windbreakers with pockets stuffed with tissue—who is she to be their guru? What qualifies her?

She twists off the top of her water bottle and takes a long glug. It's true that her throat is dry from all of the talking, but she's also fighting a dull ache at the front of her forehead and a queasy stomach from last night's wine. After ten or fifteen people, all of them start to run together. As she guessed, most of them are women in the retiree bracket, people who have time to tour a convention center on a weekday morning to hear about books and antiaging strategies and natural menopause remedies.

She closes the cover on a book, sliding it across the table to the woman in a floral-patterned T-shirt, who thanks her again and steps aside for the next guest.

She looks up, and the pen falls out of her hand.

He takes a step forward. She hasn't seen him in twenty years.

"Charlotte," Reese says, holding her book.

"Oh my—"

"I didn't mean to shock you," he says. "I knew you wouldn't expect me, but . . ."

He is just as she remembers him. Older, of course, but still with his same crooked smile. The same . . . He's the same. *Maybe better*, she thinks, noticing the salt-and-pepper hair above his temples, the way his gangly, boyish frame has filled out.

"You're at the Southern Women's Show," she says.

"Uh-huh." He nods and laughs. "I am."

He's still wearing his wedding ring, she notices.

"Yeah," he says, holding his hand up. "Haven't taken it— I assume you heard?"

"You know my mother."

He smiles. "That I do."

"I'm sorry," she says. "It must be hard."

He shrugs. "But now I have this." He holds up the book.

"Oh, God," she says, waving a hand at him. "Don't—"

"What? Charlotte, it's great. I read it the day it came out, cover to cover. And"—he leans toward her—"I had a full roster of patients that day."

"Thank you," she says, studying his face. His same, stupid, handsome face. He hurt her so much.

"I'm so happy for you," he says. "Not that I'm surprised. Maybe more than anyone else I know, you're doing exactly what you should be doing. You found your calling. And you were always going places."

There's a forlornness in the way he says it, and she wonders if he means it the way she's heard it; meaning she was going to all the places he wasn't. Her mind zips back to the letters he sent, begging her to come home to him.

She closes her eyes for a moment, trying to refocus. "Well, the bad news is all I do now is go places. If you ever need frequent-flier miles . . ." she says, grimacing at her own bad joke.

"Will you sign my book?" he says, placing it on the table between them, and she notices that it indeed looks read. "I hope you don't mind that I showed up like this. I just . . . I saw an advertisement for the conference on the bulletin board in the office." He shoves his hand in his pocket and jingles his keys, just like he used to, and the familiarity of the gesture floods her with a feeling that makes her dizzy. "I just had to come see you," he's saying. "I hope you don't—"

"I don't mind," she says, fumbling to open to the title page. *What the hell am I supposed to write?* Her heart is beating in her ears, so strongly it seems like the entire convention center can hear it.

To . . . she starts. She looks up at him, and he immediately looks away, understanding that she's self-conscious. *To my old friend*, she writes, pleased that she came up with it on the spot.

She scrawls her name, like she's done thousands of times without a thought over the past two years, and when she looks up, Reese is staring at her in a longing, far-off way. She knows the reason why they never married is because she couldn't forgive him. They both know that.

"I've taken up too much of your time," he says, gesturing back to the crowd gathered behind them. "But, uh . . ." He pulls a business card out of his back pocket and flings it on the table like an afterthought.

She stands, taking it, and holds a finger up to the crowd, smiling contritely. "So sorry!" she mouths. "Just one more second!" She walks around the table, offering her arms out for a hug, and he pulls her in, just like he used to. He always hugged her like he meant it.

She closes her eyes, taking in the moment. She'd thought, if she ever saw him again, that the anger would overtake her, and in the early years, when she'd come home to Savannah and they'd be out somewhere, she'd search the faces around her just in case, wanting to avoid him. Later, when she didn't run into him, she thought that if she ever saw him again she'd still feel angry, but also vindicated. She could gloat about the great life she'd built without him. But she doesn't feel that way at all. She's not angry or vengeful. Regardless of what happened, he is her history, and a big part of it at that. She feels a wonderful sense of peace, seeing this part of her past laid to rest.

"Thanks for coming," she says, sensing the crowd behind them as she lets go. She takes a step back.

"I wouldn't have missed it," he says, holding up the book. "Doin' good, Charlotte!" And then, just like that, he disappears into the crowd, and he's gone.

EIGHT

Jason and Jamie are sitting on a bench outside the Asia Trail exhibit, eating sandwiches from the cafeteria.

"So I spent the morning guiding a group of fund-raisers around my exhibit trying to charm them into a big donation," Jamie says. "How's your day been?"

"Eh," he says. "Better than yours, it sounds. I spent the past hour doling out bamboo to the red pandas. Ace hasn't been eating well." He watches a field trip walking by, a single file of preschool-aged kids in matching bright blue T-shirts. Their little chubby hands grip a red rope, the front end of which is being held by two teachers. The kids remind him of Birdie once upon a time. He can almost feel the clammy stickiness of their skin, watching them, and his stomach clenches, thinking of the blowup fight he had with Birdie this morning, how she left for school in tears, her face blotchy and red.

"Not eating?" Jamie says. "Not even the bamboo?"

"Yeah, I don't know," he says. "We'll keep an eye on him. Anyway." He leans back on his bench.

"I wanted to check in . . . How are things with Charlotte?" she asks.

"She's in Savannah," he says. "Well, she comes home today."

"Visiting her family?"

"And giving a speech."

"Mm," Jamie says. "Sounds like Charlotte."

He smarts a little, even though it's just a tiny dig. It's one thing for him to bitch about her, but another thing for somebody else to; still, he lets it go. "It's annoying, having her gone so much, but lately, it's just easier. And it's not bad having the bed to myself, or having full control of the remote. I'm kind of enjoying being alone, to be honest."

"Then you should try widowhood!"

"Oh, God." Jason slaps a palm to his face. "Jamie, I'm so sorry." He angles his body toward her. "That was a stupid thing to say."

"No, no." She laughs and pops an apple slice into her mouth. They've always joked that her food preferences resemble those of a lot of the animals in their care. "I was the one making the joke. I get it. It's nice having the place to yourself. I used to feel that way when Warren worked late."

"I remember that, how his hours were long."

"Yeah," she says, an uncharacteristic whine in her voice. She looks off into the distance.

"What?"

"I never shared this with you when he was alive, but I guess it doesn't matter now." She glances at him for a moment. "Warren had a pretty serious problem with depression."

"What?" Jason drops his hand to his lap. "You're kidding."

"Yup," she says. "It sort of waxed and waned. When it was bad, he'd spend days in bed, just staring up at the ceiling."

"Whoa," he says. "Jamie . . ."

"I know," she says, crunching down on another piece of apple. "You never would have guessed it given how successful he was at work, and all of the working out. The ultramarathon stuff was actually a good way for him to cope. It sort of focused him."

"How long had it been going on?"

"He'd always had—" She hesitates. "I don't want to say *moody*, that seems too light a word, but it was always there, in the background, and then it got worse over the years. There were times when he could manage it well, and times when he couldn't. So, anyway, yes, when he was working late, it was actually a bit of a relief, because it meant that he was on an upswing. He was at his best when he was wrapped up in a project, whether that was work or training for a race."

"Jamie, that's a lot to deal with. It must have been hard on you."

"I'm okay," she says. "Like I've told you, lots of good therapy. I've decided that the healthiest thing for me is to choose to remember my favorite version of him, when he was feeling good."

"Yeah," Jason says, taking a sip of his soda. "I totally get that." He thinks about his *favorite version* of Charlotte. Like when Sylvie was a puppy, and they'd walk for hours around DC with no particular destination in mind. Or when Birdie was a baby and they were always sleep-deprived, and they went through a fun, stupid stage where they made bloody marys and giant brunches for themselves during her morning naps on the weekends, eating their omelets in bed while they watched *House Hunters International* marathons. She used to tuck her feet around his as they slept, their ankles crossed over each other's. She'd leave him little notes on his nightstand.

He looks at Jamie, her attention on a couple who've just dropped a giant bag of popcorn all over the walkway, and thinks to himself that those memories of how he and Charlotte used to be are so distant that she may as well be as dead as Warren. But then—*Jesus, Jason*, he thinks—*what the fuck? How can you be so melodramatic?*

Jamie turns back to him. "You know what?" she says, wiping her nose with a napkin.

"Huh?"

"The loneliness actually sucks."

"Yeah." *I know*, he thinks.

"I'm, um . . ." She makes a face like she's not sure she wants to continue.

"What?"

"I've started online dating." She raises an eyebrow.

"Nuh-uh!" he says. "Really?"

She nods, her eyes widening. "Yup."

"Oh," he says, squeezing his paper sandwich wrapper into a tight ball between his palms. "Great! What site are you on? Tinder or Match or . . . eharmony? Do people still do eharmony?" He taps his feet against the pavement, looking down at the space between them.

"Bumble." Jamie laughs. "You sure know a lot of them for a married person." She leans over and elbows him, and he notices that after she does it, she doesn't scoot back to where she was. She stays close, not touching him exactly, but she might as well be.

"Commercials," he says. "Radio commercials when I'm driving in the morning. What's Bumble?"

"It's the one where the women have to write the guys first; at least, you know, when it's hetero."

"Ohh," he says, wondering to himself what kinds of guys she'd reach out to.

"Here, I'll show you. I did Tinder for a while," she says, swiping around on her phone's screen. "But I felt like I was twenty years older than everyone else on it. At least. And it seems like it's just mainly for sex." She pauses. "Not that that's a bad thing." She glances at him for a second, and he feels himself flush. "Sometimes an itch needs to be scratched, know what I mean?"

He clears his throat. "Uh-huh," he says, straightening up in his seat and leaning forward, his elbows on his knees. "Sure."

"Sorry," she says, laughing low. "Don't mean to . . . I guess that's oversharing. Okay," she says. "Here."

She nudges closer to him, so close this time that their thighs touch, and hands him her phone. She's leaning over his shoulder, so close that he can smell the garlic on her breath from the hummus she was eating earlier. "Tell me what you think of my profile," she says.

He should move away but he doesn't. "Where is that photo from?" he asks, squinting at the tiny image of her on the screen, feeling her leg against his own.

"Oh," she says. "I'll show you."

She taps on the circle surrounding a head shot, and a larger screen opens, revealing the full image. Jamie is sitting on the edge of a rock, in a cream-colored tank top that shows off the delicate line of her collarbone. She's wearing khaki shorts, rolled up to almost the tops of her thighs, and he realizes that he's never seen her legs before (she always wears pants to work, with a carabiner or two attached and lots of pockets), and she has *great* ones, strong and lean from all of that biking. She has a coiled bandanna tied loosely around her neck, sunglasses. Behind her is an expanse of green and blue, hills rolling out behind her.

"Where was this taken? The scenery is beautiful," he says, though his focus has pulled, after just a second or two, back to her. He can almost feel the sun shining on her in the photo, the way she must have felt, healthy and happy.

"Hiking outside of La Jolla," she says. "It's from a couple years ago, a business trip of Warren's. Do you remember? He had a conference out there once a year and I usually tagged along. That's in Torrey Pines."

"It's beautiful."

"Okay, okay, but what about *me*?" she jokes. "What do you think of the photo? If you were on the market, would you swipe right?"

"Yeah," he says, feeling his voice break. "Of course. You look great."

"Great like a mom in her mid-forties or great like you'd like to fuck me?"

"Jamie!" He hurries the phone back into her hands like it's a hot potato.

"Sorry!" She puts her hand to her mouth, giggling behind it.

"It's okay." He laughs but his heart is pounding like he's just been sprinting. He takes a napkin from his pocket and wipes his forehead.

"But . . . seriously," she says, her eyes meeting his. "I actually want your opinion. Would you?"

"Yeah," he says, letting their eyes lock for a few seconds longer than they probably should. "Definitely."

She bites her lip like she's mulling something over, then looks away, breaking the moment.

"Is it weird that the photo I put on my dating profile is one that my dead husband took while we were on a romantic vacation together?" she says, gazing off into the distance.

"No," he says. "No. I'm sure Warren would be—"

"He'd want me to be happy." She hands him the phone back. "Here," she says. "Scroll down and read my profile. Tell me if there's anything that would give you pause."

He takes the phone and reads:

> **Jamie, 44.**
> Zoologist who loves the outdoors, cycling, hiking, pizza and red wine, old dogs, prefers Adam Sandler to artsy films. Raised on the coast, now living in the city. Widowed mother of two. Looking for fun, friendship, or something more.

He looks up at her, a stirring in his stomach that he doesn't expect. "It's perfect," he says.

"Really?"

"Yeah. It really is." It *really* is.

"You would be psyched if I got in touch with you?"

"Um . . ." he says. She's smiling at him in a way that feels like innuendo, like she means more than she's saying. "Yeah," he says. "I mean, if I was single."

"Of course." She rolls her eyes. "Obviously. Don't get weird, Jason."

"I'm not—"

"What part did you like?" she asks, cutting him off.

"All of it," he says. "Really."

"But . . ." She leans in again, quite close, and he glances around. To any casual observer, he's sure that they look like a couple, and to be honest, he thinks, glancing over at her, feeling the warmth of her radiating next to him, if it wasn't a coworker who saw them, just one of the field trip leaders, say, or a group of tourists, he actually wouldn't mind. "Was there anything in *particular* that stood out?"

"No," he says. "It's perfectly you. It's honest. It's attractive. I mean, it's really . . . It's really, really great."

She looks at him and smiles, and the twisting inside of him gets more intense, pleasantly so. "Thanks," she says, taking the phone from his hands. "Now I just have to find someone to go out with me," she says, her eyes meeting his. "I'm just going to keep an open mind, you know? If there's one thing I've learned from the past year, it's that anything can happen."

"Yeah," he says, and looks away before she can say more. "Well, I don't think you'll have any problem," he says. "You deserve someone great, Jamie."

She stands and holds out her hand for him, and he takes it, letting her pull him up. They're practically eye to eye, and they stand there for just a moment longer than they should, their hands still clasped together.

"So do you, Jason," she says, and then her hand leaves his. "Come on," she says, as casually as any regular day, which this clearly isn't. "I'll come back to the panda yard with you for a few minutes, see if we can get that boy to eat some bamboo."

"Okay," he says, his legs wobbly. He follows behind her, watching her, looking at her, her words—*anything can happen*—ringing in his ears.

The door slams, then Jason hears the sound of Charlotte's heels coming down the hall, the dull thrum of her roller bag dragging behind her.

He shakes the water out of the colander full of pasta, then dumps the noodles back into the pot, drizzling them with olive oil. He hears her keys clatter into the bowl on the table in the hallway. Her motions sound deliberate, sharp, signaling her mood, and he braces for the worst.

"Hi," she says coming into the kitchen. She's wearing the yellow dress she wore on Easter Sunday last year. It feels like a lifetime ago, the three of them sitting around in the family room, golf on the TV in the background, eating the candy out of Birdie's basket together after brunch at his parents' house. It had been one of their better days in recent memory.

Charlotte kicks off her shoes, pushing them against the wall and out of the way with her foot, and leans down to say hello to Sylvie, who's wagging her tail eagerly. "Where is she?" she asks.

"Upstairs," he says.

"Did you—?"

"We had a big fight this morning when I confronted her. Ran out of the house. Then charged up the stairs when she got home."

"You didn't follow her up there?" she asks.

He pauses, eyes boring into hers. "No, Charlotte. I didn't. I wanted to wait for you."

She rolls her eyes. "Would have been nice to hear from you today," she says. "Did you forget to call me?"

"No," he says. "I texted you. I figured you were getting ready for your talk."

She shakes her head. "I never got a text, Jason."

"I sent you a . . ." He puts down the wooden spoon he's holding and fishes his phone out of his pants pocket. *Fuck.* "Okay, sorry," he says. "It looks like I never sent it. But I meant to." He holds his phone out, screen facing her, presenting the draft as evidence.

She shakes her head a second time, then goes to the refrigerator. "All right, well," she says. "Let's get this over with." She pulls the wine bottle from the slot in the refrigerator door. "And I'm about to have a glass of wine," she says sarcastically. "Apologies if that bothers you."

"Do you really have to act like that?" he says, picking up a block of parmesan to grate over the pasta.

"You're the one who told me I have an alcohol problem."

"I didn't tell you—I don't think you have a problem, Charlotte, I just think you could slow down a little. And I've noticed that we always fight when you drink."

"We always fight, period," she says.

It sounds so matter-of-fact, the way she says it, like it's as set in stone as their blood types. He thinks of Jamie earlier today, and he feels a wave of guilt. And then he thinks of what Jamie's actually going through this year, how scared and alone she must feel.

He doesn't want that.

"Charlotte," he says, walking across the kitchen to her before he can talk himself out of it. He puts his palm on her back, and then he puts his hands on her shoulders. He notices immediately how she tenses up, and the next thing he knows, she's pulled away from him and walked out of the room. "Birdie!" she yells. "Birdie, come down here!"

Jason leads them, like the grand marshal in a parade, into the family room. He puts his arm out, allowing Birdie to go first, and she skulks past him. She takes the couch across from them, her arms wrapped defiantly across her middle, her body sunk so low against the cushions that her chin touches her chest, and he and Charlotte take the armchairs opposite her.

"You're grounded," Charlotte says, and Jason cringes. *What kind of opener is that?*

"I thought I was already grounded," Birdie spits back.

"You are," Charlotte says. "But now it's going to be much worse. You owe us an explanation."

Birdie purses her lips into a thin, tight line.

"Birdie!" he says. "Answer your mother."

She stays quiet, the expression on her face miserable, like they've done something to her. It's unbelievable to him, how quickly she's changed. How easy it seems to be for her to behave this way. "Birdie, skipping practice is unacceptable," he says. "And so unlike you, especially on a week when you have this big match coming up. What's going on?"

She looks back at him with a sharpness that reminds him of Charlotte. "Maybe I don't want to play tennis anymore," she says, in a way that feels like it's meant to hurt him, which it does. He can just picture it now, Birdie sitting on a barstool when she's twenty-five, a tattoo on the back of her neck, her eyes bloodshot, trying to convince the idiot regulars around her that she used to be an athlete.

"Are you kidding me?" Charlotte says, her volume rising. "You love tennis! You've always loved tennis!"

"People change," she says.

"Oh, come on," Jason says. "Don't be silly."

She bursts into tears. "I'm not being silly!" she wails. "Just maybe you guys don't understand what kind of pressure it is! To be the best one on the team when you're only a freshman! I mean, it's not like other sports, where the team works together. These older girls, the juniors and seniors, they are out to get me! You don't have any idea!"

"Well, how could we have?" Charlotte says, sounding more like her old self.

"Why didn't you say anything?" he says.

Birdie wipes her nose with the sleeve of her shirt. "I don't know."

"So is that why you skipped practice?" he says. "You didn't want to deal with the other girls?"

She nods.

Jason and Charlotte exchange a glance. This morning, he

kept waiting for Birdie to admit she was with Tucker. It doesn't appear she's going to do it now either.

"Where did you go?" Charlotte asks.

Birdie bites her lip. "I just hung around school for a little while," she finally says. "I did some homework in the library, but then I didn't want to run into anyone so I came home."

Charlotte sits forward in her chair, her wineglass balanced between her two hands. He notices that she's nearly drained it in the few minutes they've been sitting there.

"Are you sure, Bird?" she says.

"Yeah." Her eyes widen.

"Birdie, tell us the truth," Jason says, squeezing his armrest.

"Last chance," Charlotte says.

Five seconds pass, then ten.

"Birdie," Charlotte says, the warning in her voice unmistakable. "Let's go. Tell us."

Her lip starts to quiver. "I was at Tucker's, okay?"

"Well, of course you were!" Charlotte stands. "I can't believe you'd sit here and try to lie to us! Who are you, Birdie? What has happened? I just don't understand these decisions you're making! You never would have done this before you met him!"

"What the *fuck*?" Birdie suddenly wails, looking at the ceiling. "This has nothing to do with him!"

"Birdie!" Jason says, stunned by her language. Outside of the occasional slip or when she's singing along to a song lyric in the car, he's never heard her curse like this. Not like she means it.

"I asked Tucker if we could hang out, okay? It was all me, Mom! Why do you blame everything on—"

"I don't want you to see him anymore," Charlotte says,

wagging her finger like a teacher in an old cartoon. "I don't want you to have anything to do with that boy!"

"Mom!" Birdie continues to wail. "Mom, stop it! You can't do that! I'm too old for you to tell me—"

Charlotte laughs. "You are fourteen," she says. "Barely a teenager. If you think for a minute that—"

"He makes me *happy*, Mom! Isn't that enough for you? Or are you too busy with your stupid fans to notice?"

"Birdie!" Jason says. "Don't talk to your moth—"

"*What mother?*" she screams, standing, and his heart lurches. "I hardly remember my mother!" Birdie's eyes are wild. "My mother used to spend time with me! This woman—" She flings her hand toward Charlotte. "This woman is never around anymore, and even when she is, she's not really here, is she, Dad? Isn't that what you said a few days ago, or last week, or during one of the zillion fights you guys don't think I hear? It isn't really a fucking picnic around here, so excuse me if I'd rather spend time with the one person besides Hannah who makes me feel good."

Jason's mouth drops open. "Birdie . . ."

"Go to your room," Charlotte says, her voice shaking. When he looks over at her, she has her head lowered, her hand to her forehead like she's shielding her eyes from the sun.

"Gladly!" Birdie says.

They're both silent as they listen to her footsteps up the stairs, her door slamming.

"Are you okay?" he asks.

"No," she says, and then she hoists herself out of her chair and leaves the room, taking her glass with her.

NINE

To say that you have changed my life is nothing short of an understatement, the email begins. I watched your TED talk last month, and something just clicked! I realized that the only person who's been holding me back is ME! I stopped making excuses. I stopped—as you would say—waiting for happiness to find me. I put the mantra on my bathroom mirror—Action first, feelings later—and it's worked! In the past two months, I've quit my crappy job and got a new one that is so much better, cleared my house of clutter, and ran my first 10K! Just wanted you to know that there's a forty-something in Houston, Texas, who considers you her guardian angel! I don't know where I'd be without you!!

Charlotte rubs her hand against her mouth, scanning the email a second time. *Guardian angel*, she huffs under her breath. *Please.* She used to save all of these messages in an Outlook folder labeled "Feedback" and sometimes, on a shitty day, she'd visit it like she was dipping into a box of chocolates, the praise a balm for her pride. But somewhere along the way, the messages started having the opposite effect. She felt envy at her own expense, like she'd loaned a dress to a friend and discovered that it looks much, much better on her. *10K . . . new job . . .* She puffs her cheeks out like she's about to vomit and deletes the message.

Ms. McGanley, the next one starts. I can't help but write to express my concern about the misguided, and possibly even life-threatening, assumptions you espouse in your book. I am a psychologist with thirty-seven years of experience, and I am surprised that you, a PhD with a position at a fine school, would choose to cash in by dumbing down our work for profit.

Delete. Charlotte puts her phone facedown on the white tablecloth. It is nearly a week since the blowout with Birdie. She is sitting in the window of a quaint bistro on Wisconsin Avenue in Georgetown, waiting on Wendy, her agent, who is in town for the day from New York, and she does not have the bandwidth for criticism. She glances at the phone, tempted to google this so-called experienced expert, but she stops herself. For a bunch of people supposedly devoted to mental wellness, no group is more neurotic than the psych community. She thinks back to the time a year ago when a coworker invited her to join an online chat to weigh in on some new research about the whole "actions before emotions" theory she'd based her book on, and a professor from Indiana used it as an opportunity to call her a sellout, a moron, and so on. When she looked up his bio, she discovered that his research specialty was, of all things, empathy.

She grabs her phone and checks Instagram. @KGPartyof5 hasn't written her since Savannah. A few nights ago, after the blowup with Birdie, Charlotte actually considered messaging her to vent about it, and even began typing a note under the guise of asking how her own kid was doing, but then she deleted it, quelling the temptation.

Her phone dings. A text from Wendy: Sorry I'm late. Uber stuck behind maybe a motorcade??? The president????

Can you see the license plate? Charlotte types back. 800–002 if it's prez, and there will be a couple dozen cars around. Big black car, almost a limo, flags and the seal on the side.

No, not a bunch of cars, Wendy writes. Five-ish? A light on top, like on a police car.

Prob just a cabinet member then, Charlotte types.

HA! Who knew? Wendy types back, adding the shoulder-shrugging, palms-in-the-air emoji to the end of her text. Sorry again—see you soon.

No problem, Charlotte says. I don't teach another class today, so I have all afternoon. We're good.

It's funny, given all that they've been through over the past few years, that Charlotte and her agent have met in person only twice. Wendy is a dynamo, quick-witted and funny and a terrible gossip—and as much as Charlotte is desperate for her brand of distraction, she can't deny the dread looming in the back of her mind because she knows why Wendy's made the special trip.

It's not that she doesn't want to publish a follow-up. It's just that she doesn't want to write one. And therein lies the problem. She thinks of Birdie screaming at her the other night, and a phrase pops into her head: *time affluence*, which means feeling like you have enough time for all of the things you need and want to do. It's a central tenet of happiness, per the research, and there's a whole chapter about it in her book, with a dreamy opener about how she always felt like she never had enough time to catch up with extended family until she started her daily morning check-ins with her mother, which "has the double bonus of making me feel like I'm strengthening our connection and helps me start the day more relaxed, all for the simple act of a ten-minute phone call." It might be the biggest line of BS in her whole book, one that made Jason laugh out loud when he read it for the first time. But the book's release, and everything that had ensued, had actually dissolved any actual sense of time affluence she had. She wonders now, how she can write another book, when the success of the first one has been so damaging to her actual life?

She looks out the window, watching an older woman with a coiffed pompadour and big black sunglasses shuffle past the restaurant. The sidewalks seem more crowded than normal, almost certainly because it's an outrageously beautiful day: bright blue sky, a slight breeze, the temperature just warm enough for short sleeves. Her eyes lock on a woman about her age in front of the Mexican restaurant across the street, who's wrangling the leash of a large black Lab trying to access the smattering of broken tortilla chips underneath one of the iron tables out front. People shuffle to maneuver around her, stepping off the curb and bumping into one another, but the more the dog pulls in one direction, the more she rears back, trying to get her footing like they're playing a game of tug-of-war.

Charlotte watches as a busboy who's clearing the table says something to the dog owner, laughing good-naturedly before disappearing into the restaurant, and then another woman approaches from behind and starts chatting with the woman, pulling something from her pocket and offering it to her dog.

The woman looks vaguely familiar. Long, curly hair, khaki pants, sneakers . . . and then Charlotte realizes: *Of course! Jamie!* The last time she saw her was at her husband's funeral. *How awful that was*, she thinks, feeling a pang of guilt for how she treated Jason the other night; when, first, he tried to hug her, and then comfort her after Birdie blew up. In the moment, she just couldn't talk to him. It felt easier to walk away and sulk in private, with the aid of a glass of chardonnay.

Jamie's talking animatedly, waving her hands, laughing with the other woman, and Charlotte smiles to herself, pleased that she looks like she's doing so well. But then a split second later, she notices someone sidling up beside her. *Jason? What is he doing in Georgetown?*

The three of them begin chatting easily, like old friends. Jason points to the dog, now lying at his owner's feet, and says something that makes Jamie throw her head back in laughter.

And then she clasps Jason's upper arm, threading her hand around his bicep.

Charlotte freezes. This doesn't faze him. He doesn't stop talking, he just keeps going, like Jamie's hand on him doesn't even register. *But she's his coworker* . . . The gears turn in Charlotte's head, piecing something together. *They look so . . . Anyone might think . . . What are they doing in Georgetown?* Jason never leaves the zoo's campus during the workday, not ever. *What are they doing, period?*

She tries to swallow but her mouth has gone dry. They're walking away now, waving goodbye to the dog lady, still laughing, but walking slowly—strolling, really—like they have all the time in the world. A wave of nausea passes over her. Jamie's hand goes back to Jason's arm, just like before, and Charlotte can see, even from here, how Jamie squeezes it, just above his elbow, before letting go.

Charlotte flies out of her seat, her chair knocking the one at the table behind her, and rounds the corner down a couple of steps toward the entrance of the restaurant, forcing a waiter in a starched pin-striped shirt to press himself against the wall as she bolts past. "Is everything okay?" she hears him call after her. She has to catch them! She has to find out— She pushes the heavy wooden door open with both hands and, chest heaving, scans the block, but they're gone. *How could they have disappeared so quickly?* She can't find them anywhere. *I'll go anyway,* she thinks. *I'll try the side street.* She starts toward the crosswalk, but then she hears a voice behind her, calling her name.

She turns. "Wendy!" she manages, gulping in air like she's just been underwater. She feels dizzy, her thoughts spinning. Wendy, in her black on black, is walking toward her, one shoulder slumped low to balance the weight of her huge leather tote.

They hug and air-kiss, and Charlotte wishes, as Wendy pulls away, that she could lean on her to steady herself. A million questions buzz in her head; blaring, zipping, Times Square billboard thoughts: *Did I actually just see what I thought I did? Where were they going? What were they doing? Or about to do?* She sees Jamie's hand again. *On his arm. On his shoulder.*

"I'm so sorry I'm late!" Wendy's yakking. "This place looks adorable. How are you? I'm starved!"

They'd looked like a couple. Anyone passing them on the street would think they were a couple. "Char, are you okay?"

"Yeah, yeah," she says, shaking herself back into the present.

"I'm sorry. I thought I saw someone I knew so I hurried out to say hello and then you—" She waves her hands in front of her face. "Never mind." She forces a smile, knowing she must look deranged. "It's so good to see you, Wendy! Let's go eat." She gestures toward the door, letting Wendy go first, but just before she steps inside, she turns to scan the sidewalk one last time.

As they sit, Wendy oohs and aahs about the restaurant's homey decor, smacking her lips like it's literally delicious: "Oh, this scrumptious wallpaper! And this fabric on the chairs!" Charlotte notices some of the other diners turning to see who's cooing with such enthusiasm. With her loud Chicago accent, her hair dyed bright cherry red, the hyperglow lipstick, Wendy makes an impression. Charlotte has always secretly believed that aside from her obvious acute business sense, one reason why she is so successful—she started her own agency three decades ago, when she was just twenty-seven years old, with a roster of bestselling clients who've made her millions—is because she is impossible to forget.

"God, you're gorgeous as always," Wendy says, flopping down into her seat. "If you would just let me put you on a book cover, I swear you'd sell double."

"Please," Charlotte starts, wiping her hand along her damp forehead, feeling her blouse cling to her back.

"I know, I know." Wendy shoos a hand at her. "Not your style. I know!"

The waiter she almost knocked over is now patiently standing off to the side, a sweating silver pitcher of water in his hands, and seeing him, Wendy taps her copper-colored fingernail to her chin. "I think just a seltzer for the moment," she says. "Just plain. No lime, no lemon, nothing." She looks at Charlotte and pats her hand against her middle. "I feel a little queasy. Not the best Uber driver. Hit the brakes every five seconds and the car *reeked* of smoke."

"Water still okay for you?" the waiter asks Charlotte.

She looks down at the menu, *really* wanting the viognier she spotted when she first arrived. "Yes, it's fine."

"So!" Wendy says. "How are you? It's been what . . . almost a year?"

"Something like that," Charlotte says. "Since the 92nd Street Y talk."

"Right, right, of course!" Wendy says. "What a boon that was!" She clicks her tongue. "Anyway, how have you been? Such a beautiful day here. I saw the cherry blossoms from the plane! Breathtaking!"

"Yes," Charlotte says. "You're lucky you caught them. The bloom season is so short."

"That's right." Wendy raises her finger to the air. "Here today, gone tomorrow. Which . . ." She wiggles her eyebrows at Charlotte, a mischievous look on her face. "Is also a good metaphor for what we *don't* want to happen to your career." She clasps her hands on the table and leans in. "As I can imagine you've gathered, that's why I'm here."

Charlotte smiles. "Wendy, listen, before we go any further, I really don't have anything new for you yet. Like I said when we talked last week, I just need to get through this semester and the Montana talk. Once it's summer break, I can start thinking seriously about a follow-up."

Wendy leans back and raps the fingers of both hands against the table, studying Charlotte like they're opposing players at a poker game. "We need to get you working on another book sooner than that. You don't want to be a one-book wonder, do you?"

"Of course not," Charlotte says, rearing back a little. "You know I don't." She also knows that she's been promising a proposal for over a year now. "I was mulling that workbook idea. You know, workable exercises and strategies based off the info in the last—"

"Yeah, yeah," Wendy says, waving her hand back and forth. "But that's more of an ancillary thing, a supplement. Not a *follow-up.* We need your next bestseller and we need it now. I know it might not seem like it given how busy you are but if too much time passes, people will forget about you. Remember my client Todd Marshall?"

"No," Charlotte says.

Wendy leans forward. "My point exactly. He was a former Navy SEAL. His book was a health guide, it sold at least as well as yours. And then he never wrote anything again." She flicks her fingers in the air, like *poof.* "One-book wonder."

The waiter arrives and sets down Wendy's seltzer. "Have you had a moment to look over the menu?"

"We haven't even looked yet," Charlotte says.

"I'll give you another minute."

"Actually," Wendy says, holding up a finger. She narrows her eyes at Charlotte, as if considering something. "Could we have a couple glasses of champagne?"

Charlotte's ears perk up. *Champagne is exactly what I need,* she thinks. *Also a shot or two of tequila.*

"Certainly," the waiter says, walking off.

"You can handle a glass of wine at lunch," Wendy says.

"Apparently I'm going to," she says. "Thank you!"

"I'm trying to butter you up." Wendy rubs her hands together then clears her throat. "So here's the thing: I'm not going to make you sit here and promise me a second book idea that I know you don't have yet."

"You're not?" Charlotte says, feeling at once relieved and sheepish.

"Nope," she says. "Because I actually have one *for* you."

"You do?"

"I do. You know my new assistant? Noelle? You've spoken to her on the phone."

Charlotte nods, wondering where on earth this might be going.

"She is a *bulldog. So* smart. She actually reminds me quite a bit of myself at that age!" Wendy laughs. "She's been doing a lot of research."

"Okaaay," Charlotte says. "What kind of research?"

"You wouldn't believe it actually," Wendy says. "She had these spreadsheets on her iPad . . . she's looked at the demographics. The people buying your book, the people attending your talks, the people attending your talks and *then* buying your book, and not that this is any big surprise—I mean, we know this just by looking at your social media—but Noelle and I really believe that the evidence shows that the secret to your success with the next book is . . ." She puts her palms up, mouth open, waiting for Charlotte to answer for her.

"Women between the ages of twenty-five and fifty?" Charlotte guesses.

"Well, yes," Wendy says. "Yes. But more specifically, it's moms."

"Moms?" Charlotte says.

"Yes."

"Well, that isn't exactly surprising."

"No, it's not," Wendy says. "But think about it: You've got your exhausted working moms, your exhausted stay-at-home moms, your moms in the sandwich generation, caring for both their kids and their aging parents. Noelle—" She raises a finger. "Hold on." She reaches into the tote bag hanging on the back of her chair and rustles around for her phone, then taps on the screen a few times. "Okay. Here we go. According to a study that Noelle found, it is moms between the ages of thirty-four and fifty who are most likely to be diagnosed with depression."

"Right," Charlotte says, straightening up in her chair. "I've reviewed that research. There was a study out of UC Davis just last week that said as much."

Wendy runs her finger along her phone's screen. "And also," she recites. "Another study says that mothers in midlife are the fastest-growing group when it comes to abuse of alcohol and prescription drugs."

"That one is from polling out of UNC," Charlotte says. "It was all over the news a few months ago," she adds, thinking of Jason's accusation about her wine drinking last week. *How could he*, she thinks now, *when he's cheat*—She shakes the thought away, not ready to go there. "You know, the drug thing, that was on *Oprah*, like, twenty years ago."

"Well, *Valley of the Dolls*, 'mother's little helper,' we can go back even further, can't we?" Wendy says. "But it's worse now than ever. By far. *You* know that."

Her pointed manner lands in a way that stings Charlotte, even though she's sure it was unintentional. "Right."

Her agent's face falls. "This doesn't seem to excite you," she says.

"No, no," Charlotte says. "It's not that. I guess that it's just not exactly breaking news."

"Well, not to you, of course, but you're mired in this stuff every day, Charlotte. It's your life's work."

"True," she concedes.

The waiter arrives with two flutes of champagne, and Wendy gestures for Charlotte to take a sip. Charlotte lifts the glass to her mouth, feeling the exquisite tingle of the tiny bubbles against her lips. It tastes like relief.

"You're a mom, Charlotte," Wendy says. "You're right in this. You're busy, at the top of your game at work, and raising this wonderful girl, too . . ."

Charlotte takes another sip.

"You know *exactly* what the challenges are. And the solutions!"

"So what are you thinking, then?" Charlotte asks. "A happiness guide for moms? That just seems a little . . ."

"It's not *just* anything," Wendy says. "You have a platform, Charlotte. This could inspire real change. You could really help a lot of women."

Charlotte raises her eyebrows.

"Why are you so resistant?" Wendy asks.

"I'm not resistant," Charlotte says. "It just seems a little . . . maybe, in a way—" she says, her thoughts taking shape. "Is it a little shortsighted? Because women who haven't chosen motherhood feel a lot of the same pressures."

"Right, but if we're talking about families—traditional ones, at least—women still shoulder so much of the crap at home, right?"

"Well, sure. Statistically."

"And statistically, they're the ones suffering. Stealing pills out of the medicine cabinet. Drinking their 'mommy juice.'"

Charlotte rolls her eyes.

"True, though, isn't it?"

"Well, sure," Charlotte says. "I can guarantee I wouldn't be depressed if I wasn't responsible for so much."

Wendy cocks her head. "Are you depressed?"

Charlotte stiffens. "Jesus, no!" she says. "You know what I mean. Just busy and stressed, the usual, you know."

Wendy considers her, and then her eyes drift toward Charlotte's glass, which is nearly empty now, and Charlotte feels herself flush. "Exactly," Wendy says, lowering her head and looking into Charlotte's eyes like she's giving her an ultimatum. "So why not use your expertise and personal experience?"

"Wendy," Charlotte says, feeling her stomach churn. "I don't know . . ."

"All right, listen," Wendy says. "I'll be straight with you. I thought you were going to love this idea."

"It's not that I don't love—" she starts but Wendy stops her.

"Maybe this will help," her agent interrupts. "I spoke with your editor a few days ago and I mentioned the mom idea, and once we started talking, the thing just snowballed. The publisher loves the idea, and they even have a title: *Perfect Happiness: Family*," she says, flicking her fingers in the air like she's putting the words in lights. "They think it'll be big. That's why . . ." She gestures toward the champagne.

Charlotte feels a thrum in her chest, her heartbeat pulsing. *A book about family*, she thinks. *And I'm the expert.*

Wendy continues her pitch, which begins to feel more and more like a demand. "You could do it however you want," she's saying. "The stages of family life, different types of families, geared toward moms, dads, single-sex parents, parents of special-needs kids . . . there are a million different directions you can go in, Char."

"I assume, like last time, they'll want anecdotes from my own life?" she asks, trying to sound casual.

"Well, yes," Wendy says, finally taking a sip of champagne. "But that should be easy for you. Gorgeous husband, gem of a kid. And you're the spark, my dear." She reaches and clinks her glass against Charlotte's. "Is there any reason this wouldn't work?"

Charlotte glances out the window. "And what if my family life isn't perfect?" she says. *"Perfectly happy?"*

"Even better!" Wendy says. "Books are built on the backs of dysfunction!" Charlotte can see the searching question behind her agent's eyes. "But you're an expert, so you could balance it out. People don't just want their own shitty lives reflected back at them." She puts her hands out. "Not that your life is shitty, you know what I mean, but your shitty is different because you project a certain authority. You have a brand, and if you confess that your home life isn't all *Leave It to Beaver* and *Donna Reed*, people are just going to love you more for it. A year ago, everything was about *authenticity*, but now, *vulnerability*'s the thing."

Charlotte nods.

Wendy narrows her eyes. "I thought for sure this would be a home run. I assumed I'd be calling your publisher on the way to the airport, that we'd have a deal by the time I touched down at LaGuardia."

Charlotte puts her hand to her chest. "It's not that I'm not grateful," she says. "It's not that I don't appreciate their enthusiasm. I guess I'm just daunted by the idea of taking on the next thing, and if it's going to talk about my family, you know, Birdie is in such a precarious stage of life. I wouldn't want to embarrass her. I'd need to talk to Jason, too." Her eyes slide toward the window again.

Wendy twists in her seat and pulls a folder out of her bag. "I had my assistant print this out." She pushes the piece of paper across the table. Charlotte sees that it's an email from her editor.

> We've spoken as a team about PH: Family. We think it's exactly where we should go, and the sooner the better. We'd love to have a finished manuscript within the next six months or so. Is Charlotte amenable? We can offer $750,000.

Charlotte's eyes widen. The numbers swim on the page.

"That's what you're worth to them," Wendy says. "That's how special you are, Charlotte."

Charlotte takes a deep breath, rereading the text. *$750,000?*

Wendy leans across the table. "And listen," she says, stabbing a finger onto the page. "Given how long your book's been a bestseller, I can probably get you more. Not to speak out of turn, but if you're worried about Birdie, that's college tuition right there."

"It's a lot more than . . ." Charlotte's voice drifts off, the reality sinking in. Wendy's right. She'd be a fool to turn this down.

"The bottom line is that they're not going to wait forever, and you need to do something before this train loses steam or leaves the station." She cackles. "You know what I mean! But, come on, Charlotte, why wouldn't you say yes?"

Images flash before Charlotte's eyes. Jason, his barely perceptible goodbye mumbled as he races out the door in the morning in a way that feels like an escape. Birdie, hysterical, essentially screaming that she's a terrible mother. Jason, laughing with Jamie on the street in a way that Charlotte can't remember him doing with her in years. She looks up and finds Wendy staring at her.

"This is the thing that people work their whole lives for," Wendy says, holding up her champagne. "You've earned this, Charlotte. It's the brass ring. Take it."

Charlotte inhales deeply and snatches her own glass from the table. "Okay," she says, tossing back the glass as Wendy yelps. She closes her eyes, feeling a tingling in her nose like she might cry, and she wills the tears to stay back. When she looks at Wendy, she tries to match the excitement in her expression, but she feels out of body, like she's some other person looking down at herself, asking what the hell she is doing. She looks again at the figure on the page, and wonders if it is enough, if anything could be.

Back in her office, Charlotte's not sure what to do with herself. She fingers the leaves of the peace lily on her desk and checks whether it needs water. When her eyes catch on the photo of her and Jason and Birdie at the beach a few summers ago, he in the center, his arms around the two of them, she turns it over, then picks it up and shoves it into her bottom desk drawer, slamming it closed, shaking with anger.

She turns to the window, watching the students pass below, envying how easy their lives look from this vantage point, how small their problems seem.

She needs to get it together. She needs to stop circling the drain with this misery, stop living every day like a martyr, "shift her focus," "see her own possibilities," she thinks. She needs to start following her own advice. *What could I do right now?* she asks herself. *What's the one thing that could make me feel better in this instant?* She sits, swiveling back and forth in her chair, a thought occurring to her. She shouldn't, she *knows* she shouldn't, but like going back into the kitchen for another glass of wine after everyone's in bed, it's exactly what she wants.

She finds her wallet in her bag, pulling out the card from the slot behind her driver's license. Emailing would feel safer, she knows, but she picks up her phone anyway, tapping in the numbers before she can talk herself out of it. It rings, twice and then a third time, and she considers hanging up, but then a voice comes on the line.

"Hello?"

"Oh!" she says, startled. "Hi, it's—"

"Charlotte?" Reese says, sounding confused.

"Yes," she says, her face on fire. "I didn't think I'd get you in the middle of the workday."

He laughs. "So you called hoping not to get me, or . . . ?"

"I don't . . . I don't know exactly," she says. "You're not in surgery?"

"Nope," he says. "Not today. Cleared my calendar for the afternoon."

"Well, that sounds nice," she says.

"Mmm," he says, doubt in his voice. "I actually just left my lawyer's office. Trust me when I tell you that I would rather be *on* an operating table than going through divorce proceedings."

"I'm so sorry," she says, the word he just used—*divorce*—reverberating.

"Nothing for you to be sorry about, it's not your fault." He laughs. "Though apparently it's one hundred percent mine."

"So it's not amicable?"

"That's not the word I would use."

"What happened?" she says, realizing how forward the question is only once it's out of her mouth. "I mean, you don't have to tell me."

"No, no," he says. "I'm surprised you don't already know, given how word spreads in our fair city. She cheated on me."

"Oh, Reese," she says, her face going hot, thinking of the parallel to her day. If she'd learned this a few weeks ago, before she saw him, or any day other than today, she'd probably feel some sort of vindication, but now . . .

"With our next-door neighbor, of all people," he says. "He's a pilot who moved up from Jacksonville. Thought he was a good friend, but . . ." He sighs. "It's probably karma for what I did all of those years ago."

A jolt runs through her body.

"You know I still hate myself for doing that to you," he says.

"No, Reese, no," she says, swallowing. "It's—"

The silence hangs between them. She doesn't want to say it's okay, because it's not. "It was a long time ago," she finally says.

"You're too forgiving," he answers.

She starts to say something about how the research shows that forgiveness is one of the best routes to contentment, but then she stops herself. He doesn't need to hear her shoptalk.

"So what's happening with you?" he says. "How are you? Where are you?"

"Oh," she says. "I'm at work."

"The famous Dr. McGanley," he says. "Is there a little plaque on your door?"

"Well." She laughs. "Yes."

"And do your students all call you Dr. McGanley?"

"They do." She laughs again. "And some of my colleagues, occasionally. But yours do, too. I don't know why you're making fun."

He chuckles. "I'm not making fun," he says. "I'm just happy for you, doing exactly what you set out to do."

"More or less," she says.

"What do you mean?"

"I don't know. Sometimes I second-guess myself."

"I do, too," he says. He lowers his voice. "Even sometimes in the middle of surgery, but don't tell that to my patients."

"Reese!" She laughs, and it feels good, especially because it feels familiar. They could be sitting on the dock behind her parents' house right now, shooting the shit like they did for so many years. She realizes how much better she feels after just a few minutes of talking with him, and remembers how it was so often like this between them, the world shrunk down to its simplest, and its best.

"But you're so good at what you do," he says.

"It's changed," she says. "I feel a little blindsided by it . . . and I worry about what it's doing to the rest of my life."

"Really?" he says.

"Yes," she says. "Sometimes I just wish I could escape. Chuck it all. Run away."

"But I bet you'll look back years from now and be so happy about everything you accomplished."

"I don't know," she says, her mind drifting to Birdie, who's probably on her way to practice now.

"Maybe you just need a vacation?" he says.

She laughs. "I won't get one anytime soon. I actually just agreed to write a second book."

"What?" he says. "That's amazing! I'm so happy for you!"

"Thanks," she says, wondering what Jason's reaction will be.

"Charlotte, seriously," he says. "That's fantastic news. You need to celebrate."

"It's really not that big—"

"It's a huge deal," he says. "Come on. You've always sold yourself short. Don't be so damn modest. Charlotte, you're amazing," he says. "Don't you know that?"

Tears suddenly come to her eyes again. It's been so long

since anyone who mattered said something like this to her. She squeezes her eyes shut, trying to stop the tears.

"You really, really are," he says. "I'm so proud of you. If I were there, I'd take you out for champagne."

"I'd love that," she says, but the moment the words are out of her mouth, she realizes how wrong this is. She thinks of Jason, of Birdie. This feels too dangerous, too good.

"I should go," she says.

"I'm glad you called," he says. "It totally turned my day around."

She closes her eyes, not wanting to say it. "Mine, too."

TEN

SOS! SOS!

Amanda's text arrives just as Charlotte's pulling into the parking lot of the high school. She'd decided to blow off the rest of the day and leave work early to watch Birdie's practice, hoping the gesture might smooth things between them.

What is it? she types, scanning the groups of students milling between the parking lot and the practice fields. School's been out for over an hour, but with all of the activities that these kids have these days, few of them will be home before dinnertime.

A warning that your mother came by an hour ago and mentioned the idea of us walking that horrendous dog of hers down the aisle at her and E's vow renewal.

Oh, Jesus, Charlotte types. And are we walking down an aisle?? Does she think this is a royal wedding?

She also wants us to all give toasts.

No! I already weaseled my way out of helping her write her vows.

Says she will call you about it in the am to discuss.

God help us all.

Charlotte starts to get out of the car, then hesitates, deciding to check Instagram quickly. Right before she left the office, she'd posted a photo of the cherry blossoms, a caption about noticing the little things because they are so fleeting. Almost 16,000 likes. She taps over to her profile page and checks her follower count. Almost 94,000. *Another book might double it*, she thinks, and then she thinks again about the money, recalling those studies that occasionally pop up in her psych journals about it—the misery of lottery winners, the correlation between income and happiness. There's a sweet spot, around $100,000, she thinks she remembers, past which people just become more miserable as their incomes grow. And then she thinks of Jason. And Jamie. Would he be happier with her? *Is he already?*

She walks across the grassy swath that separates the parking lot from the tennis courts, and has a momentary panic that Birdie won't be there. But then she hears the familiar thwack of Birdie's racket against the ball, and sees her daughter racing across the court, her arm slicing through the air. The sight itself is a comfort to Charlotte, because *this*—the grace, the strength, the speed—*this* is her Birdie.

She barely knows the other parents from the team, but she

smiles at them as she climbs the metal bleachers, nodding hello. A woman in a green Masters Tournament baseball cap turns to her from her spot two rows beneath. "She's yours, right?" she says, pointing at the court, where Birdie is getting ready to serve.

"Yes," Charlotte says, slipping her feet out of her flats and resting them on the warm metal of the step in front of her. She wishes she was dressed like this woman is, in exercise shorts and a tank top, the unmistakable sheen from sunscreen on her skin. She looks like summer vacation.

"She's only a freshman, right?"

Charlotte nods.

"Wow," the woman says, though the expression on her face shows no enthusiasm. She turns away and raises her eyebrows at the woman sitting next to her, who hasn't bothered to greet Charlotte. She immediately wonders if they're the mothers of the upperclassmen on the team who are giving Birdie a hard time.

They watch Birdie's serve zoom over the net, the player across the court just missing the return, and the other woman leans back. "How long has she played?"

"Oh," Charlotte says. "Forever. Since she was a toddler."

The woman's eyebrows shoot up. Charlotte knows what she's thinking, that she and Jason pushed Birdie into it, that they made this Birdie's sport. She turns back around to the court, whispers something in the other mother's ear. Charlotte laces her hands together, squeezing.

"How old is she?" asks Green Masters Cap, leaning back again.

"Fourteen," Charlotte says.

"Did you play?"

"No," Charlotte says, happy for this question. "My husband either. We had nothing to do with this."

"Mm," the woman says, clearly not buying it.

"She used to sit in front of the TV for hours watching matches, and not just the U.S. Open and Wimbledon, but the Australian Open, the French Open, random regional matches on the Tennis Channel."

She wishes she could go on and on, but she doesn't want to seem defensive. She could tell them about the walls of Birdie's bedroom, plastered with so many Serena posters that Jason joked that it looked like a stalker's bedroom in a horror movie. Or about how, in fourth grade, while her friends wrote book reports on Harry Potter, Birdie wrote about *Open*, Andre Agassi's autobiography, a book she read so many times that the spine broke.

Another mom farther down the bleachers turns around. "You're that happiness person, right?" she says, her hands above her eyes to shield the sun.

Charlotte smiles. "Yes," she says. "I am."

All three women now appraise her, and she waits for one to say something but they don't. *What is this about?* Eventually they turn around, and she shakes the encounter away, turning her focus to Birdie.

Birdie bounces a ball on the court, preparing to serve again, and then hits it with such force that a dad on the far end of the bleachers gasps. The ball zooms past the tall, pale redhead on the other end of the court, so fast that the girl whirls around, twirling like a pinwheel. Charlotte scans the reaction of the other girls on the court, and sees a couple whisper to each other, watching Birdie all the while. It could be nothing, or it could not be, she thinks, eyeing the women who just spoke to her, waiting to see if they'll say something.

Birdie hasn't seemed to notice her mother there or is pretending not to, but after a few minutes, while she's grabbing a ball out of the basket on the edge of the court and tucking it into her skirt, she looks over to scan the stands. Charlotte gives her a little wave, not wanting to embarrass her, and Birdie lifts her hand like she's about to wave back, but then something catches her eye. When Charlotte follows her gaze, she sees it: *Tucker.*

He's approaching the bleachers. He sits on the bottom row and watches Birdie for a minute, chin in his hand, then turns to his phone. Before long he's laughing, God knows at what. What do fifteen-year-old boys laugh at on their phones? Fart jokes? Girl jokes? Porn memes? *Put your phone down, Tucker, and watch her play,* she thinks. He doesn't deserve her.

Birdie, meanwhile, keeps looking over at him, smiling a little, in stark contrast to the way she looks at Charlotte lately. Coach Noah notices that she's distracted and calls to her, looking exasperated, whispering something in her ear that apparently does the trick because seconds later, the focus is back on her face and in her shots. Even at practice, and with her mind somewhere else, it's evident that she can outplay anyone on this team.

Tucker finally puts the phone down and leans back, arms resting on the bleacher behind him, and Charlotte can't take it anymore. She keeps imagining that Instagram video. She has to seize the chance to say something to him. She steps carefully down the four rows between them, and sits next to him.

"Hi, Tucker," she says, as casually as she can.

"Oh!" he says, surprised. "Mrs. McGanley! Hi! I didn't see you." He immediately grabs his phone from the space between them and begins to tap at it, an unconscious habit, she's sure, one she sees her students do all the time. It's a tic, disappearing into the phone when you get uncomfortable, like raising an invisible privacy screen.

"Tucker," she says. "I need to ask you about something."

He puts down the phone, but his eyes stay on the court.

"Look at me, please," she says, in a tone that Birdie once dubbed her "mean teacher voice."

He does, and Charlotte notices the gold flecks in his eyes, the tiny crusting pimple beside his temple, the chapped corners of his lips. He feels like such a villain in her mind, but she sees now that he's just a kid, not even old enough to drive a car.

"You don't have practice today?" she says.

"It's in twenty minutes." He stutters a little, looking unsure.

"Listen," she says, smiling, aware that Birdie or the other parents might be watching them. "I know I don't have to tell you that it's not okay with me or Birdie's dad for you to take her back to your house when there aren't adults there."

"What are you talking about?" he says, though his cheeks immediately turn pink.

"Tucker, we know she was over at your house. We know about her skipping practice."

He leans forward, elbows on his knees. Charlotte waits for him to say something, but he doesn't. She wonders if he's ever been reprimanded for anything before. She gets the feeling he hasn't, that he's actually the kind of kid she hates most when they come sauntering into her classroom, the ones whom she is sure could get out of anything in exchange for a big donation to the school from their parents.

"Was it your idea to go back there?"

He huffs and looks away, shaking his head like he's disgusted, confirming her suspicions about him. She glances at the court. Birdie's back is to them but it's only a matter of time before she turns around.

"Tucker, please answer my question," she says, and he tilts his head toward her.

"Let me guess," he says. "You found out because you saw my Instagram story, right? Why are you so obsessed with my account, Mrs. McGanley? It's kind of weird, isn't it? For an adult to be following a kid's account the way you do?"

"Tucker!" she snaps, but then her mind goes blank, not finding the words. What is there to say? He's got her. And from the look on his face, the self-satisfied, nothing-will-ever-stick-to-me smirk, he knows it. Every cell in her body pulses with anger. This *kid. This fucking kid!*

"Tucker, I'm going to say this once," she says, her voice low, aware of the parents around her. "You do anything like that again and I promise you, you'll regret it."

He whips his head back around, surveying the people behind them on the bleachers. "Are you threatening me, Mrs. McGanley?" he says, loudly enough for everyone around them to hear.

She shifts on the bench, not daring to look around. "Don't be silly, Tucker." She leans back like they're having a casual conversation, crossing her legs and letting her shoe flip off her heel, bouncing it as she watches the kids on the court, now breaking apart for their next drill. Birdie looks over, sees them sitting together, and a nervous grin materializes on her face.

Charlotte's heart is beating triple time. She knows she has to tread carefully. Anything she says to him will circle back to Birdie, probably embellished.

"Birdie likes you, Tucker," she says, just under her breath as she waves casually at her daughter. "And she's a good judge of character, so I know some part of you must be decent enough, because she's a smart girl." She puts her hand out and touches his arm, just for the briefest moment, to make her point. "But hear me on this, Tucker: You may care about my daughter. Or I'm going to assume for the sake of this conversation that you do, let's put it that way, and she may have feelings for you, but it is nothing compared to the way that I feel about her. And the kind of love that I have for Birdie means I'll do anything for her. Anything."

She waits for him to say something but he doesn't. Birdie races across the court to return a volley and slams it over the net.

"Do you understand?" she says.

He picks up his phone. "Right," he says, hopping up. He saunters to the tennis court, looking back for a moment at Charlotte as he does it, like he's challenging her. He leans against the metal fencing and calls Birdie's name. Her eyes widen, embarrassed by the attention, but the thrill on her face is undeniable. She checks to see what her coach is doing, and seeing that his head is dipped, discussing something with another player, she jogs over to Tucker. He puts his palm up to the fence and she matches hers to it, their fingers interlacing for the briefest moment. Seconds later, she's jogging back to her teammates, and a couple of them make goofy faces at her, giggling. Tucker walks off, not looking back, seeming like he doesn't have a care in the world, because—Charlotte's sure of it—he doesn't. And nothing worries her more.

"Nice for your mother to come to practice, huh, Bird?" Jason says, tipping his head sideways to take a big bite of his sandwich. Charlotte's not sure what to make of it, but Birdie was mercifully, finally cordial to her after practice. Whether it was because of her showing up, Tucker showing up, or something else entirely, she's relieved that something might be normalizing between them.

They stopped at the Italian Store (Birdie's choice) on the way home and picked up a sub for Jason, a couple of slices of pizza for Birdie, and pasta salad from the deli counter that Charlotte is pushing around her plate. She watches Jason across the table, and takes a sip of the deep, rich chianti she picked up in the wine section while Birdie was surveying the cannoli. A forty-five-dollar bottle, easily double what she normally spends, but as she was turning the bottle in her hands, examining the label, she heard Reese's voice in her head, telling her she should celebrate her book offer, and so she grabbed it, deciding she could have herself a little party of one. It is a stupid amount of money that they're offering her. A ridiculous amount. She looks at Jason across the table, strategizing how to tell him. The wine, for all that she spent, tastes terrible.

His phone keeps vibrating on the counter across the room,

which is not unusual in and of itself. Her father-in-law has a habit of texting his son every time a thought materializes in his head that he believes Jason might find interesting; about the new shortstop for the Nats, the weather conditions at the beach, or asking him to check on the bird feeders/water filter/thermostats at the house. Normally Charlotte can ignore it, but not tonight. Because what if it's—

"You feel ready for the match tomorrow?" Jason says, wiping a slick of vinaigrette from his chin.

"Mm-hmm," Birdie says through a mouthful of pepperoni.

"She looked great out there this afternoon," Charlotte says, attempting to act normal.

"What were you and Tucker talking about?" Birdie asks, her mouth turning up, a shy smile.

"Tucker was at practice?" Jason says, cocking his head at Charlotte. "You spoke to him?" Charlotte hears the phone buzzing again, the sound corkscrewing into her eardrum.

"Just for a minute," Birdie says. "Before his own practice. Mom, what did you say to him?"

"You haven't texted him forty times already since you got home?" Jason says, raising an eyebrow at her. Under normal circumstances, this could have been typical dad-joke teasing, Birdie laughing at him to stop, but instead, she looks down at her lap, seemingly still chastened by the trouble she's gotten into.

"Well," Jason says. "I'm glad you had so many spectators. And I'm glad that you actually made it to practice so they could see you."

Birdie grimaces, and Charlotte tries another sip of her wine, remembering how Tucker looked back at her this afternoon. Can a fifteen-year-old really be that malicious? With his girlfriend's mother?

"Bird, it's okay," Jason finally says, glancing at Charlotte, as his voice softens. "I know it was a onetime offense."

She nods and takes a bite of her pizza, and Charlotte studies her, looking for some signal that she's okay. "I tried to tell Tucker as many embarrassing stories as I could in the five minutes we talked," she jokes.

"Mom!" Birdie smiles, and Charlotte instantly feels it, the reward centers, as she might say in class, going off in her brain. The phone buzzes again and Charlotte sees Jason look briefly in its direction before turning back to his sub.

"I told him about the time you took off your dirty diaper during Thanksgiving dinner and handed it to Grandma," Charlotte says.

"Mom!" Birdie screams, her ears turning deep red.

The phone buzzes again and Charlotte can't take it anymore. She dips her head back, looking up at the ceiling. "Could you *please* answer that, Jason?" she says.

"Yeah, yeah," he says, hopping up like he's just hearing it for the first time.

"Oh, geez," he says, leaning against the counter, crossing his feet casually at the ankles. She watches as he scrolls through the texts, a nervousness passing over her like the slightest breeze.

"What is it?" Birdie says, twisting in her seat.

He puts his hand to his mouth, continuing to read. "It looks like there's something going on with the new orangutan baby."

"Oh, no!" Birdie says, looking over at Charlotte with alarm.

"Yeah," he says, scrolling faster now. "I'm going to have to go in."

Charlotte puts down her fork. Jason rarely needs to go into work off-hours. Maybe once every few *years.* "But you don't even work in the ape house anymore," she says, barely getting the words out. She knows, of course, who does.

"I know." He scratches his head. "But there's something going on with his heart rate. And Lucy, the mom, is freaking out."

"Again," Charlotte says. "What does that have to do with you?"

He looks at her, clearly miffed by this comment. "Besides Jamie, I'm the only keeper Lucy's most comfortable with. She's going nuts," he says, holding up the phone like it's proof. "Jamie needs help. I'm sorry, I need to go."

"I guess if Jamie needs help . . ." Charlotte says. He looks at her in confusion but then he shoves his phone in his pocket and starts out of the room.

"Dad, text me and let me know how the baby is when you get there, okay?" Birdie says, watching him go. "The poor thing!"

Charlotte looks at her daughter, so innocent and oblivious, and jumps up from her seat. "I'll be back in a sec," she says, her heart racing. "Just need to go ask your dad one more thing."

She meets him in the hallway just as he's heading out to the garage.

"Are you seriously giving *me* a hard time for having to go into work?" he says before she can speak.

She pauses, her arms dropping to her sides. "Jason," she whispers. "I saw you today."

"What?" he says, shaking his head like he doesn't understand.

"I saw you," she repeats, opening and closing her hands at her sides.

"You saw me where?" he says, frustrated and impatient.

"I saw you on Wisconsin with Jamie, in front of that Mexican place," she says, her heart pounding in her chest.

"Oh," he says. "Yeah." He looks away then, a move that seems suspicious to her somehow, and she wishes she could remember what she learned in undergrad about reading people's expressions, something about how if they look down, they're lying.

"Since when do you leave the zoo for lunch?" she asks.

"It's Jamie's birthday," he says, reaching for the door.

"So you went all the way to Georgetown? Just the two of you?" she says. "What happened to crappy grocery store cake in a conference room, just like at every other workplace in America?"

He turns back, his face hard. "It's not that far to Georgetown from the zoo," he says. "Seriously, why do I feel like you're accusing me of something?"

"Should I be?" she says. Her heartbeat feels like it's crawling up her throat.

"We went to America Eats, that José Andrés place. A few of our coworkers met us. Our boss made the reservation."

She studies him. His explanation came out quickly, so maybe he is telling the truth. "It surprised me," she says. "To see you."

He puts his palms up. "I don't know what to tell you."

"You looked . . ."

"What?" he says, sounding impatient. "What, Charlotte? We looked what?"

"I said *you*," she says. "Not *we*."

He closes his eyes and sighs.

"Is there something going on with you two?" she asks.

"You've got to be kidding me," he says. "Me and Jamie?"

"She kept touching you."

"How long were you watching us?"

"That's beside the point!" she says.

"She's like that with everyone, Charlotte. Not just me."

"Seriously?"

"Yes!"

"Why was it just the two of you? Where were the rest of your coworkers?"

"At the restaurant! We rode over together because we'd been with the baby right before we had to leave."

"How cozy," she says sarcastically.

"I don't know what you want me to say!" he says in a frustrated stage whisper, looking over her shoulder toward the kitchen. "But I can guarantee you that I am not having an affair with my coworker whose husband died barely a year ago! My God! If anything, I can't believe you would think such a thing!"

She closes her eyes. *Okay*, she thinks, *calm down*. "It surprised me," she says, her voice trembling. "Okay? I've never once run into you during the workday, in a totally different neighborhood from the zoo. It was . . . jarring."

He nods, but he's clearly pissed off. Maybe she *is* being irrational.

"She just looked . . . The two of you looked . . . Anyone who saw you might have thought you were a couple."

"I don't know what to tell you," he says. "Besides that this is ridiculous."

"Okay," she says, taking a deep breath. "Okay," she repeats.

"I have to go," he says, looking at her pointedly. "To work."

She nods, biting her lip, feeling a little embarrassed.

"Where were you anyway?" he says. "When you saw me?"

"Oh," she says, envisioning Wendy, the email printout from her publisher on the table between them. She can't tell him now, not like this. "Just a lunch meeting. Nothing important."

She hears the garage door closing behind him as she walks back into the kitchen and finds Birdie rinsing her plate. She searches her daughter's face for any sign that she'd heard them but Birdie is humming along to something, singing to herself, as she wipes her hands on the kitchen towel hanging by the sink.

"Sorry, Mom," she says. "Don't mean to leave you, too, but I have a crap ton of homework."

"Birdie—" she starts.

"I mean *ton*!" Birdie laughs. "*Ton*, sorry."

"No, it's—It's not that. It's fine."

"What is it, Mom? Is something wrong?"

"No, of course not," she says, fighting back tears. "Come here."

"What is it?"

Charlotte wraps her arms around Birdie, embracing her in

a tight hug. "A mom can't hug her daughter?" she says. Over Birdie's shoulder, she sees the nearly full wineglass on the table. *Maybe I'll—No.* She stops herself. *No, not tonight.* She holds Birdie tighter, one final squeeze.

"Hey, Bird," she says, when she finally releases her. "Do you mind if I go for a quick run?"

"Of course not," she says. "Go for it."

"I'll be back in thirty minutes, tops," Charlotte says. "Just want to clear my head."

ELEVEN

The following afternoon, Jason leaves work early (a reward for being there half the night before, he tells himself), and is grabbing a quick coffee on the way to Birdie's tennis match when his phone rings.

"Dad!" Birdie yells.

"What is it, hon?" he says. "I'm headed over right now."

"Shoot! You are?" she says, panic in her voice. "You're already on your way to school?"

"Yeah, what is it, Bird? Is everything okay?"

"Uh-huh, it's fine," she says. "But I need you to do me a huge favor. I somehow forgot to pack my uniform shirt. I have everything else I need but it isn't in my bag! Can you run home and see if it's in my room? Coach will kill me if I don't have it!"

"Yeah, yeah, of course," he says, pulling his seat belt back around him, the latch clicking into place as he inserts the buckle and starts the car. "Where in your room?" he asks, picturing the piles that never leave her floor. Years ago, he and Charlotte stopped nagging her about it, deciding it was easier to just close the door.

"It's probably on the floor. Or in the hamper in my closet," she says. "Hurry, Dad! We're already warming up."

"On my way," he says, a determination in his voice like he's the action hero in a movie about to defuse a ticking time bomb. "I'll find it. Don't worry."

Minutes later, he bounds up the stairs in the house, leaving the front door wide open, and flips on the light in Birdie's room, the purple butterfly switch plate scratched and grimy with age.

There's stuff everywhere. He scans the room and then dives in, rifling through the balled-up jeans, the flannel pajama pants and dirty socks, books and papers and scrunchies, stuffed animals she's had since she was a toddler, but he comes up short. No uniform.

He moves to the dresser, thinking maybe Charlotte washed it and put it away, and combs his fingers through the rumpled T-shirts from tennis camp and the pool and the surf shop down on the Outer Banks. *Nothing.* He pulls his phone out of his pocket, getting ready to dial Charlotte, but then realizes, looking at the time, that she's in class. *Probably better anyway,* he thinks to himself, knowing how annoyed she gets when he asks her where something is, as if he's supposed to intuit where she wants everything to go.

He opens the bottom drawer of the dresser and files through a stack of exercise shorts and leggings, his hopefulness waning, when something scratches against his finger. He pushes the pile aside and sees the corner of a piece of paper, tucked underneath a tie-dye shirt that Birdie made at the art camp where she worked as an assistant teacher last summer.

Oh my God. His chest seizes up, all of the air leaving his lungs as he pulls out the pamphlet and sees the words on the front of it. *How could it—*

Everything You Need to Know About Birth Control, it reads in mauve block letters. A thousand thoughts zip through his mind all at once, like he's traveling in one of those cartoon vortexes in an animated movie: *Where did she get this? Why does she need this? Did she seek it out because she needs this? Did a friend give it to her? Did Tucker give it to her? Did Charlotte give it to her? Did she just get it in health class?* He remembers now, vaguely, a conversation with Charlotte a long while back, toward the end of elementary school (or was it middle school?) about the sex ed unit they'd do in health class. Maybe this is all this is. Maybe there's a high school version they take now? And she got it there? And she tucked it away for later—*much later . . . much, much later*—until she needs it. Birth control. *Everything you need to know.*

What a stupid phrase. He shoves it back in its spot, telling himself that the smart thing to do now is to not freak out over this. He goes on autopilot: *Just find the shirt, get to the tennis match. Find the shirt. Find the shirt.* He leaves Birdie's room (flees it, really) and hustles downstairs to the basement laundry room. *Everything you need to know. It isn't everything you need to know*, he thinks, *it isn't even half of it. How could you fit everything a kid needs to know about sex into a three-page pamphlet like the flimsy mailers advertising window replacements and lawn care? How? How? How?* He remembers when Birdie was in fourth grade and she asked Charlotte how babies were made. The three of them sat down together—Charlotte always stressed how important it was for him to be involved, how research shows it is the girls whose dads made sex seem like a weird thing who end up weird about sex themselves—and told Birdie how it happens, and she immediately fell back on her pillows in a fit of hysterical laughter, shocked and grossed out in equal measure, the way he guesses he hoped she would always be about the subject.

The shirt is folded on top of a stack of laundry next to the washing machine. He grabs it and races back up the stairs, poor Sylvie jogging beside him, looking up at him expectantly, the tags on her collar jangling, wanting to understand why the hurry, and then flies out the door, slamming it behind him.

The drive is a blur. He's at the high school in five minutes. Birdie sees him and races toward him, snatching the jersey from his hand, hardly breaking her stride as she runs toward the doorway that leads to the locker room, calling out that he's a lifesaver, that she'll be right out, to go find a seat. *Thank you, Dad!*

His chest is heaving. He hunches over with his hands on his knees, trying to catch his breath, as she disappears behind the heavy metal door, her ponytail swinging behind her.

The match is good. Birdie is playing at her very best, the proof of her skill evident in how easily she is beating her opponent, a junior whom somebody down the bleachers says is a potential recruit for Georgia, the number one women's team in the country last year. Jason tries to concentrate but it's difficult. His mind keeps snagging on the question of what he's going to do about the pamphlet. *She won't get a tennis scholarship anywhere if she's a teen mom*, he thinks, irrationally, then shakes the thought away.

It could be nothing. After all, he kept condoms hidden between his mattress and his box spring for years before he even came close to learning how to unlatch a bra, the contraband courtesy of his buddy's older brother's stash, which they found in the compartment between the seats of his car. Then he thinks of Tucker. *What does he have hidden?*

That little piece of shit. He'd been defending the kid to Charlotte for so long now, and for what? He supposes he wanted to believe that Birdie would never date anyone who didn't meet his own high standards for her, and that they should let go of the leash and let her figure things out, but now he feels like an idiot.

He knew Charlotte was right: He really had kissed Finch Cunningham's ass at their house that night, and what the fuck for? What had he been trying to prove? How was he just now *really considering* the connection between the Finch Cunningham he'd known in high school and Tucker Cunningham, whom his daughter was now dating?

He claps as Birdie hits an ace.

Finch Cunningham had been a dick in high school. Not the worst of the worst—that title went to Josh Lerner, a guy who'd terrorized Tate, Jason's older brother, almost as much as he harassed their female classmates—but Finch had still been plenty bad, the kind of guy who might not be the first to broadcast his conquests but always chimed in to try to one-up whatever story someone was spinning. Would Tucker be like that? And could the subject be *his daughter*?

He'd scanned the bleachers for Tucker as soon as he arrived, but then remembered that this morning, when Charlotte had asked Birdie if he was coming to the match, she'd said that he had a lacrosse game himself, out in Sterling.

He thinks of the drive home after the match, wonders how the hell he'll act normally, if he should say something or wait for Charlotte. Surely, Birdie would rather talk to her mother about this. He knew logically that the day would come, of course, when he'd have to reckon with the fact that his daughter was sexually active, but he'd assumed it would be later, much later. Someday, when he got gray and needed hearing aids and Birdie was married, she would announce that they were going to be grandparents, and they could just sweep the rest of it under the rug.

The match ends, Birdie winning easily. He stands with the rest of the parents on the bleachers and claps, noticing how a few of them look back at him, and he feels a surge of pride when he sees a woman a couple rows beneath him wolf-whistle and throw her fist into the air. Birdie shakes her opponent's hand. She walks toward her teammates (all of them clapping for her, he notices), grabs a towel from the stack just off the court and wipes the back of her neck, and looks up and scans the crowd for him. She waves, smiling mostly with her eyes, not wanting to seem too boastful, he knows, even though she smeared that other kid.

He gives her a quick thumbs-up, forgetting, for the briefest moment, about the pamphlet. She is such a good kid, such a humble kid. He really—he knows this in his heart—has nothing to worry about.

There's another match Birdie needs to stay and watch before they can head home, so while Birdie convenes with her teammates,

Jason hops down from the bleachers and walks over to the patch of grass just beyond the courts.

He calls Charlotte, not sure exactly what he's going to say but needing to unload, and gets her voicemail almost immediately. He tries her again, and then again, but each time it goes to voicemail. She must be talking to someone as she drives home—Stephanie, her mother, Amanda. He looks back to the court, to where Birdie and her teammates are standing in a circle, singing out a cheer. *Y-O-R-K . . .*

He looks back down at his phone, turning it in his hand, worrying over the car ride home again, and then tonight at the dinner table . . . He wants to talk to Charlotte before he has to be alone with Birdie, to figure out what to do. He nibbles at the inside of his lip, wondering who else to call. He could try Tate? His brother would surely tell him to laugh this off and say that it's a good thing that Birdie is educating herself, but as reasonable as that is, it's not what he wants to hear, even if he doesn't know what it is exactly that he does want to hear.

He looks back down at his phone. He paces a few steps through the grass and dials.

"Hi!" Jamie says, a cheery brightness in her voice.

"When do kids start having sex these days?"

He hears the sound of her gasp, and then her laugh. A mellifluous wave, like the sound that a xylophone makes when you run a mallet across it.

"Sor . . . sorry," he says, stuttering. "Sorry. I . . ." He sighs. "I found something."

"Hold up," she says, still laughing. "You're not making any sense."

"Sorry. I found something in Birdie's room. I was looking for her tennis shirt and I found a pamphlet about birth control."

"A pamphlet?" she says.

"Uh-huh."

"But you didn't find any *actual* birth control?" she says, obviously amused.

He feels his face redden. "Right."

"Oh, Jason," she coos. "Jason, Jason, Jason."

"What? It wouldn't freak you out?"

"No, no, I get it," she says. "I totally get it."

"I just thought you might have some insights."

"I . . . Well . . . Hmm," she starts. "This is giving me pause, actually." He hears clanking in the background, the comforting sounds of pots and pans and making dinner. "Warren and I talked to the boys, of course, did the whole birds-and-bees thing, but that's it. They're just twelve. Maybe I'm naive, though . . ."

"Okay," he says. "Okay. Sorry to bother you," he says, feeling embarrassed. "I couldn't reach Charlotte so I thought you . . ." His voice trails off, thinking of Charlotte's accusation from the night before.

"Don't be sorry!" she says. "It would rattle any parent, but I don't think it's anything to be alarmed about if that's the only evidence. I mean, I'd talk to her, obviously."

"Of course," he says. "I mean, obviously."

"I think . . . hmm . . ." she says, and he can picture her, thinking it over, squeezing her bottom lip between her thumb and the knuckle of her forefinger in the way she does when she's puzzling something out at work. "I'd just try to be as normal as you can about it. Talk to her calmly, without freaking out. That's the best thing you can do, I think, because if you make it weird, or blame her, God forbid, she'll never talk to you about this stuff again, and that's the last thing you want."

"Right," he says. "That's good advice."

She sighs. "I don't envy you."

He groans. "Why do they have to grow up?"

"I know," she says. "It's the worst. It really is."

He laughs, feeling his tension loosen just a touch, a spring uncoiling. He hears water running, a hollow knocking. "Are you making dinner?"

"Yeah," she says. "The world's most thankless task. Well, that's not true. The laundry might be worse. Scratch that—bathrooms. You haven't lived until you've cleaned a bathroom shared by preteen boys, no offense."

"None taken," he says. "What are you making?"

"Two pounds of spaghetti and sauce from a jar. *Très gourmet.*"

He laughs. "Did you say *two* pounds? Are you having people over?" *A guy*, he wonders, remembering the dating app from the other day.

"Oh, no," she says. "It's just the three of us. And when two are these boys, and one of them runs cross-country . . . Honestly, I'm not sure if this will go far enough. I just pulled a second loaf of garlic bread from the freezer."

Jason pictures the steam rising from a silver pot, the comforting smell of butter and garlic wafting through the air, this morning's newspaper on the kitchen table, the sound of a basketball dribbling in the background. Jamie sipping from her water bottle on the counter, happily humming to herself.

"You going to be okay?" she says, snapping him back to the

present. He immediately feels guilty, thinking about Charlotte's face last night. But he knows he downplayed what she saw, too, because if the shoe was on the other foot, if he saw some co-worker of hers touch her like Jamie's always touching him lately, it would freak him out. He supposes he could ask Jamie to stop, but . . . well, that would be weird, he tells himself. She'd probably think he was going to report her to HR or something, and he doesn't want to overplay it, he thinks, ignoring the other thought lurking in the back of his mind: that he doesn't want it to stop because he likes it.

Also, maybe he liked that Charlotte acted the way she did last night, as fucked up as that is. "Yeah, I'll be fine," he says. "I'm sorry to have bothered you. Get back to your evening."

"Jason, no, don't apologize. I'm glad you called. I really am. Anytime. You know that, right?"

"Yeah," he says, swallowing. "Uh-huh. Thanks."

"I owed you one anyway, for your help last night at work."

"Of course," he says. "I'm glad it all worked out. Was everything okay today?"

"Oh yeah, she's fine."

"Good," he says, turning back to the court. "Well, I should go."

"I'll see you tomorrow," she says, and there's something about the lilt in her voice that makes the back of his neck tingle.

"Thanks again," he says, ending the call quickly.

He starts walking back toward the court, feeling better, though it troubles him to think about the reason why.

TWELVE

Charlotte returns to her office after class, tailed by a student who wants to borrow a book that came up during her lecture. Her phone buzzes with a new text, and she fumbles to look at it, assuming it's Jason, who'd called during class but hadn't left a voicemail. It's a local number she doesn't recognize. She slips the phone into her bag, telling herself she'll look at it later, and fishes out her keys.

She unlocks the door and flips on the light. The student, Valeria, steps in behind her, and runs her finger along the spines of the books in her bookcase. "Ah, here it is!" Charlotte says, coaxing out the copy of *Stumbling on Happiness*, Daniel Gilbert's bestseller. She hands it to the girl, who immediately flips it over to read the description on the back cover, and Charlotte watches her for a moment, thinking how lucky she is to be so young, the endless options she has in front of her. Valeria is as stunningly beautiful as she is sharp, and one of the thousands of international students that make up a chunk of Georgetown's student body.

"Are you headed back to Madrid right after finals?" Charlotte asks, walking to her desk and glancing at the time, noting to herself that Birdie's match must be over by now.

"No," she says. "First to Barbados."

"Barbados?"

She nods, the corner of her mouth turning up. "My boyfriend's family has a place there."

"Boyfriend?" Charlotte asks, imagining a tall, dark Dolce & Gabbana model type.

She shrugs. "For now."

"That's the right attitude," Charlotte says, shuffling the papers on her desk into a neat stack. "Don't pin yourself down."

Valeria hugs the book to her chest. "How long have you been married?" she asks, a question that would probably strike another professor as too forward, particularly in this post-#MeToo era, when everyone's especially careful not to cross a line. But after teaching the happiness class for so many years now, Charlotte's grown accustomed to a certain familiarity between herself and the students, many of whom talk openly during their class discussions about their overbearing parents, their antianxiety medications, even, a few times, their suicide attempts. More than once, Charlotte has called the campus's mental health services on behalf of somebody.

"Too long," Charlotte spits out, realizing her mistake when she sees the shocked expression on Valeria's face. "It's a joke!" she says. "We've been married fifteen years. Why do you ask?"

"Just wondering," her student says. "I don't know if I want to get married."

"Then you shouldn't," she says. "Unless you're absolutely sure. It's not something you can feel wishy-washy about. But you've got all the time in the world."

Valeria nods.

"Are your parents married?" Charlotte asks.

"Oh, yes," she says. "But they shouldn't be."

"What?" Charlotte says, taken aback. "Why?"

Valeria flips her long black hair over her shoulder. "Did you know that Spain has the highest divorce rate of anywhere in Europe? The government enacted this 'express divorce' law a while back, and now three out of every four marriages end in divorce."

"You know a lot about this," Charlotte says.

"I've researched it. On my mother's behalf." She frowns. "My father has always had girlfriends, for as long as I can remember."

"Really?" Charlotte says. "How does that even work?"

"My mother is . . . what can I say? She's a devout Catholic. She gets up and makes him breakfast every morning. Irons his shirts. Cleans up after him, literally and figuratively. They just celebrated their thirtieth wedding anniversary. There was a big party, and he made a big speech." She rolls her eyes. "Two of the ex-girlfriends were there."

"It doesn't bother her?"

"I guess you just get used to what you're used to. It's strange, I know, but it's their arrangement. Anyway, I'm sure that's why I feel the way I do about marriage."

"That makes sense."

"How about you?" she asks. "What was your family like? Were your parents always together?"

"They were," Charlotte says. "My dad passed away many years ago, but yes, they were married for a long time."

"Were they happy?" Valeria asks.

Charlotte turns and picks up a pen off her desk, remembering how she'd lie in bed at night, Aaron sometimes crawling in beside her, and they'd hide under the covers while their parents raged at each other downstairs. "No," she says. "Not really at all."

"And did that affect you?"

Charlotte gasps out a laugh. "I'm sure. I was sort of the peacekeeper."

"I can see that. Keeping everyone happy?" Valeria raises an eyebrow.

"I guess so."

"Well . . ." Valeria says, holding up the book. "Thanks for this."

"Of course. See you in class next week."

Charlotte sits down at her desk, hearing the door click shut, and thinks again about her father, the counterweight to her mother's mercurial rage, always making a joke to tamp down the tension her mother filled the room with just by her presence.

She jiggles her computer mouse, looking up at her monitor as it springs to life out of sleep mode, and feels an instant wave of shame. During her lunch break today, she'd been putting the final touches on her Montana speech, suddenly just two days away, when she found her mind drifting, and typed Jamie's name into her search bar.

As the results popped up, she instantly felt awful about it, because seventy-five percent of them were links to local news articles and announcements about her husband's fatal accident. But there was one particular picture, on the second page of hits, from a press release that ran eight years ago about Lucy the orangutan. In the photo, Jason and Jamie stand on either side of her, each with one palm faced up, Lucy between them with her hands resting on theirs. It's a silly picture, one that Jason probably complained about at the time. He hates anything that smacks of humanizing animals—raincoats on dogs, cats in strollers—and in this photo, the three of them look very much like a weird little family. Charlotte leans forward, examining it, looking for some clue she could have missed if she saw this back when it was taken, and then she hears her phone buzzing in her bag. *Jason*, she thinks, but when she looks down, she sees a 912 area code. And she feels a flutter in her stomach that she knows she shouldn't.

How's your day?

She holds the phone in her hands. Perhaps she shouldn't answer the text at all, she thinks, realizing the hypocrisy of it given her accusation to Jason last night, but then she looks up at the screen, seeing Jamie's smile, and she thinks about her hand on Jason, how he rushed into work last night . . .

Just finished teaching. It's a totally innocent response. Totally innocuous. Then, unable to help herself, she adds: And you?

Two nose job consults, breast reconstruction surgery prep, calf implant follow-up.

She can't help herself. She hits the call button. He's laughing before she says anything.

"Did you say calf implant?" she says.

"Well, *calves*, technically," he says.

"What exactly do you implant? Actually, never mind. I don't want to know."

"All in a day's work," he says. "Aren't you impressed?"

"I don't know," she says, laughing. "I'm not sure." Her eyes drift to the monitor, where Jason and Jamie stare back at her. She reaches for her mouse and closes out of the browser. "So," she says.

"So," he echoes.

"Are you still at the office?" she asks, leaning back in her chair, and kicking off her shoes under the desk.

"Just leaving," he says.

"What does it look like?"

"My office?"

"Yeah," she says, stretching her arms over her head. "I'm picturing all dreamy blues, gorgeous supermodel assistants walking around in white lab coats."

"Oh, yeah," he says. "It's just like that."

She laughs, feeling relaxed for the first time all day.

"How about you?" he says. "Still at work?"

"Trying to leave," she says. "But I have to talk to my department head first and I don't really want to so I'm stalling."

"Oh yeah?" he says. "Why's that?"

"I need to break the news about the new book."

"Ah," he says. "Won't he be happy for you?"

"*She* will not be pleased."

"Sorry," he says. "Why not? I don't understand why she wouldn't be."

"She doesn't like anything that has to do with me, but that's another story for another time."

"Mm," he says. "Sounds like fun."

"And what do you have planned for the rest of the night?"

"Well," he says. "I'm headed over to my mother's house."

"For dinner?" she says, remembering his mother, whom she ran into years ago when she was home for the holidays. Birdie was just a toddler, and Reese's mom leaned down and cooed at her in her stroller, albeit in her polite, reserved way.

"I'm actually staying there now. Just for a little while. The ex is still in our house."

"She cheated on you and you were the one who had to clear out?" Charlotte says, remembering how, last night, when she went to bed, Jason still not back from the zoo, she imagined what it would be like if the room was always just hers.

"I was," he says. "Stupid, I know, but she's supposed to be out next week. I might just put it on the market. Too many memories."

"That makes sense," she says, weighing whether to ask the question she really wants to. "How did you know?" she finally asks.

He groans. "To be honest, I wasn't that surprised," he says.

"You weren't?"

"I guess I always sort of knew it wasn't exactly right, between me and her," he says. "I hoped it would *become* right."

"I understand," she says, though with Jason it felt right at first. The cracks began to show later, with age.

"I also noticed when we were with our neighbor. She always

seemed to be having more fun with him than with me. Laughing louder, smiling bigger, that sort of thing."

"Right," she says.

"Why?" he asks.

"Oh," she says. "No reason. I'm, uh . . ." She pauses. "Asking for a friend."

"Oh, really?" he says, the concern in his voice unmistakable. "A friend?"

"Yup," she says, taking a deep breath.

A beat of silence passes between them, and then another.

"Huh," he says.

"Yeah," she says. "I thought we were just having growing pains. Typical, married-for-a-while stuff, lots of changes with my job. I'm not sure, but . . . It could all be my imagination, honestly."

"Wow," he says. "Wouldn't that be . . . Are you worried about . . ."

"I don't know," she says. "I probably shouldn't have said anything."

"Well, if you ever need to talk . . . Not that I'm the person you'd probably want to talk to, but, anyway. I'm here."

"Thanks," she says, feeling uneasy as she recalls the days after she found out about his cheating, how Amanda practically had to drag her out of bed.

"It was good to hear your voice, Charlotte."

"Yeah," she says, rapping her fingers on her desk. She's let things get too comfortable, too fast. "I should go," she says.

"Okay," he starts, but she hangs up before she hears him say goodbye. She stands at her desk, and then she pulls up the image again, Jason and Jamie, just one last time before she leaves.

She's halfway down the hall to Tabatha's office when she hears her phone buzzing again. She fishes it out of her bag to turn it off and sees a text from Jason: When will you be home?

Soon, she types back, walking slowly down the hallway. Just have to chat with Tabatha quick. Birdie win?

Yes, played great, he writes back. Was easy for her. But need to talk to you about something.

OK, she types. She stiffens, locking her knees. Oh, God. It suddenly occurs to her: *Could their confrontation last night have precipitated something? Is he going to confess?* She hears Tabatha shuffling around in her office. Her doorway is just a few feet away. Wait till I'm home? she types. Need to catch her.

She glances toward the open doorway, wondering whether she should just leave. It seems crazy, that she would just yesterday have this Jason/Jamie thing pop in her head, and now . . . *No*, she thinks. *He said it was nothing. It's Jason, for God's sake. It must be something with Birdie, or some other—*

"Hello?" she hears Tabatha bark from inside her office. "Charlotte, is that you?"

"Yes," she says, peeking her head into the dimly lit space.

"What are you doing lurking around out there?" Tabatha says, her chin hunched into her shoulders.

"I was just finishing—"

"Never mind," she says, holding out her hand. "Just give me five, okay? Need to—" She taps her pen to the papers in front of her. "Give me five minutes."

Charlotte dips into the hallway and leans against the wall. She looks down at her phone and sees the text notifications from the unfamiliar number she ignored earlier. She taps on it, then freezes. It is not, as she'd assumed, an auto-message from a local business who values her patronage.

THIS IS DAYNA CUNNINGHAM, it reads in all caps. I AM VERY CONCERNED! TUCKER JUST TOLD ME ABOUT WHAT HAPPENED AT TENNIS!

Charlotte's hand flies to her chest. *What happened? Is this what Jason wanted to talk about?* She thinks of what Birdie said about the upperclassmen on the team picking on her. *Did something happen at the match?*

I'm sorry, she types back. I'm at work.

She bites her lip, trying to figure out what else to say. She doesn't want to appear like she's in the dark if something happened today, but she remembers Jason saying Birdie played great. She shakes her head, frustrated with herself. Fill me in, she types, then waits as the three dots flash across her screen.

> HE SAYS HE SAW U AT PRACTICE. I CANT BELIEVE U R PRETENDING U DONT REMEMBER!

Ohhhh. Charlotte blinks. *Fuck.*

> HE SAYS YOU THREATINED HIM! YOU ARE LUCKY I HAVENT CALLED THE SCHOOL! IF YOU THREATIN MY SON I WILL MAKE YOUR LIFE HELL!

Oh, God, Charlotte thinks. She taps her foot against the nubby industrial carpet, trying to remember exactly what she said to Tucker.

I promise you, Dayna. I didn't threaten him, she types, then pauses, deletes a word and writes it again in all caps—THREATEN. Sure, it's petty, passive-aggressively pointing out her misspelling, but *fuck her*. Charlotte glances toward Tabatha's office. What she would give for a nip from the bottle of whiskey she knows Tabatha keeps in her desk. I was going to reach out to you, she types. The kids skipped practice and hung out at your house the other day. Did Tucker tell you that? When I saw him, I simply explained that that was unacceptable for Jason and me. Nothing threatening in the least. I just don't want my daughter alone at your house w/out adults. Sure you understand.

"Charlotte?" Tabatha calls from her office.

Please call me if you need to discuss further. She hits send and puts the phone in her bag.

Charlotte is not the first person in the department to publish a bestselling book. Her colleague Juan has had a book on the *Wall Street Journal*'s list for over a year now about cynicism in modern culture, something he still talks about on cable news on a regular basis. But Charlotte is the department's cash cow. She reminds herself of this as she sits down, placing her bag carefully beside her chair.

Tabatha is leaning over the paperwork in front of her on her desk. "What can I help you with?" she says, pushing the end of her ballpoint pen and depositing it in the silver cup next to her monitor.

It's such a Tabatha thing to say, Charlotte thinks. Of course, she assumes that Charlotte needs something from her. "I've had something come up," she says, deciding to just rip off the Band-Aid. "My publisher has offered me another book deal."

"Really?" Tabatha says in a disbelieving way, as if she hasn't closely followed Charlotte's success.

Charlotte nods, her heart racing beneath her white button-down. "It's another happiness book—"

"Obviously," Tabatha interrupts, retrieving her pen and clicking the top a few times. She does this during department meetings, too, and Charlotte wonders if it's truly a tic or something she does on purpose, just to irritate the people around her.

"But it's a happiness book for families," she says.

Tabatha's eyebrows shoot up. Charlotte doesn't have to guess what she's thinking, that the family subject is soft, silly. She has three grown children herself, and her husband has been a producer on the political desk at NPR for several decades now, but Charlotte can only assume she approached raising children with the same dull sobriety she exudes in the halls of their department. She never talks about her kids, and none of them have ever been to the office to visit. It's obvious that she was never a rolling-around-on-the-floor-laughing kind of mother.

"The manuscript is due later this year so I'll do the bulk of the writing while school's out this summer," she says, hearing her voice rise, thinking to herself that she sounds like Minnie Mouse. She clears her throat. "I don't suspect this will affect my course load next term—"

"You don't *suspect*?" Tabatha interrupts again.

"No," Charlotte says more forcefully. "I don't. Though because I don't know the book's publication date just yet, I can't be entirely firm on when I might need to travel for a book tour or speaking engagements related to the release. But that's a ways off."

Tabatha taps her pen against the papers on her desk, which look like the draft of an academic paper, a journal article that she and/or one of her students must be submitting somewhere. Her one saving grace in Charlotte's eyes is that she appears to be a very good teacher. The only time Charlotte ever hears a trace of enthusiasm in her voice is when she's talking to one of her advisees.

Charlotte shifts in her seat, noticing out the window behind Tabatha's desk that dusk is just beginning to fall.

"Let me ask you something," Tabatha finally says, leaning across the desk toward Charlotte, a move that can only be meant to intimidate her, which it does. "Do you want to be a college professor, an academic psychology expert at one of the best universities on the East Coast, or do you want to write . . . *these books*?" she says, the distaste so clear that Charlotte may as well have told her that she is leaving Georgetown to write for a tabloid. "Because it's not clear to me."

The pen clicks in the heavy silence, the sound like Charlotte's ratcheting anger. She has given her entire life to her work over the past couple of years. She thinks of Birdie, screaming at her just a week ago about never being around, of Jason, who so clearly resents what she needs to do for her job. How dare Tabatha suggest that she isn't committed?

"I got tenure over a decade ago," Charlotte says, fighting to keep her voice even. "I'm not going anywhere. And I'm certainly not going to apologize for my success, which has done a lot for this university and for this department in particular."

Tabatha smiles at her in a bored way, like she's being forced to sit through a children's dance recital.

"By telling you about the book I was simply doing you a courtesy," Charlotte says, her heart banging in her chest. "Any other department head might be thrilled at the prospect of more attention. Oh—and before you ask, a reminder that I'm out for the rest of the week because I'm heading to Montana. The Grey Browning symposium."

"Why?" Tabatha asks, taking a sip from her NPR travel mug.

"Why what?" Charlotte begins. "Why was I invited to the symposium?"

"No, no." Tabatha grins, like Charlotte's confusion amuses her. "Why do you do it? This work? Why do you run yourself around, like a little . . ." Her voice trails off, and she wiggles her two fingers, making them running legs. "Your class is the most popular course in Georgetown's history. Isn't that enough for you?"

Charlotte's mouth falls open. She's caught off guard. "I . . ."

"Oh, wait," Tabatha says, pointing a finger toward the sky. "The money! That must be it. You must like the money."

"No, no!" Charlotte says. "That's—I do it because—" Her mind races, her face flushing as her boss studies her. *Why?* she thinks. *Why do I . . .*

"And the attention," Tabatha says, scooching forward in her chair, her hands on the armrests. "You seem like the type who needs that," she says, almost as if she's saying it to herself.

"Tabatha, I—" Charlotte begins. "I don't know what to say. I'm appalled that you—"

"Is there anything else you really *need* to say, Charlotte?" Tabatha says, smiling at her in the dim yellow glow of her lamp.

Charlotte stares back at her, feeling utterly stuck, because there are a lot of things she'd like to say, but can't.

"It's getting late," Tabatha says. "You should go home to your family."

Charlotte stands, practically shaking from their interaction. "As should you," she says. She begins to walk out but then she pauses and turns back. "You're lucky to have me," she says. "You know that, right?"

"Oh, sure," Tabatha says, her eyes not leaving her papers. Charlotte stands there for a moment, waiting, as if she could expect some other outcome, and then she turns to go.

THIRTEEN

Charlotte should go right home, but slamming the car door and turning on the ignition, she remembers that the only wine left in the house is a dusty bottle of a horrid-looking riesling that Jason's aunt brought them months ago.

She stops at the local wine store that is conveniently on the way home, picking up two bottles, and when she finally walks in the door, she finds Jason and Birdie sitting side by side at the kitchen counter, both of them picking at the quesadillas Jason's made.

"What's going on?" she says, fishing the wine opener out of the drawer. Birdie's expression is hard to read. She's upset, it's clear, but is she angry? Feeling guilty?

"What happened?" she says. "I heard you played great, Bird. I wish I'd been there to see it." *Is she mad I wasn't there?* she thinks.

Jason opens his mouth and closes it, his eyes sliding toward Birdie, and Charlotte realizes that the expression on his face isn't anger. He looks worried, fearful even.

"What is it?" she says, walking around the counter and kissing the top of her daughter's head. "Tell me." She squeezes her shoulder but Birdie wiggles away.

"Birdie and I talked on the way home from tennis about this, but . . . We need to . . ." He stammers like he can't find his words. "Birdie, why don't you fill your mother in?" He flips a palm toward the ceiling, inviting her to speak, and Birdie frowns, hunching into herself.

"It's really not a big deal!" she exclaims, looking down at her lap. "I don't know why you're making a thing out of it!"

"Well, it *is* a big deal, Birdie," Jason says, his voice measured. "It's a very big deal."

"Whoa, whoa!" Charlotte says, looking back and forth between the two of them as she fills her glass. "Can someone tell me what's going on?"

Jason fiddles with a triangle of quesadilla on his plate, then finally speaks. "I was looking for Birdie's tennis jersey in her room before her match and I found that," he says, nodding toward something on top of the pile of mail on the counter.

Charlotte picks up the pamphlet, and she only needs to read the heading before it all becomes clear. *Oh, no. No, no, no, no, no.* A dizzying shiver runs up and down her body, from her head to her toes. *Her Birdie? Having sex? If Dayna thinks she was threatening Tucker before, she hasn't seen anything yet.*

"You're only fourteen," she says, dropping the pamphlet on the counter. "You're *fourteen*, Birdie." She had assumed the worst of Tucker, but she hadn't expected this. Kissing, yes. Second-base stuff, maybe. *But this?* No. *How?* "I don't understand," she says. She lifts her glass, downing at least half of it, and stares at her daughter, thinking that this is one of those do-or-die moments in parenting that she must get right. *Okay*, she thinks, steadying herself. *Information is power. This is a good thing. She's educating herself. It doesn't mean she's actually doing anything.* "Birdie, where did you get this?" she asks, trying to inject some gentleness into her voice despite her alarm. "Why didn't you talk to me about it?"

She looks at Jason, who seems as morose as Birdie does. She wishes he would chime in and help her, but he just sits there, clenching his jaw.

She turns back to Birdie. "Are you . . . having sex?" she asks. "Or are you . . . thinking about it? Are your friends?" She remembers a *Dateline* report she saw a few years ago, about the horrid game that teenagers play at parties now, an amped-up version of spin the bottle involving blow jobs and—She shakes away the thought.

Birdie bends forward, holding her balled fists to her eyes, and Charlotte realizes how mortifying this must be. "I haven't done anything," Birdie says, head still bowed, eyes firmly on her lap. "I just . . . I got it at school, in the counselor's office. I thought I was being smart. I thought I was doing the right thing, thinking things through, getting information, the way you've always told me to."

Charlotte looks at Jason and exhales a heavy sigh. He rubs his hands up and down over his face like he's just woken up. Birdie's shoulders start to shake. "Oh, honey," Charlotte says, racing to wrap her arms around her daughter. Jason leaps up to retrieve the box of tissues from across the room. "It's okay, it's okay," Charlotte says, shushing her. "You did exactly the right thing." She takes Birdie's hands, feeling the ever-present calluses on her palms, from gripping her racket. "You absolutely did the right thing, getting information from the counselor, but is this something you really need to worry about right now? You're just getting used to high school, honey. You're so young. You have all the time in the world."

"Mom, I don't . . ." Birdie huffs hard, sighing through her teeth, and squeezes her eyes shut.

"We just want to help you," Jason says, putting a hand on Birdie's back. *This must be so hard for him*, Charlotte thinks, and she reaches and squeezes his shoulder. He looks at her, his mouth turning up in a reluctant half-smile, acknowledging the gesture.

"Bird?" Charlotte says. "How can we help?"

Birdie shakes her head, the same exasperated expression on her face that she makes when things aren't going right on the tennis court. "I'm not actually doing anything!" she suddenly shrieks. "I don't actually intend to do anything!"

Charlotte looks at Jason, the surprise on his face matching her own.

"Okay, well . . . that's good, honey," Charlotte says tentatively. "But then . . ."

"Is he pressuring you?" Jason says.

"Dad!" Birdie throws her crumpled napkin onto her plate.

"Because if he's pressuring you—" Charlotte puts her hand on Birdie's shoulder but her daughter jerks away from her and stands.

"I don't . . . *No!*"

"Then . . . If it's not about Tucker . . ." Charlotte starts. "Is it . . ." She can't bear to think it. "Another boy? Is there someone else?"

"Oh my God!" Birdie yells and starts out of the room.

"Birdie!" Jason says. "Honey, talk to us!"

She spins around. "It's nothing, okay? Just trust me! I just got it from the counselor! That's it!"

"We just want to help," Charlotte says, feeling helpless.

"We just want to understand," says Jason, taking a step forward.

Birdie could nod, understanding, assure them that she's fine and that everything's okay. But she turns, running up the stairs to her room once again. Her door slams.

Charlotte looks at Jason, the defeat in his eyes matching her own.

"I don't . . ." She takes a step toward him but he turns away, his hand over his mouth.

"Jason," she says, putting a hand on his back. "What do we do now?"

He turns to her. "I don't think there's anything we can do."

She should answer emails, take a bath, pull out her neglected yoga mat and do some stretches, anything else, but she refills her wineglass instead. Jason retreats to the backyard, watering plants, making himself busy. She goes upstairs and knocks on Birdie's door but Birdie says she doesn't want to talk. She promises she's fine, it's "just awkward."

She starts to call Stephanie, to ask her what she thinks, but there's a part of her that's afraid to, because what if Hannah isn't talking about any of this yet? What if it's just *her* daughter? Birdie's the first one with a boyfriend, after all. She decides against it—to respect Birdie's privacy, she tells herself. She looks out the window at Jason.

She'd always told herself that she would be the kind of mother who would be open and talk these things through with her kid, ensuring that her child would never have to weather these things alone. *Easier said than done*, she thinks, remembering a morning, years and years ago, sitting in the pediatrician's office when Birdie was a newborn in her carrier, and confessing to the older mother next to her that she was nervous that Birdie was going to need to eat soon and would have a meltdown, disturbing everyone around them. The woman leaned toward her. "Little kids, little problems," she said. "Big kids, big problems." It had felt like a comfort and a warning all at once, and now, in what feels like the blink of an eye, here they are.

When Jason finally comes inside, his hairline wet and spiky with sweat, she's pouring her third glass. She is losing the day's edges, finally, like somebody is rubbing their palms along her skin, smoothing out the nervous energy on the surface.

"Did you talk to her?" he says, washing his hands. She sees speckles of dirt along his forearms.

She shakes her head. "I tried but she doesn't want to talk." She takes a sip of her wine. Her last glass, she tells herself, and looks at Jason, relieved he hasn't said anything about it yet.

"How was your meeting?" he says.

"What?"

"With Tabatha. You said you were talking to Tabatha before you left?"

"Oh," she says, leaning against the counter. "That."

"What?" he says.

She takes a deep breath and looks at him. *Now or never.* "I have some news actually."

"Oh?" he says. "Good news, I hope?"

"Well," Charlotte says, scratching the back of her head. "That depends."

"Depends?"

She wrinkles her nose. "It looks like I'm writing another book."

"Another book," he says, in a way that feels a little bit like a question.

She nods and takes a sip of her wine. It tastes too syrupy now, with the faintest musky scent, but she doesn't care. "Yes," she says. "You know they've been on me for a while to do a follow-up."

He dips his head and runs his thumb against his brow. "Do you really want to write it?"

"I don't think it's something we can say no to," she says. "Wendy was here. That's who I was having lunch with, when I—" She pauses. "In Georgetown."

He looks away.

She sucks in her lips. "They're offering me $750,000."

He pitches forward a little bit, the number registering. "Seriously?"

She nods.

"Oh." He lets the news settle over him. "Wow." And then: "Congratulations." The way he says it sounds like he's somehow on the other side of her good fortune, the one losing out, the runner-up.

"Well, it's not just . . . It's for all of us, Jason. It's not just *my* thing. And—" She takes a deep breath. "They came to me with the idea. It's a follow-up but focused on family. *Perfect Happiness: Family.*" She takes another drink.

"Oh," he says again, and she notices his eyes trailing her glass as she puts it down. "Will you—"

"I assume they'll want me to write about us, yes," she says, biting her lip.

"Right."

She twirls the stem of her glass, watching it skitter against the counter. "Jason," she starts. "I don't . . ." She looks at him. *Is this when he confesses?* "What's going on with us?"

"I don't know," he says. "I don't know how we got here."

"I don't either," she says. "I thought it was just a rut at first."

"Me, too," he says.

"But it seems like—"

"We just can't connect," he finishes for her.

She thinks again of him laughing with Jamie, and about what Reese said on the phone earlier about his wife, and how it always seemed like she was having more fun with the other guy. "Do you want to try to make things work?" she asks, bracing herself for his answer.

He looks at her like the question surprises him. "Of course I do," he says. "I'm the one who suggested counseling not that long ago."

"Right," she says, remembering that night.

"I want *you* back," he says.

"You have me, though, Jason," she says, tearing up, the unexpected words hitting her like a strong gust of wind. "I'm right here."

"No," he says. "No, things have been different ever since—"

"My work," she finishes for him, swiping a tear from her face.

He nods. "You seem like two different people, Charlotte," he says. "The one at home and the one giving the speeches, posting the shiny happy stuff on Instagram."

She knows he's right, but it stings to hear him say it, and realize how obvious it is. "It's just a lot of pressure," she says and picks up her glass again.

"How much have you had to drink tonight?" he says.

She puts it down, the stem clattering against the counter. "Jason."

"It can't be helping," he says.

"Every woman I know has a glass of wine at night."

"A glass."

"Oh, come on!" she says. "Why are you . . . Don't you see all of the jokes online? The wine memes and stupid T-shirts? Wine o'clock and whatever? I'm hardly alone on this."

He shakes his head. "I don't know what you're talking about."

"Well, trust me."

"Fine," he says.

"Jason, everyone drinks. It's not like I'm shooting heroin."

He stares back at her.

"I'm doing my best," she says, trying to hold back more tears. "You know that, right?"

"I do actually. I know you are. But we're both miserable, and to what end? I just don't know how you think you're going to do this. Don't we have enough to deal with?"

"I don't know, either." She wipes a tear from her cheek and looks at the clock. It's only eight but she is so, so tired. "What do you want me to do?"

"Does it matter?" he says.

"Jason . . ."

"None of this has been good for you," he says. "Or for us."

"It's been good for our bank account, hasn't it?"

"Oh, come on." He slaps the counter and turns away.

"Well, hasn't it, Jason?"

He whips back around, suddenly angry. "And at what expense?"

"That's easy for you to say!" she says, her voice rising. "While I'm off busting my ass, running a million miles an hour to be successful for our family, and you just get to sit back and reap the rewards."

"Is that you or your mother talking?" he says, wincing out the words.

He's right. She knows he's right. But they also both know that invoking her mother is about as low as it gets. They stand there, facing off, both of them too stubborn to give in.

"Just think this through, Charlotte," he finally says. "Make sure it's worth it. Make sure you can do it."

"*Of course* I can do it," she says.

"If the past couple of years are any indication, no. I don't want more of that."

"It will more than pay for college, Jason," she says, trying to be logical. "And if Birdie gets a full ride because of tennis, even better. Imagine what kind of shape we'll be in, heading into retirement." She realizes the irony of her words the second they're out of her mouth.

"I can only imagine," he says. "The shape we'll be in."

She eyes her wineglass, which is almost empty now. "Jason, it's not an either-or. It's not either I write the book or our family stays together. There are gray areas, there are options."

"What's going on?" Birdie says, suddenly appearing behind them in the doorway. "Are you guys fighting?"

"No," they both say, nearly simultaneously.

"We're not fighting," Jason says.

Birdie continues into the kitchen. She goes to the refrigerator to fill her water glass. "I can get that for you, honey," Charlotte says, moving past Jason. "Let me." The words in her mouth feel suddenly jumbled. She's slurring a little, she realizes. Just a *little*, she thinks. *Not enough for anyone to notice.*

"Oh," Birdie says, moving aside. "Okay. Thanks, Mom."

Charlotte hands her the glass.

"Mom," Birdie says, confused.

"What? Oh!" she realizes. "Oh my God." She laughs it off, taking the wineglass from Birdie's hands. "I gave you my . . . ." She hurries for the water glass she's just poured, refusing to look anywhere in Jason's direction.

"Are you okay?" she says to Birdie, running her hand along her back. "About earlier?"

"Uh-huh," Birdie says, pulling away from her. "I was just reading for school, and I heard you guys talking."

"Everything's fine," Jason says.

"Okay, good night then," Birdie says, slipping out of the room as quickly as she arrived.

Jason looks at her, just for a moment, but it's long enough to see the disappointment in his eyes. "I'm going to take Sylvie for a walk," he says.

Charlotte listens as he grabs the dog's leash off the hook by the garage door and they leave. She takes her glass and walks to the window over the sink, where the trees are silhouetted against the denim sky. *There are just a few sips left*, she thinks, swirling it in her hand. *I could just dump it*. She considers it for a moment, tipping the glass toward the drain, and then, hardly thinking about it, she swallows it down in one gulp, the taste on the back of her throat acrid and sour, like bad medicine.

She rinses the glass and puts it in the sink, aware of her reflection in the window. She closes her eyes. She doesn't look up.

FOURTEEN

Sylvie sniffs something in the neighbor's yard, and Jason thinks how nice it must be to be a golden retriever, to be so gloriously clueless. Eat, sleep, shit, walk. It's a thought he has often while he's working with the animals. He really believes that they have something to teach people, that watching the way they live, their simplicity, their presence, is a good lesson.

It is just beginning to get dark out, the streetlights coming on up the block. The young mother who recently moved in a few doors down is getting out of the car, dressed in a black skirt suit, hoisting a grocery bag onto her hip. Across the street, Will, a lawyer for DHS, waves as he heads into his house. Sylvie, straining on her leash, stops in front of a house owned by people Jason doesn't know, an older couple—not as old as his parents but older than him, with twirling lawn ornaments in their yard. She digs her nose into their mulch, seeking out something, and he notices the flickering light of the TV inside their window. *How long have they been married?* he wonders. *And has it always been smooth sailing?*

He walks, thinking that he doesn't really *know-know* anyone on his street anymore, not in any significant way, and especially since Birdie grew out of selling Girl Scout cookies and trick-or-treating, lemonade stands and riding her bike in circles around the cul-de-sac at the end of the block. He feels a lump in his throat, realizing it. Mourning her childhood.

He turns the corner and takes his phone from his pocket. He doesn't even know who to call. Charlotte was always the person he went to, the person he talked to. When they were first dating, she marveled at how different the DC area was compared to Savannah, and even Atlanta. *Capital-S serious*, she said, laughing about how weird it was to discover that the woman who speed-walks down the street on Saturday mornings in an old grubby windbreaker is the former ambassador to France, or that the person behind you in line at the grocery store, grumbling about the slow cashier, is the manager of a presidential campaign. Arlington, she said, was full of Serious People doing Serious Things, Type A's who spouted off acronyms when you asked them where they worked: OPM, DARPA, DOJ, HHS. As hard as she worked back then, trying to get tenure, she wasn't so hardened, so intense. She could laugh things off and let them go at the end of the day.

He misses that part of her. And he wonders if she does, too. When he picks up the book she wrote, as he sometimes does, opening to any old page, he finds the woman he fell in love with, the one who says in the TED talk that started it all, "Life, when it comes right down to it, is not something you should grit your teeth through. It's meant to be cherished. You *are* meant to be happy."

Promoting all these ideas, in her big, big way, has cost them a lot: time, connection, energy for the things that should matter, like just being together, just hanging out. He knows that she is stressed about the conference in Montana, but she hasn't even mentioned it to him. She doesn't acknowledge the part he plays in this machine she's created. He feels like they're circling a drain.

He looks up at the sky, feeling helpless, then down at his phone. His brother answers on the second ring.

"To what do I owe the honor?" Tate says.

"I'm just out for a walk," Jason says. "Thought I would call my dear brother to say hello."

"How nice," Tate says. "I'm actually walking, too. Headed to meet Paul for dinner but I'm exhausted. And we have to be up early to drive to the coast."

"Vacation?" Jason says.

"No, I wish," Tate says. "Seeing about a project for work."

"I don't know how you do it."

"What?"

"Work with your spouse."

"Ugh, that word," Tate jokes.

"Work, or . . . ?" Jason jokes back.

"You know what I mean."

"Actually," he says. "Speaking of that . . ."

"What?"

"I need your help," Jason says, knowing it very well may be the first time he's ever said the words to his brother. He worries he's called the wrong person. Tate doesn't believe in marriage, and only married his partner, Paul, a few summers ago because he was given an ultimatum.

There is silence for a moment. "Is it Mom? Dad?" he says, and Jason thinks back to that day, when he was fifteen and Tate was eighteen, when his brother came out to his parents. Jason knew. He'd suspected first and then Tate had told him on the back patio under the bug zapper, late at night after they'd both been out drinking with their individual groups of friends. He wonders, still, how his parents had been so surprised when Tate told them, because they must have known on some level, even if they didn't want to. They had come around. It had taken time (their father's exact words were "This will take some time to get used to") but Jason knows that there is still a strain there. Tate will probably always resent their parents a little bit (and how could he not?) for not completely accepting him as he is. It's not surprising that he chose to live all the way across the country.

"No, it's not them," he says. "It's Charlotte." He fills his brother in, telling him what it's been like. "She doesn't seem intent on changing anything, even though I can see how unhappy she is. And she's drinking a lot."

Tate laughs. "She's always liked a drink," he says. "That's one of the things I love about her. When we're at the beach house, I always know I can count on Char to join me in a breakfast margarita."

"Perfect," Jason says. "Thanks, Tate."

"Oh, come on. So, what? Is she day-drinking? Getting drunk every night? What?"

"No, not day-drinking but maybe . . . I think she had three glasses tonight."

"That really doesn't sound like a lot," Tate says.

"And maybe it wouldn't be, if the two of us were hanging out and having drinks or something. But it's like she's desperate to jump into the bottle the minute she gets home. It doesn't look so much like she's enjoying it as needing it. Does that make sense? I know she's doing it because she's unhappy. It's like she's trying to numb herself or something."

"Well, I never would have known that from her Instagram feed."

"Yes, well, all part of the act," Jason says.

"And you've tried everything?"

"Yeah," he says.

"Are you having sex?"

"No," Jason admits, rubbing his brow. "Not really."

"Mm," Tate says. "You know they say that when that goes, it's all downhill."

"Thanks, Tate."

"Why don't you take a break? I know you can't *Eat Pray Love* it because of your responsibilities with work and Birdie, but maybe a little absence to make the heart grow fonder might help?"

Jason thinks of Jamie, who suggested the same thing. "You can't really take a break from your marriage."

"Tell me about it," Tate says. "Honestly, though, you'd be surprised. We have a coworker here who did it and it worked like a charm. After their kids went off to college, he and his wife got separate apartments. They'd meet for dinner a few times a week, like they were dating again. And now they're fully back together, though they do keep the separate places. Maybe you could do something like that?"

"You'd think, with the amount that she travels, that we

wouldn't need to do that. I don't know, Tate. It seems weird. And Birdie, she'd freak out. I just don't like how it sounds."

"For someone who's supposed to be a typical straight dude, you're far more sensitive than your gay brother." Tate laughs. "You realize that, don't you?"

"I guess."

"Take a break, Jason."

"I don't know if Charlotte . . ."

"Well, exactly my point," Tate says. "Maybe you should focus less on what she's doing and more on you. What is it that she says? Action first? Follow your instincts? See if that does the trick."

"Yeah," Jason says. "I could. I guess I hadn't thought of it that way."

"Well, there you go," Tate says, sounding pleased with himself. "I'll send the bill later. Listen, though, I do need to run. I just got to the restaurant and Paul's already seated. He just did that annoying pointing to his watch thing." He lowers his voice. "He's so fucking impatient."

They hang up. Jason knows he should head home soon, he can't walk forever, but he thinks of his brother's advice.

What would make me feel better?

He stands there for a moment, with Sylvie looking up at him, and then he looks down at his phone. *Fuck it,* he thinks, putting it to his ear. He doesn't think she's going to answer, but then, just as he's about to give up, she does.

"Hi!" she says in a loud whisper. There's music in the background, the clattering of dishes.

"Where are you?" he says.

"On a date!" Jamie says. "A horrible, awful date!" She laughs. "The picture the guy posted on his profile must be twenty years old! I feel like my eyes are going to be permanently damaged from staring at the glare bouncing off his bald head."

"Oh my God," he says, chuckling, though he feels a yearning, too. Envy, he realizes, picturing this guy, whoever he is, who's out with her right now.

"Do you think I could escape from here? I'm in the bathroom now. I could just climb out the window."

"Oh, that's so mean," he says. "You can't do that. Not unless it's really bad."

She groans. "I guess you're right. He's not awful. Just boring as hell! Don't you want to come rescue me?"

"Yes," he says, blurting it out. "Actually."

They're both silent for a moment, his words settling over them. "Well," she says. "Me, too."

He shuffles his feet, kicking a piece of gravel on the sidewalk. "Well," he says.

She makes a funny sound, somewhere between humming and clearing her throat. "He's in a band," she says.

"That's cool."

"No, no. It's a dad band," she says. "He plays the ukulele."

"Ohh."

"Sexy, right?"

"So he has kids?"

"Three. He's divorced."

"Mm." Jason feels a knot in his stomach. "Do you know why?"

"No," she says. "But I'll find out."

"I should let you go," he says.

"Wait, is everything okay?"

"Yeah," he says, continuing to walk. "Just called to say hi."

"Oh," she says. "Well, I'm glad you did."

"Me, too," he says, closing his eyes when Sylvie looks up at him. If the dog's making him feel guilty, he definitely shouldn't be doing this. "I'll see you tomorrow."

He gets to the curb and sees how far he's gone, much farther than he anticipated. He should turn around and go home, but he sees a street sign up ahead and his adrenaline kicks in as he realizes where he is. He should go home, he knows this, but he hears his brother's voice in his head—*follow your instincts*—so he keeps walking.

Jason has been gone for over an hour. His usual walks never last more than twenty minutes, maybe thirty if he gets lost in a good podcast, and Charlotte is starting to worry. *Maybe he's been hit by a distracted driver,* she thinks, sitting up on the couch in the family room, *or some asshole on one of those motorized scooters that have popped up on every corner like swarms of locusts.* Charlotte pictures him splayed out on the ground at the awful pedestrian walkway on George Mason where nobody ever stops, Sylvie panting hopelessly next to him.

And then she has another thought: *Could he be with Jamie? Maybe he'd used the dog walk as an excuse to go meet her somewhere . . . but no, that couldn't be. Jamie lives all the way in*

Bethesda. Of course, she could have driven over here . . . but . . . no, she thinks. *With two kids, no one else to help her . . .* They'd been to her house years ago for a cookout when all of the kids were small. It had been blazingly hot, a Sunday afternoon, and at one point, Charlotte retrieved a bottle of Coppertone baby sunscreen from her diaper bag and started applying it to Birdie's cheeks. She sensed Jamie watching her with a kind of pensive bewilderment. Hesitatingly, Jamie walked over, pulled a little tube of something from her back pocket, and asked if Charlotte would like to try it because it was "natural" and "less scary," she said, pointing to Charlotte's brand-name sunscreen. Charlotte had waved her off with a laugh, saying they'd take their chances, and that had been the end of it, but later in the car on the way home, she was pissed, though Jason insisted that Jamie couldn't have possibly meant anything by it because she was quote "so laid-back." Thinking it over, she remembers how Jason has used that phrase lots of times when referring to his coworker, whether it's describing her way with the animals at work or how she is at home. What did that imply? That she, by contrast, is not?

She pictures him somewhere nearby—on his phone, most likely, she decides—talking to Jamie about what's transpired in their house tonight. Talking about *her* and her apparent drinking problem. She pictures him, standing the way he does when he's on the phone, his free hand crooked into the fold of his other elbow, pacing casually, laughing about her, bitching about her.

She hears Tabatha's voice in her head. *You seem like the type who needs attention.* Why does everyone around her—her husband, her boss—have an opinion on who she is, on what she should do? Isn't she doing enough?

She looks down at her phone, where, a little while ago, she Instagrammed a photo of a book, placed artfully on top of a pretty woven throw blanket she keeps folded over one of the armchairs in the living room. Taking time for me at the end of a long day, her caption reads. What do you do to fill your tank? No matter that the book, *The Poisonwood Bible*, is Birdie's, and that Charlotte slid it out from under her daughter's arms when she went to check on her and found her asleep on top of her covers. She saw that Birdie's nails were painted light blue and felt a guilty pang for not noticing it until now. *What else have I missed recently, big or small?* She looked around Birdie's messy room, thinking of the panic Jason must have felt in discovering that pamphlet, and her heart aches, knowing that despite everything she feels about him right now, watching Birdie grow up is hard for him in a different way than it is for her. She ran her hand over Birdie's head, kissed her on the forehead, and as she walked downstairs, she had the sensation that her daughter had slipped away from them, become an autonomous person, so separate from them in her daily life. *Maybe this is something I could write about for the book*, it occurs to her now, and as soon as it does, the thought repulses her. *This* is the thought that she has about her daughter? That it's fodder for the next bestseller? *Then again, maybe* . . . she thinks, pulling down at her phone's screen, watching the likes rack up like points on an arcade game, *maybe it might actually help things if I write this book? It could help us all.*

I fill my tank with CHARDONNAY! a commenter's written, which has led to a slew of replies with little wineglass emojis, two champagne flutes clinking "cheers." *See?* she thinks, feeling redeemed. She goes to the kitchen. One more, she tells herself, ignoring the guilt that comes as she empties the rest of the bottle she bought just a few hours ago into her glass. She knows she's drunk. It was awful, when she slurred earlier, handed Birdie that glass by accident. *But it's been a really long awful day*, she tells herself, sinking back into the couch. She shoots off a reply text to her brother, who messaged earlier about their mother's idea for a wedding-like send-off on the Savannah River, with everyone holding sparklers and bidding the couple farewell. Couldn't we just toss them both in the river? she types, and then opens another window on the phone to check in with Stephanie, whom she hasn't spoken to in a week. *People with close social connections are happiest*, she hears in her head, thinking of how, at the start of each semester, she makes her students commit to logging at least five face-to-face interactions with friends each week.

Hey, she types. Taking a poll. How much do you drink during the week?

Oh, God, don't tell me that I'm not allowed to drink wine anymore, Stephanie writes back. Don't tell me that it's bad for my happiness, please, I don't want to know. She types three wineglass emojis. This is what I've had tonight. More than usual, but it's not UNusual, know what I mean?

Charlotte nods to herself.

Hey, it's either this or Valium, Stephanie adds, along with a laughing-through-tears emoji.

Exactly, Charlotte types. Her fingers hover over the screen. She could tell Stephanie about Dayna's message to her today—

she wants to—but then she'd have to confess what she said to Tucker.

Why do you ask? Stephanie says.

Just a thing for a lecture, she types, then goes back to Instagram.

Now she has 42,619 likes. Not bad for an average weekday night, she thinks, sipping from her glass. She looks at the time and tells herself that if Jason's not back in ten minutes, she'll call him. Suddenly, a DM notification pops in the corner of her screen.

Ahhh. She smiles, seeing the username. @KGPartyof5 is back.

I hated that book, she's typed. Poisonwood Bible?

Why does that not surprise me? Charlotte responds. You're a tough critic.

You sound like my daughter, she writes.

How is she doing? Charlotte types. I've been thinking of her.

Better, she says. Much better. Tho Im afraid it's because of her new boyfriend, who Im not real fond of.

Charlotte sits up and reaches for her wine. Oh? she types. Why not?

Kid seems like a loser, the woman responds.

Sounds familiar, Charlotte writes.

Really? says the response.

I can't stand the kid my daughter is dating, Charlotte writes. She hesitates for a moment, knowing how stupid it is to vent to a complete stranger, but she does it anyway. The kid is such a prick, from this ostentatious family. The mom actually texted me to accuse me of threatening him.

No way! The text comes back, along with a couple of siren emojis. You? Little Miss Sunshine? I'd love to see that! Did you actually threaten the kid?

Charlotte bites her lip. Well . . . she types.

The response is instant: I love it! Who would've guessed?

Action first, feelings later, I guess, Charlotte types. I wasn't thinking. And you shouldn't mess with mama bear.

I like this side of you! the woman writes.

Well, don't believe everything you see online, Charlotte adds. There's more to me than you know.

What are you saying? KGPartyof5 replies. You don't wake up every day and piss rainbows, bluebirds hovering around you?

Ha! But gotta keep up the image, you know? Charlotte writes. Being happy is the brand. Gotta do what you gotta do.

I love it! So are you actually reading that book you posted, or . . . ?

Charlotte swipes along her phone's keyboard, taps out a wineglass emoji. Yes, I'm lounging. No, I'm not relaxing, she types. Actually waiting on my husband to get home. No idea where he is.

Whoa! The response comes back instantly. That doesn't sound good!

Charlotte frowns. No, it doesn't, does it? she adds.

She hears the door opening, the sound of Sylvie's tags jangling on her collar. Gotta go, she types and, leaping up from her seat, she finishes her glass, then hurries to the kitchen to put it in the sink.

An hour and twenty-five minutes after Jason left, Charlotte enters the family room just as he's sitting down on the couch, the collar of his T-shirt wet with perspiration. He tosses his phone down on the coffee table, making the screen come to life. His wallpaper is a photo of Birdie from last fall, sitting in the backyard in an old Georgetown sweatshirt of Charlotte's, her cheeks flushed from the cold. They'd been raking leaves together. Charlotte had made a pot of chili and her father's famous cornbread, flecked with bacon and jalapeños. It had been a good day.

She sits down in the chair across from him.

"So I went over to the Cunninghams'," he says.

"*What?*" Charlotte says, her eyes widening. "Why? What happened?"

"I didn't mean to, exactly," he says, shoving off his shoes with the toes of each foot. "I just found myself headed in that direction, and the next thing I knew, I was standing in front of their driveway."

"Did you go in?" Charlotte says. "Did you ring the doorbell?"

"No," he says. "Finch was actually outside. Putting stuff in his car. Tucker was with him. It was really strange, actually."

"Why? What did you say? What happened?"

He shakes his head like he's still trying to figure it out. "Tucker was in his lacrosse uniform, and when Finch saw me, he walked right over, and launched into a story about the game and his son's performance."

"Of course," she says, her tongue thick in her mouth. Her stomach growls and she realizes she never ate, that her dinner was a bottle of wine.

"I waved hello to Tucker. I mean, after today, I wanted to punch the kid, and he barely waved back before he slipped inside. I didn't know what to make of it at first—" *I do*, Charlotte thinks, guessing what Dayna may have told her husband. "But then Finch walked closer to me and gestured back toward his car. He was putting *suitcases* in the car."

"A trip?" Charlotte says. She rubs her fingers across her forehead, feeling a headache coming on.

"No," Jason says, looking concerned. "No. He said he's moving out."

"Moving out?" Charlotte says. "Like out-out?"

"I guess so," Jason says, leaning forward, his elbows on his knees. "He made a joke out of it."

"A joke?" Charlotte says.

"He said Dayna found something on a company credit card receipt."

"What?"

"He didn't say and I didn't ask. But he was laughing, almost like it was nothing new."

"Wow," she says.

"He also said too bad about Birdie and Tucker."

"What?" she says.

"Yeah," he says. "But he didn't elaborate. I would've asked him what he meant but he said it like I should know, and then all of the sudden, he was waving goodbye and slipping into his car."

"Huh," she says. "Well . . ." She mulls it over, weighing whether to say more. "I did get a text from Dayna today."

"You did?" he says.

"Yeah. She, um . . . She accused me of threatening Tucker, when I saw him at Birdie's practice. She was really angry. She said she almost called the school."

"Threatening him?" he says, his eyes widening. "Charlotte, why would she say that? I don't understand."

"I didn't threaten him," she says, aware of the stutter in her voice. "I just . . . it was right after she skipped practice and they went to his place. I just wanted him to know that it wasn't okay with us. That's all."

"And you worked it out with Dayna?" he says, a slight panic in his voice.

"Jesus, Jason. Don't overreact," she says. "I handled it."

He takes a deep breath.

"What?" she says.

"Nothing," he says. "You're just . . ."

"I'm what, Jason? What? What am I that's so . . . Why do you have that look on your face?"

"You're drunk, Charlotte."

"I'm not . . ." She rakes her fingers through her hair. "I just didn't eat. I need to—" She hoists herself up and staggers, knocking her shin into the side of the coffee table. The pain radiates up her leg but she plays it off as best she can, stepping forward, gritting through it. "I need to get some crackers or something . . ."

A moment later, she hears Jason's footsteps on the stairs. He doesn't even say good night.

FIFTEEN

"So this is your first time in Big Sky?" Leo says, unlocking the door to Charlotte's suite. She's not quite sure what she would call him—he's not exactly a bellboy, given that this is a private home, but *butler* seems too antiquated a term. Even *house manager* seems too stuffy for this gorgeous twenty-something in a plaid button-down and jeans.

"Yes, my first time," she says. Everybody she's encountered since she arrived on the grounds has been unnaturally beautiful, like genetically perfected robot people. Leo has the kind of olive skin she's always coveted, piercing green eyes, and hair that hangs down just past his chin in a way that looks unintentionally stylish. He told her on the walk across the grounds that he was born and raised in Montana and never intends to live anywhere else. He's worked at the ranch for over a year, and he loves it because it provides ample time for him to be outside, skiing and fly-fishing and whatever else Grey Browning likes to do when he's here.

He opens the door to the suite and when she steps inside, her jaw drops. What she'd pictured during the plane ride over was something rustic and luxurious; Ralph Lauren plaid and Pendleton blankets and handsome wood furniture. The sitting room she's now standing in is certainly that, but the ceiling is double-height, featuring a round chandelier that must be eight feet in diameter, with dozens of flickering candle lights. The far wall is actually a floor-to-ceiling window that frames a breathtaking view of the Northern Rockies. She takes in the massive, cloud-like white wraparound couch, the elegant paintings on the walls, the impeccably plush rug, the antelope-skin chairs flanking the sleek carbon-colored fireplace, where a fire is crackling invitingly.

He looks at her and laughs. "Yeah, it's pretty nice," he says, and starts rolling her bag down the hall. She follows.

"There's a small kitchen here," he says, gesturing toward a room on the left, where Charlotte sees gleaming marble countertops and luminous white cabinets. A bowl overflowing with fruit sits in the center of the counter. "I assume somebody had you fill out the questionnaire?"

"Yes," she says, remembering an email that came weeks ago with involved questions about her preferences for everything from the type of water she'd like in her suite (still? sparkling? room temp? iced?), to the kind of coffee and tea and breakfasts and snacks she enjoys.

"Good," he says. "Then the fridge should be stocked with things to your liking, but of course you can call down to the main kitchen at any time, day or night."

"I'm sure it will be fine," she says, laughing a little at the extravagance of it all. She's barely going to be here for twenty-four hours.

He flips on the light to the bedroom and she can't hide it anymore, she gasps. "This is . . ."

"I know," he says. "Everyone has this reaction when they stay here. But, you know, Montana. And the owner. Everything's big." He shrugs.

"I'll say!" she says, gawking. The bedroom is grand and decorated impeccably. There's another massive fireplace, this one gray stone, and across from it is a carved-wood canopy bed the size of a boxing ring, set on a pedestal. She has to resist the urge to swan dive into it, the way people do in the movies.

Outside a wall of sliding doors is a patio with a settee, two lounge chairs, and a fire pit. It's only forty degrees outside—spring in Montana, apparently—but there are gorgeous cement planters teeming with evergreens, trailing ivy, and mountain laurel.

"There's a robe and slippers your size in the closet," Leo says, setting her suitcase next to the door. "Please take them with you, as our gift. And the bathroom is just beyond that door," he says, holding out his arm. "Any of the toiletries you requested should be in there. You sent your toothpaste preference?"

She laughs. "I think so, on the questionnaire."

"We have more of everything. Whatever you need."

"Thanks very much," she says, looking around in a daze.

"Is there anything else I can get you at the moment?" he says.

Her phone buzzes in the pocket of her coat, and she feels a pang in her stomach, thinking of home.

"No," she says, putting her hand on it. "I think this will do just fine."

"Well, you should have just received a text with my contact information," he tells her, starting for the door.

"Oh!" she says, pulling her phone from her pocket and seeing the 406 area code. "Isn't that efficient?"

He smiles. "Well, you know . . ."

"Right," she says, nodding, thinking of who invited her here. "Of course."

"If you need anything at all, just shoot me a message. Or give me a call."

"What I need is to never have to leave this place," she says.

He smiles and heads for the door. "Enjoy your stay."

After the door closes behind him, she turns a circle around the sitting room, trying to decide what to do with herself in the couple of hours until the symposium begins. She heads toward the kitchen for some water, perhaps a snack. She woke up at four o'clock this morning, an hour before her alarm was set to go off, feeling nauseous and puffy. Now she has a splitting headache, and she's sure she's dehydrated, from last night, and the plane, and the bloody mary she ordered during the flight after she saw a guy across the aisle drinking one, telling herself, as she poured the mini-bottle of Smirnoff into her plastic cup, that it would settle her nerves.

She wanders around the suite, wishing she had somebody to share it with. Jason and Birdie were still asleep when she left the house, and as she drove to the airport along the GW Parkway, the sunrise pink behind the Washington Monument, she felt a sinking uneasiness like she used to feel when she left Birdie at daycare when she was a baby, like she should turn around and call off the trip.

She notices a leather folder placed neatly in the center of the glass coffee table in the sitting room, and realizes her name is embossed on the front, in gold letters. She lifts the front cover and sees the agenda that was emailed to her a few days ago. She'll speak just before cocktail hour, right after a mega-famous Hollywood actress who has become one of the most vocal proponents of CBD.

When Wendy called her three months ago, screaming into the phone that Grey Browning's people had called requesting that she give the keynote at this year's symposium, she thought she was going to faint. She'd read for years about the annual meeting, which brought some of the biggest names in business, politics, and entertainment together for two days of "cutting-edge idea exchange and next-level thinking." But what really made it so exciting was Grey Browning himself, a former hippie who dressed exclusively in white linen tunics and flowy pants whose venture capital group had funded the biggest things coming out of Silicon Valley, many of them related to healthcare. His people told Wendy that he was interested in Charlotte's thoughts on happiness and how it might translate to technology, possibly in the form of an app or a media channel. Charlotte and Wendy didn't quite know what to make of this idea, but they surmised that the speech she would give tonight was a kind of audition.

She walks to the window and steps outside, the wind whipping her hair into her face as she takes a few photos of the view. She starts to send one of them to Birdie but stops herself, thinking it better not to appear as if she's having a good time away from her, and Instagrams it instead with a simple caption, Northern Rocky Mountain High.

She takes the water glass back to the kitchen and opening the refrigerator to peruse the snacks, she notices a bottle of Piper-Heidsieck, her favorite champagne, chilling on the wine rack. A drink would loosen her up before her talk, she knows, but then she thinks of Jason, the night before, and how she couldn't even look at him after she stumbled getting out of her chair. She grabs the plastic-wrapped plate of cheese and fruit instead, telling herself she can have a glass later, to celebrate after she's done.

She sinks back onto the couch, watching the blue flames flicker in the fireplace, and picks up her phone. Only four thousandish likes for her mountain pic so far. She taps on the little red icon notifying her that she's been tagged in other people's posts and begins to scroll through them, her confidence for tonight building as she flips through the dozens of pictures of her book set in lovely tableaus: alongside a fresh bouquet of peonies, on a beach towel in the sand, on a pretty café table next to a perfectly crafted latte, on a picnic blanket next to a wicker basket. And then she stops, moving the phone closer to her face to examine one particular post, because she doesn't quite believe what she's seeing.

It's just text, a screenshot of a message, but as she starts to read it, the room begins to shift, the words blurring as she realizes what it is.

> You? Little Miss Sunshine? I'd love to see that! Did you actually threaten the kid? . . . I like this side of you! . . . Don't believe everything you see online . . . gotta keep up the image, you know? . . . being happy is the brand. Gotta do what you gotta do. Waiting on my husband . . . No idea where he is.

She blinks, her exchange with @KGpartyof5 the night before coming back to her. *What was she thinking?* Her heart pulses in her chest. Don't believe everything you see is all the woman—Charlotte realizes that she doesn't even know her real name—has written for the caption, but she's tagged @charlottemcganley.

She lets out a big breath, trying to settle herself, angry at herself for being such an idiot, letting herself vent to an absolute stranger, knowing in the back of her mind that it never would have happened if she hadn't been drinking. *It's possible it will just blow over,* she tells herself, tapping at the forty-three comments that have appeared so far, some of them questioning what the "threaten the kid" statement means, others saying things like "I always knew she was a fake!"

She's going to have to fix this, but she can't deal with it now, not here. She feels the familiar pressure again, the weight settling itself on her chest, and although she knows she shouldn't—it's what got her into this mess in the first place, isn't it?—she needs to relax. It's a big night ahead. She goes to the kitchen and gets out a glass.

The glass of champagne that she'd drunk had turned into half the bottle by the time she left her room, but it turns out to be exactly the liquid courage she needs to get through the talk. When she first steps onstage and looks out over the crowd, the faces staring back at her include not just a bunch of overpaid tech geeks but also a legendary national news anchor, a huge Hollywood director, and a former vice president who is rumored to be considering a run for the presidency. For the first time in a long time, she is standing at a podium where she feels out of her depth, like she maybe can't just charm her way through it. After running through her usual intro, citing the studies on how behavior shapes emotion, she notices some of the faces in the crowd assessing her in a bored way, a few checking their phones. She pauses and fans through her notes, shifting her weight from side to side. She's buzzed, but she's going to make it work in her favor this time, like rocket fuel, muting her inhibitions. It feels like permission.

"You know," she says, grinning out at the crowd. "Forget it. I'm going to lose these notes. The truth is, I have a bone to pick with you." A few heads in the crowd immediately shoot up, standing to attention, like gophers popping out of their holes. "You know, there's a lot of research out there now—more and more each day—showing that technology is making people feel more unhappy than ever. Lonelier, more insecure." She scans the crowd and notices a guy roll his eyes a few rows back. "You've read it, too, right?" she asks, pausing to point directly at him. "But you don't care, or . . ." A few murmurs pop throughout the crowd. "My students sometimes do a tech fast. It's become quite popular, actually, among the millennial set. And without exception, they feel better afterward. Why do you think that is?" She waits for a response. "Seriously, anyone want to chime in?" The room is painfully silent, until she hears the snap of a phone camera somewhere off to the right. "You've seen the suicide rates, right? Among teenagers especially? Don't you think you have something to do with that?" The news anchor, holding a pen to her chin just like Charlotte's seen her do during her TV interviews, laughs and shakes her head. "All right, well, if nobody's going to chime in, I will. Earlier today, somebody posted something horrible about me on Instagram. There were, I don't know, maybe four hundred comments on it before I left my room? It made me feel terrible, like maybe I am a fraud and don't have any idea what I'm talking about. Sometimes I think, Wouldn't it be nice if we snapped our fingers and all of the phones and social media and everything just went away?" *Shit.* She thought a minute ago that she might—*Jesus, what was she thinking?*—inspire some kind of thoughtful discussion or debate, but clearly she's gone off the rails. These people—Stanford and MIT engineers, Ivy League grads—must think she's an idiot. She takes a breath, clears her throat, and finds the place where she's abandoned her talk. She'll start over. "Okay, so . . . back to happiness. A study out of UCLA showed that . . ." she begins.

"Phenomenal," Grey Browning says, golf-clapping, his eyes sparkling behind asymmetrical glasses that remind Charlotte of something she might have seen in an eighties music video but probably cost more than her plane ticket here. "Just wonderful."

He is standing where the sixty guests he's invited to this year's event are mingling for cocktail hour. It's been just over an hour since Charlotte stepped off the stage, which provided a relief that was almost orgasmic. She completely bombed, and it is all over Grey Browning's face. She can tell he is faking his enthusiasm. He is probably counting the seconds until he can make her disappear.

He bows slightly in front of her, his hands pressed together in prayer. "You weren't quite what I thought you would be," he says. "But it's always good to be surprised, isn't it?"

"I hope I didn't—"

He cuts her off. "Please, come with me." Grey leads her into the cocktail hour, down a couple of stairs into a solarium, which looks like a botanical garden in outer space. There are palms of varying massive heights, and thick cords of blooms—plumeria, bougainvillea, camellias—strung on some sort of fishing line to make it appear as if they're floating and swaying in midair. The lighting has been adjusted to cast a golden hue over everything, and the perfume from the flowers hangs heavy in the air. Charlotte hears the faintest hint of music in the background, something that sounds vaguely tropical or tribal. It is a weird choice for Montana, she thinks, but then again, Grey Browning is a weird guy. And she knows from her research that he spends part of the year in Bali. Maybe this is a nod to that.

"Did you give your phone to the attendant?" he asks.

"Yes," she says, remembering how she'd stopped at a rope line on the way over from the compound's theater and was asked to leave her phone at a check station.

"I'm sure *you* can appreciate that we prefer to be without distractions here, to be able to exchange ideas with purity and freedom," he says, leaning in and peering into her eyes in a way that is aggressive and off-putting, invasive somehow, like he's wanting to check the spaces between her teeth. She takes what she hopes is a subtle step back and looks away, breaking the intense eye contact.

"Yes, always nice to go off the grid," she says. "Though I suppose that I alluded to my feelings on that during my talk," she says, attempting to make light of it.

He nods once, taking her arm. "Let me walk you around. There are several people here who I'm sure would love to speak to you."

Oh, I'm sure, she thinks, cringing inside.

"But first," he says, waving over a waitress. "A drink? We're serving only natural, biodynamic wines tonight. Nothing with additives. *Terroir* blends," he says, handing her a glass of cloudy white. "See," he says, holding it up to the light. He taps his finger on her glass. "That sediment means no hangovers."

"Even better," she says, clinking her glass to his. *Maybe the talk wasn't so bad*, she thinks, assessing his smile. As they weave through the crowd, she drinks, and begins to finally relax and enjoy herself, deciding to ignore the odd looks she gets from many of the attendees. *Screw them*, she thinks, remembering her father's old advice, that being universally liked is a sign you're not risking enough. She'll probably never have another opportunity like this, to interact with this kind of crowd, and so she gives in to the moment, forgetting whether or not they think she's a moron, just like she would tell her readers to do.

It's a whirlwind, and thirty minutes in, she finds herself disappointed by her encounters. It seems like most people here are interested in making money or pushing their own brands.

An executive at one of the television streaming services corners Charlotte, asking if she would be interested in doing a reality show where she would give participants "happiness makeovers." He's a big guy, with coal-black hair that matches his coat, and at first, she finds herself drawn to his charismatic pitch about how they could "focus on the internal rather than the external," but before long, he leans over, his rank cheese breath in her face, and says, "But we'd of course do physical makeovers, too, because no matter what anyone says about regular people on TV, pretty sells."

Before long, she feels like she's been twirled around the room, do-si-doed from one conversation to the next, and she realizes that she needs to eat. She's continued to accept glasses of organic wine as they've come around, but only nibbled at a single shrimp wonton when a server passed by with a tray. "Do you know if there's any more food?" she asks another guest as she's walking by, and the woman kind of laughs, mentioning something about dinner being served soon and making a face at the person she's with. Seeing the exchange, the way their eyes widen at each other, about her, she realizes she's had more to drink than she thought. She weaves among the crowd. There's no way she can make it through a dinner like this. She remembers the cheese tray in her room. She'll go back there, catch her breath, eat something and sober up, and then she'll be fine. She'll go to the dinner and redeem herself and *everything will be fine.*

She retrieves her phone, then walks down the long hallway that leads to her suite and punches her code into the keypad on the door, then realizes, looking at the name carved into a little piece of framed wood on the door—Elk—that this isn't her room at all. She's in Lynx, she remembers, because she took a photo of the little plaque and sent it to Amanda, making a joke about what a perfect match it was for her, and Amanda immediately wrote back teasing that she should actually be in Cougar. Charlotte replied with an eye roll emoji.

She finds herself at the end of another hall less than ten minutes later, and then, wobbling a little, she walks back to the central hall, and realizes that, *of course*, she needs to take the elevator up two floors.

She steps in, and there is Leo, the assistant-bellboy-whatever, leaning against the wall, looking like a cologne ad.

"Having a good night?" he asks. She notices his forearms, bare beneath the rolled-up sleeves. *How did she miss those before?*

"Yes," she says. "It was great." She's warm suddenly, and takes a deep breath to try to settle herself.

"Your talk was fantastic."

"You heard it?" she says.

"Oh yeah," he says. "Perk of the job. I wouldn't miss any of them. Really, though, yours was great. Pretty bold, saying what you did in front of this crowd."

"I don't know, maybe it was a mistake," she says. "Wasn't my smoothest."

"You okay?" he asks, narrowing his eyes at her.

"Yeah, of course," she says, leaning back against the wall.

"The altitude can get to people if they're not used to it," he says. "Especially if you just had a couple glasses of wine."

"That must be it," she says, smiling sheepishly.

"Anyway, your talk. Even though I'm part of this," he says, waving his hand around. "That's what I love about being here in Montana. You really do feel unplugged, separated from a lot of the real world in a good way. Not, like, a Unabomber way." He winks at his own joke, and she feels herself flush. He really is so handsome. If she were younger, and single . . .

The elevator slows, coming to a stop, and he lunges and reaches his arm out to hold the door for her.

She steps toward the threshold as the doors part, falters a little, and it happens so fast. She falls, her knee skimming the floor just as he grips her arm, scooping her up.

"Whoa," he says, steadying her.

"Oh my God, I—" She takes a step forward, wanting to shake him off, but the hallway ahead is spinning, the ground like a fun-house floor changing under her feet.

"Let me help you," he says. "May I help you get to your room?"

"Okay," she says, trying to laugh it off. "I think you were right about the altitude. I'm so embarrassed."

"Don't be." He reaches, threading his arm around her waist, and holds her hand with his free hand. They walk slowly, and it's nice, she thinks, her weight leaning into him. She lets her head loll against his shoulder, allowing him to guide her. "Thank you," she says.

"Of course," he murmurs. "Just slow and steady. One step at a time."

"Okay," she says. He's practically carrying her. *Right, left*, she thinks. *Right, left*.

Back in her room, she closes the door, insisting she'll be fine. She chains the lock although she knows it's unnecessary and then she stumbles for the bathroom. The motion sensor light comes on as she enters, startling her, and she lurches for the vanity, grasping for the edges with both hands. Once she catches herself, she turns on the faucet and splashes cold water on her face, and when she looks up at herself in the mirror, and sees her makeup running down her cheeks, her bloodshot eyes, she begins to cry.

She gets herself into the bedroom and lies on the bed for a few minutes, the room spinning. Her phone buzzes in the distance, and she gets up and walks back to the sitting area, where she'd dropped it on a chair as she came in. It's Reese.

How did it go? his text reads.

And then another from Birdie: How was it, Mom? Me and Dad want to know.

She holds her phone to her chest. What has she done? What on earth has she done? She goes to the kitchen and pours herself a glass of water, downs it, and then her eyes lock on the open bottle of champagne that she left in the ice bucket several hours ago. She yanks it out, hesitating for just a moment, and empties it into the sink.

The phone buzzes, Reese again. Call me if you can. I'm up.

Charlotte walks back to the bedroom and climbs onto the bed, remembering when she first saw it today, how she looked forward to the way she'd feel when she came back here this evening, filled with relief and pride (she hoped) after a successful night.

The phone buzzes once more, and she considers whether to take Reese's invitation, knowing the right answer. She gets up and unzips her dress, stepping out of it, knowing there's no way she can make it to dinner, and hopes that nobody will notice that the keynote speaker who just insulted most of the room has also decided to skip the evening's main event. She remembers the robe in the closet and slips it on, then goes to the bathroom to brush her teeth. The phone buzzes yet again but she ignores it. She splashes water on her face, brushes her teeth, ignores her sinking shame. *What have I done? What have I done?*

She gets in bed, sits with her back against the headboard, pulling the blanket up tight to her waist. She begins texting Birdie, but is interrupted when Reese calls.

"I was just about to return your text," she says.

"Sorry." He laughs. "I was going to leave a voicemail, just to say congratulations. Was it everything you thought it would be?"

"It was," she says. "It was interesting. I don't . . . I think I offended them."

"Oh, come on."

"No, I really do." She feels tears welling up in her eyes but she brushes them away. She takes a deep inhale through her nose. She won't break down, she tells herself. Not now. Not like this. "I was maybe more than they bargained for," she says, speaking slowly, extra-careful to enunciate her words.

"Well, better to be memorable," he says. "You've had a few drinks, I believe."

"Well—" she starts, prepared to defend herself. "I—The altitude, I think."

He laughs. "It's okay," he says. "You've been so nervous about this."

She traces her finger along the embroidery on the duvet, feeling both soothed by his words and troubled by them, because he shouldn't be the one saying these things to her. "It's late there," she says.

"Yeah," he says. "But I never go to bed before midnight. Just not my nature."

"I remember that," she says, thinking of all of the times in college and graduate school when she'd wake up in the middle of the night and find him at his desk, hunched over a book.

"You okay?" he says.

"Yeah," she says, her voice breaking.

"What is it?" he says. "What's wrong?"

She squeezes her eyes shut.

"Charlotte," he says, his voice soft. "Come on, tell me."

"I just . . ." She shakes her head at herself, thinking of everything that has happened over the past several days. Birdie, seeing Jason and Jamie, the interaction with her boss, tonight . . . "My life hasn't worked out quite the way I thought it would, Reese. I thought if I . . . I don't know what happened. I just . . . I miss my peace of mind. I don't have that anymore. I don't recognize myself."

"I know just what you mean," he says.

"You do?"

"Yup. I know what people think about my marriage. I knew on my wedding day that people thought she was too young, or just after my money. And maybe she was. But it's like I told you the other day: I thought it would just continue to grow into what it was supposed to be, you know? Like a picture coming into focus? I thought we'd make it work. I wanted it to work." He pauses. "I wanted it to be the way it was with—" *Don't say it,* she thinks, but he does: "With us."

"Oh," she says, her mind racing.

"I'm sorry," he says. "I shouldn't say—"

"No." She stops him. "I think about it, too," she says, knowing that she shouldn't. "I think about what it was like, growing up together, being on the water, all of the—"

"How it was supposed to be," he says. "Before I—"

"Reese."

"I'm sorry," he says again. "You don't need this now. You should get some rest. A good night's sleep."

"Right," she says. She can't remember the last time somebody spoke to her like this, the last time somebody encouraged her to rest. She realizes how desperate she is for somebody to comfort her, for somebody to tell her that everything will be okay. "Thank you, Reese."

"Good night, Charlotte," he says. "Get some sleep."

"Good night."

As soon as they hang up, she dials Jason's number, telling herself that if there's one thing she should do tonight, if for no other reason than to assuage her guilt, it's this. Even though she knows deep down that she would have rather stayed on the phone with Reese than speak to her own husband.

"What time is it?" he grumbles.

Shit. It didn't even occur to her, she'd been so wrapped up in the conversation with Reese that she forgot the time. "I'm so sorry, I forgot the time change."

"It's okay," he says, his voice muffled from sleep. "How was it?"

"Good," she says. "It went really well." She can hear the thick cotton in her voice, the way she can't get her words out, and when he doesn't respond, she's sure he can, too.

"Guess who I met?" she says, trying to sound cheery, but it's hard to keep the words straight. "The . . ." *Shit. What's his name again? The sneaker guy?* "Nike," she says. "The CEO?"

"Huh," he says, not as impressed as she'd hoped. *But he was sleeping*, she tells herself.

"I miss you," she says, tears burning in her eyes.

"We miss you, too." He hurries out the words; she can tell there's no feeling behind them. "Listen, it's late here," he says. Shame settles over her. She feels heat rise to her cheeks, thinking of the way she must sound. The room spins around her. "Okay," she says.

"Be safe, Charlotte," he says.

"I miss—"

He's hung up before she can finish.

She thinks of the words he said—*be safe*—and thinks to herself: *Too late.*

SIXTEEN

When Charlotte arrives home, she throws her keys on the kitchen counter and walks around the house, trying to ignore the thoughts that have been banging around in her head since she left Montana. She straightens the pile of mail into a neat stack on the table by the front door, puts the cereal bowls in the sink in the dishwasher, and, upstairs, puts the cap back on the toothpaste that Birdie left on her bathroom counter. When she enters her bedroom, she sees that Jason has left the bed unmade, the sheets tangled in a pile at the end of the mattress, his *National Geographic* magazine left open, facedown, on his nightstand.

She sits for a moment, then changes into shorts and an old T-shirt from years ago, when she and Birdie ran a 5K at her elementary school together—and finds the Advil, taking three to combat the splitting headache she woke up with after a couple of hours of fitful sleep in the beautiful suite that was supposed to be a reward. Jason and Birdie will be arriving home any minute now, and she thinks to herself that maybe they can all go out to dinner, or that she might order takeout from their favorite Lebanese place, something. Anything to erase the past few days. An image of herself stumbling down the hall pops into her head again, and then her fumbling onstage, the way she may have embarrassed herself at the cocktail party, the way she spoke to Reese, all of the images relentless.

She takes her laptop out to the table on the back porch, and lets her cursor hover over her email inbox, where there are messages from two of her doctoral advisees freaking out over various aspects of their dissertations, a note from Wendy about coming up with a deadline for the next book proposal, and an official schedule from Tabatha for final exams coming up in two weeks.

She opens her browser and looks at Instagram, where @KGPartyof5's post now has over six hundred comments. She needs to alert Wendy about this—some of the sentiments expressed are truly vile, and Charlotte tells herself, trying to make herself feel better, that the people who leave the worst of the worst must be venting their own frustrations. *Sticks and stones*, she thinks, though the truth is, it does hurt her, being called a fraud and a fake and a phony, and it's humiliating, the implication about her marriage. *No idea where he is*, she'd typed, the words pricking at her because she knows they're true on so many levels. She checks her Google alerts and is relieved to see that nobody from the symposium has posted or written anything online about her talk, though she knows it's probably only a matter of time. She reminds herself that she is not her image, that none of these people—online, in Montana—know what she is at her core, but that troubles her, too, because she herself is the one who's most aware that she is not the person she presents to the world. She's not even close.

The phone rings, a local number she doesn't recognize.

"Ms. McGanley?" the woman asks, a hint of New England in her voice. "I'm calling from the counseling office over at Yorktown High School. I have Birdie here, and I know it's short notice, but any chance you can come in?"

Charlotte leaps out of her chair. "Yes, of course," she says. "I'll be right over."

A million thoughts fly through her head as she races into the school, not just why Birdie might be in the counseling office, but why she's there after school hours when she's supposed to be at practice.

A secretary leads her back to the counseling office, where Birdie sits in a plastic chair at a round table on one side of the room, the woman who is presumably the counselor next to her, and—*what is this?*—Coach Noah next to the counselor. She wonders if this has something to do with the older girls on the team giving Birdie a hard time.

Her daughter's face is splotchy. It's clear that she's been crying.

"Ms. McGanley," the counselor says, standing and shaking her hand. She looks about Charlotte's age, though she's at least a head taller. "I'm Ms. Loren," she says, smiling in the apologetic, slightly self-effacing way a doctor might just before revealing your horrible diagnosis. Coach Noah stands, too, shaking her hand, but his eyes barely meet hers. Charlotte looks at Birdie, who starts to cry again, covering her face with both hands.

"What's going on?" she says, scooting through the space behind the counselor's chair to sit in the empty chair next to Birdie and gripping her daughter's arm. "What happened?"

Ms. Loren looks from the coach to Birdie and then back to Charlotte. "Well," she says, twirling her pencil between her hands. "We had something come up today. Birdie, do you want to tell your mom, or would you like me to?"

Birdie's face crumples again and Charlotte pulls her close, feeling her body shake with her sobs. "What is it? Tell me," she says to the counselor.

"A student brought this to our attention," she says and pushes her phone across the table. Charlotte picks it up and puts her hand to her mouth. *"Oh, Birdie,"* she says. This is much worse than anything she could have imagined. Much, much worse.

It's an Instagram photo posted yesterday. A black-and-white shot of Birdie, taken from the side, her hair mussed and hanging down her back. She is topless (*her arms crossed over her chest, at least*, Charlotte thinks, a wave of nausea coming on) and wearing her team tennis skirt, the school's logo clearly visible on her thigh. In the background of this shot, which looks, sadly, like it was meant to be artful, there is a figure outside the frame, but his hand—a clammy, callused, teenage boy's hand—is resting on Birdie's waist, his fingertips grazing her hip bone.

Charlotte sucks in her breath. "Okay," she says, trying to make sense of what she's seeing. "Okay." She can't find any other words. Her arm is still around Birdie and she pats her back, not knowing what else to do, then lets her hand slide away.

"So," Ms. Loren says, scooting forward in her chair, seeming to choose her words carefully. "This is obviously a problem on several levels."

"Birdie," Charlotte says. "Why would you—" She sees that the username on the account isn't one she recognizes from the pool of Birdie's friends that she stalks online. "Whose account is this?"

Birdie stares down at her lap. Charlotte looks at the counselor and the coach, neither of whom say anything.

"Birdie," Ms. Loren finally says.

"It's mine," Birdie says, her voice barely above a whisper.

"It's— Wait," Charlotte says. "But you don't have an Instagram account. You know that's a rule in our house, Bird."

"It's mine," Birdie repeats.

"A lot of kids have secret accounts," Ms. Loren explains, her expression sympathetic. "Under obscure usernames, or shadow profiles . . ." She trails off.

"Oh my God." Charlotte shakes her head. She knew some other kids did this but— She feels so stupid. "Oh, no."

Coach Noah clears his throat. "One of the upperclassmen on the team brought it to my attention. When I arrived at practice today, a bunch of the girls were looking at it."

Birdie's eyes are still pinned to her lap, her cheeks flaming red.

"Now, school policy is that kids aren't supposed to use their devices during the day, and certainly this is . . ." The counselor stops and flips through a stack of papers in front of her, then passes one to Charlotte, where a passage has been highlighted. The words *Expulsion . . . lewd content . . .* jump out at Charlotte, though she's hardly able to process them. She looks at her daughter, the sweet kid who used to draw smiling suns on any available surface. *What the hell happened?*

"We've asked Birdie to remove the post, of course, but it's probably been shared by other students at this point. We've also . . . we've considered a suspension. This incident is problematic not just because of the photo itself but because it so clearly shows the school logo. I've discussed it with the administration, however, and because Birdie is in her freshman year, and she's such a bright kid, and this seems to be atypical for her, Coach Noah and the administration and I are not going to suspend her. However." She puts her hands out, inviting the coach to jump in. "Would you like to . . . ?"

He leans forward in his seat. "We are going to have to put Birdie on athletic probation. She won't be able to play for the rest of the season." Charlotte hears Birdie begin to sniffle beside her. "Obviously, this is a huge blow to the team. As you know, Birdie is among our strongest players." *Your* strongest *player*, Charlotte thinks. "And losing her isn't something any of us want, but consequences are important. We'll have to see—" he starts, his leg bouncing rapidly under the table. "We'll have to see about next year."

"See about next year?" Charlotte says. "There's a chance this could continue into next year?"

"We hope not," he says. "But that will depend on Birdie. We have certain expectations for our players, you have to understand."

Charlotte sighs. "I do." She nods. "And Tucker?" she says, trying to imagine how Finch and Dayna will react to this news. "I assume he's off the lacrosse team for the rest of the season."

Ms. Loren tilts her head to the side, her brow wrinkled in confusion. "Lacrosse?" she says.

"Yes," Charlotte says. "Tucker Cunningham." She points to the phone, now facedown on the table in front of them. "The boy in the—"

Birdie suddenly speaks. "That's not Tucker, Mom."

A sharp pain bolts through her chest. "What?"

Ms. Loren gives Charlotte a look that is meant to be compassionate but feels like a punch to her gut. "The boy's parents have been contacted as well," she says.

Charlotte's hands shake, gripping the steering wheel.

"His name is Micah," Birdie says through her hands. She is leaning into the passenger-side door, like she might try to jump out at any moment, and Charlotte wouldn't blame her if she did.

"Who is Micah?" Charlotte sputters. "What about Tucker? I thought—" She wipes a sweaty palm across her forehead. "None of this makes sense, Birdie! Who is this boy? Why would you do such a thing? And a secret Instagram account? I can't even . . . !" She shakes her head. "I can't even believe this is *you*, doing this!"

"Mom, *all* of my friends have secret accounts!" Birdie wails. "And I wouldn't have ever gotten one if you'd only let me get on social—"

Charlotte jerks the steering wheel, pulling to the side of the road and slamming the gearshift into park. Birdie jolts back. "Don't you dare tell me that this is our fault!" Charlotte screams, leaning over the armrest toward her daughter. "Don't you dare try to put this on me! *I'm* not the one who did this! How on earth could you think this was a good idea, Birdie? *How could you be so stupid?*"

"A lot of my friends—" she yells. "It's not that unusual, Mom, for kids to send pictures like this to their—"

Charlotte puts her hands out. "Birdie, stop!" she yells. "Stop! You can't begin to try to explain to me why this is okay! On *any* level! You are *fourteen*! Was this *his* idea? This *boy*? Is he your boyfriend now?"

"It was my idea," Birdie says.

Charlotte grips her hands tighter against the steering wheel. "But *why*, Birdie? Why would you do this?"

"I wanted to make Tucker jealous, okay?" she yells, sobbing again.

"I don't understand. Birdie, I just don't understand!"

"I wanted to make him jealous, Mom!" she screams again. "He broke up with me! Last week!"

"He broke up with you?" Charlotte says, remembering what Jason said Finch had told him when he walked by the Cunninghams' house the other night, and how, with everything going on, she must've forgotten.

"Yes," Birdie says, her voice a whine. "Yeah, Mom, he did. He broke up with me the day after he came to my practice, Mom," she says. "When you talked to him?"

"But . . ." Charlotte starts, an uncomfortable tingling creeping up her legs. "Why? What happened?"

"I don't know," Birdie says. "He said he . . . he said things were getting too intense for him, that he didn't want anything so serious. But he's already seeing somebody else. The girl he was with before me." She starts to say something else but then stops.

"What?" Charlotte says.

"He also said his mom didn't want him seeing me anymore."

"What?" Charlotte says. "Why?"

"It doesn't matter," Birdie says. "Tucker and I are done. It doesn't matter. Mom, I'm so sorry. I'm so so sorry."

Charlotte straightens in her seat. "Birdie, let's go home."

Jason is so angry he can't speak.

For hours after Birdie goes up to her room, he sits at the table in the backyard, staring into space, barely moving. Charlotte made Birdie tell him herself, and it was gut-wrenching to witness both the shame in her daughter's voice and the disappointment on his face. He was so quiet that it was worse than if he had yelled and screamed. Charlotte stalks him from the kitchen window, where she sips a cup of chamomile. There is a bottle of wine in the refrigerator and every time she opens the door, her eyes slide toward it, but she won't let herself. Not tonight.

Her mother calls, leaving a message asking about her travel plans for the vow renewal, and she ignores it. Stephanie calls (*she's probably seen the photo*, Charlotte thinks, *or at least heard about it from Hannah*), and she sends it to voicemail. And then finally, unable to wait any longer for Jason to come in, she sits down at her desk in the home office, surrounded by family pictures and mementos (a sand dollar Birdie found on the beach, a picture she drew of their family when she was little), and discovers that her old friend @KGPartyof5 has messaged her. So you're just not going to respond? it says, and Charlotte hits delete. *Game over.*

She emails Wendy to tell her about the woman's post, but

doesn't feel so concerned now that she has her daughter's to compare it to. What happened to Birdie (or what Birdie made happen to herself) is a big deal. This—a critic, a nameless person whom she should have known better than to tussle with—means nothing. She'll deal with the repercussions of Montana later, if she needs to.

She thinks of Reese again. She's been thinking of him all night, wanting to text him, to call him and tell him what happened because she knows he'll make her feel better, the way he did the night before. He'll tell her it's going to be okay. Finally, she relents, opening up her email inbox.

You won't believe what happened today, she starts. It's bizarre, how simple it is, to fall back into this easy shorthand with him, as if they're twenty again and there was no rift in their relationship. She tells him everything, about how drunk she actually was in Montana and how awful she felt on the plane ride home, about how she knows how unfair it is to Jason for her to talk like this with him, about Birdie and how much she worries that her unraveling is a direct result of her parenting or lack thereof.

She's getting up from her desk, about to turn off the lamp, when Jason appears in the doorway.

"Can we talk?" he says.

"Sure."

He pulls out the ottoman next to the armchair in the corner of the room and sits, and she swings around in her desk chair to face him, hugging her knees to her chest.

"Are you okay?" she says, sipping her tea.

He nods. He didn't want to see the photo, he said earlier. The description was enough.

"I'm hoping this is rock bottom for her," she says, repeating what she just emailed to Reese. "I don't think she'll go any further. Losing tennis is too big a risk. I think that's going to scare her straight."

He has his arms leaning on his knees, his hands clasped in front of his mouth.

"What do you think?" she says.

He looks at her, then looks away, and in the reflection of the fading light out the window, she sees the tears in his eyes. They've always joked about the fact that he only cries during dog movies. Funerals, graduations, even the birth of their own daughter didn't faze him. "Jason," she says.

He finally looks at her. "I'm tired," he says.

She nods, not totally understanding what he means.

"I can't—" He pauses and presses his lips together, a pained expression on his face. "I can't do this anymore, Charlotte."

"What do you mean?" she says, fear building inside of her.

"Charlotte, I need a break."

"A break?"

"I need some time." He looks at her again, his jaw shifting behind closed lips, and this time she sees it. The blankness. Through all of their fights and disagreements and storming out of the room, she has never quite seen him look at her in a way that sends a shiver down her spine like this does, because there is nothing behind it. He looks at her like he has no feeling at all.

"Time for . . . what?" she says, her voice small.

"I'm going to go stay at my parents'," he says. "They'll be at the beach until the week after Memorial Day."

"But what do we—" She feels a sudden panic, letting his decision settle in. "I don't understand how this will work."

"I just think some distance will do us some good. All of us. Maybe it will help us get some perspective." His eyes meet hers then.

"Give *me* some perspective? Is that what you're saying?"

"Both of us."

"Jason, we're married. We're not . . . teenagers. We can't take breaks."

"I'm not saying . . . I'm not sure what else to do, Charlotte. I don't know, exactly, what this looks like. But I need some time away to clear my head."

She studies him, watches as he shifts his feet on the floor, plays with the paper clip he's picked up off the desk.

"Does this have anything to do with Jamie?" she says.

"What?"

"Jamie," she says again, feeling stupid when she sees the genuine surprise on his face.

"You're kidding, right?"

"I don't know," she says, knowing how hypocritical this is, when she was just baring her soul over email to her ex-fiancé.

"Listen," he says, scooching farther up in his chair. "This has nothing to do with anyone except me and you. I would never cheat on you. *Ever.* I would leave you first."

The words feel like a slap across her face. "Is that what you're doing now?"

"It's not," he says, standing. "Okay? I promise you, it's not. I'm just taking some space."

He looks at her in a way that tells her she can't change his mind.

"When will you go?" she asks, the reality sinking in. Jason isn't someone to do something like this. It's one of the reasons she married him.

"Tomorrow, I guess."

She squeezes her shaking hands together, her panic building. "How do we explain this to Birdie? Especially after what happened today? It's not great timing, Jason."

"There's never going to be a good time," he says. "And if it will help us, it's the best thing for her."

She gasps.

"I don't know what else to do, Charlotte. It's not like I feel good about it."

"But this will kill her," she says quietly.

"I'm right here," a voice suddenly says from just outside the door. Birdie is standing in the hallway, tears streaming down her face.

Charlotte freezes. Jason jumps.

"I heard everything!" she wails. *"Everything!"*

"Birdie, honey. We just—" Charlotte starts.

"We're trying to do what's best for us, Bird," Jason says, placatingly. "What's best for all of us as a family."

"Are you kidding me?" she says, convulsing into sobs. "You guys are actually trying to convince me that the best thing for our family is for you to live somewhere else?"

"Birdie, it's—" He tries to put an arm around her but she flinches and moves away. "We're not separating," Charlotte says, feeling lower with each passing second.

"How could you do this to me!" Birdie screams. "How could you!"

"We're just not getting along right now, Bird," Jason tries.

"It's the healthy thing for us to do," Charlotte says.

"Just stop, Mom!" she yells. "Just *stop*!"

"Birdie—"

"You know what? I don't even care what you do anymore! I don't even care if you never come back!" she screams at her father.

"You don't mean that, honey . . ." Charlotte says, seeing how his face falls.

"Don't tell me what I'm supposed to feel!" Birdie says. "I'm not a kid! I'm not stupid!"

"We know you're not—" Charlotte begins.

"Just stop!" She backs away from them, shaking her head. "What's the point?" she says, crying. "Really? Why do I even care anymore?"

She runs up the stairs and Charlotte starts after her, racing down the hall, but then halfway up the staircase, she stops. What is there to say?

She turns, and Jason is standing at the foot of the stairs. She takes a step toward him.

"I'm sorry," he says.

She nods. "Me, too."

The next afternoon, as she's driving home from work, her mother calls. Charlotte didn't call her on the way into work this morning because she couldn't bear to fake it, not after last night. Jason had left before she awoke, and while she was getting dressed for class, she noticed what he'd taken with him: his toothbrush and razor were gone, along with the suitcase she'd used for Montana, which she'd emptied but hadn't put away. Birdie told her that she was going to walk to school and left without another word, the door slamming behind her. Charlotte had gone back upstairs then, her emotions overtaking her as she thought about what Birdie would go through at school that day and how she and Jason, instead of being a safe harbor for their daughter, had only made it worse. She pulled the shoebox off the linen closet shelf that they used as a medicine cabinet and found the in-case-of-emergency bottle of Klonopin she'd been prescribed years and years ago when she was in the thick of her infertility struggle.

The phone rings again, Nancy's name on the dashboard screen like a warning sign, and Charlotte finally answers, knowing that if she doesn't, her mother may just call back. They haven't spoken in several days because of her trip, and according to texts from both Amanda and Aaron, this vow renewal has turned her mother into an unbearable silver-haired Bridezilla.

"Well, finally," Nancy says, in lieu of *How are you?* Or *How was your trip?*

"Hello, Mother," Charlotte says.

"You're tough to get ahold of."

"Remember, I had that trip out to—" she starts but Nancy cuts her off.

"Even I have time to make a phone call, dear, and I'm planning a major event."

Charlotte takes a deep breath. "Everything going okay?" she asks.

"Oh, splendid. It's going to be fabulous."

"Good," Charlotte says. "I'm sure it will be."

"So we're having dinner tonight at Husk and I was just starting to plan an outfit," she says. "And I was sitting here in my dressing room and it occurred to me that I haven't asked you yet about what you're thinking about wearing to my vow renewal." It's not lost on Charlotte that every time her mother brings up the vow renewal, she refers to it as her own, and not hers and Emmett's. "You know, it would be nice if we all coordinated," her mother says. Charlotte pictures her sitting in the anteroom between her bedroom and master bath, enough makeup for a magazine photo shoot laid out on the glass table in front of her.

"Remind me what your colors are again?"

Nancy sighs. "Charlotte, we talked about this just last week."

"I know, I know, I'm sorry," she says, remembering how she'd tuned out during her drive into work that day. It had been so easy. She'd hardly had to say a word during the monologue about the merits of silk shantung table coverings versus linen.

"Well, it's spring down here, you know," Nancy says. "Goodness, I saw your weather up there," she adds. "Still just in the sixties? I don't know how you stand it. So I think I've settled on a lilac and then a very, very subtle vanilla to complement it. You know, I've always looked good in purple."

"Mm-hmm," Charlotte says. "The color of royalty," she says, knowing her mother will love such a comment.

Nancy laughs. "Yes, yes!" she says. "That's right, isn't it?"

"Marie Antoinette," Charlotte mutters.

"I'm sorry?" Nancy says.

"Never mind," Charlotte says. "So if I do a deep blue dress, will that work for you?" she asks, thinking of the Veronica Beard dress she borrowed from Rent the Runway but didn't end up wearing for the Montana trip.

"Oh, honey. It's not a funeral. Can't you think of a *happier* color?" Nancy says, her emphasis on the h-word. Another one of her digs. "I had this lavender in mind . . . Kind of the same tone as that lavender dress you wore to your senior prom with Reese? Oh, it was darling."

Charlotte feels a burn in the back of her throat at the mention of Reese's name, though she shouldn't be surprised. Her mother still has their prom picture in a little oval silver frame on an antique oak table in her living room, Charlotte in a strapless Jessica McClintock, her hair a weird yellow-white from the Sun-In that she and Amanda had applied before they laid out on Charlotte's dock each day after school in anticipation of the event.

"I'll find something," Charlotte says.

"I'll send you a link," Nancy says, finally circling around to what she wanted to say all along. "I have the perfect thing. Now, Birdie and Jason . . ."

"I don't know yet," Charlotte says, swallowing, not wanting to tell her mother that the reason her family isn't coming with her is not because of Birdie's imaginary "big match" but because Jason wants space, and she doesn't want everyone back home finding out about it, which would almost certainly happen even if she just brought Birdie. "You know, it's the height of Birdie's tennis season, and her team is quite dependent on her," she says, her mind flashing back to the meeting at school the day before. "And Jason—" She pauses, imagining the field day that Emmett would have if she made up any sort of zoo-related excuse, but goes for it anyway. "He has a lot going on at work right now."

Her mother is silent on the other end. One beat, and then another, and then another. "Oh, Charlotte," she says. "Your priorities . . ."

Charlotte closes her eyes. After a lifetime of it, her mother's commentary shouldn't hurt anymore, but even at her age she still pines for the kind of comforting, cookie-baking mother she never had. She thinks again of Birdie, hoping that her daughter never feels this way about her, and wishes she could believe that she's done everything she could to be the kind of mother she didn't have.

"Aaron and Amanda's boys will all be in khaki summer suits. She found the most darling lavender-and-white bow ties. Just perfect . . ." Nancy says, the words, they both know, like little drops of arsenic being deposited on Charlotte's tongue.

"Let's assume for now that it's just me," Charlotte says. "I'll let you know if anything changes."

"Talk to Amanda about a dress," she replies. "She'll know the right thing. *She* always does."

"Okay, I will," Charlotte says, thinking of Amanda's noisy house, the messy boys leaving trails of tortilla chip crumbs everywhere, shouting and wrestling, drums banging, balls being thrown despite Amanda's warnings. And then she thinks of her own deadly silent house, what she's about to arrive home to, Birdie locked in her room, Jason not there at all. "I'll talk to Amanda. You'll have final approval."

"Oh, Charlotte," Nancy says, laughing. "You know better than to lie to me."

SEVENTEEN

Jason is sitting at the ancient Dell computer in the basement of his childhood home. His parents have turned one corner of it into an office, delineating the space with an old green carpet remnant and a row of metal file cabinets where his mother still methodically files all of the paper copies of their bills after she pays them each month.

He takes a sip of his beer, turning in his chair, a shaft of late afternoon sunlight beaming through the little rectangular window at the top of the wall in front of him. Beside him is the old couch facing the TV where he and Tate played their first Nintendo, where he and his friends slept until noon on Saturdays in high school, where he made out with a girl for the first time.

Being here is horribly depressing, and several days into the so-called break, he's started to think he may have made a terrible mistake. Charlotte doesn't seem to think so, though. She's been oddly cheery since he left, her voice taking on a chipperness the few times they've talked that makes him uneasy, in part because it doesn't seem like she's faking it. Their conversations so far have been solely logistical, neither one of them broaching the actual problem of their relationship, treating it like a bruise they know is going to hurt if they touch it.

This week they took turns picking up Birdie, who barely speaks to either of them, making him feel even worse about what he's done and worried about what lasting impact this might have. Two days ago, after he met her in the parking lot behind the gym, where other kids were sauntering off to their various practices, arms swinging, heads tipped back in laughter, he tried to get her to go out for frozen yogurt, or to the driving range over on Hains Point, something they used to love to do together. He knew, on some level, that it was wrong to treat her suspension from the tennis team and the free time it afforded her as an excuse to have some fun, but he wanted to make it better, this thing that he'd done. He wanted everything to get better. Finally she asked if they could go to Bluemont Park for a little while, and he thought she might want to go for a walk or a run, maybe talk some things over, but instead, when they got out of the car, she slung her racket bag over her shoulder and marched determinedly to the tennis courts, where she hit balls for forty-five minutes straight, never saying a word to him, banging each shot into the wall with impossible force.

When Charlotte called earlier, she said she had just been planting some flowers in the front yard, and he pictured her, her favorite Emory cap pulled low over her eyes, singing to herself the way she sometimes used to when she would garden. She sounded so relaxed, and there was music playing in the background; country, he could tell, which he had never been able to stomach so she usually listened to it alone, in her car or when she went running. She asked if it would be okay with him if Birdie went to Hannah's to sleep over tomorrow night. With all of the lightness that would suggest she was talking about something as inconsequential as the sandwich she was about to eat for lunch, she said, "I think it's fine if we give her a pass, Jason. What we've done to her this past week is punishment enough, not to mention what she's probably been through at school. You know how cruel kids can be."

He looks up and stares at the computer screen, clenching his jaw as he scrolls through the site he googled a little earlier. The face staring back at him looks so happy, so smug.

He rubs his eyes. He hasn't been sleeping well. Last night, he tried moving into the guest room. He'd been staying in his childhood bedroom, but he discovered, not that it should have surprised him, that it felt truly pathetic to be forty-four years old and sleeping in your old twin bed, under the same quilt where you first learned how to jack off, with the same soccer trophies on the shelves, the same Heather Locklear poster on the wall. He'd said as much to his brother on the phone late last night. It was just past midnight in Arlington, only nine out in Oregon, and Tate was walking to that same sushi place where he and Paul are regulars. Tate snickered that it was funny how their mother hadn't touched Jason's room since he left home, but had no problem turning Tate's room into a sewing room. Jason said that it was only because Tate's room had the good windows, but they both knew that wasn't true, and they laughed, making guesses about whether either of their parents ever caught on to the fact that the *Rambo* poster that had hung in Tate's room for the entirety of his teen years was purchased because of Sylvester Stallone and the beefcakey picture of him, skin glistening and that headband around his forehead, and not because Tate had any interest in the actual movie.

Jason kept waiting for him to say something about Charlotte, to confirm that he'd made the right decision to take his advice and try a sabbatical, but Tate was oddly silent about it. When they got off the phone, Jason wondered if, in some small way, Tate was pleased that this had happened to him, if only because it might show their parents, who've never fully embraced his partnership, that he is every bit as stable and committed to their family values as Jason is, maybe even more so.

Jason looks at the screen again and takes another sip of his beer. When he first saw the name in bold at the top of Charlotte's email inbox that other night, it took a few beats for him to register it. And then he saw the subject line, a simple *Re: Hey*, telling him that she had composed the email he was responding to, her "Hey" telling him, like a burn singeing his skin, that there's a familiarity between them that is recent.

He'd walked into the office after Birdie had slammed her bedroom door, after he and Charlotte had stood there in the hallway, staring at each other, the weight of what their daughter had just experienced settling over them. He'd paced in the kitchen for a while after that, not knowing what to do with himself, and when he went upstairs to brush his teeth, he heard Charlotte crying on the other side of their bathroom door despite the running faucet, which never muffled noise like she thought it did. He went back downstairs to turn off the lights and lock up the house for the night, and seeing that the lamp in the office was still on, he went to turn it off and collect Charlotte's teacup from earlier.

And then his eyes landed on the computer and he saw the email. Reese Tierney. *Re: Hey. Reese Tierney, MD,* he sees now, looking at the home page for Reese's medical practice. He remembered vaguely that Reese had become a plastic surgeon, a factoid he'd forgotten because it was inconsequential. Reese Tierney was a relic from his wife's past, he thought, irrelevant to the present, as pertinent to their lives today as the old high school yearbooks he'd found in his childhood dresser a few days ago.

He clicked open Reese's email and scrolled down, the oxygen seeming to leave his lungs as he read what his wife had written her ex-fiancé just an hour earlier, about how he made her feel, about her mistakes. He takes a swig of his beer now, thinking of what Reese had replied. I'm here for you, always, the last line said, and then he'd used the salutation *Yours,* which sounded like a declaration, staking ground.

He'd known before he read Charlotte's email that she was distracted. He knew that she felt stretched too thin and scattered, because she'd said as much over the past several years, and it had shown in the way that she pinballed through the day, often with a glass of wine nearby to soften the edges. He looks at her Instagram now, where he sees the container of flowers she's planted, pink and white, green leaves hanging down the side of a pot, captioned "Spring's my favorite," and his blood roils. How can she do this? How can she compartmentalize like this when he is sitting here seething?

She wrote to Reese that she had humiliated herself in

Montana, that some twenty-something kid named Leo had to walk her back to her room. He couldn't wrap his brain around it, he'd had to read the message several times before the words made sense to him, because he had never thought his hyper-capable wife could blow it the way she said she had. ("Leo Montana" he'd googled in stupid desperation, finding only horoscopes from the local paper as a result.) Worse, she had chosen to confess the disastrousness of her trip not to him but to her ex-fiancé. She felt guilty, she said in the email, for her behavior, for flubbing her talk, for drinking so much, and for turning to him instead of her own husband. But not guilty enough to do something about it, it seemed.

I'm here for you, always, Reese replied.

Jason had thought that the break would give them a chance to sort through their thoughts, to come back to their marriage with fresh eyes. A few weeks, he thought, but maybe, he worried now, he was just giving Charlotte the out she wanted, deep down. She sounds lighter than she has in so long, and maybe it's because he's the deadweight.

He closes out the browser, making Reese's face disappear from the screen. What else is he going to do? He can't sit here any longer. He can't wait for her to come confess to him, and actually, he thinks, his frustration brewing, he's spent enough of the past few days thinking about her. It's not doing him any good. He tugs the skinny chain that turns off the lightbulb hanging from the basement ceiling and starts up the creaky wooden stairs, fishing his phone from his pocket.

"Hey," Jamie answers as he's closing the door to the basement and walking into the kitchen. "What's up?"

"Not much," he says. "I know it's last minute but any chance you want to grab dinner? Pizza or something? I remember you said that the kids are at your parents' for the weekend. I can head toward you."

"Oh," she says, the slightest hesitation in her voice, and he suddenly feels embarrassed. *This was a stupid idea.* "You know, I'd love to, but I'm actually heading out the door."

"No," he says. "It was last minute. No problem."

"You okay?" she says. "Living it up at your bachelor pad?"

"Yeah, yeah," he says, scratching his head, thinking that he shouldn't have told Jamie about the break. He feels pathetic now, imagining himself sitting in front of the TV alone again tonight, a container of some greasy takeout balanced on his lap. "Where are you headed?" he asks, trying to sound casual.

She laughs. "Actually, I'm meeting Heath for drinks."

"Heath? The dad-band ukulele player?"

"Yes," she says. "And you know, I have to tell you, I went and saw them play the other night at a bar and they weren't half-bad. The ukulele thing is quirky, one hundred percent, but actually weirdly endearing."

"Huh," he says, surprised by this development.

"I know," she says. "Who woulda thought? Hey—" She laughs. "Does Birdie still have that birth control pamphlet lying around? I might need some info."

He sucks in his breath.

"Too soon?" she says. "Sorry, Jason. That was bad. I shouldn't have—"

"It's fine," he says, forcing a chuckle. "Totally fine. Go, have fun," he says, sinking into the couch in the living room and reaching for the remote. "You deserve it."

"You know, I do!" she says, with a little too much exuberance. "That's exactly what my therapist keeps telling me and I think I'm finally starting to get the message. Thanks, Jason. I hope you have a good night."

"Thanks, yeah, I will," he says, swallowing. "All good here."

"Well, call me if you need anything."

"No, I'm good," he says. "All good. Have fun!"

Charlotte ends up having Birdie's leftover macaroni and cheese from the day before for dinner. She'd had grand plans to try to enjoy her Saturday night alone, to try to see it as an opportunity to pamper herself and relax, *practice self-care*, like she's advised her readers to do so many times. But ever since she dropped Birdie off at Stephanie's house, biting her tongue to keep herself from reminding her daughter that they are not to leave the premises, she's been frittering away, puttering around, biding her time.

She pours herself a glass of the rosé that she bought at Whole Foods this afternoon, when she and Birdie were picking up groceries. She'd slipped it into the cart while Birdie was browsing the cookie case in the bakery department, tucking it under a plastic clamshell of microgreens just as a text came in on her phone. Seeing the name, she turned away from her daughter, muttering something about how she'd forgotten something over in the dairy aisle, and furtively typed back to Reese that she was looking forward to talking later. He replied that he'd call her at nine. She slipped her phone back into her tote and proceeded to let Birdie fill the cart with whatever she wanted—the fifteen-dollar tubs of sliced mango they never bought because they were rip-offs, the chocolate–peanut butter cereal that's essentially candy for breakfast, several bags of chips, a couple of bath bombs, a new shampoo.

It's so quiet in the house, and strange to be alone. When she first started traveling for work, she loved the time to herself. Walking the threshold from the jet bridge onto a plane felt like pressing pause, suspending her reality. Her life then was a daily series of crossing things off lists: wake up, make lunches, get Birdie off to school, work-work-work, get Birdie home from school, tennis practice, monitor homework, dinner, more work, bed. At a conference in Philly or St. Paul or wherever, though, she could bow out of a reception early and order a burger from room service, eating it in bed by herself with a glass of wine while watching HGTV makeover shows. Once, she woke up in a pitch-black hotel room after a talk, the shades pulled tight over the windows. She sat up in bed, assuming that she'd awoken in the middle of the night, but it was actually nine-thirty in the morning. She'd slept for twelve hours straight, something that hadn't happened since before she became a mother.

Now, looking around the house, she is lonesome and on edge. She picks up a paperweight that Amanda gave her a few years ago, when she got into that "cozy quote" decor trend. Amanda has enough money to buy anything she wants, but instead of cashmere throws and fine art, her weakness is a fifteen-dollar

"This house runs on love, hugs, and strong coffee" sign from Michaels, a "Kiss Me Good Night" placard over her bed. The paperweight is a smooth stone, etched with "These are the good old days." Charlotte turns it in her hand, that sinking feeling returning to her, and puts it back on the table, facedown.

She gets herself another glass of wine, ignoring her conscience as she fills it nearly to the rim. She hasn't had a drink since Montana, but it's her first night alone in the house and not the time to deny herself. She heads upstairs and sits on the floor of Birdie's room, in the center of the mess, and starts snooping. There is a lip gloss she didn't know about (Buxom, it's called), a silly note from Hannah with abbreviations that Charlotte doesn't understand stuffed into the back of her sock drawer, and a romance novel that Charlotte didn't know she was reading, but otherwise, nothing incriminating. She thinks of Birdie's secret Instagram account, which she watched Birdie delete the other night. The good news is that aside from that one photo, the rest of it was pretty tame. Pictures of her and Hannah making funny faces, moody black-and-white photos of her dirty tennis shoes, a shot of Sylvie with a tennis ball in her mouth, a few of Tucker, including one of their hands, pinkies linked, with a caption that made Charlotte's breath catch when she read it, because it had been lifted directly from the conclusion of her TED talk: "Small moments make up a life. Make sure yours count."

Thinking of those words now, in this empty house, Jason doing who-knows-what at his parents' house or wherever he is, she's never felt like more of a fraud. Then again, she's not the one who took off. That's on him.

She turns on the television and has a couple more glasses of wine, knowing all the while that she's numbing herself, waiting for Reese's call, like she did so many years ago. They haven't spoken since she poured out her heart to him over email the other night, telling him how unhappy she was, and that was before Jason broke the news that he was leaving, before Birdie overheard and ran screaming from them, a vision Charlotte can't shake. She thought for sure he would write back right away, and it troubles her a little; she feels embarrassed, knowing that she has been so vulnerable with him and he hasn't acknowledged it. She'd hoped he would at least mention the email in his text earlier today.

Finally, when she can't take another minute of Chip and Joanna Gaines, Reese calls, at nine o'clock on the dot. She opens a second bottle for the occasion.

"Cheers to Saturday night," he says, reciting something they used to say way back when.

"How is your weekend going?" she says.

"It's okay," he says. "Saw patients at the clinic this morning."

"Let me guess: boob job, boob job, tummy tuck?" she teases.

"No." He laughs. "Actually a cleft palate surgery that I'm doing for free, on a four-year-old, and then reconstruction—yes, a boob job—on a woman who had a double mastectomy after eight rounds of chemo."

"Oof, I'm sorry. I stand corrected."

"But then I managed to get outside for a little bit. Played nine holes with my cousin."

"That sounds nice," she says, feeling the tension she's been holding all day fall away, a fist unclenching.

"It was," he says. "Hot as blazes, though."

She laughs.

"What?"

"'Hot as blazes.' You sound like my grandfather."

"Hey!" He laughs.

"I just haven't heard that expression in a long time."

"Maybe you've been gone too long."

"Maybe you sound like my mother," she jokes, though his words hit her hard. She takes a sip of her wine. It's cool and sharp. She takes another sip.

"You there?" he says, his voice gentle.

"Yeah, I'm here," she says.

"You holding up okay?"

"Mm," she says. "Yeah. But . . . I have to ask . . ."

"What is it?"

"Did you see my email? From last week?"

"Of course," he says immediately. "I wrote back right away."

"You did?" she says.

"You didn't get it?"

"No," she says. "I thought—"

"Oh, Charlotte," he says. "You *didn't get it*? I'm so sorry."

"No, I just—I felt kind of stupid, laying it all out there like that."

"But I did—Hold on, let me check." He pauses. "Yes, I sent it."

"Strange," she says. "I never got anything."

"I'll send it again, but the gist of it was . . ." he says, letting the words roll out slowly. "I said that I'm here for you. I'm here to help."

"Thank you," she says. "The thing is—"

"What is it?"

"Well, the shit's kind of hit the fan since then."

"Oh no."

"Jason. He . . ." She hesitates. "I guess there's no nice way to say it. He left."

"What do you mean he *left*?"

"He says he needs a break. From me."

"Oh, come on."

"And our daughter overheard us fighting and hates us both."

He's silent for a moment, and she wonders what he's thinking, whether he's judging her. "Well, being optimistic here, but maybe it is the best thing for you to take some time and think things through," he says. "Though it's obvious I'm not an expert on any of this."

She thinks of how many times the description has been attributed to her—happiness *expert*—and how proud she was of it once, how awful it makes her feel now.

"Where is Birdie tonight?"

"Sleepover," she says. "I'm hoping they won't sneak out again, like they did the last time."

He laughs. "You know they're probably going to try."

"Reese, come on." She smiles despite herself. There's something about the playful way he says it.

"How old is she again? Fourteen?"

"Yes."

"We were fourteen once, too, if I recall . . ." He chuckles a little under his breath, and the memories come racing back. She'd spend the night at Amanda's house, where her mother hardly noticed they were there, and they'd walk down to the waterfront on Reese's family's property and pair off with Reese and whichever friend of his Amanda was dating at the time. Sometimes it was just the four of them, sometimes dozens of kids, but for Charlotte, all that mattered was the two of them.

"Thanks." She laughs. "Now I'm worried."

"Oh, don't be," he says. "It's all good memories, isn't it?"

"Yes," she admits, remembering the thrill of their first kiss, after they finally admitted that they both wanted more than friendship. All of her early milestones, every last formative moment of her teens, were with him, and she never doubted whether that was exactly the way it was supposed to be. Memories like gifts, rare and precious, she knows now.

She hears ice clinking. "Still a bourbon drinker?" she asks, reaching for her own glass.

"Mm-hmm," he says, chewing an ice cube. "One a day, doctor's orders."

"I wish—" She feels a hitch in her chest and stops herself before she says it.

"What's that?" he says, his voice soft and gentle.

"Never mind," she says.

"I wish we were together right now, too," he says. "Is that what you were—?"

"Yes." She closes her eyes tight, a feeling rising up through her body that she knows she should have only about her husband. "I can't . . ." she starts.

"I'm sorry," he says. "I'm sorry, Charlotte. I don't mean to complicate things for you. It's just been so nice, reuniting with you like this. Maybe not the healthiest thing, I'll admit, given the timing, but please don't confuse my intentions. Just old friends, right?"

"That's right. Just old friends." She feels the looseness of the words in her mouth, the slight slur. "You know . . ." she starts, weighing whether to say it. *But they're just old friends, so . . .*

"What is it?"

"I'm going to be in Savannah in a couple of weeks."

"You are?" he says.

"I am," she says, leaving it at that. She wants him to say it first, but he doesn't, so she continues. "Would you like to . . ."

"I would love to see you," he says.

"I would, too," she says, knowing that it's wrong. She thinks of Jason, who walked out on her, who's . . . *where?* "I would love to see you."

"It's a date," he says, and she cringes, wishing he hadn't worded it that way. "Or it's . . ."

"Old friends," she says, the phrase somehow absolving her. "Just old friends."

EIGHTEEN

It's 11:45 when Charlotte's phone rings next to her bed, waking her. Sylvie's curled up against her legs, and the television across the dark bedroom is playing yet another episode in the *Law & Order: SVU* marathon she'd settled on before promptly passing out. As she fumbles for the phone on the nightstand, she nearly knocks over the half-empty glass of chardonnay and the pile of crumpled tissues she put there when she got into bed.

She sits up and squints at the name on the screen, the photo of her beautiful, beautiful girl, five years old, holding hands with Jason as they walked along the National Mall. *Her beautiful—* Mesmerized by the photo, she doesn't register who's calling until it's almost too late.

"Hello!" she yelps, wiping her face. "Birdie? It's Mom!" she says, nonsensically, since Birdie's the one who called her.

"Mom!"

Immediately, Charlotte hears the panic in her daughter's voice, a sound that tears through her. "Birdie, what is it?" she says, jumping out of bed, reaching for the edge of the nightstand when she stumbles, shoving her feet into her slippers. "Where are you? Who are you with?"

"Mom!" she says, still urgent but more calmly now, like she's catching her breath. "We're at . . . me and Hannah . . . we're at Tucker's house."

Tucker's house?

"That pool party, Mom," she says tentatively. "I mentioned it a while ago? Mom, I'm *sorry*," she moans. "I'm *so* sorry. But you always said . . . if I ever needed anything . . . if people were drinking or something and I got stuck . . . We need you to pick us up, Mom. I'm *so* sorry! I know we shouldn't have snuck out, but this junior girl drove us. We can't find her anywhere."

"Okay," Charlotte says. She fumbles down the steps, holding on to the wall on one side. *Am I okay to drive?* she thinks, and then she hears Birdie's pleas in her head again.

"It's okay, it's okay," she says, lifting her keys off the hook by the back door. "It's okay," she says, her heart pounding. "I'm on my way."

She isn't out of the garage before she knows.

Backing out, she almost rams the passenger-side mirror into the side of the garage, jerking the steering wheel just in time. She reverses down the driveway slowly (too slowly? she's not sure) and even though it's wide enough for two cars to park side by side, she has trouble staying straight. The steering wheel feels unsteady in her hands, like she's in one of those motorcycle-ride arcade games careening from side to side.

But Birdie . . .

She puts her foot on the gas. *Shit!* Too hard. The car rears back into the street, and when she slams on the brakes her head bounces against the back of the headrest. The Browns across the street have family visiting and there are cars parked in front of their house, making the space to navigate even narrower. She puts the car in drive and presses the gas again, slowly. *It's just two miles, not even*, she tells herself, beginning to ease down the street. *BirdieBirdieBirdie.*

She takes a deep breath and turns up the fan. The street is dark—too dark. *Wait.* She forgot to turn on her headlights. She fumbles, reaching for the dial, and in the process, hits the gas, again with too much force. As soon as she realizes it, her foot leaps off the pedal and she jams on the brake, turns the wheel too hard. *Shit!* The car fishtails like it's on ice. *What did Jason tell me, when he taught me how to drive in the snow? Turn in to the skid? Or is it turn out?*

She stops mere centimeters from the Marchettos' mailbox. *I can't do this.* The realization comes at her with a punch. *I'm too*—She reaches for her phone, squinting against the fuzziness that comes in waves.

He answers after two rings. "Jason?" she cries. "Jason! I need—"

"What's wrong?" he says. "Charlotte, are you okay? Where are you?"

"I'm okay," she says. "I'm . . . I'm at home. Jason, go get Birdie. Can you go get Birdie? At the Cunninghams'."

"What?"

"She just called me, she's with Hannah, she has her phone. She's at Tucker's and she wants to come home, Jason. Go get her!" The words come out slick, thick with tears and phlegm.

"Okay!" he says. "I've got it, okay." She can hear him moving, the muffled hustle, banging the door open. "Charlotte, are you— Why aren't you—?"

They both know. He *must* know.

"Jason, I . . ." The humiliation falls over her, heavy. "Jason," she says. "I can't."

Several minutes later, she manages to get back into the garage, pulling dead in the middle of the empty space meant for two cars, hitting the garage door button as quickly as she can, hopeful that the door will close before anybody sees her. When she gets in the house, she moves quickly back upstairs, where she runs a cold washcloth over her face and smooths her hair and gargles from Jason's big bottle of Listerine, and then hurries back down to the kitchen, where she puts her wineglass in the dishwasher and tosses the empty bottle into the recycling bin under the sink. She walks to the front of the house, bracing herself against the sill of one of the family room windows, and she waits.

Minutes later, the front door opens. *"Go, go, go!"* Jason screams. The girls tumble into the hallway ahead of him, and then Hannah hunches over, her arms splayed out to her sides, and retches all over the area rug in the foyer. Charlotte's first thought is how grateful she is that it's not Birdie, but then she looks up and sees the dead-eyed stare her daughter is giving her, the way she's leaning into the wall, and she realizes that Birdie's drunk, too. Jason is the only sober one among them.

She hurries to the kitchen for a roll of paper towels and cleaning spray. "I'll do that," Jason says, grabbing them from her hands, looking at her a beat too long. "You go with the girls."

She starts after the two of them, who are now halfway up the stairs, and he stops her, putting a hand on her shoulder as if to steady her. "You okay?" he asks, but his tone is almost businesslike.

"Yes," she says, brushing past him. Her fuzziness has faded, the intensity of the moment making her feel focused and clear.

When she gets upstairs, she sees that Birdie isn't as bad as she thought. Hannah's another story. Birdie helps her friend out of her dress and gets her into the shower. She sits her down into the tub, and hands her a spray nozzle to rinse her hair and then closes the curtain, kneeling on the pale yellow bath mat on the other side, telling Hannah she's right there, to let her know if she needs anything, and Charlotte is reminded of a time, just last year, when Birdie had a stomach bug and she did the very same thing.

"What did you girls drink?" Charlotte asks quietly, handing Birdie an extra towel from the linen closet.

"They had some kind of punch," Birdie says, her eyes not meeting her mother's. "I didn't have any of that, but Hannah—"

"Right," Charlotte says. "Do you know what was in it?"

Birdie shakes her head, staring down at the floor.

"But . . ." she begins. "Somebody had Jell-O shots. I had two of those. And Asher gave me a beer. I only had a few sips, though."

"Asher? Who's . . . Never mind," Charlotte says. "I'll leave you two. I'll be just outside if you need help."

"Mom, I'm so—" Birdie starts to cry.

"We'll talk about it tomorrow." She pulls her phone from the waistband of her pajama pants and goes out to the hallway to call Stephanie, but she doesn't answer. Charlotte shoots off a quick text, part of her relieved that she won't have to see her friend tonight: Girls are here, she types. Everything's fine but they snuck off to the Cunninghams' pool party and had too much to drink. Everything is okay. Have it covered. Call in the morning.

She puts the phone away and looks up. Birdie's standing in the threshold of the bathroom, staring at her. "Why didn't you come get us?" she asks. "Why did you send Dad?"

"Oh," she says. "He called right after you did. He was already out so it was faster."

Birdie nods, and Charlotte can tell that they both know she's lying.

"I'm going to go get some clean clothes from your room for Hannah," she says.

"Mom, I'm so sorry," Birdie says again. Charlotte takes a step forward and hugs her hard.

Jason is standing in the hallway when she comes downstairs with Hannah's soiled clothes for the laundry.

"I can take them," he offers, holding his hands out.

"I've got it," she says. "It's okay."

He presses his lips together. "I'll just sleep in the guest room, okay?"

She nods. "Thank you."

NINETEEN

In the photo, they must be twelve. She is barely developed, still a kid really, with two long low ponytails hanging over her scrawny shoulders. She is squinting into the camera, barefoot on the dock, in hot-pink terry-cloth shorts and a white T-shirt. Just from looking at the photo, she can smell the marsh—its musky, loamy sourness—and feel the heat on her cheeks, her arms, the part in her hair. In one hand, she holds a net. Her other arm is around her father's waist, his squinty smile identical to hers beneath his cap. Reese is on the other side of him, an old tackle box in his hand, grinning beneath the bangs that nearly cover his eyes, one of his sneakers untied.

Reese had texted the photo at four in the morning. Found this—one of my favorites.

Lying in bed, Charlotte is so ashamed that she can hardly bear to look at herself, this former self, this innocent self. She woke up warm, damp with sweat, the taste in her mouth rancid, a dull ache pulsing just behind her temples. She looks at herself at age twelve, and knows with a stony certainty that she has let this girl down.

She remembers the day the picture was taken, even though it wasn't any particular occasion, there were simply so many days like it. Summer weekday mornings, Saturday afternoons. Arguing with Reese and Aaron over who had to tie the chicken back to the crabbing net, her dad laughing to himself a few feet away, casting out with a Camel cigarette between his lips. Flicking sea snails at each other on the side of the shore. Teasing when one of them caught a stingray and couldn't lift it to the surface. Lying side by side, mushy Sunbeam bread tomato sandwiches between them, their arms over their eyes to block the sun.

This was long before they knew what would happen between them, when *love* was a word that you used for parents, your stuffed animals, the dog who slept beside your bed. Everything was simple and clear, even easy.

What became of her?

She's nauseous, looking at herself, thinking of what that girl would think of her and how she's turned out. Her stomach burns. *What a mess she's made*, she thinks, and then the phone rings. Her hands shake as she answers.

"What happened?" Stephanie says.

"They're fine." She runs her tongue along her teeth, which are filmy. "Still asleep but I suspect it won't be pretty when they wake up." She knows how hypocritical this is, the disapproving tone in her voice when she is so clearly just as guilty. More so.

"I don't know how the hell they Houdinied themselves out of my house again, Charlotte," Stephanie says. "I'm so embarrassed."

"You shouldn't have to lock up your house like a fortress when my daughter sleeps over," Charlotte says, walking to the bathroom for the Alka-Seltzer she's started keeping next to her toothpaste and face wash. "They're the ones who should know better."

"I guess so," Stephanie says. "But still."

"You are the last person who should feel guilty right now," Charlotte says.

"How drunk were they?"

"It wasn't pretty," Charlotte says. "Hannah threw up."

"Oh my God!" Stephanie groans. "I'm so sorry."

"Come on, don't be silly," Charlotte says, her cheeks burning, thinking of herself last night in the car. "They did Jell-O shots and drank some sort of punch."

"Are you kidding me?" Stephanie says. "If there's one thing I've told Hannah to stay away from—"

"I know," Charlotte says. "I know." She lies back on her pillows and massages her forehead with the heel of her hand.

"Do you think it's the first time they've drank?" Stephanie says. "I mean . . . probably not, right? I don't know. What do you—?"

"Maybe not," Charlotte says. "Probably not . . ." Her voice trails off.

"I thought kids didn't really drink anymore," Stephanie says. "I thought they just got together and stared at their phones in a group."

"Apparently not."

"Remember when we used to go to Kindermusik together on Saturday mornings?" Stephanie says. "How they used to wiggle their big diaper butts, clapping, singing along to 'The Wheels on the Bus'?"

Charlotte presses her thumb and forefinger to the bridge of her nose, trying to stop it, but the tears come anyway, hot and fast.

"Are you crying?" Stephanie says. "Oh, Char . . ."

She sniffs and clears her throat. "I'm fine," she says. "It's okay. They're supposed to do this stuff, right? We did this stuff . . . Hopefully this is the one bad time, the one big mistake . . ." She thinks of the photo of herself again, all of the things that girl didn't know she'd do, all of the things she would take back if she could. *This has to stop.*

"I'll throw some clothes on and come get her," Stephanie says.

"No hurry," Charlotte says. "I think they'll sleep for a while. Why don't I text you when they start to stir? Probably good to let them sleep it off a little, for all of our sakes."

"Sounds good," Stephanie says. "Thanks so much for everything you did last night. Dealing with all of it."

Charlotte turns on her side, remembering the blur of the shower running, of carrying Hannah's clothes downstairs. Jason turning his car keys in his hands, asking if she was okay and insisting he sleep over. In the guest room.

"Oh!" Stephanie says. "Not to bring this up now, but I keep meaning to ask what you're wearing to the auction."

Auction? "Oh, fuck," Charlotte says. "I totally forgot about it." They'd bought the tickets months ago, before the holiday break. Were she and Jason really going to attend a school auction together when they couldn't even live under the same roof?

She inhales deeply. "I need to check my calendar to see if we can still make it."

"I'll kill you if you don't go," Stephanie says. "Who will I talk to?"

"Okay, I'll see," Charlotte says.

"I'll see you in a little bit," Stephanie says. "Thanks again."

Charlotte stares at the ceiling after they get off the phone, the room rocking a bit. She tries to tell herself that it's no big deal, people get drunk all the time. Parents all over Arlington are waking up hungover right now. But her old excuses, the ones she's used so many times over the years, feel flimsy now. It occurs to her that for the past several years—five? Ten? Twenty?—the only time she's made it through a weekend, or a week, without at least a little bit of a hangover was when she was pregnant or trying to be. Sure, they weren't all as bad as this one, but how could she think that is okay? How could she call it normal? Every bad decision she's made in her adult life, including reaching out to Reese when she should have been reaching for her husband, has happened when she's been drunk. She looks at the photo Reese sent one last time, stares into that little girl's eyes, whispers, to herself, "I'm sorry."

When Charlotte walks past the guest room, she finds the bed made and the shades pulled open, as if Jason hadn't been there at all. But when she gets downstairs and turns in to the kitchen, she discovers that he has put out breakfast.

She clenches her fist at her chest, thinking how much she doesn't deserve this. There is a pot of coffee brewing and her favorite mug—chipped, with a photo of Sylvie as a puppy—set next to it. There are sliced bagels, fanned out on a plate. A bowl of strawberries with the stems lopped off. Bacon slices on a baking tray on the stove. She looks for a note but he hasn't left one. Why would he? Why should he?

But still. There is something about this gesture. Maybe he meant it more for Birdie, but there's the coffee cup left just for her. It's a little thing, but it's everything. He wouldn't do this if he didn't care.

The girls finally stir, neither of them able to look Charlotte in the eye as they shuffle downstairs and nibble at strips of bacon before they retreat back to Birdie's room. Minutes later, Stephanie comes to retrieve Hannah, apologizing once again.

"Did Jason see her throw up?" Stephanie whispers, standing in the entryway in an old Turkey Trot T-shirt and exercise leggings while Hannah is finding her shoes.

Charlotte hopes Stephanie can't see the worry on her face at the mention of her husband. She should be able to tell her that Jason isn't living here right now, but she can't. It's too much to explain, there will be too many questions she doesn't want to answer. She nods her head consolingly, letting Stephanie believe that Hannah vomiting on the very rug they're standing on is the worst thing that happened last night. "It's fine!" she says, reaching to squeeze Stephanie's arm. "Trust me, his mind is on Birdie."

Stephanie gives her a guilty look. "I really don't know how they snuck past me."

"Stop," Charlotte says.

Stephanie sighs, then reaches out and grips Charlotte's

shoulders. "We will make it through this," she jokes, her hands squeezing. "When they're heading off to college, we might even *miss* this."

"Speak for yourself," Charlotte says.

Stephanie laughs. "We might, though! Because when they're gone, we'll be left all alone with our husbands." She widens her eyes in mock terror.

"Scary," Charlotte manages to joke along, then turns before Stephanie can see the emotion on her face. "Birdie?" she calls up the stairs.

Hannah comes down alone. "Birdie's in the bathroom," she says, her Converse sneakers hooked into two fingers at her side. "Mrs. McGanley," she says, her eyes downcast. "Again, I'm so sorry. I'm so—"

Stephanie puts her hand on her daughter's back, guiding her out the door. "We'll talk in the car, Hannah," she says, then turns to Charlotte. "We'll wash these and bring them back," she says, nodding at Birdie's T-shirt and pajama pants that Hannah's wearing.

"No hurry," Charlotte says. "Least of my concerns."

Stephanie gives her a morose look, as if to say *Tell me about it*, and Charlotte shuts the door behind her.

After Birdie comes downstairs, Charlotte asks her to join her at the table on the back patio where so much of their family life has occurred. Lazy weekend breakfasts, Sunday afternoon cookouts, long late-night talks between her and Jason when their marriage was young and they didn't know what lay ahead of them, Birdie falling asleep in Jason's arms, the fireflies twinkling around them.

"Let's talk," Charlotte says, pulling out a chair and forcing those memories from her mind.

Birdie sits across from her, tucking her knees up under her chin.

"I'm not going to punish you," Charlotte begins, picking up a shiny green leaf that had fallen onto the table and turning it between her fingertips. "We don't need to go over why it was wrong for you to sneak out of Hannah's house again but I'm proud of you for calling us when you needed help."

Birdie looks up at her, and when she does, her glare shoots right through Charlotte. "You were drunk last night, weren't you, Mom? That's why you couldn't pick us up?"

Shame courses through Charlotte's body. "I need to apologize to you," she says, weighing her words.

Birdie's expression remains stern and determined, waiting for an answer.

"I did have too much to drink last night, that's true."

"So what did you do? You called Dad to get us?"

Charlotte nods. No need to tell her daughter that she tried to come get her, or how humiliating it felt when she realized she couldn't.

"Are you going to get a divorce?" Birdie asks.

Charlotte looks down at her lap, trying to collect herself as she figures out how to handle Birdie's questions. It's difficult to look at her daughter. She has the same aggression on her face as when she's lobbing a tennis ball over the net.

"No," Charlotte says, although the truth is, she doesn't know now. "Bird," she continues, "I haven't been available to you in the way that I want to be. This first year of high school is such a big transition, and instead of helping you through it, walking with you . . . figuratively at least . . . I've been . . ."

"You've been distracted?" Birdie says.

"Yes." Charlotte looks at her daughter, stunned by her intuitiveness. "That's exactly it."

"By stuff with Dad? With work?"

"Yes," Charlotte says. "That's right."

"It's just weird, Mom," Birdie says, sitting up in her chair. "Because you're always so stressed. You have this expression on your face all the time like you're worried about something."

Charlotte feels tears come to her eyes. She's always believed that kids see and hear more than their parents realize, but it doesn't make it any easier to see the truth of it staring right back at you, asking for answers.

"But then I see you out in public somewhere, like talking to Hannah's mom, or in a video I find on YouTube of one of your talks, and you're like this totally different person."

"Well, that's just, with work—"

"I'm not talking about work, Mom," Birdie interrupts, clearly frustrated. "You always use that as an excuse but I'm not talking about work. I'm talking about *you*." She runs her hands through her hair, pulling it into a ponytail at the nape of her neck and then letting it go. "I'm just wondering, which one of you is my real mother? The one in the videos or the one I see here? Because I'd like to know. I think I can guess, but it's not fair to me, Mom, to give the world one person and leave me with . . ." She looks away, and Charlotte can tell from the expression on her face that this is far from the first time she's thought about this. "It's not fair to any of us."

"Birdie, I—" Charlotte begins. "You have to understand that I'm doing the best I can."

"Are you, though?" Birdie says.

"What?"

"Is that what you were doing when you talked to Tucker that day at my practice? Doing your best?"

"Birdie, I don't understand where this is going."

"You know Tucker broke up with me because of you, Mom. That's what I didn't tell you in the car the other day. He said you threatened him, and it was all just a little too much. It was so humiliating, Mom. He broke up with me at school, in front of everyone."

Charlotte tenses. "What do you mean?"

"Well, he posted this video online when we were still together. It was so stupid," she says. "Of a girl's back, out by his pool. She was wearing a yellow bikini top, the kind that ties in the back?"

"Okay," Charlotte says, pressure building in her chest, wondering where this is going.

"And the video showed Tucker's hand—though he tried at first to claim it wasn't his—pulling the string on the tie until it came undone."

"Did she—Was it like a joke?" Charlotte says. "Did she want him to do that, or—"

"Yes, she definitely wanted him to," Birdie says. "So everyone was talking about it the next day at school, the day after that practice, and when I saw him in the hallway, I confronted him. He was with a bunch of his friends, all the lacrosse guys, and she was there, too."

"The girl?"

Birdie nods. "She put her arm around Tucker's waist and he kind of looked at me and then looked away."

"Honey, I'm so sorry."

"I just . . . I didn't know what to do. I froze," she says. "He just stared at me and said, 'I guess I should have told you, but I don't think it's going to work out.' And everyone laughed. It was so terrible, Mom. You can't even imagine how embarrassing. And then later that day outside school, when he wasn't in front of his stupid friends, he told me about what you said to him."

"Oh, Birdie, why didn't you tell me? I could've—"

"*Helped?*" Birdie deadpans.

Charlotte's heart sinks. "I would have liked to know," she says. "I would have liked to have been there for you."

"That would have been impossible, Mom," Birdie says. "Because you're never around. And you have no idea what it's like to be me. The pressure at school, the pressure with tennis."

"If it's too much pressure, you can stop playing tennis," Charlotte says. "We've always said that, Bird."

She rolls her eyes. "And have you heard Dad when he starts talking to someone about college and the scholarships, like at the Cunninghams' that night? Have you heard Coach Noah, constantly on me about my potential?"

"But we've always said—"

Birdie shakes her head and looks away, like she doesn't want to hear it.

Charlotte leans forward. "I really am trying to do my best," she says, grabbing for Birdie's hand across the table. Birdie lets Charlotte take it, but it lies limp in her hand. "You have to understand that, Bird. I'm trying really, really hard to hold everything together." *Hold myself together*, she thinks.

Birdie looks up at her, not an ounce of understanding on her face. She removes her hand from Charlotte's and stands.

"I'm trying so hard to do what's best for us, Birdie," she says, almost pleading. "I really, really am."

"Try harder, Mom," Birdie says, the words hitting Charlotte with such force that she feels like she's had the wind knocked out of her. And then Birdie is gone, leaving her, too.

TWENTY

"Well, if it isn't my favorite task," Jason hears her say, then feels a hand on his shoulder. He turns.

"You want to help?" he says, holding up one of the bottles of glitter.

Jamie sighs. "Oh, why not?" She takes it, and he slides over a metal tray of raw meat he's just cut into cubes. "Blue glitter on that one. I'll do the silver here," he says. When elementary and middle school groups come to visit the zoo, they completely lose their minds when they learn that zookeepers examine animals' poop to monitor their health, even occasionally adding glitter to their food so that when it comes out the other end, they'll know which animals produced which specimens.

"So how was the date?" he asks, though he's not sure he really wants to know.

"Good enough," she says, a smile on her face like there's more to the story.

"Good enough?" he says. "That's it?"

She tick-tocks her head back and forth. "Yeah." She winks.

He reaches for the cap for his glitter container and fumbles as he twists it on, trying to ignore the picture that's just materialized in his head of Jamie writhing under some out-of-shape middle manager whom he's sure isn't good enough for her.

"And how was your weekend?" she says, putting down her bottle and leaning against the counter behind them.

He lets out a sigh.

"That good?"

"Long story," he says, thinking of Saturday and the apologetic texts Charlotte has sent since. Everything is going to change now, she wrote this morning, a statement as meaningless and vague as if she'd written it in hieroglyphics. He wanted to believe her, but how could he, when he knew she was deceiving him? He'd done something he never could have imagined himself doing and logged in to her Gmail, using the password (her father's birthday) that he knew she used for everything, and sure enough, she'd written Reese, telling him everything about Saturday night and the conversation she'd apparently had with Birdie the next morning, and Reese had written back with bland platitudes ("It's going to be okay." "Hold your head up") that he couldn't believe his wife—or at least, the Charlotte he'd fallen in love with—could possibly find useful.

More than anything, he'd wanted to drive over to the house and see Birdie, whom he hadn't seen or spoken to since he peeked in on her before he left the house the morning before. She was sound asleep, Hannah passed out next to her. He felt helpless, wanting to be the father he knew she needed right now.

"Do you want to tell me about it?" Jamie says.

"Not really." He turns and grabs a pen to label the trays, thinking of how he'd filled his Sunday afternoon. He went for a run but abandoned it twenty minutes in because his back hurt so bad from tossing and turning in the guest room the night before. He went to the grocery store and bought a few things, but the very act depressed him. Everybody around him was filling their grocery carts for the week with big bags of chips and popcorn for the lunch boxes they'd pack, shrink-wrapped trays of chicken and ground beef for the family dinners they'd cook, giant clamshells of greens, gallons of milk. He felt a crushing sense of not belonging, with his sad basket of food for one: a plastic bag of sliced turkey from the deli, a couple of frozen burritos, a plastic jug of iced tea.

Jamie's looking at him expectantly. "What's going on?" she says. "Your face just changed twenty different times. Something's gnawing at you."

He sighs and throws the pen down on the counter. "Okay," he says, and he ends up telling her everything. By the time he's done, tears are rolling down her face.

"I'm sorry," she says, wiping her cheeks. "Ugh." She shakes her head at the ceiling. "Life just sucks sometimes, doesn't it?"

"Yup," he says. He feels no sense of relief from having spilled his guts. If anything, he feels worse.

"All right," she says. "Well . . . Do you want to know what really happened with my date? It may make you feel better."

"Sure."

"We met at Del Mar."

"Well, well," he says, remembering the review he'd read of the sleek Italian seafood place on the Wharf.

"His choice," she says. "And it wasn't worth the price of admission. He talked and talked and talked, going on and on about his work, and as I sat there, all I could think about was how much I missed Warren."

Jason's shoulders slump. "Oh, Jamie. I'm sorry."

"Yeah," she says. "So the truth is, I left. I just got up, put my napkin on the table, told him I couldn't do this, and I walked out."

"Ugh."

"Yeah," she says. "It was awful. And then, to make it even more pathetic, I walked down the block to Ben & Jerry's, stood in the massive Saturday night line of teenagers and cute families and couples on dates that were actually going *well*, and I sat on a bench by the water, eating my huge waffle cone, and cried like a crazy person."

"No," he says. "Oh, Jamie. That just sucks."

"Sorry . . . I . . ." She moans at the ceiling. "I just sometimes wish things weren't the way they are, you know? Simple as that. I mean, I'm an adult. Life is hard. I get it. I just didn't know it would be as hard as this. *Why me?* Know what I mean?"

He nods, and they stand there, staring at each other for a moment, and then he walks two steps across the tiny room and wraps his arms around her, hugging her hard, nestling his head against the top of hers, feeling her fingers against his back through his shirt. They are so close that he feels her deep exhale, her heartbeat against his, their hips fused so neatly together, and before he knows what he is doing, he kisses her. He tastes the mint from her gum and the salt from her tears and he doesn't think of anything else in that moment, he just kisses her, and it feels good, to be wanted, to feel her hands against his back, the way she presses herself closer to him, and then—

"Oh my God," she says, her palms against his chest, pushing herself away.

He holds his hand to his mouth like he's been stung. *Oh my God*, his thoughts echo.

Her eyes widen, but then she takes another step toward him, like she wants this to continue.

"No," he says. "I'm sorry, I can't—Jamie, I—"

She steps back and turns for the door, fleeing before he can finish.

He goes outside to get some air, and sees one of the zoo's famous pandas wrestling with a piece of bamboo, flopping onto her back and hugging it to her chest. A family standing a few feet away watches her and laughs, and then all four of them—the parents, two teenagers—pull out their phones, yelping to each other about getting pictures, about which of them will take a video. It depresses him, how many people he sees doing this each day, observing the animals through their screens instead of taking them in with their eyes, missing anything outside of their shot, all of the things on the periphery that are every bit as, if not more, compelling.

He thinks of Charlotte then, always on her phone, always feeling the need to project the right image, and he feels an intense wave of guilt, thinking of what he's just done. He thought he might feel vindicated somehow if it happened. It wasn't as intentional as that—he didn't know he was going to do it until it actually happened—though leveling the playing field had crossed his mind over the past couple of days. But kissing Jamie unlocked something he didn't expect: He just misses his own wife that much more. He misses her more than ever.

Charlotte's standing in the kitchen in her sweaty running clothes, taking a long swig of water, when Wendy calls.

"Sooooo . . ." she says, uncharacteristically quiet.

"What is it?" Charlotte says, pulling her hair from her ponytail and shaking it out. She looks at the clock. Birdie will be arriving home at any moment, she hopes. Charlotte took the afternoon off, telling Tabatha she planned to work at home and prepare for final exams, but she really intends to take Birdie out to dinner, anywhere she wants, if Birdie is up for it.

"I got an email," she says. "From someone I worked with ages ago. She used to be in magazines—I used to pitch her my books all the time—but now she works out in California at a marketing agency for some of the tech firms."

"Uh-huh," Charlotte says, the subject of the conversation dawning on her. *Montana.* She'd told Wendy about the social media thing, and her agent had written it off as nothing to worry about, something that would go away if they just ignored it. And she'd been correct. But she'd skirted over the details of the Montana talk when she emailed Wendy, not being entirely truthful about how it had gone. She wanted to erase the trip from her memory, to never think of it again.

"She said she saw your talk," Wendy begins. "How did it . . . You said it went okay, correct?"

"Uh-huh," Charlotte says. "Yup."

"Okay," Wendy says, sounding relieved. "You're sure? This woman was always a bit of an exaggerator, and cynical, kind of a pain in the ass. The type of person who complains about the sun being too hot during a day at the beach. But she said . . . she said your talk was . . ."

"What?" Charlotte says, worried now because Wendy is never at a loss for words.

"Lackluster."

"Lackluster?"

"That's the word she used."

"Well . . . I was nervous, so maybe I wasn't my best."

"I figured as much. But I watched the video this morning. I thought it was odd that they hadn't posted it on the symposium website, because they always do. Every year."

"Right," Charlotte says, pulling out one of the chairs at the kitchen table and sitting.

"So I called my contact there and she sent it to me. She said they'd decided not to put it up."

"Oh," Charlotte says, not sure whether to feel disappointed or relieved. "Okay."

"You weren't your best on it, Charlotte, I gotta say. You seemed really off. Did you take an anxiety pill or something beforehand? Did you have something to drink? Because you seemed kind of, I don't know, dopey."

"Ouch," Charlotte says.

"I'm sorry. I'm sorry, Char, I really am, but it just didn't seem like you. Is there anything you're not telling me? I want to make sure as we head into this next book that everything's okay."

Charlotte bites her lip. She's done a pretty good job of ignoring the next book since Wendy's visit to DC, telling herself that she'd focus on it after school gets out, as if her family issues would be resolved by then. "I think I was nervous, Wendy," she says. "Really. I know it wasn't my usual caliber. I think I just airballed, you know? I'd really worked myself up about the audience."

"Okay," Wendy says, but she doesn't sound like she's buying it.

"It won't happen again," Charlotte says, resting an elbow on the table and putting her head in her hand.

"It's all right," Wendy says. "As long as you're honest with me."

"Of course," Charlotte says, closing her eyes.

A moment passes, and then another. "All right, all right," Wendy says. "I'm just gonna . . . This is really uncomfortable, Charlotte, because I don't have any desire to get involved in my clients' private lives, but this is an instance where I think I need to."

"What is it?" Charlotte asks, clenching a fist in her lap.

"This is really uncomfortable. But the woman I know who was at the talk?"

"Yeah?" Charlotte says, her anxiety ratcheting up.

"She also mentioned that she saw you walking back to your room. With a man."

A feeling like water rushing into her ears comes over Charlotte, her adrenaline spiking as she realizes what this is about. Wendy is waiting for her to say something.

"Oh, God," she says. "Wendy, I can—I had too much to drink. It happened really fast. I don't . . . I can't really explain it; I think it was the altitude. The man was Leo. The . . . house manager, I guess? He helped me find my room."

"And that's it? That's all he—"

"*What?*" Charlotte says. "Of course that's it! Did you think—"

"I didn't know."

"No!" Charlotte says. "No, absolutely not, Wendy. He just walked me to my room."

"Charlotte, just tell me before we officially sign these papers that you're capable of writing a happy family book. You really stalled on me when I was down there and presented it to you, and if this is the reason why, I need to know. Is your marriage on the rocks? Because those texts that woman posted on Instagram made me worry, too."

"Everything's going to be fine," Charlotte says, surprised by how forcefully she wants to fight for this deal now that it's precarious. "I promise you, there is nothing to worry about."

Wendy sighs heavily into the phone. "Okay. I'm taking you at your word."

"You have it," Charlotte says. "I promise."

TWENTY-ONE

I'm inside, Jason's text reads. Charlotte pushes through the double doors into the darkened ballroom on the ground floor of a bland office building in Ballston where the Yorktown High School auction is being held. She feels nervous in a way that she hasn't in some time, keenly self-conscious that this is the first time she will face Jason since last weekend. She wants to tell him that she hasn't had a drink since then. At night, she makes big bowls of ice cream for Birdie and herself, not caring if they both know that the whipped cream and caramel sauce and rainbow sprinkles on Birdie's bowl are an obvious ploy for forgiveness. Her daughter still isn't really speaking to her, but her silence this time feels less like animosity and more like a strategy to see if Charlotte will live up to the expectation she set during that morning-after conversation. Charlotte gets it: Actions speak louder. And so every night, she hands Birdie her bowl and nudges her over on the couch, pulling an edge of the blanket Birdie usually has over her lap onto her own, and they sit there together, silently eating, watching whatever Birdie's chosen. It is slow, incremental, but it feels like progress. In part because, instead of floating into the wine haze she'd become so accustomed to, Charlotte is there. She is present.

But she wants to drink. Badly. After the phone call with Wendy, she went straight for the kitchen and opened a bottle, and then she paused. She *paused*. She saw herself again, swerving, wobbling. She saw herself knocking her shin into the coffee table in front of Jason. Accidentally handing Birdie her wineglass instead of the water she asked for. Unable to drive her own car, to mother her daughter in her time of need. She poured the entire bottle down the drain, and then gathered up the three remaining bottles in the house and emptied them, too. She doesn't know if she's done drinking forever, if she is finished for good, but she knows that the role that drinking plays in her life can no longer be a leading one. *Try harder*, Birdie had said that day on the back patio. *Try harder, Mom.*

The auction committee has clearly gone to great pains with the decor, but to Charlotte's relief, at least there isn't a theme. No jungle safari fake palms in the corners, no shining sparkling cardboard cutout stars hanging overhead. There are silver and blue balloon arches and tasteful bouquets on the skirted tables, a five-piece band playing palatable jazz on the stage on the far end of the ballroom. Dozens of people mill about, and Charlotte waves to some of the familiar faces, looking for Jason, who should be the most familiar face of all but feels like just the opposite.

A woman—pretty, young, her wavy hair clipped back from her face—stops in front of her with a tray of drinks in clear plastic cocktail glasses. "Can I offer you a drink?"

"What is it?" Charlotte asks, desperate to quell her nerves.

It's a pinkish red, like the drink she used to order in college, vodka and soda with a splash of cranberry, a selection she thought was so sophisticated at the time. She felt grown-up, leaning across a crowded bar, shouting her order to a bartender while everyone else ordered Bud Light and Jäger shots.

"A . . ." The waitress glances down at the note she's pulled from her black pants. "A patriot, they're calling it."

"Ah, like the school mascot," Charlotte says.

The woman shrugs. "It's vodka and pomegranate juice."

Charlotte shakes her head and steps away. She scans the room, holding her chain-link evening bag in front of her middle, in a matronly way, she realizes, then tucks it under her arm.

"There you are!" Stephanie says, appearing at her side with her husband, Joe. "We just saw Jason," he says, hooking his thumb back over his shoulder. "He's looking for you."

"You didn't come together?" Stephanie says, furrowing her brow. Charlotte eyes the glass of wine in her friend's hand.

"I had a work thing that I knew would run late," she says, reciting the line she'd come up with this morning, after she asked Birdie, again, if she'd told Hannah that Jason wasn't living with them right now, and Birdie insisted, again, that she hadn't ("Why would I want to embarrass myself like that, Mom?").

"This place looks nice, doesn't it?" Charlotte says, changing the subject. "Have you checked out any of the auction items?"

Stephanie nudges Joe in the side. "This one already bid on, like, six different things," she says. They give each other a teasing look, and Charlotte feels a pang in her stomach, envying their closeness. She searches past them, looking for Jason, and suddenly spots him.

"Oh, yeah. There he is." Stephanie makes a face at her. "Talking to Finch Cunningham."

Jason is wearing the jacket they bought together on a Saturday morning at Nordstrom a few years ago, when he finally acknowledged that the sport coat he'd had since college had seen better days. Charlotte can picture him standing in front of the bathroom mirror, the air humid with steam from the shower.

"You heard about Finch and Dayna, of course?" Stephanie takes a step toward Charlotte, dipping her head.

"I know that he left," she says, her eyes still on Jason.

Stephanie raises her eyebrows. "I heard that she found out he was a frequent customer at some quote-unquote spa in McLean."

"That doesn't surprise me in the least," Charlotte says, waving and smiling at a mom she remembers from Birdie's elementary school years.

"He's disgusting," Stephanie says, and takes a big swig of her drink. Charlotte watches, wanting her own, and crosses her arms over her chest. She takes a deep breath, and then another.

"Is Dayna here?" she asks, thinking of Birdie and what she'd told her, how Dayna didn't want Tucker seeing her because of Charlotte.

"Oh, yeah," Joe says. "Over there." He points his chin toward the banquet tables, where Charlotte sees her, dressed to the nines in a tight silver sheath, hunched over one of the silent auction tables.

"Of course my husband noticed her," Stephanie jokes, but Charlotte's eyes are back on Jason, whose expression is serious, matching Finch's. They almost look like they're arguing, and Charlotte feels a hitch in her chest. Finch takes a step toward

Jason, a step that looks aggressive. And then Jason does something he never ever does; it is so unlike him that it almost doesn't seem as if it could be him, but he takes his own step forward, closing the distance between them.

"Uh-oh," Stephanie mutters, leaning into Charlotte's side, their shoulders brushing against each other's. "What's—"

"I'm going to go find out," Charlotte says, her nervousness over seeing Jason now replaced with a fear that her husband is about to make a scene. The people around them start to notice, how one of Finch's friends pats his shoulder, easing him away, and then Jason turns, and he's staring right at her. She starts toward him.

"What was that about?" she says under her breath, smiling like everything's fine so that people won't be compelled to keep watching as they meet beside the parquet wood dance floor.

"Never mind," he says.

"Jason—" She waves at another familiar face.

"He was just being an asshole," he says. "Said something about you bothering Tucker."

Charlotte looks down at her feet.

"It's not important," he says. "Forget it."

They stand there, pretending that this is normal, the two of them together, and Charlotte thinks to herself that it's like that odd pressure when you try to push the wrong sides of magnets together, each side repelling the other. The closer she stands to him, the stranger it feels.

"Do you want to—?" Jason points to the banquet tables, arranged in a U-shape, where the silent auction items are displayed.

"Sure," she says, and they wander over. As they browse the

offerings, Charlotte finds herself thinking of every prize description as a reminder of their uncertain future. With whom would she use a gift certificate to the Inn at Little Washington? Season tickets, right on the ice, to the Capitals? A Fourth of July fireworks viewing party on a yacht in the Potomac?

"I'm going to get a beer," he finally says. "Can I get you something?"

"No," she says.

His eyebrow twitches, almost imperceptibly, but she notices.

"I'm really trying—" she starts, but he cuts her off. He shakes his head, and then he turns like he's about to walk away, but then he stops himself and faces her.

"I kissed Jamie," he says.

"What?"

"I did," he says, his eyes cast downward, the saddest expression on his face. "I didn't mean to," he says, almost like a boy confessing that he broke a window with a baseball. "It was this past week, at work."

"Jason—" she starts, feeling dizzy. "I don't—"

"I wasn't lying to you," he says. "There's never been anything between us before, but I did it. I'm the one who kissed her. I wanted to do it."

Charlotte takes a step toward him, not wanting anyone to overhear. "I don't understand."

"I read your email," he says.

"Oh." It's just one syllable but she can barely choke it out, realizing what he's saying.

"Why is it easier for you to talk to your ex than it is to talk to your own husband?"

"Jason, I—" She looks at him and then around the room.

"I'm not trying to be argumentative," he says, leaning in and whispering. "I really want to know. Is *he* who you want? Is that what you want?"

"No," she says, and she knows it's true, every part of her knows. "No, I don't."

"Then why?" he says, but before she can answer the lights begin to flicker and the band stops. An emcee appears on the stage, and he introduces himself over the static-filled microphone as a trigonometry teacher at the school, then announces that the live auction is beginning.

A sizzle of excitement moves like a wave over the crowd and one of the dads, already too many drinks in, whoops like he's on a spring break booze cruise. Laughter and groans ripple through the room, and the crowd feels like it tightens around Charlotte, everybody wanting to inch closer to the stage as the emcee explains that the silver stars scattered on the tables throughout will serve as bidding markers. She feels woozy and wishes she could escape, but it's too late now.

The emcee begins with a private tour of the National Gallery of Art, which goes quickly and without incident to a couple Charlotte knows from a drama camp that Birdie used to attend every summer. Next, Nationals box seats for a game over Memorial Day weekend, and the bidding goes on longer than Charlotte would have expected, with four groups of people vying for them before they go for just over three thousand dollars. Charlotte glances at Jason once, yearning to feel some connection with him, but his eyes are locked on the stage, his expression hard.

"Okay, this next one is a biggie," the emcee begins.

He pulls an index card off of the podium beside him and holds it in front of his face, twirling it between his fingers. "Are you ready?" He's met with more whooping and applauding.

"We have . . ." he starts. "A weekend for two at the Ritz-Carlton in Lake Tahoe, California." He clears his throat and continues reading. "Your weekend features your own private suite with spectacular lake views, round-the-clock butler service, full access to all of the resort's facilities and award-winning spa, plus more." He wiggles his eyebrows. "The bidding starts at one thousand dollars."

Instantly, several hands shoot up. "Fifteen hundred!" someone shouts.

"Eighteen hundred!" another exclaims. Within seconds, the price is up to $2200, and Charlotte wonders, watching the crowd, if these people are so hot to outbid each other because they actually want the prize or because they want to show they can afford it. And then suddenly, a familiar voice yells out, "Five thousand dollars!" silencing the room.

Charlotte turns to see. It's Dayna, waving her spindly arm above her head, her bracelets jingling on her wrist.

"Five thou—" The emcee barely gets it out before a hand shoots up on the other side of the ballroom.

"Six thousand."

Somebody shrieks, but then the crowd falls deadly quiet. Charlotte cranes her neck. *Finch.*

"Ten thousand!" Dayna's voice rings out over the crowd.

The emcee's mouth falls open.

"Ten five," Finch barks.

Every head in the room whips in unison to Dayna, who

throws her head back and laughs. "Fifteen," she says and turns to glare at Finch. Out of the corner of her eye, Charlotte sees someone lift a phone and when she turns back, she sees it's one of the tennis moms she recognizes from practice, actually recording this marital breakdown.

"Okay," the emcee starts, his eyes darting back and forth, his voice a little less certain since he picked up on the fact that this isn't just friendly competition. "Fifteen thousand. That's fifteen . . ." He pauses. "Fifteen thousand, going once . . ."

"Dammit!" Finch yelps. "Okay, sixteen!" he yells.

"Twenty thousand dollars," Dayna exclaims before the emcee can continue, her voice clear and proud.

The crowd erupts with some laughing, some gasping, but above it all, there is the sound of Finch bellowing.

"Goddammit, Dayna!" he yells. "What the hell are you doing? You know this is my money either way! Just give it up! Stop!"

She doesn't even look in his direction.

"That's twenty thousand," the emcee begins. "Twenty thousand going once . . ." The crowd falls silent, all eyes on Finch, waiting to see what he'll do. "Twenty thousand going twice . . ."

"Argh!" His strangled groan fills the room. "Jesus, *twenty-five*!"

"Sir, is that twenty thousand, and five hundred, dollars?" the emcee says, an impish grin appearing on his face. "Or twenty-five thousand?"

Before he has a chance to answer, Dayna's voice calls out: "Thirty thousand dollars!"

"Oh my God," the emcee says, echoing the crowd's thoughts. "Okay! *Thirty. Thousand. Dollars.*" He pauses. "Going once." He turns to Finch, holding the microphone away from his mouth, waiting for him to make a move. "Thirty thousand going twice . . ."

Charlotte looks around the room at the sea of wide-eyed spectators, some of them familiar but most of them not. They're like the fans at a bloody bullfight, their mouths gaping. Another phone goes up, and then another. *It's easy to just watch, isn't it?* she thinks. She looks at Jason, whose expression is so agonized he looks like he's in physical pain.

"Sold!" the emcee screams, pointing in Dayna's direction. "To the woman in the silver dress."

"You bitch!" Finch yells, sputtering and screaming like a dying motor, veins popping from his head, his buddies reaching for him, trying to calm him down. The crowd erupts, drowning out the sound of his outburst.

Out of the corner of her eye, Charlotte sees her husband's head dip down. She brushes her hand against his, and their fingers interlace, finding each other for the first time in what seems like forever. He squeezes his hand around hers, and it's only a few seconds before he lets go again. "I have to get out of here," he says.

"Okay, I'll come—" she says.

The band starts up again.

"No," he says. "I have to go. I can't—" He starts to walk away.

"Jason, please!" she says, but he doesn't turn back. She watches as he disappears through the double doors beneath a glowing red exit sign.

She lies to Stephanie, saying that Jason isn't feeling well, and when she gets outside, she searches the sidewalk for him, but he's gone.

He kissed Jamie.

He's gone.

She walks for a while, even though her car is parked in the garage down the block. She needs the activity, the feel of the cool fresh air on her face. She passes apartment buildings where people are heading out for the night, and bars and restaurants from which music is spilling, the sounds of laughter and clinking glasses and celebration. She wants a drink. Her phone buzzes in her bag and she fumbles to get to it before the call goes to voicemail, hoping it's Jason.

It's Reese. She waits a moment, the phone buzzing in her hand. She's standing just outside a restaurant, twinkling candles on the tables, crisp white tablecloths. Through the glass, she can see a young couple having a drink at the bar, the woman twirling the stem of her glass between her fingertips. It is clear through their body language—the way he looks at her, the way she's angled toward him—that it's a date, maybe a new relationship. She turns away just as the woman's eyes meet hers, and she presses the play button on her voicemail.

Reese's voice in her ear: "Hey, stranger," he says, sounding hopeful, a little shaky. "It's been a few days. Miss talking to you. Wondering if you're still headed this way. I'd love to see you." She thinks of Jason then, the look on his face a little while ago, confessing to her, and then she thinks of Birdie, and then of Dayna and Finch, the people watching them tear each other apart in that ballroom, the delight in their eyes, watching them battle, their truth laid bare.

She thinks of the people who come to hear her talk and their searching faces, of her students, their fingers poised over the keyboards of their laptops, hanging on her every word. She tells them not to feel, to push through, and there is validity in that, she still believes it, but she also knows that there is a big difference between faking a good mood, a good day, a good attitude until it comes to be like conjuring a spell, and pushing through because you're too scared of what lies beneath. Numbing with wine. Numbing with work. Numbing with the distraction of what might have been instead of facing what's right in front of you and has been all along.

She looks back at the woman through the window, how she tilts her head and takes a sip of her drink, and then another, and then Charlotte notices her own reflection in the glass, the straight slit of her mouth, the exhaustion, now unmistakable. She is so, so tired.

She pulls out her phone and taps a message. Reese, I'm sorry, she says. I can't see you. She turns away and heads toward home.

TWENTY-TWO

Jason looks up from his bowl of mint chocolate chip when he hears the sound of the garage door opening.

Birdie, next to him on the couch, slides her spoon from her mouth. "I guess Mom thought the auction was boring, too," she says.

"I guess so."

"Do you want me to go upstairs?"

"Of course not."

"Dad?" she says, the question in her voice making her sound younger than she is. "I don't want you to go."

"I know," he says. "I don't want to go either."

"You don't?"

He shakes his head. "No," he says, reaching an arm around her. "I don't."

He had left the auction rattled and frustrated, and driven back to his parents' house, but as soon as he pulled the car into the driveway, he knew it wasn't where he was supposed to be.

This place of limbo he had put himself in, he realized, was what hurt most of all. He needed to go home.

When he walked in the front door of his house, the wellspring of every defining moment of the last fifteen years, every joy and sorrow, the place where he slept on the left side of the bed, and opened presents on Christmas morning, and had a thick stack of old Father's Day cards tucked in his nightstand, he found Birdie in the family room, watching a Netflix rom-com. The delight in her eyes when she saw him nearly brought him to his knees.

He hears Charlotte come into the house, the door closing behind her. "Hello?" she calls from the hallway. "Birdie?"

"In here," Birdie says.

"Hi," Charlotte says, surprise on her face when she enters the room, her heels in her hand. "I didn't expect to—" She points a thumb back behind her. "I saw your car in the garage."

"I'm sorry I left you there," he says.

"Dad said it was lame," Birdie interjects, and the faintest hint of a smile appears on Charlotte's lips.

"Yes," she says, looking at him with a tenderness that she hasn't felt in some time. "It was." Birdie must sense something passing between them because she puts her bowl down and rises from the couch, hitching up her oversized sweatpants after she stands, and says she's going to go upstairs for a while. Just before she does, she leans down and hugs Jason.

"See you in the morning, right?" she says.

He looks at Charlotte. "See you in the morning."

Charlotte sits in the chair across from him, the TV flickering shadows between them.

"I'm sorry I left," he says again. "I couldn't be there. That whole scene with Finch and Dayna . . . I couldn't . . . I don't want to be like them, Charlotte. I don't want to end up like that."

"I don't either," she says, relief in her voice like she's been holding her breath.

"I just need to know what you want," he says.

"You," she says. "I want you."

"Are you sure?" he says.

She starts to cry. "I'm so sorry. I'm so, so sorry."

"I am, too," he says, and sighs. "We really fucked things up."

"Yes," she says. "We have a lot of work to do."

"But I think . . . if we try . . ."

"I think so, too."

"I want to come home," he says.

"You're sure?"

"Absolutely."

She nods. "Stay."

TWENTY-THREE

Charlotte is sitting on the dock behind her brother's house. It's over ninety degrees, and it's barely eight o'clock in the morning. Her mother has already texted her twice to remind her that the last-minute dress she found for Birdie might need to be steamed one more time, and that Jason must wear a tie.

Inside, Birdie is still sleeping. Jason, too. Charlotte stretches her arms over her head, yawning wide, and looks down at her journal, open on the dock in front of her. She's been writing every day, the words coming out in a flood now that she's stopped smudging her thoughts out with wine. She looks down at the gratitude list she wrote this morning, marked with her bulleted ballpoint stars:

- Waking up to see the sunrise after a solid night of sleep
- My family here with me

- Starting to nail down exactly what to say in the next book

She bends her head from side to side, working out the kinks in her neck from the long drive the day before. The plane tickets they looked at for Jason and Birdie were astronomically priced at such short notice so they drove instead, just like they used to, years ago, when they couldn't afford to fly. A crash on I-95 meant that it took them thirteen hours instead of the usual nine, and they got off the highway three different times, trying the back roads. It was frustrating, testing all of their patience, and it felt like they were barely moving at some points. Around dusk, they stopped at a gas station somewhere in South Carolina, a little dusty side-of-the-road place. While Jason was outside filling the tank, and Birdie had her eyes closed, listening to something through her headphones, Charlotte snapped a photo of the rearview mirror just outside her window. Sometimes to look forward, we have to look back, she wrote in the caption before she posted it. Sometimes we're doing so much, trying to get to the next thing, that we forget why we're doing it in the first place. I've spent a lot of time charging ahead this year, and for all of my talk of action, there is something to be said for presence, for paying attention, something that's hard to achieve when you're doing life with a phone in your hand, or a glass of wine, or whatever it is you use to escape into. I am trying instead to opt for the slow road. To take my time and pay attention. It isn't easy. It's testing every bit of my patience. But I have a feeling it will be worth it, so I'm going to take a break from this for a while. Reflexively, she swiped down on the screen, watching the likes rack up once again, the comments peppered with hearts and smiley faces, praying hand emojis, thumbs-up. She glanced out the window, then back down at the screen. She read her post one last time, and then she closed out the app and deleted it from her phone.

She looks down at her journal, where she's scrawled a few notes for the book.

Marriage starts with a vow, a promise, but it's actually a series of promises, over months and years, commitment and recommitment. Family is also about noticing, about the little things, she'd written, thinking of Amanda's silly paperweight, *that we miss when we distract ourselves with the things that seem bigger, more urgent, in the moment.*

She hears a noise behind her and turns. *Jason.*

"Hi," she says.

"Good morning." He sits down next to her and rubs his eyes, then plays with the hem of his old T-shirt. There is still a distance between them, but it's closing, slowly but steadily, a little bit each day.

"What are you doing?" he says, motioning toward the journal.

"Oh, nothing," she says. "Just thinking." She puts down her pen. He reaches across her for her mug and takes a sip from her coffee, and she narrows her eyes at him, jokingly. He puts it down between them, smiling just a little. He holds out his hand, and she takes it.

Acknowledgments

I feel like the luckiest author in the world to have worked with the same editor, Emily Griffin, since I published my first novel almost ten years ago. Emily, you are such a sharp, skilled editor and I am so fortunate to get to collaborate with you once again. Katherine Fausset, my literary agent, has been wonderfully enthusiastic about this particular story from the start, and is a guiding force throughout my fiction career, and I couldn't be more grateful to have her in my corner. (More lunches in New Orleans, please.)

Thank you to everyone at HarperCollins, particularly Falon Kirby, a PR pro who makes the nerve-racking work of book publicity fun, Megan Looney, Amber Oliver, Suzette Lam, and Amanda Hong.

Special thanks to Dr. Laurie Santos, an *actual* happiness professor at Yale University, who bears zero resemblance to the main character in this book but gave me such great information to work with as I was writing.

Independent bookstores do so much for authors, and I can't miss the opportunity to thank the teams at my two locals: One More Page in Arlington, Virginia, and Bard's Alley in my hometown of Vienna, Virginia. I could not be more grateful to you all for getting my books into readers' hands.

Finally, to Jay and the girls: I love our happy life. Thank you for cheering me on.